The House of Sounds and Others

THE HOUSE OF SOUNDS AND OTHERS

by M. P. Shiel

Edited and with an Introduction by S. T. Joshi

Hippocampus Press

New York

Published by Hippocampus Press
P.O. Box 641, New York, NY 10156
http://www.hippocampuspress.com

Cover illustration by J. T. Lindroos.
Cover design by Barbara Briggs Silbert.
Hippocampus Press logo designed by Anastasia Damianakos.

First Edition
1 3 5 7 9 8 6 4 2

ISBN 0-9748789-6-0

Contents

Introduction

In the original version of "Supernatural Horror in Literature," H. P. Lovecraft wrote:

> Matthew Phipps Shiel, author of many weird, grotesque, and adventurous novels and tales, occasionally attains a high level of horrific magic. *Xélucha* is a noxiously hideous fragments [sic], but is excelled by Mr. Shiel's undoubted masterpiece, *The House of Sounds*, floridly written in the "yellow nineties", and re-cast with more artistic restraint in the early twentieth century. This story, in final form, deserves a place among the foremost things of its kind. It tells of a creeping horror and menace trickling down the centuries on a sub-Arctic island off the coast of Norway; where, amidst the sweep of dæmon winds and the ceaseless din of hellish waves and cataracts, a vengeful dead man built a brazen tower of terror. It is vaguely like, yet infinitely unlike, Poe's *Fall of the House of Usher*.[1]

It is evident that Lovecraft had not yet read Shiel's true masterpiece of weirdness, the novel *The Purple Cloud* (1901). Frank Belknap Long lent this book to Lovecraft in May 1927, referring to it as "the most unutterably terrible book ever written."[2] Lovecraft's own response, when he read the book shortly thereafter, was equally enthusiastic:

> "The Purple Cloud" was magnificent, despite a perceptible weakening or letting down of the tone in the latter half. . . . It deals with vague Black Powers & White Powers battling for the earth's supremacy—how the former were released by the visit of a man to the frightful lake & carven column at the North Pole, & how all the human race save him & one other were thereupon wiped out with prussic-acid vapour. But it is in the *details* that the power lies. Ugh! What pestilential death-ships & dead cities! This book is worth buying if you can possibly get it.[3]

Lovecraft accordingly felt obligated to augment his discussion of Shiel when "Supernatural Horror in Literature" was scheduled to appear in a revised version in the *Fantasy Fan* (1933–35):

> In the novel *The Purple Cloud* Mr. Shiel describes with tremendous power a curse which came out of the arctic to destroy mankind, and which for a

---

1. "Supernatural Horror in Literature," *Recluse* No. 1 (1927): 48–49.

2. Lovecraft to August Derleth, 22 May [1927] (ms., State Historical Society of Wisconsin; hereafter abbreviated SHSW).

3. Lovecraft to August Derleth, 28 May [1927] (ms., SHSW).

time appears to have left but a single inhabitant on our planet. The sensations of this lone survivor as he realises his position, and roams through the corpse-littered and treasure-strown cities of the world as their absolute master, are delivered with a skill and artistry falling little short of actual majesty. Unfortunately the second half of the book, with its conventionally romantic element, involves a distinct "letdown".[4]

This is (with one exception) the extent of Lovecraft's public discussions of Shiel, and yet it was sufficient to bring Shiel's work to the attention of his young disciple August Derleth, who would later reissue Shiel's tales under the Arkham House and Mycroft & Moran imprints.

As with several other writers, Lovecraft owed his initial reading of M. P. Shiel (1865–1947) to the generosity of others—in this case, W. Paul Cook, the amateur associate from whose extensive weird library Lovecraft would make many discoveries. In the fall of 1923, Cook lent Lovecraft Shiel's *The Pale Ape and Other Pulses* (1911), containing "The House of Sounds" and other tales that caught his fancy. So taken with that story was he that he immediately wrote what can only be described as a fan letter to Edwin Baird, editor of the recently founded *Weird Tales*:

> Every once in a while I discover some weird masterpiece by an author either wholly unknown or unknown in America, which I wish could be popularised. Just now I am enthusiastic about a tale called 'The House of Sounds', by M. P. Shiel, which occurs in a book of short stories named after the first one, 'The Pale Ape', and published by T. Werner Laurie, Clifford's Inn, London. This is the most haunting thing I have read in a decade—a creeping horror and menace trickling down the centuries in a sub-Arctic island off the coast of Norway, where, amidst the sweep of daemon winds and the ceaseless din of hellish waves and cataracts, a vengeful dead man built a brazen tower of terror. It is vaguely like—yet infinitely unlike—'The Fall of the House of Usher'. I wish there were a way of getting republication rights from the publisher—for it would surely be a sensation in *Weird Tales*."[5]

The similarity of language between this letter and Lovecraft's subsequent discussion of the story in "Supernatural Horror in Literature" is patent. *Weird Tales* did not in fact reprint the tale, but, as mentioned, a seed may have been planted in August Derleth's mind to do so—first in the anthology *Sleep No*

---

4. *The Annotated Supernatural Horror in Literature* (New York: Hippocampus Press, 2000), p. 56. This segment did not actually appear in the *Fantasy Fan*, as the serialisation ended in the middle of Chapter VIII, whereas this passage is included in Chapter IX. It first appeared in print in *The Outsider and Others* (1939).

5. *Weird Tales* 3, No. 1 (January 1924): 88; rpt. in *H. P. Lovecraft in "The Eyrie,"* ed. S. T. Joshi and Marc A. Michaud (West Warwick, RI: Necronomicon Press, 1979), p. 19.

More (1944), then in the Arkham House collection *Xélucha and Others* (1975), the last major assemblage of Shiel's short stories until the present volume.

Lovecraft initially announced his discovery of Shiel in a letter to Frank Belknap Long, in which he wrote:

> Some of the things [in *The Pale Ape*] are mediocre, though all are smooth. One is diabolically clever, though hardly weird. Three or four are superfine—"Huguenin's Wife", "The Bride", "The Great King", and "The House of Sounds". Yes—this last is the masterpiece! How can I describe its poison-grey "insidious madness"? If I say it is very like "The Fall of the House of Usher", or even that one feature mirrors my own "Alchemist", (1908) I shall not even have suggested the utterly unique delirium of arctic wastes, titan seas, insane brazen towers, centuried malignity, frenzied waves and cataracts, and above all hideous, insistent, brain-petrifying, Pan-accursed cosmic SOUND . . . God! but after that story I shall never write another of my own. Shiel has done so much better than my best, that I am left breathless and inarticulate. And yet the man is virtually unknown in America—and almost so in his native Britain.[6]

Lovecraft cannot claim especial acuity in detecting the resemblance of "The House of Sounds" to "The Fall of the House of Usher," for Shiel, profoundly influenced (like Lovecraft) by Poe from an early age, consciously sought to duplicate that fusion of human souls to the fate of a physical structure that is at the core of both stories. It is a bit surprising, in fact, that Lovecraft did not detect the similar parallel between his other favourite, "Xélucha," and Poe's "Ligeia."

Lovecraft manifestly preferred the more subdued, less flamboyantly baroque prose of "The House of Sounds" to its original, "Vaila," first published in Shiel's early collection *Shapes in the Fire* (1896), and here printed in an appendix. It is not clear when Lovecraft read the earlier version,[7] but it is likely that he did so at a time when he was himself in the process of conducting an overhauling and simplification of his own prose style, eschewing the floridity of his earlier work for the scientific realism of his later tales. Lovecraft owned the radically revised edition of *The Purple Cloud* (1929)—it was given to him by Richard Ely Morse in 1932—but it is unclear whether he actually read it.[8]

---

6. Lovecraft to Frank Belknap Long, 7 October 1923; *Selected Letters 1911–1924*, ed. August Derleth and Donald Wandrei (Sauk City, WI: Arkham House, 1965), p. 255.

7. In a letter to August Derleth (c. 1933) he writes: "As for Shiel—he is undeniably clever, but exasperatingly uneven. The florid flamboyancy of some of his prose is painful—& yet at times he becomes virtually peerless. His indubitable masterpiece— "The House of Sounds"—is a revision (made in 1908 [*sic*]) of a vastly weaker & more effusive tale written in 1896. I saw the original (whose title I forget) once, & was certainly glad that the author saw fit to do it over" (ms., SHSW).

8. In a letter to Morse acknowledging the book (30 August [1932]; ms., John Hay Library), Lovecraft speaks of his intention to read it, but there is no definitive evidence that he ever did so.

There is lively debate among enthusiasts of weird fiction as to whether these later versions of Shiel's work are in fact superior to the earlier ones, many contending that Shiel's distinctive subject-matter is best suited to the euphuistic prose he cultivated in his early years.

Curiously enough, Lovecraft first read Shiel at the exact time when Shiel's reputation was in the process of undergoing a revival. His career can be neatly divided into two periods—1895–1913, when he published his first twenty books, and 1923–37, when his remaining ten titles appeared. In the interim, Shiel published nothing in book form, although pseudonymous or anonymous publications have long been suspected. In the United States, Shiel was indeed little known until 1929, when Vanguard Press issued the revised *Purple Cloud* and also published the novel *Dr. Krasinski's Secret*, followed the next year by *The Black Box*. Lovecraft also owned Shiel's *The Lord of the Sea* (the edition of 1924, an exhaustive revision of the original edition of 1901); this novel—about a modern-day superman who attempts to control ocean traffic by means of innovative military devices—was given to Lovecraft in 1935 by Richard Ely Morse, and he read it late that year, noting: "'The Lord of the Sea' has a curious power—& its opening chapters sound almost prophetic in these days of Nazidom & sporadic anti-Semitism." (Shiel's novel has also been accused of anti-Semitism.) Samuel Loveman gave Lovecraft a copy of Shiel's early short story collection *Prince Zaleski* (1895), but Lovecraft was unenthusiastic: "I own Shiel's 'Zaleski', but cannot get very deeply excited over it. It consists of three medium length tales—none of which impressed me as 'The House of Sounds' did."[9]

Lovecraft's preference, in consonance with his view that weird fiction works best in short compass, was manifestly for Shiel's short stories. His letter to Frank Belknap Long of 1923 contains, however, a number of peculiarities and ambiguities. What is the "diabolically clever, though hardly weird" tale to which Lovecraft refers? My feeling is that this is "The Case of Euphemia Raphash," a skilful murder mystery with a well-hidden twist at the end. Lovecraft does not specifically note enjoying "The Pale Ape," but it would be difficult to imagine him not relishing this tale of anomalous hybridity, so similar to his own earlier work, "Facts concerning the Late Arthur Jermyn and His Family" (1920), soon to be embalmed in *Weird Tales* under the give-away title "The White Ape" (April 1924). "Huguenin's Wife," another tale of a hybrid monster, accomplished something that Lovecraft had perhaps hoped for much of his career to do: to draw upon the latent weirdness of classical myth. Of the other stories Lovecraft singles out, "The Great King" is an artfully told tale of a revenant, but "The Bride"—never reprinted since its original appearance—is an odd tale for Lovecraft to have enjoyed, being largely a romance, even a melodrama, with a supernatural element slyly inserted only at the very end.

Of *The Purple Cloud* it is difficult to speak in small compass. The novel is the second component of a very loose trilogy—the other volumes being *The*

---

9. Lovecraft to August Derleth, 12 November 1926 (ms., SHSW).

Lord of the Sea (1901) and *The Last Miracle* (1906)—purporting to be visions of the future as transmitted through a psychic, Mary Wilson. Each volume contains a nearly identical introduction recounting this highly contrived premise, but the reader quickly forgets it in Shiel's gripping tale of what appears to be the last man left alive on the earth, following the explosion of a volcano that produces a deadly purple cloud of cyanogen gas. This detail must have amused Lovecraft, for in an early letter he speaks with whimsical misanthropy of his hope that the entire human race "could be mercifully blotted out by a whiff of cyanogen gas in some comet's tail!"[10] Shiel achieves a true sense of cosmicism by his lonely protagonist Adam Jeffson's traversal of the entire globe in what appears to be a vain search for any remaining members of his species. Whether the last portion of the book really constitutes a "letdown" will depend upon the temperament of the reader. Lovecraft's comment is of a piece with his general lack of interest in the portrayal of human character in weird fiction, and specifically with any admixture of "romance" that might diffuse the depiction of cosmic horror. In reality, the romance element comprises only the final quarter of the novel (in the 1901 edition); moreover, Shiel's handling of Adam's tortured relationship with the young woman, Leda, is far from conventional, and his gradual shedding of his ferocious cynicism and misanthropy in the face of her naive and winsome optimism is managed with exquisite skill and psychological acuity. But Lovecraft is probably correct in suggesting that the cataclysmic vista of a dead world littered with the suddenly meaningless tokens of humanity's relics—its cities, its art, literature, and science, its religions, its hopes and aspirations all apparently gone for naught—will linger far longer in the reader's mind than Adam and Leda's ultimate decision to renew the human species.

Shiel's revision of *The Purple Cloud* deserves a treatise in itself. In sheer wordage, the novel has shrunk from the 103,000 words of the 1901 edition to 93,000 words in the edition of 1929; but this does not begin to tell the whole story, for scarcely a sentence has been left unaltered. In general, Shiel has pruned what might appear to be excess adjectives and adverbs, in accordance with his echoing, in the essay "On Writing" (1909), of Voltaire's remark that "the adjective is the enemy of the noun, even though it agrees with it in gender and number."[11] Once again, individual temperament will dictate whether the loss of precision and nuance is deemed sufficiently offset by the gain in concision. David G. Hartwell maintains: "This cutting and revision has the subtle and pernicious effect of removing the work from a firm grounding in its own period and casting it adrift as a literary-historical hybrid,"[12] but this criticism seems a bit captious: Shiel was under no obligation to preserve his novel as an

10. Lovecraft to Rheinhart Kleiner, 25 June 1920; *Selected Letters 1911–1924*, p. 120.

11. "On Writing," in *Science Life and Literature* (London: Williams & Norgate, 1950), p. 89.

12. "Introduction" to *The Purple Cloud* (Gregg Press, 1977); rpt. in *Shiel in Divers Hands*, ed. A. Reynolds Morse (Cleveland: Reynolds Morse Foundation, 1983), p. 115.

historical artifact, and in many ways his revisions do tighten up the work and render it more idiomatic and smooth-flowing. However, since Lovecraft's judgment of it is evidently based upon his reading of the 1901 edition, that is the text we present here.

It is difficult to detect any clear influence of Shiel upon Lovecraft. Even "The House of Sounds," although it perennially made Lovecraft's lists of his favourite weird tales,[13] may have been of significance only as a stellar example of the sense of the cosmic in literature. One telling detail, however, may be worth noting: its mention of a "door, half a mile wide, flat on the ground" seems highly suggestive of the entrance to Cthulhu's suddenly risen city of R'lyeh, which Lovecraft describes in "The Call of Cthulhu" (1926) as an "immense carved door with the now familiar squid-dragon bas-relief," later remarking: "It was . . . like a great barn-door; and they all felt that it was a door because of the ornate lintel, threshold, and jambs around it, though they could not decide whether it may flat like a trap-door or slantwise like an outside cellar-door."[14] (This detail, however, might also have been derived from the "moon-door" featured in A. Merritt's "The Moon-Pool.") Shiel's account of the preparations for the voyage to the North Pole in the opening pages of *The Purple Cloud* may perhaps have had some minimal influence upon Lovecraft's similar description of the preparations of the Miskatonic Expedition to Antarctica, although the parallels are very loose and general.

Suffice it to say that, in Shiel, Lovecraft found a weird writer working along surprisingly similar lines—one who cultivated a mannered, almost *recherché* style to create a kind of incantatory effect upon the reader; one who scorned conventional character portrayal to depict Poe-like protagonists full of quirks, eccentricities, and scorn of mundane morality; and one who looked upon his early work with disfavour and chose to amend it by shearing away some of its grotesqueries of style and incident in light of a newer aesthetic that sought to convey more with less. Lovecraft never got the chance to revise his work in the wholesale manner in which Shiel transformed "Vaila" into "The House of Sounds" or the *Purple Cloud* of 1901 into its leaner version of 1929; but the chances are that, had he been given that chance, he might have pruned away some of the excrescences in his early tales to match the tightly knit rigour of his later ones. Lovecraft in effect performed the same function by taking the core of such plots as those of "Dagon" and "Facts concerning the Late Arthur Jermyn and His Family" and transforming them into "The Call of Cthulhu" and "The Shadow over Innsmouth," respectively. Whether he would have taken a scalpel to those latter works, had he lived another decade or more, is a question that must forever remain unanswered.

—S. T. Joshi

---

13. See "Favourite Weird Stories of H. P. Lovecraft" (*Fantasy Fan*, October 1934); in *The Annotated Supernatural Horror in Literature*, p. 73.

14. *The Dunwich Horror and Others* (Sauk City, WI: Arkham House, 1984), p. 151.

A Note on the Texts

Of the stories in this volume, "Xélucha" and "Vaila" are taken from *Shapes in the Fire* (1896); "The Pale Ape," "The Case of Euphemia Raphash," "Huguenin's Wife," "The House of Sounds," "The Great King," and "The Bride" are taken from *The Pale Ape and Other Pulses* (1911). The 1901 edition of *The Purple Cloud* (not available since its original edition, aside from the Gregg Press edition of 1977) has been printed here, as it is presumably the edition read by Lovecraft.

I am grateful for John D. Squires for his assistance and encouragement in the compilation of this volume. David E. Schultz provided valuable aid in many particulars.

—S. T. J.

The House of Sounds and Others

Xélucha

"He goeth after her . . . and knoweth not . . ."

[FROM A DIARY]

Three days ago! by heaven, it seems an age. But I am shaken—my reason is debauched. A while since, I fell into a momentary coma precisely resembling an attack of *petit mal.* "Tombs, and worms, and epitaphs"—that is my dream. At my age, with my physique, to walk staggery, like a man stricken! But all that will pass: I must collect myself—my reason is debauched. Three days ago! it seems an age! I sat on the floor before an old cista full of letters. I lighted upon a packet of Cosmo's. Why, I had forgotten them! they are turning sere! Truly, I can no more call myself a young man. I sat reading, listlessly, rapt back by memory. To muse is to be lost! of *that* evil habit I must wring the neck, or look to perish. Once more I threaded the mazy sphere-harmony of the minuet, reeled in the waltz, long pomps of candelabra, the noonday of the bacchanal, about me. Cosmo was the very tsar and maharajah of the Sybarites! the Priap of the *détraqués!* In every unexpected alcove of the Roman Villa was a couch, raised high, with necessary foot-stool, flanked and canopied with *mirrors* of clarified gold. Consumption fastened upon him; reclining at last at table, he could, till warmed, scarce lift the wine! his eyes were like two fat glow-worms, coiled together! they seemed haloed with vaporous emanations of phosphorus! Desperate, one could see, was the secret struggle with the Devourer. But to the end the princely smile persisted calm; to the end—to the last day—he continued among that comic crew unchallenged choragus of all the rites, I will not say of Paphos, but of Chemos! and Baal-Peor! Warmed, he did not refuse the revel, the dance, the darkened chamber. It was utterly black, rayless; approached by a secret passage; in shape circular; the air hot, haunted always by odours of balms, bdellium, hints of dulcimer and flute; and radiated round with a hundred thick-strewn ottomans of Morocco. Here Lucy Hill stabbed to the heart Caccofogo, mistaking the scar on his back for the scar of Soriac. In a bath of malachite the Princess Egla, waking late one morning, found Cosmo lying stiffly dead, the water covering him wholly.

"But in God's name, Mérimée!" (so he wrote), "to think of Xélucha dead! Xélucha! Can a moon-beam, then, perish of suppurations? Can the rainbow be eaten by worms? Ha! ha! ha! laugh with me, my friend: *'elle dérangera l'Enfer'!* She will introduce the *pas de tarantule* into Tophet! Xélucha, the feminine! Xélucha recalling the splendid harlots of history! Weep with me—manat rara meas lacrima per genas! expert as Thargelia; cultured as Aspatia; purple as Semiramis. She comprehended the human tabernacle, my friend, its secret

springs and tempers, more intimately than any *savant* of Salamanca who
breathes. *Tarare*—but Xélucha is not dead! Vitality is not mortal; you, cannot
wrap flame in a shroud. Xélucha! where then is she? Translated, perhaps—rapt
to a constellation like the daughter of Leda. She journeyed to Hindostan, accompanied by the train and appurtenance of a Begum, threatening descent
upon the Emperor of Tartary. I spoke of the desolation of the West; she kissed
me, and promised return. Mentioned you, too, Mérimée—'her Conqueror'—
'Mérimée, Destroyer of Woman.' A breath from the conservatory rioted among
the ambery whiffs of her forelocks, sending it singly a-wave over that thulite
tint you know. Costumed cap-à-pie, she had, my friend, the dainty little completeness of a daisy mirrored bright in the eye of the browsing ox. A simile of
Milton had for years, she said, inflamed the lust of her Eye: 'The barren plains
of Sericana, where Chineses drive with sails and wind their cany wagons light.'
I, and the Sabæans, she assured me, wrongly considered Flame the whole of
being; the other half of things being Aristotle's quintessential light. In the
Ourania Hierarchia and the Faust-book you meet a completeness: burning
Seraph, Cherûb full of eyes. Xélucha combined them. She would reconquer the
Orient for Dionysius, and return. I heard of her blazing at Delhi; drawn in a
chariot by lions. Then this rumour—probably false. Indeed, it comes from a
source somewhat turgid. Like Odin, Arthur, and the rest, Xélucha—will reappear."

Soon subsequently, Cosmo lay down in his balneum of malachite, and
slept, having drawn over him the water as a coverlet. I, in England, heard little
of Xélucha: first that she was alive, then dead, then alighted at old Tadmor in
the Wilderness, Palmyra now. Nor did I greatly care, Xélucha having long
since turned to apples of Sodom in my mouth. Till I sat by the cista of letters
and re-read Cosmo, she had for some years passed from my active memories.

The habit is now confirmed in me of spending the greater part of the day
in sleep, while by night I wander far and wide through the city under the seda-
tive influence of a tincture which has become necessary to my life. Such an existence of shadow is not without charm; nor, I think, could many minds be
steadily subjected to its conditions without elevation, deepened awe. To travel
alone with the Primordial cannot but be solemn. The moon is of the hue of the
glow-worm; and Night of the sepulchre. Nux bore not less Thanatos than
Hupnos, and the bitter tears of Isis redundulate to a flood. At three, if a cab
rolls by, the sound has the augustness of thunder. Once, at two, near a corner,
I came upon a priest, seated, dead, leering, his legs bent. One arm, supported
on a knee, pointed with rigid accusing forefinger obliquely upward. By exact
observation, I found that he indicated Betelgeux, the star "*a*" which shoulders
the wet sword of Orion. He was hideously swollen, having perished of dropsy.
Thus in all Supremes is a *grotesquerie*; and one of the sons of Night is—Buffo.

In a London square deserted, I should imagine, even in the day, I was
aware of the metallic, silvery-clinking approach of little shoes. It was three in a
heavy morning of winter, a day after my rediscovery of Cosmo. I had stood by
the railing, regarding the clouds sail as under the sea-legged pilotage of a moon

wrapped in cloaks of inclemency. Turning, I saw a little lady, very gloriously dressed. She had walked straight to me. Her head was bare, and crisped with the amber stream which rolled lax to a globe, kneaded thick with jewels, at her nape. In the redundance of her décolleté development, she resembled Parvati, mound-hipped love-goddess of the luscious fancy of the Brahmin.

She addressed to me the question:

"What are you doing there, darling?"

Her loveliness stirred me, and Night is *bon camarade*. I replied:

"Sunning myself by means of the moon."

"All that is borrowed lustre," she returned, "you have got it from old Drummond's *Flowers of Sion*."

Looking back, I cannot remember that this reply astonished me, though it should—of course—have done so. I said:

"On my soul, no; but you?"

"You might guess whence *I* come!"

"You are dazzling. You come from Paz."

"Oh, farther than that, my son! Say a subscription ball in Soho."

"Yes? . . . and alone? in the cold? on foot . . .?"

"Why, I am old, and a philosopher. I can pick you out riding Andromeda yonder from the ridden Ram. They are in error, M'sieur, who suppose an atmosphere on the broad side of the moon. I have reason to believe that on Mars dwells a race whose lids are transparent like glass; so that the eyes are visible during sleep; and every varying dream moves imaged forth to the beholder in tiny panorama on the limpid iris. You cannot imagine me a mere *fille!* To be escorted is to admit yourself a woman, and that is improper in Nowhere. Young Eos drives an *equipage à quatre*, but Artemis 'walks' alone. Get out of my borrowed light in the name of Diogenes! I am going home."

"Far?"

"Near Piccadilly."

"But a cab?"

"No cabs for *me*, thank you. The distance is a mere nothing. Come."

We walked forward. My companion at once put an interval between us, quoting from the *Spanish Curate* that the open is an enemy to love. The Talmudists, she twice insisted, rightly held the hand the sacredest part of the person, and at that point also contact was for the moment interdict. Her walk was extremely rapid. I followed. Not a cat was anywhere visible. We reached at length the door of a mansion in St. James's. There was no light. It seemed tenantless, the windows all uncurtained, pasted across, some of them, with the words, To Let. My companion, however, flitted up the steps, and, beckoning, passed inward. I, following, slammed the door, and was in darkness. I heard her ascend, and presently a region of glimmer above revealed a stairway of marble, curving broadly up. On the floor where I stood was no carpet, nor furniture: the dust was very thick. I had begun to mount when, to my surprise, she stood by my side, returned; and whispered:

"To the very top, darling."

She soared nimbly up, anticipating me. Higher, I could no longer doubt that the house was empty but for us. All was a vacuum full of dust and echoes. But at the top, light streamed from a door, and I entered a good-sized oval saloon, at about the centre of the house. I was completely dazzled by the sudden resplendence of the apartment. In the midst was a spread table, square, opulent with gold plate, fruit, dishes; three ponderous chandeliers of electric light above; and I noticed also (what was very *bizarre*) one little candlestick of common tin containing an old soiled curve of tallow, on the table. The impression of the whole chamber was one of gorgeousness not less than Assyrian. An ivory couch at the far end was made sun-like by a head-piece of chalcedony forming a sea for the sport of emerald ichthyotauri. Copper hangings, panelled with mirrors in iasperated crystal, corresponded with a dome of flame and copper; yet this latter, I now remember, produced upon my glance an impression of actual grime. My companion reclined on a small Sigma couch, raised high to the table-level in the Semitic manner, visible to her saffron slippers of satin. She pointed me a seat opposite. The incongruity of its presence in the middle of this arrogance of pomp so tickled me, that no power could have kept me from a smile: it was a grimy chair, mean, all wood, nor was I long in discovering one leg somewhat shorter than its fellows.

She indicated wine in a black glass bottle, and a tumbler, but herself made no pretence of drinking or eating. She lay on hip and elbow, *petite*, resplendent, and looked gravely upward. I, however, drank.

"You are tired," I said, "one sees that."

"It is precious little that *you* see!" she returned, dreamy, hardly glancing.

"How! your mood is changed, then? You are morose."

"You never, I think, saw a Norse passage-grave?"

"And abrupt."

"Never?"

"A passage-grave? No."

"It is worth a journey! They are circular or oblong chambers of stone, covered by great earth-mounds, with a 'passage' of slabs connecting them with the outer air. All round the chamber the dead sit with head resting upon the bent knees, and consult together in silence."

"Drink wine with me, and be less Tartarean."

"You certainly seem to be a fool," she replied with perfect sardonic iciness." Is it not, then, highly romantic? They belong, you know, to the Neolithic age. As the teeth fall, one by one, from the lipless mouths—they are caught by the lap. When the lap thins—they roll to the floor of stone. Thereafter, every tooth that drops all round the chamber sharply breaks the silence."

"Ha! ha! ha!"

"Yes. It is like a century-slow, circularly-successive dripping of slime in some cavern of the far subterrene."

"Ha! ha! This wine seems heady! They express themselves in a dialect largely dental."

"The Ape, on the other hand, in a language wholly guttural."

A town-clock tolled four. Our talk was holed with silences, and heavy-paced. The wine's yeasty exhalation reached my brain. I saw her through mist, dilating large, uncertain, shrinking again to dainty compactness. But amorousness had died within me.

"Do you know," she asked, "what has been discovered in one of the Danish *Kjökkenmöddings* by a little boy? It was ghastly. The skeleton of a huge fish with human—"

"You are most unhappy."

"Be silent."

"You are full of care."

"I think you a great fool."

"You are racked with misery."

"You are a child. You have not even an instinct of the meaning of the word."

"How! Am I not a man? I, too, miserable, careful?"

"You are not, really, *anything*—until you can create."

"Create what?"

"Matter."

"That is foppish. Matter cannot be created, nor destroyed."

"Truly, then, you must be a creature of unusually weak intellect. I see that now. Matter does not exist, then, there is no such thing, really,—it is an appearance, a spectrum—every writer not imbecile from Plato to Fichte has, voluntary or involuntary, proved that for your good. To create it is to produce an impression of its reality upon the senses of others; to destroy it is to wipe a wet rag across a scribbled slate."

"Perhaps. I do not care. Since no one can do it."

"No one? You are mere embryo—"

"Who then?"

"*Anyone*, whose power of Will is equivalent to the gravitating force of a star of the First Magnitude."

"Ha! ha! ha! By heaven, you choose to be facetious. Are there then wills of such equivalence?"

"There have been three, the founders of religions. There was a fourth: a cobbler of Herculaneum, whose mere volition induced the cataclysm of Vesuvius in 79, in direct opposition to the gravity of Sirius. There are more fames than *you* have ever sung, you know. The greater number of disembodied spirits, too, I feel certain—"

"By heaven, I cannot but think you full of sorrow! Poor wight! come, drink with me. The wine is thick and boon. Is it not Setian? It makes you sway and swell before me, I swear, like a purple cloud of evening—"

"But you are mere clayey ponderance!—I did not know that!—you are no companion! your little interest revolves round the lowest centres."

"Come—forget your agonies—"

"What, think you, is the portion of the buried body first sought by the worm?"

"The eyes! the eyes!"

"You are *hideously* wrong—you are so *utterly* at sea—"

"My God!"

She had bent forward with such rage of contradiction as to approach me closely. A loose gown of amber silk, wide-sleeved, had replaced her ball attire, though at what opportunity I could not guess; wondering, I noticed it as she now placed her palms far forth upon the table. A sudden wafture as of spice and orange-flowers, mingled with the abhorrent faint odour of mortality over-ready for the tomb, greeted my sense. A chill crept upon my flesh.

"You are so *hopelessly* at fault—"

"For God's sake—"

"You are so *miserably* deluded! Not the eyes *at all!*"

"Then, in Heaven's name, what?"

Five tolled from a clock.

"*The Uvula!* the soft drop of mucous flesh, you know, suspended from the palate above the glottis. They eat through the face-cloth and cheek, or crawl by the lips through a broken tooth, filling the mouth. They make straight for it. It is the *deliciæ* of the vault."

At her horror of interest I grew sick, at her odour, and her words. Some unspeakable sense of insignificance, of debility, held me dumb.

"You say I am full of sorrows. You say I am racked with woe; that I gnash with anguish. Well, you are a mere child in intellect. You use words without realisation of meaning like those minds in what Leibnitz calls 'symbolical consciousness.' But suppose it were so—"

"It is so."

"You know nothing."

"I see you twist and grind. Your eyes are very pale. I thought they were hazel. They are of the faint bluishness of phosphorus shimmerings seen in darkness."

"That proves nothing."

"But the 'white' of the sclerotic is dyed to yellow. And you look inward. Why do you look so palely inward, so woe-worn, upon your soul? Why can you speak of nothing but the sepulchre, and its rottenness? Your eyes seem to me wan with centuries of vigil, with mysteries and millenniums of pain."

"Pain! but you know so *little* of it! you are wind and words! of its philosophy and *rationale* nothing!"

"Who knows?"

"I will give you a hint. It is the sub-consciousness in conscious creatures of Eternity, and of eternal loss. The least prick of a pin not Pæan and Æsculapius and the powers of heaven and hell can utterly heal. Of an everlasting loss of pristine wholeness the conscious body is sub-conscious, and 'pain' is its sigh at the tragedy. So with all pain—greater, the greater the loss. The hugest of losses is, of course, the loss of Time. If you lose that, any of it, you plunge at once into the transcendentalisms, the infinitudes, of Loss; if you lose *all of it*—"

"But you so wildly exaggerate! Hal ha! You rant, I tell you, of commonplaces with the woe—"

"Hell is where a clear, untrammelled Spirit is sub-conscious of lost Time; where it boils and writhes with envy of the living world; *hating* it for ever, and all the sons of Life!"

"But curb yourself! Drink—I implore—I *implore*—for God's sake—but *once*—"

"To *hasten* to the snare—*that* is woe! to drive your ship upon the *lighthouse* rock—that is Marah! To wake, and feel it irrevocably true that you went after her—*and the dead were there*—and her guests were in the depths of hell—*and you did not know it!*—though you *might* have. Look out upon the houses of the city this dawning day: not one, I tell you, but in it haunts some soul—walking up and down the old theatre of its little Day—goading imagination by a thousand childish tricks, vraisemblances—elaborately duping itself into the momentary fantasy *that it still lives,* that the chance of life is not for ever and for ever lost—yet riving all the time with under-memories of the wasted Summer, the lapsed brief light between the two eternal glooms—riving I say and shriek to you!—riving, *Mérimée, you destroying fiend*—"

She had sprung—*tall* now, she seemed to me—between couch and table.

"Mérimée!" I screamed,—"*my* name, harlot, in your maniac mouth! By God, woman, you terrify me to death!"

I too sprang, the hairs of my head catching stiff horror from my fancies.

"Your name? Can you imagine me ignorant of your name, or anything concerning you? Mérimée! Why, did you not sit yesterday and read of me in a letter of Cosmo's?"

"Ah-h . . .," hysteria bursting high in sob and laughter from my and lips— "Ah! ha! ha! Xélucha! My memory grows palsied and grey, Xélucha! pity me— my walk is in the very valley of shadow!—senile and sere!—observe my hair, Xélucha, its grizzled growth—trepidant, Xélucha, clouded—I am not the man you knew, Xélucha, in the palaces—of Cosmo! You are Xélucha!"

"You rave, poor worm!" she cried, her face contorted by a species of malicious contempt. "Xélucha died of cholera ten years ago at Antioch. I wiped the froth from her lips. Her nose underwent a green decay before burial. So far sunken into the brain was the left eye—"

"You are—*you are* Xélucha!" I shrieked; "voices now of thunder howl it within my consciousness—and by the holy God, Xélucha, though you blight me with the breath of the hell you are, I shall clasp you,—living or damned—"

I rushed toward her. The word "Madman!" hissed as by the tongues of ten thousand serpents through the chamber, I heard; a belch of pestilent corruption puffed poisonous upon the putrid air; for a moment to my wildered eyes there seemed to rear itself, swelling high to the roof, a formless tower of ragged cloud, and before my projected arms had closed upon the very emptiness of inanity, I was tossed by the operation of some Behemoth potency far-circling backward to the utmost circumference of the oval, where, my head colliding, I fell, shocked, into insensibility.

*   *   *   *   *

When the sun was low toward night, I lay awake, and listlessly observed the grimy roof, and the sordid chair, and the candlestick of tin, and the bottle of which I had drunk. The table was small, filthy, of common deal, uncovered. All bore the appearance of having stood there for years. But for them, the room was void, the vision of luxury thinned to air. Sudden memory flashed upon me. I scrambled to my feet, and plunged and tottered, bawling, through the twilight into the street.

The Pale Ape

"A big thing of a pig."—ARISTOPHANES.

Yesterday again I stood and looked at Hargen Hall from the lake; and it is this that has brought me to write of my life in it. Wintry winds were whistling through the withered bracken and the branches, whirling withered birch-leaves about the south quadrangle; and no birds sang.

When I first entered it I was a girl, one might say—gay enough; but now I have known what one never forgets; and the days and the hairs grow grey together.

Five titled names among my friends gained me an entrance to Hargen in the fall of the year '98. 1 arrived on the evening of 10th November; and shall never forget the strangeness of the impression made on my mind that night: for even ere I rounded into sight of the house, the sound of the waters far off filled me with a feeling of the eerily dreary—the house being almost surrounded with mountain and cliff, down which a series of cascades shower; and that night I had some difficulty in catching quite everything that was said to me, though in two or three days, maybe, my ear became used to the tumult.

It was four days before I met Sir Philip Lister himself—Davenport, the old butler, told me that his master was "indisposed"—but Sir Philip sent me a polite missive inviting me to take things carelessly a little: so I spent the first days in learning my pupil's moods, and in roaming over the place from "Queen Elizabeth's Room"—behind the bed still hung a velvet shield broidered with the royal arms in white wire—to the apes and the cascades. A sense of forlornness pervaded it all, for scarcely ten of us were in all the desert of that place, with an occasional glimpse of two or three gardeners, or a groom. The kitchen was now a panelled hall like a chapel, with windows of painted glass containing the six coats-of-arms of the Lister-Lynns, a hall in whose vastness the cook and her assistant looked awfully forlorn and small; and hardly even a housemaid ever now entered all that part of the east wing which had been singed by a fire fifty-five years since.

It was on the fourth forenoon, a day of "the Indian summer," that my pupil took me to see the apes. There were three of them—two chimpanzees, one gibbon—in three rooms of wire-netting close to the east line of cliffs, i.e., about six hundred yards from the house. There, chuckling and chattering in the shadow of chestnuts, they lived their lives, anon speculating like philosophers upon their knots, or hearkening to the waters which chanted near in their ears. And there was a *fourth* room of netting in the row, but empty; as to which my pupil said to me:

"The one that used to be in this fourth room was huge, Miss Newnes, and had a pale face. He died some time before I came to Hargen: but his ghost walks when the moon is at the full."

"Now Esmé," I muttered. (Her name was Esmé Martagon, daughter of the Marquis de Martagon and of Margaret Lister, Sir Philip's sister; the child being at this time twelve years of age, and an orphan—a rather pretty elf with ebon curls, but as changeable as the shapes of mercury, now bursting with alacrity, and now cursed with black turns of sadness.)

"But if I have seen it?" she gravely, replied, gazing up at me with her great eyes.

"The ghost of an ape, Esmé," I muttered.

For answer, flying off into vivacity, she cried to me: "Come, you shall hear it!"—and she led the way northward through the park, until we walked down a dark path tremulous with spray, where one of the smaller waterfalls came down. By stepping on the tops of rocks in its froth, one could get, in the rear of the torrent, into a grot, where the greenery grew very vigorous and gay from the perpetual spray; and when I had followed Esmé's career into this hollow in the rock, she hollaed into my ear in opposition to the tons of thunder sounding down: "Now, listen a little: this one is named 'The Ape.'"

For some minutes—three to six—I heard nothing but the burden of the cascade's murmur, and was now about to say something sceptical, when there sounded what I am bound to say affected me in a rather startling way—a sound very sharp and energetic—the *chuckle, chuckle* of a monkey—most pressing, most imperative, in its summons to the attention. It was over in a moment; but presently came again: and in the course of half an hour's listening it came altogether five times, not quite at regular intervals, but still with a kind of periodicity: and I concluded that some small cause, perhaps only a condition of the wind, acted ever and anon to modify the cataract's tract, and produce this curious cackling.

My pupil hollaed to me: "And if you kept on waiting to hear, and listening to it, do you know what would happen to you, Miss Newnes?"—and when I asked what, she called: "You would go stark mad!"

"Not I," I said.

One of the shadows darkened the child's face; and presently she remarked: "I should, I know. Three of the ladies of the Listers, and one of the Lynns, have—among them my mother's mother. It is in the blood, I think."

I started!—for I now suddenly believed her. Indeed, to my consciousness, there was something ironic in the torrent's chuckle, and at once, taking the child's hand, I said: "Come."

Later in the day when we were together in what is called "the Great Hall," Esmé, ever sage beyond her age, again spoke of the chuckling cascade, begging me not to mention, or show it to her Cousin Huggins when he came: for a young man of this name, who had hardly been at Hargen since he was six, was coming from India in some months, and was expected to spend a month with us.

It was that night that, for the first time, I saw Sir Philip Lister: for he dined with Esmé and Mrs Wiseman and me in the main building dining-room, the old Davenport waiting upon us in state with his silent footsteps, we five making a pretty insignificant group in that great room, whose array of windows have a south aspect upon the south quadrangle. It has (or had) tapestry all round, and rows of Jacobean carving-tables, which give the room an air of very gloomy state; and a wood-fire bickered on the iron-work fire-back, under whose oak overmantel Sir Philip sat with Esmé and me ten minutes then took himself away into his own sequestered nook of the house.

Two days after this he again had dinner with us, and again the day after that; but that third time the child, in one of her chatterbox fits, chanced to observe that "Uncle Philip is lending his presence since Miss Newnes has come"—and like a bird that shies Sir Philip showed himself no more to us for many days.

I regretted this, for his presence interested me, his manners were in such a high degree grave, dignified, and gracious. He was big, and, if not handsome, interesting to the eye—quaint, one might say—his face smooth like an actor's, his hair longer than usual, with great owl-eyes, whose glowering underlook was thronged, to my thinking, with mysteries of sorrow—something shifting, though, uncandidly shy, in them. His age I guessed to be about forty-five.

He was engaged in the writing of what I heard was "a great work," six volumes long, on "The Old Kingdom" (fourth to sixth dynasty of Egyptian Kings), and lived a life of such privacy, that it was three weeks ere I met him afresh. Meantime, Esmé and I entered upon the course of our adventurous studies—"adventurous," for never for two hours together was my pupil the same girl. Esmé had fits of headache; and she had fits of reading, when she feasted upon volumes with a hungry vulture's greed; and she had fits of indolence, dormouse torpors, fits of crying, dark-minded lamentations, fits of flightiness, of crazy dissipation, of craving for—wine. As for her knowledge, it was astonishing in such a child, and she anon plied me with queries to which I could find no reply.

On a forenoon in the fourth week, when she was feeling out of sorts, we were sauntering in the park, when, for once, I saw Sir Philip out of doors. We came upon him with his face against the ape-house netting, gazing in at the gibbon—so eagerly, that we were near him ere he seemed to hear us. When he suddenly saw us, he stood struck into a posture as of suspense, but presently was very affable in his reserved manner, and conversed with me some minutes about the apes and their various traits. They had the names of Egyptian kings, the chimpanzees being Pepy II. and Khety, and the gibbon Sety I.; and at the gibbon Sir Philip shook his finger, saying with a playful solemnity: "*That fellow! That fellow!*"—I had no idea what he meant.

Suddenly, in the midst of our talk, he—with a certain awkwardness of his lids—proposed a picnic-luncheon out of doors to which Esmé and I readily assented. But three minutes afterwards he started, furtively murmuring the words: "I must be getting back to work," and was gone—to my astonishment!

After this he again made himself very scarce for three weeks. Esmé and I, meantime, got into the habit of spending our hours of labour in the great hall, sitting on a day-bed that lay in the solar-room gallery there—the gallery from which of old one gazed down upon the retainers at table below; and those days of my life, that I whiled away in that place, are to me at present days touched with much strangeness and a tone of Utopia. But the great place was quite plain and empty—a plain ceiling, plain white walls, oak-panelled half-way up: only, as it was lighted by fourteen great windows with shields of painted glass, when the sun glowed through them, it transfigured that old room into glory-land. . . . But it is gone from me now like a dream, and I shall not see it again.

It was on the Thursday afternoon of my thirteenth week at Hargen that I received from Sir Philip Lister a singular missive: he had injured his thumb, he said, and wished to know if I would "kindly write from his dictation." But what, then, I asked myself, was to become of Esmé meantime? I did not wish to leave the child! However, I could not say no: and so entered that day the sacred den. He, with his fingers in a sling, instantly jumped up with a gush of apologies, showering upon me a thousand thanks that were at once gushing and shy, till the shyness triumphed, and he was suddenly silent and done. Then, I sitting at an old abbey-table, he on an old farm-house settle, he dictated to me with his eyes closed, in a low tone, all about Khufu, and Khafra, and the things of "the Pyramid Age," until I had the impression that he was himself something Egyptian and most ancient, and I with him, and in which age of the world we were I was not at some moments certain. In the midst of the dictating he all at once pressed his left palm upon his forehead, as if tired or muddled, his eyes tight shut; and, jumping up, he muttered to me, "thank you! thank you!" offering me his hand. Some of his actions had a wonderful swiftness and suddenness; and that hand of his which I touched was as chill as snow: so that I made haste from him.

That night I retired, as usual, soon after eleven to my room, which was in a rather remote and lonely region of the house; and was soon asleep. Two hours later I awoke terrified—I could not quite tell why—but so terrified, that I found myself sitting up in bed—with a singular sound, or the memory or dream of a singular sound, lingering about my ears: and I was trembling, my brow was wet with sweat. Through my two windows, which stood open, shone the full moon's light, lying over the floor, lighting the stamp-work tapestry on my right; and I could hear the night-breeze breathing drearily through the leaves of the cedar, some of whose branches, held up with chains, brushed my panes. For some minutes I sat so, hearing my heart beating in my ears, the breezes shivering through the tree, the streams showering, the soundlessness of the house and hour, and as conscious of some living spirit hovering round me as though I saw it. If it had lasted long, I must have lost consciousness, or else cast off the oppression of it with a shriek: but presently something reached my ear—a chuckle, a little giggle of glee, just distinct enough to convince me that it was due to no lunacy of my ear: and immediately, with a creeping in my hair, but a species of rage and desperation elevating me, I was out of bed, and at one of the windows: for just after the chuckle a sharp rush through the leafage of the cedar seemed to reach me, and I rushed to see.

What I saw made me faint—whether instantly or after some seconds I cannot say: I know that when I came to my senses I was seated on the floor with my forehead leaning on my old oak chair, and the tower-clock was now sounding the hour of three. But however soon I may have swooned after seeing it, it was not so instantly that I could have the slightest doubt as to the actualness of what my eyes saw. For though the moonlight left the interior regions of the tree's leafage in some obscurity, I was sure that some brute of the ape species with a pale face was hanging there in the cedar—hanging head-downward among the network of chains and branches in such a way as to see into my chamber; and I have an impression of hearing—either before I fell, or through my swoon afterwards—a succession of chucklings; and then a voice somewhere remonstrating, pleading, commanding, in a secret species of shout; and then a strangled outcry of horror, of anguish, somewhere, all mingled with a dream of the chuckle of the chuckling stream.

But the strongest of my impressions was undoubtedly that drowning outcry of horror—an impression so strong, that I could hardly believe it to be a dream, or all a dream. This cry was somehow connected in my mind from the first with old Davenport; and this feeling was confirmed in me when Davenport was nowhere to be seen the next day, nor for four days after. Mrs Wiseman, the housekeeper, who for days was pale, and occasionally fell into a vacant staring, told me that Davenport was "suffering." She asked me no questions as to the night, but I twice caught her eye piercingly bent upon me with a meaning of inquiry, of anxiety, in it; and the same thing was true of Sir Philip when, three days later, he appeared towards evening: for he took my hand with a tender solicitude, and a lingering look of question in his gaze. As for Davenport, when I next saw him it was under a tree in the park, where he sat like a convalescent, in his flesh that pathetic pallor of the flesh of aged people who have passed through an illness; and the wrappings round his neck could not wholly hide from my eyes that his throat had been most brutally bruised.

During those days it was as if a blow had fallen upon Hargen. Esmé no longer laughed, and a lower tone of talk overtook us all. It was obvious that each held the consciousness of a secret which none dared breathe to another; and in vain I consumed days of musing in seeking to see into the meaning of these things. For my part, I was ailing, nor could quite hide it. I had the thought of moving out of my room, which I now shrank from entering even in the day-time, but did not care to show so openly that I was afraid. Through the nights I burned a light, but slept with my nerves awake. Not that I was ever of a very nervous temperament, I think: but terror infected me like a sickness in those days; the stare of eyes of affright in the night was ever present in my imagination; and Hargen soon grew to be to my haunted heart the very home of gloom. Then one day, on a sudden, all this trouble of mind rushed away from me like a shadow; and my being galloped into a mood of gladness in which gloom was abolished, and I forgot to be appalled in the dark.

I will tell of it very briefly. It happened that one afternoon when Esmé and I were sitting listlessly in that solar-room gallery, an open grammar lying idle between us, suddenly behind us, there rose out of the floor, as it seemed, a young man who clapped his fingers over Esmé's eyes, smiling with me the while. "Cousin Huggins!" the child cried out—much surprised, for Huggins Lister was not expected at Hargen for some days yet. He caught her up in his big arms, and bussed her like a gun, for he was a being made all of ardours and horse-play: and then he looked into my eyes, and I looked into his eyes.

It was as if I had always known him—long before I was born; and what hurried me more into the sort of maelstrom in which I was now caught was the circumstance, that on the day after that first day Esmé took a chill, remained in bed, and I was all alone with Huggins Lister in that wilderness of Hargen. The young man was, or pretended to be, interested in old things, and would have me show him all the cassone and old needlework, the Spanish glasses giving their glints of gold, the old girandoles with their amorini. He dined with me, we two alone, and Mrs Wiseman: for Sir Philip more than ever kept himself to himself. Only, on the fourth evening when Huggins Lister and I were walking in the park, Sir Philip suddenly appeared before us, walking with precipitate steps the other way; did not pause, nor utter a sound, as he passed by us with a bowed brow, his hat raised; but when he had gone some way beyond us, he stopped, and—shook his finger at us! was going, too, I am sure, to venture to say something, but failed; and suddenly was gone on his way again. I remember being very offended at the moment: but a moment more, God forgive me, had forgotten that Sir Philip Lister lived.

I showed the young man the apes, and the Queen's Room, and the cascades, save one, and the ivory inlay of the two Spanish chests, and the Tudor fireplaces, and what was in "the long gallery"; and still he wished to see things. And just under the window that lights the great staircase, there stands on the landing a sedan-chair painted with glaring variegations, the window-glass casting the gauds of the six coats-of-arms of the Lister-Lynns upon the already gaudy chair: in which chair he got me to sit—it was high noon, on the open stair, but we were as solitary there as if night veiled us in a monastery; and, indeed, all that waste of Hargen seemed but made to beguile and mislead our feet to our fate—he got me to sit in it, I say, and then, having me well in his bondage in the sedan-chair, began to sob to me with passion; and when I hid away my face for pity of him there in his passion on his knees, and dashed one wild tear from my eyes, the young man ravished my lips with his lips, there in the chair on the stair that day. I could not help it, for in respect of me Huggins Lister came, and saw, and conquered! and I was as one drugged with honey-dew, and dancing drugged, in Huggins Lister's hands.

Also, the young man persuaded like a hurricane! and hurried me as madly into marriage as those sand-forms of the sand-storm which madly waltz into oneness. Within six months, he said, he would arrange everything so as to proclaim the marriage; but meantime it must be secret, and must be immediate! Against this tyranny I made a feint of resistance; but half-heartedly; and it availed me nothing: indeed, he was dear to me, and near, and had me all in the hollow of his hand and heart. And so one forenoon I stole out of Hargen gates, and met him at a house in St Arvens townlet, the place of our marriage; but, as we were passing out, married, from the door of the house, my heart bounded into my mouth to see Sir Philip Lister walking hardly ten yards away. Yes, he who never left home was there before my eyes in the broad light in St Arvens street with his oak-stick—walking away from us, indeed, seeming unaware of our presence: yet I have an impression, too, of his head half-turned toward us a moment, of a face ashen with agitation: and my heart, for all its warmth, shivered as with a mortal chill in me.

My reeling feet led me back to Hargen in a kind of dream, a wedded wife, as wild with thoughts as with wine that day, for I was my beloved's, and he was mine: and in what way I spent that day I could not say, since I was new in heaven, and can but remember my fruitless efforts to hide from Esmé's eyes the state of my mind: for she had lately risen from her ailment, and I made a pretence of study with her, and I was severe with my dear, denying him my presence until the evening; and even then retired betimes, leaving him sighing.

My chamber-door I barricaded with a chair—a bridal childishness, since, to secure the room, I should have locked it. And I lay awake for a long hour, looking at the luminosity of the full moon, until, wearied out by the reel of my day's dream, I fell into a brief sleep.

From this a roar awoke me: and may a sound like that sound never more come to me to summon me with its trump. I understood that some soul was *in extremis*, and out of the deeps of grief and horror was horridly appealing to his God; and, finding myself on the ground, I knelt one wild second, crying aloud: "Almighty God, guard my love from harm in this house of horror." A moment more I had thrown a gown round me, and was gone out of the door.

As I ran along the corridor, trying to strike a light to the candle that I carried, there seemed to reach my ear from somewhere a chuckle very hushed and low, like the jackal chattering over its carrion; and my fingers were so shaken by this thing, that they failed to bring the match into relation with the candle's wick. When the heat reached my hand I dashed down the match. Still running, I lit another—or half lit it: for in the instant when the match fused at the scratch, I saw—or in some manner knew—that some mad and monstrous animal was with me; at the same moment the match went out, or was puffed out; and a thing most chilly cold touched my skin. I felt pain then, the pain of the awe of the darkness; and I stood palsied. But within some seconds, I think, I was rushing afresh toward the corridor-end, without the candlestick now, which had dropped from me; so that I could not see that the portal at the end, which I expected to be open as usual, was shut; and I rushed with a shock upon it. It was not only shut, but locked!—finding which, I, standing there, piled the passion of my whole soul into cry on cry, crying "Huggins! Sir Philip! Davenport! Huggins!" then I stood, hearing the streams murmuring as through eternity in the silence of the night, and the strong knocking of my heart against my side—but no reply to my calls.

This was not very astonishing, as my room was in such a solitary part of the mansion: and I stood imprisoned, suffering, expecting every second the coming upon me of that which would strike me dead with fright. The stillness lasted half a minute, perhaps, and then I became aware of a sound outside the door, a bumping going down the stairs in a regular way, like something massive being dragged down, with bump, bump, bump: and such was the solemnity and mystery of this thing to me in my solitude there in that gruesome gloom, that to linger any longer there in my pain soon grew to be impossible to me; and before I knew what I was doing I was out of a window, moving along a ledge fifty feet aloft toward the next window. The ledge was scarcely more than a foot wide, I think, and how I dared it, and why I did not fall, I can't now say. With my nose close to the wall—conscious all the time of drizzle tossed by high winds, conscious of the night full of a wild light, though the moon was quite hidden—I stepped flutteringly along over thin snow in dizzy suspense, keeping my sob until I should reach the next window: and there, as I leapt, I gave it vent, and fainted at my safety. I did not cease to hear, though, the bumping sound going down; and when it got to the bottom, something in me gave me the dauntlessness of heart to go after it.

Down I crept, haltingly, crouching, stair by stair. Half-way down I seemed to hear something being dragged over the floor below. I went on down. The sound had now gone out through a doorway, and I knew which doorway; but as I followed that way, my bare toes struck upon something cold, and I dropped upon my hands over it. I moaned then for pity of myself, because it was dark, and because I did so suffer. But I was conscious, as I dropped, of a rattle of matches, for I still had the match-box in my hand, without knowing that I had it: and the desire took me to strike a light. It was some time, though, before I would, or could, and when I eventually ventured, I saw the sight of the body of the old butler in his night-attire lying wildly before me on the floor: and I knew by a look that was in his eyes that they were for ever sightless.

At the same moment I was aware of the slamming of a door some way off; and again I knew which door—the little side-portal by the kitchen-entrance, leading out northward into the park—and again something gave vigour to my knees, and lifted my feet, to go to see. I made my way to the little portal; opened it slowly; my soles were out on the snow. And before me on the short gravel-path going north into the park I distinctly saw the pale ape, bearing a body against his breast. A moment later he laid down his heavy load, and bent over it; and when I saw him horribly muttering over it, something in me stooped, took up a stone and threw it at the brute.

It went straight to his head.

After some seconds the creature raised himself slowly, and raced with reeling feet into the darkness of the park.

I staggered then to the body, and saw that it was Huggins Lister strangled; and on the body of my beloved my senses left me.

It was ten in the day before I knew anything more; and then I lay on a bed, on one side of it Esmé, on the other side Mrs Wiseman.

The latter had a fixed stare; and from the manner in which Esmé was smiling, with her face held sideward, while she persistently counted on her fingers, I could make out that the child was now insane.

I lay still, I said nothing; little I cared.

Presently a girl named Bertha entered to murmur the words: "He isn't found yet"; and from some words murmured in reply by Mrs Wiseman, I gathered that Sir Philip Lister had disappeared.

Little I cared, I lay still and sullen, with closed lids.

Near noon again came the news that the men seeking for Sir Philip Lister could even yet discover no trace of him; but at about five in the evening he was found dying in the hollow of the rock that lies behind the cascade that they call "The Ape," and was brought to the Hall.

Very soon afterwards Mrs Wiseman, who had then left my side, flew in again to me with crying eyes, imploring me to try and go for a moment to the dying man, who was hungering to have one sight of me; and I let her throw some clothes over me, and was led by her to the death-bed.

By this time I knew—for Mrs Wiseman during the day had revealed it to me in a flood of tears—that Sir Philip Lister's mother had too much listened to the chuckling cascade, and so had borne him the being he was—a being capable at any agitation of shedding his human nature to resume the nature of the brute, and hurling away human raiment with his human nature in the murderous turbulence of his nocturnal revels—he who in my eyes had been so perfect in gentleness, so shy, so staid! But none the less I shuddered to the soul when he touched my hand to pant at me through the death-ruckle rolling in his throat: "I have loved you well"—a shudder which perhaps saved me from death or from madness, for I had lapsed that day into a mad apathy. It was nearly night then, and the light in there was very dreary; but I could still see that the hair which overgrew the ogre's frame was considerably more than an inch deep—greenish, and gross as the gorilla's. It clasped him round the throat and round the wrists in lines perfectly defined, like a perfect coat of fur that he wore; and it did not thin, but continued no less thick where it abruptly ended than everywhere else.

But he had "loved me well," and I him now—for if he had been perniciously jealous, it was for love of me that he had been jealous; and in dying he looked into my eyes with human eyes, kindly, mildly, looking "I have loved you well"; and when with his last strength he pointed to where the pebble I had flung had sunk into his skull, then I lifted my voice and wept to God because of him, and myself, and Hargen Hall and all, not caring any longer if my face was buried in the horror of his hairy breast. And so he died, and Huggins Lister, and I was left alive.

The Case of Euphemia Raphash

"Man's goings are of God: how can a man, then, understand his own way?"—PROVERBS.

Oh, Mr Parker, he is coming at last, sir!" the housekeeper said; and I: "God! the Doctor?"

"The Doctor, sir," she said—"saw him myself—he is on foot—must have passed through the north-park gates, and is at this moment coming up the drive!"

I ran to the lawn; saw him slowly coming in the old frock-coat of flimsy stuff, his gaze on the ground.

"Ah, Parker,"—he glanced up and held out a limp hand—"Well, I hope."

"*I* am well enough, thanks, Doctor."

"But why the accented *I*? My sister, Parker?"

I was astounded! "You have not, then, heard?" I asked.

"I have heard nothing."

"In heaven's name! In what land have you, then, been?"

"Parker, in a land fairly far away."

I said nothing more, nor he. He felt fear—fear to ask the question which I felt fear to answer; and we moved together into the gloomy home, an ancient place in ruins, the home of a race most ancient; till in the room we called "study" he seated himself on our sofa, and with complete composure said: "Now, Parker—my sister."

"Miss Euphemia, Doctor, is no more."

His face was stone; after a minute I distinctly heard him murmur: "I thought as much. So it happened once before."

What had? Heaven knew! I only added: "Three weeks ago, Doctor."

"Of what?"

"She was—"

"Say it."

"Doctor, she was—"

"Oh, say it, man—she was murdered."

"Doctor, she was murdered."

I see him again now—spare and pigmy, grand in forehead, which at the top bristled with a scrub of iron-grey; yellow shaven face; and those eyes, grey, so unquiet, never an instant still, a name high in the eye of the world among the hierophants of learning. During the fifteen years of my secretaryship, we had produced ten books, every one monumental in its way. His energies, in fact, might be called vast—though I don't say steady, or at least not steady so far as I was concerned: for anon, perhaps in the midst of some work, he would suddenly vanish from Raphash, without warning, nor at such times did I ever know whether it was some Old Dynasty "find" that had enticed him overseas, or excavations at Mycenæ, or at Khorsabad, or at Balbec: I knew only that he was gone, and that in due course he would as quietly be back again at his labours.

An old "lady-housekeeper" and myself, besides the Doctor and Miss Euphemia, were the only inmates of the old place, for we occupied only an insignificant nook of the ground-floor of one of the wings. Never a visitor broke in upon our solitude, except one man, whose calls always corresponded with the Doctor's absences. The lengthy *tête-à-têtes* of this gentleman with Miss Euphemia led me to suspect an ancient flame, to which the Doctor had had objections.

Miss Euphemia was a lady of forty-five years, taller than her brother, but remarkably like him. She, too, had become learned by dint of reading the Doctor's books. I cannot now say how it was, for they hardly ever exchanged a word, but I had arrived at the certainty that each of these lives was as necessary to the other as the air it breathed.

Yet for three weeks the newspapers had been discussing her disappearance, and he knew nothing of the matter! He looked at me through half-closed lids, and said, with that dryness of tone which was his: "Tell me the circumstances."

I answered: "I was away in London on business connected with your Shropshire seat, and can only repeat the depositions of Mrs Grant. Miss Raphash had, strange to say, been persuaded to attend the funeral of a lady, known to her in youth, at Ringlethorpe; and, staying afterwards with the mourning friends, did not return till midnight. She wore, it seems, some of the old jewels. By one o'clock, however, the house was in darkness; and it was an hour later that a shriek reached Mrs Grant's ears. She managed to light a candle, and had opened her door, when she saw a man rushing towards her with some singular weapon in his hand which flashed in the half-dark—a little man, she thinks. She had but time to slam her door, when he dashed himself frantically against it, whereupon she fancies she heard the angry remonstrance of another man. Here, however, her evidence is vague; some hours later when she woke to consciousness, she rushed to Miss Raphash's room, and found it empty."

"Of the jewels?"

"Of Miss Raphash herself."

"And the jewels?"

"They lay on the dressing-table where they had been placed, untouched."

"Clearly the murderer was not a burglar."

"Clearly he *was*. He, or they, took other things, valuables from your room and mine to the amount of four hundred pounds."

"But some of these have been traced?"

"Not one. Some have been found—none 'traced.'"

"Where found?"

"In a clump of bushes immediately beneath the balcony of the south wing."

"They were singular burglars. And my sister's body was found—"

"Nowhere."

"It was buried in the park."

"Quite certainly not. The park has been subjected to too minute a scrutiny for that."

"It was burned."

"Not in the house, and again not in the grounds. It was for some ghastly reason conveyed away."

"It is not *now* in the house, for instance?"

"No—if the most recondite search in the darkest recesses of the mansion are of any value."

"There were blood-stains?"

"A few on the bed."

"No clue?"

"One. It would seem that the assassin, or one of them, before gaining entrance, drew off his boots, and, on running away, left them, for some undreamable reason, behind him."

"It is very simple. He went in a pair of yours or mine."

"No. Had his foot, as measured by his boot, been one-third as small, it could never have been forced into a boot of yours or mine."

"Yet Mrs Grant says he was a small man; it is peculiar he should have so huge a foot."

"It seems clear that there were more than one."

"Yet I incline to the one-man theory: for through some failure of courage or memory, one might have left the jewels but hardly two. Mrs Grant, being distracted, may have mistaken his stature; and in the course of my anthropological experience, I have even come across that very discrepancy between man and foot—the survival of a simian trait."

"There is another point," I said, "the boots were found to be odd."

"But that is a clue!" he said. "I have the man in my grasp. Have you now told me everything?"

"Except that a gentleman had called to see Miss Raphash that afternoon."

"Ah—what sort of man?"

"Tall, black-dressed, middle-aged, with side-whiskers. I have seen him here when you have been away. Mrs Grant says that Miss Raphash spoke to him with some show of anger, though no phrases could be made out."

"Ah!" said the Doctor, and resumed a restless walk.

"It is not impossible," he remarked after a while, "that deeps, dark to the eye of a policeman, may become visible to the eye of a thinker. Let us go over the house."

Science had habituated the Doctor to labour without the stimulus of expectancy, and in this search we spent hours in the vastnesses of the house, the stillness of wings which perhaps no step had set barking with echoes for centu-

ries, down in the vaults. We came at length to a room on the second floor of
the south wing overlooking a patch of shrubbery—a room very damp and
gloomy, its arras rotted to grey shreds. The Doctor had used it as a depository
of bones, embrya in formalin, fossils, implements of stone, and bronze. Along
one side was a chest, which, as well as a recess behind a panel in the wall, contained piles of bones, all labelled.

The lock of the door was of special construction, and the Doctor had the
key ever about him. I could not therefore but smile, when on entering, I said to
him: "Here, at least, our search is fantastic."

He glanced at me, and passed in doggedly to a gloaming where the light
that struggled through the grime of the window-glass hardly lit bits of armour,
or grave-stones of Etruria showing in the gloom grey freckles of fungus, a dank
dust covering everything.

"Someone has been here," said the Doctor.

"Doctor!"

"The catch of the window seems awry; notice the dust on the floor."

"But it is impossible, it is impossible," I answered.

He opened the window. Below was the balcony of the first floor of that
wing, from which a rain-spout ran up; and it was among the bushes of the
shrubbery just under the balcony that the stolen valuables had been discovered.

"He climbed up, you see, by the spout," said the Doctor, "the feat seems
superhuman: but there is the spout, and here the turned window-catch. We
must confront phenomena as we find them."

"But at least, Doctor, he did not climb up with a dead body in his arms?"

"No; you are right."

"And he did not enter by the door."

"No."

"Then our search here is absurd."

"Doubtless. You might look behind the panelling."

I looked, and saw only the bones of old bodies.

"She is not *in here* now?" he said, and tapped the oaken chest with his
knuckles.

I smiled. "No, Doctor, not in there. The man does not live who could
open with a key *that* lid."

"Come, then, Parker. Come—we shall find her."

We moved out, and he locked its old solitude within the room once more.

* * * * *

Men of great intellects undertake tasks which, from their very largeness,
seem simply pig-headed or silly to men of smaller gauge. The region of the impossible, indeed, is the real sphere-of-action of genius. But, on the other hand,
the crowd may be excused if, in such cases, they become incredulous, resentful,
nay, cachinatory.

And, I confess, it was not without resentment that I listened to Doctor Raphash when he said to me: "Let us find *him*, Parker, the murderer of my sister, the secreter of her body. This is a task which we must not relegate to the intellects of the recognised authorities. Let us hunt him down—and, *after* that, we shall resume our studies."

But his method, at least, was singular. To acquire personal intimacy with a whole class of individuals is an undertaking which, if possible, is the tallest order! But this was his notion; and in a few months we had learned a new language, become denizens of a new world—the language and the world of the East of London. Our dress was the dress of the navvy; our habits those of the ne'er-do-well.

And now were revealed to me the deeps in Doctor Raphash's character. The intensity of his hatred of an unknown man! "Let us hunt *him* down," he said, and his life became the incarnation of that sentence—a fury bordering on lunacy behind the scientist calm; the avenging angel *without* the flaming sword.

Days and nights we spent in public-houses, gambling-hells, cells of pawnbrokers, with roughs at slum-corners, crowds at music-hall doors. We were pals of rascals who related to each other without secrecy or shame their achievements in every species of felony. In the mornings we parted; to compare late at night notes of the day's haps. Then far into the morning I would hear the slow cheetah-step of that divine patience stealing to and fro in his chamber near mine. This, and a heightened glare in his eyes, were all the indication he gave of the mania flaming in his heart.

One day I heard something. It was in a gin-palace where two women, dissolute pigs, gossiped upon their pots.

"And how about your old man, then?" I heard.

"Oh, he must fish for hisself, he must. I took his boots to the pawn this morning, and they wouldn't take them."

"Ain't they no good?"

"They're good enough, but they're odd."

"Go on!"

"I near tore his eyes out over them same boots. I buys my lord a seven-and-eleven pair in the summer and sends him hop-picking in them; lo and behold! two months ago he turns up with his own boot on the right foot and somebody else's on the other."

"And what account did he give of hisself?"

"There's where the provoking part of it comes in. Every time I asks him, it's 'Drop it, mate.' He was on the job, you may bet, got into some scrape, and now dursn't say nothink about it."

I need not mention the steps by which, in half an hour, I had become the bosom friend of these two women. The time, place, and circumstances of the boots profoundly impressed me, and when I separated from them I doubted not that the name and address I had obtained were those of the man we wanted. When Doctor Raphash got back haggard to our garret that night, I pressed his hand.

"You have news for me, Parker."

I told him the incident.

"Let us go," he said.

"You look tired to-night; to-morrow perhaps—"

"Not at all! To-night, man—*now*—is the time to find what we seek"—and he stamped on the floor.

I glanced, startled, at him, for the action was like a sign of the break-up of that serenity which characterised him.

We passed out, I with a revolver. When, by way of a labyrinth of streets, we reached the address, the Doctor at last spoke, saying: "There is no light, you see: he is, probably, still out. Suppose you wait till he comes; then speak; take him under the lamp there, see the boots, and ask him to drink with you. I, waiting at yonder corner, will then join you."

Flakes of snow were floating downwards, while I strolled sentry-wise, and the Doctor crouched at his post. From a Swedish church near I heard the strokes of twelve, and at the same moment a working-man approached me.

"Cold to-night, mate," I said carelessly.

"Ah, that it is," he answered.

His teeth chattered—his cheeks wore a blue hue. Turned-up coat collar, and pocketed paws, and forward pose, spoke of his Polar unrepose.

"You look frozen. Come and have a drink along wi' me."

"I could do with one, mate. Not tasted grub this blessed day."

"What—broke?"

"Dead broke!"

"Come along then—the Brown Bear."

He followed me. Under the lamp I stopped.

"Like the Brown Bear? If not—"

The light fell upon him, and a sense of contempt and disappointment overcame me at the sight of his weak face, sheepish eyes. But there, at any rate, were the fellows of the two odd boots which I had handed over to the authorities.

The Doctor had been slowly approaching us, and was now in the middle of the road when Hardy, glancing, saw him.

The change in the man's face was sudden and wonderful: his eyes stared, he clung to a railing; then, suddenly taking to his heels, fled, as for life, down a side-street.

The Doctor followed, and then I. And now powers of physique, as unexpected as previously depths of soul in my old friend, stood revealed to me. He distanced me. His feet grew winged. Hardy, indeed, had an advantage in his knowledge of the intricate streets down which he dodged and sometimes for a moment disappeared; but the Doctor slowly won upon him, "hunting him down," till suddenly, Hardy dashed into a cul-de-sac, of which the house at the end was empty, every window broken. If the fugitive, then, could gain an entrance there, his escape by the back was safe, and I guessed that this was the house for which he had all along been making. And, in fact, on reaching it, Hardy dashed down the area-steps to a basement below the street-level.

"Shoot!" cried the Doctor, looking back at me: "shoot with the revolver!"

This I was far from willing to do, but it was already too late: for Hardy had disappeared. A minute afterwards we, too, had darted down the steps, and through a door sped into a cellar of which the ground was powdery dust, covering our ankles. There seemed no other means of egress, and I was looking about for Hardy, when the door banged suddenly behind us, and a bar clanged down into a staple outside.

That the man had entered the cellar was certain, also that he had had some means of leaving it other than the door. But here our knowledge ended. The blackness was Erebus itself; clouds of dust rose at our every step and choked us; and soon the intensity of the cold, after our race, made speech nearly impossible. I groped round the walls, shot off my revolver, but the flash revealed nothing but a portion of unhewn wall and low ceiling; I howled at the door; but the neighbouring houses were ruins—an echo answered me.

Towards morning I received, I confess, a thrilling experience of horror from Doctor Raphash. That he was not himself, that he suffered more than I, had become apparent. Once or twice only had he spoken through the night, seated in the dust in a corner, his knees bent up, his head buried in his arms. By palpation I knew him to be in this position.

Once I said in alarm: "Doctor, do not sleep! This cold—"

The Doctor laughed aloud. "No, no," he said bitterly; "no sleep; little fear of that to-night."

I walked for warmth to and fro, treading warily on the dust. Then a groan drew me to him, and my cold fingers touched his forehead with the sensation of contact with something hot.

"You are suffering terribly," I said.

"Leave me alone, Parker!"

An hour, and I knew that he was stalking fast up and down all the length of the cellar; swiftly! filling it with a continuous smoke of dust: and long I stood mute, noting his faint sounds on the ground as he came, losing them, following in fancy the growth of his cloudy progress, guessing that now he was here, now yonder. His mutterings guided me. He seemed to forget my presence.

When the air finally became unbreathable, I moved to go to him, and in this act my head came in contact with something, which on catching I found to be a rope hanging down. Unable to divine its purpose, I succeeded after many efforts in climbing it, my head struck the ceiling, and feeling round with my hand, I encountered what seemed the panels of a trap-door. The means of Hardy's escape now flashed upon me. I pushed with my knuckles, and some light entered. In another minute I was free on the other side—it was already day.

A strange, pale face peered up at me, rolling wild eyes. When I had drawn him up, together we passed out to the street.

Here he suddenly seized my hand.

"Parker!"—his pantings came in gasps—"be a gadfly in your tenacity, as you love, me, man! Hunt him down! Good-bye. . . . Madman! do not follow!"

And before my brain could wake from its depth of stupor, he had dashed furiously down the road, and vanished into a passing cab.

*   *   *   *   *

After Dr Raphash's mysterious desertion of our quest when success seemed near, I merely returned to the Towers, and waited. I now, in fact, considered my duty done when I had described to the authorities the fellow with the odd boots, who at this time was in hiding.

It was a month afterwards that I remarked one evening, as I was walking about the grounds, that a man, hearing my approaching footsteps, had ducked his head from me in a clump of bushes—the very bushes, by the way, in which the stolen things had been discovered.

I was accompanied by a mastiff: so, on coming close to the spot, I said aloud: "Do not run, simply rise, and hold your hands over your head. I happen to be armed—and you see the dog."

The crack of a gun would have much less astonished me than the hang-dog air with which he rose before me. I recognised instantly the insipid face of Hardy.

"No offence, master," he said, touching his hat, trembling like aspen.

"We have met before, Hardy."

He scrutinised my face, but shook his head.

"You know me better'n I know you, sir."

"Well, Charles, you must come with me," I said, and led him by the arm into a room of the house, instructing Mrs Grant at the entrance to send for a couple of the rather distant local police. I then closed the door, and proceeded to examine my prisoner. The creature wept!

"Now, Hardy," I said, "dry your tears, and tell me how you came to be in those bushes to-night."

"I was looking for the rings and things. It was hunger drove me—they've been hunting me like an animal for the last month, and I give myself up."

"What rings?"

"The rings I dropped in those bushes. I thought that, anyway, one of them might by chance be left there still."

"You admit the burglary, then?"

"Yes, master, I admit it. It was my first, and it will be my last. I haven't had a moment's peace since. I even put up a rope in an old cellar to hang myself, only I'm a coward—"

"And you admit the murder?"

"Murder, master?" he cried with a scared face. "Why, it wasn't *me* as did the murder, it was one of the other two, and didn't I nearly drop dead with fright when I see it done?"

"There were, then, two others?"

"Yes, sir, a working-man such as myself, and an old gent."

"Tell me about it."

"I and a mate of mine, sir, came down hop-picking—one of your wild chaps, and hops was too slow for *him;* so he says to me as how some of these country-houses was mere child's play, with plenty to be got, and not much danger, so one night here we stood behind a shed, waiting till the old lady was well asleep, when all of a sudden, as if he'd sprung out of the ground, this old gent stood between us. I started running; he looked like a spirit to me; but Jim, he stands his ground, whistles to me, and when I come up, he ses, "Ere's a lark, Charlie,' ses he, 'old chap's on the job hisself!' 'Partnership's a leaky ship, Jim,' ses I; but he only ses, 'Oh, bother, live and let live.' Well, I and Jim get our boots off, we all get inside, and no sooner inside, than the old cove takes the lead, showing the way, telling us what to do, me and Jim doing everything he tells us, nat'ral like. He knew every crick of the place! and first he takes us into a room, and ses he, quite wild like, 'Plunder now! raven and harry! to your souls' content!' Then he reaches down a case from a shelf, and takes out a strange, shiny knife, locks the case again—I believe he had keys to every lock in the place—and rushes out of the room into the one opposite. 'Queer chap, that,' ses Jim, looking queer hisself, 'gives me the shivers,' and before I could tell him I felt sure the cove was a devil or a ghost, we hear a struggle going on in the opposite room—someone gasping—then a great shriek which I ain't ever going to forget. Immediately after, out he flies with his wild eyes, and dashes hisself on the other old woman's door yonder. Jim, with the cold sweats on him, he plucks up courage to reason with him a bit, but no go, the old cove spurts back to the murdered lady, and dashes out again with her in his arms, a gash showing all across her chest, her grey hair trailing on the ground. And now he comes up to us, and, lofty like, ses he, 'Marshal yourselves before me— march! march! and I will show you where treasures lie thick for yer 'arvesting!' and he makes us walk before him across the building into the other wing and up two stairs, till we come to a room with a lot of bones—and, there, Great God! hide me! there—*there he is!* He'll kill me, as he killed my mate—he'll kill you, too—"

He stared wildly about, rushed behind my chair, and crouched down there, the man's shriek of panic horror thrilling me through, as the ponderous door swung slowly open on its hinges, and Dr Raphash calmly walked into the room.

"Well, Parker," he said in the old cold tone, "here I am again, you see. But whom have we . . . the murderer caught!" and triumph lighted his eyes as they rested on Hardy, who, pallid and panting, at present lay propped upon the tapestry.

"Yes, the murderer!" gasped Hardy, "but that's not me! Oh, there's plenty of proofs, if it comes to that! That coat's the very one you had on—have you washed the blood off the sleeve yet?"

Dr Raphash sat down, barely smiling, examining the face of Hardy. Presently he looked at his arm.

"Remarkable thing," he said, talking to himself: "I *have* noticed a stain here on my sleeve; it cannot be blood; Parker, see."

But, as for me, a mist hung before me: I could see nothing.

"It *is* blood," continued Hardy, gaining courage from the Doctor's calm— "you know it is, or perhaps you were too mad that night to know anything. Who but a madman would have carried the lady's body all the way to that old chest; and didn't you chase Jim round and round the room and stab him like a dog, because you said one body wasn't enough to fill the chest? And if I hadn't slipped down to the balcony by the spout, wouldn't you have killed me, too? and didn't you look out of the window and tell me to prepare myself because you was coming, and didn't I have to jump from the balcony to the ground, rolling over, and dropping all the things I had? and didn't I just have time to draw on two of the boots, and they odd, when you ran down and started after me?"

I was looking at Dr Raphash: during this categorical charge, no sound had issued from his lips; but gradually a pallor as of death had overspread his face, whose muscles became tense and fixed; his head tumbled forward, his legs stretched rigidly from his body, the stony glare in his eyes giving to his face an aspect of rhadamanthine grimness ghastly to see.

I ran and grasped the clammy fingers in mine; but he did not recognise me. So he remained for several minutes, no breath breaking the stillness there.

Then, still rigid in all his limbs, he raised his head, and let it drop heavily back over the back of the chair; and, with this action, there burst from his blanched lips—higher and higher, peal on peal, in shrillest staccato—carillons of laughter.

With creeping flesh, I seized Hardy by the arm, rushed—faint—from the room, and locked the door upon the ruin within.

* * * * *

In this way Dr Arnot Raphash hunted down the murderer of his sister; and so, with him, fell the Jewish House of Raphash in the county of Kent.

Some days later I received a letter, of which the following are extracts:—

". . . When I tell you that I am the proprietor of the private asylum from which this letter is dated, and a cousin of Dr Raphash, you will at once conjecture that his (to you) strange absences from home always corresponded with his voluntary sojourns in my establishment. He well knew the warning symptoms—head-pains, a high temperature, etc.—and he usually had two or three days grace before the definite onset of the malady. Sometimes, again, the attack was more sudden, especially when preceded by any excitement; thus, when he reached my establishment a month ago he was already mad, and I at once divined some violent agitation. . . . His first paroxysm occurred at the age of thirty when he destroyed a just-married wife by cyanide-vapour poison . . . In the sane state he had no recollection of his insane acts, which were distinguished by a mania to kill, directed mainly against those for whom he most cared. He never knew anything of his wife's doom, for he was at once placed under my care, and on returning to the Towers found her already interred. . . .

When he was leaving me 'cured' after his sister's death, I deemed it prudent to tell him nothing of that death, preferring that the journey to the Towers should intervene before the shock of the news dropped upon his newly restored powers: hence his ignorance of this thing. . . . You have probably seen me on my visits to Miss Raphash when the Doctor was away from home, my object being to give her those minute reports of her brother's progress which alone could console her. On the very day of her tragedy I had a rather angry argument with her regarding the good of putting her idol into irons, she deprecating, I insisting. Unfortunately, I permitted her to influence me, and her death was the consequence, for it is now beyond all doubt that the Doctor escaped from my establishment that night, though how he contrived to pass out of the house and grounds and then into them again without detection is still unexplained; but then to his cunning there were no bounds . . . I need only add that I shall soon have the—pleasure of telling you of the death of Dr Raphash; for the end cannot be delayed. . . ."

Huguenin's Wife

"Ah! bitter-sweet!"—KEATS.

Huguenin, my friend—the man of Art and thrills and impulses—the *boulevardier*, the *persifleur*—must, I concluded with certainty, be frenzied. So, at least, I reasoned when, after years of silence, I received from him this letter:—

"'*Sdili*,' my friend; that is the name by which they now call this ancient Delos. Wherefore has it been written, 'so passeth the glory of the world.'

"Ah! but to me it is—as to *her* it was—still Delos, the Sacred Island, birthplace of Apollo, son of Leto! On the summit of Cynthus I look from my dwelling, and within the wide reach of the Cyclades perceive even yet the offerings of fruit arriving from Syria, from Sicily, from Egypt; I see the boats that bear the sacred envoys of Pan-Ionium to festival—I note the flutter of their holy robes—on the breeze once more floats to me their 'Songs of Deliverance.'

"The island now belongs almost entirely to me. I am, too, almost its sole inhabitant. It is, you know, only four miles long, and half as broad, and I have bought up every available foot of its face. On the flat top of the granite Cynthus I live, and here, my friend, I shall die. Fetters more inexorable and horrible than any that the limbs of Prometheus ever felt rivet me to this crag.

"A friend! That is the thing after which my sick spirit famishes. A *living man*: of the dead I have enough; of living monsters, ah, too much! and a servant or two, who seem permanently to shun me—this is all I possess of human fellowship. Yet I dare not implore you, my old companion, to come to the comfort of a sinking man in this place of desolation. . . ."

The epistle continued in this strain of mingled rhapsody and despair, containing, moreover, a long rigmarole on the Pythagorean dogma of the metempsychosis of the soul. Three times did the words "living monsters" occur.

From London to Delos is a journey; yet, conquered during a long vacation by an irresistible impulse, and the fond memories of other days, I actually found myself, on a starry night, disembarking on the sands that bound the once renowned harbour of the tiny island, and my arrival may be dated by the fact that it took place just two months before the extraordinary phenomena of which Delos was the scene during the night of 13th August, 1880. I first crossed the ring of flat land that almost encircles the islet, and then commenced the ascent of the central rise, the air slumbrous with the breath of rose, jasmine, almond, with the call of the cicala, the shine of the firefly. In forty minutes I had walked into a tangled garden, and placed my hand on the back of a tall man, habited in Attic garments, who was pacing there.

With a start he faced me.

"Oh," he said, panting, and clapping his hands upon his chest, "I was awfully startled! My heart—"

It was Huguenin, and yet not he. The beard rolling over his snowy robes of wool was still ebon as ever; but the fluff of hair that floated with every zephyr over his face and neck was a fluff of wool white. He stared at me with the lifeless and cavernous eyes of a man long dead.

When we entered the dwelling together, the mere appearance of the building was enough to convince me that in some mysterious way, to some morbid degree, the past had fettered and darkened the intellect of my friend. The mansion was of Hellenic type, but nothing less than mad in extent—a desert more than a habitation, a Greek house multiplied many times over into a congeries of Greek houses, like objects seen through angular glasses. It consisted of a single storey, though here and there on the flat roof there rose a second layer of apartments, attained by ladders. We walked through a door—opening inwards—into a passage, which took us to a courtyard, or *aule,* surrounded by Corinthian pillars, and having in the middle an altar of marble to *Zeus Herkeios.* Around this court were ranged chambers, *thalamoi,* hung with velvets; and the whole house—made up of a hundred and a hundred reproductions of such courtyards with their surrounding chambers—formed a trackless Sahara of halls through whose labyrinths the most crafty could not but fail to thread his way.

"This building," Huguenin said to me, some days after my arrival, "this building—every stone, plank, drapery—was the creation of my wife's wild fancy."

I stared at him.

"You doubt that I have, or had, a wife? Come with me; you shall—see her face."

He now led the way through the windowless house, lighted throughout the day and night by the reddish ray shed from many little censer lamps of terra-cotta filled with *nardinum,* an oil pressed from the blossom of the fragrant grass *nardus* of the Arabs.

I followed Huguenin through a good number of the rooms, noticing that, as he moved slowly onward, he kept his body bent, seeming to seek for something; and this something I quickly found to be crimson thread, laid down on the floor to afford a clue for the foot through the mazes of the house. Suddenly he stopped before the door of one of the apartments called *amphithalamoi,* and, himself staying without, motioned me to enter.

Now I am hardly a man of what might be called a tremulous diathesis, yet it was not without a tremor that I looked round that room. At first I could discern nothing under the glimmer from a single *lampas* hanging in the middle, but presently a painting in oils, unframed, occupying nearly one side of the room, grew upon my sight: the painting of a woman: and my pulses underwent a strange agitation as I gazed on her face.

She stood robed in a flowing ruby *peplos*, with her head thrown back, and one hand and arm pointing starkly outward and upward. The countenance was not merely Grecian—antique Grecian, as distinct from modern—but Grecian in a highly exaggerated and unlife-like degree. Was the woman, I asked myself, more lovely than ever mortal was before—or more loathsome? For Lamia stood there before me—"shape of gorgeous hue, vermilion-spotted, golden, green and blue"—and a kind of surprise held me fixed as the image slowly took possession of my vision. The Gorgon's head! whose hair was snakes; and as I thought of this I thought, too, of how from the guttering gore of the Gorgon's head monsters rose; and then, with abhorrence, I remembered Huguenin's ravings as to "monsters." I stepped nearer, in order to analyse the impression almost of dread wrought upon me, and I quickly found—or thought that I found—the key: it lay in the lady's eyes: the very eyes of the tigress: greedy glories of green glaring with radii of gold. I hurried from her.

"You have seen her?" Huguenin asked me with an eager leer of cunning.

"Yes, Huguenin," I said, "she is very beautiful."

"She painted it herself," he said in a whisper.

"Really!"

"She considered herself—she *was*—the greatest painter since Apelles."

"But now—where is she?"

He brought his lips to my ear.

"Dead. *You*, at any rate, would say so."

Well to words so apparently senseless I would pay no attention then; but they recurred to me when I unearthed the circumstance that it was his way, at certain intervals, to make furtive visits to distant districts of the dwelling. Our bed-chambers being close together I could not fail, as time passed, to notice that he would rise in the dead of night, when he supposed me drowsing, and gathering together the fragments of our last repast, depart rapidly and soundlessly with them through the vastness of the house, led always in one particular direction by the thread of silk whose crimson lay over the floor.

I now set myself strenuously to the study of Huguenin. The name and nature of his physical sickness, at least, was clear—the affection to which physicians have given the name Cheyne Stoke's Respiration, compelling him to lie back at times in an agony of inhalation, and groan for air. The bones of his cheeks seemed to be near appearing through their sere trumpery of mummy-skin; the *alæ* of his nose got no repose from their extravagance of expansion and retraction. But even this wreck of a body might, I believed, be rescued, were it not that to assuage the rage and feverishness of such a mind the spheres contained no thyme. For one thing, a most queer belief in some unnamed fate hanging over the little land he lived on haunted him. Again and again he recalled to me all that in the far past had been written in regard to Delos: the strange notion contained both in the Homeric and the Alexandrian hymns to the Delian Apollo that Delos was *floating*; or that it was only held by chains; or that it had only been thrown up from the ocean as a temporary resting-place for Ortygia in her birth-giving; or that it might *sink* again before the spurning

foot of the new born god. He was never weary, through hours, of pursuing, as if
in soliloquy, a species of sleepy exegesis of such scriptures as we read together.
"Do you know," he said to me, "that the Greeks really believed the streams of
Delos to rise and fall with the rise and fall of the Nile? Could anything point
more strongly to the extraordinary character of this land, its far extending vol
canic constructions, occult geologic eccentricities?" Then he might recite the
punning line of the very old Sibylline prophecy—

ἔσται καὶ Σάμος ἄμμος ἔσεῖται Δῆλος ἄδηλος;

often, also, having recited it, he would strike from the repining chords of a lyre
the theme of a threnody which, as he told me, his wife had composed to suit
the line; and when to the funeral ruth of this tune—so wild with woe and
whining, that I could never listen to it without a thrill—Huguenin added the
sadness of his now so hollow voice, the intensity of effect upon me got to the
intolerable degree, and I was glad of that pallid gloaming of the mansion,
which partially hid my emotion.

"Remark, however," he said one day, "the meaning of the 'far seen' as re
gards Delos: it means 'glorious' 'illustrious'—far seen to the spiritual rather
than to the physical eye, for the island is not very elevated. The words 'sink
from sight' must, therefore, be supposed to have the corresponding significance
of an extinction of this glory. And now think whether or not this prophecy has
not been already fulfilled, when I tell you that this sacrosanct land, which no
dog's foot was once permitted to touch, on which no man was permitted to be
born or be buried, bears at this moment on its bosom a monster more loath
some than even a demon's brain, I believe, ever conceived. A literal and physi
cal fulfilment of the prophecy cannot, I consider, be always distant."

But all this esotericism was not native to Huguenin: his mind, I was con
vinced, had been ploughed into by some very potent energy, before ever this
growth had choked it. I enticed him, little by little, to speak of his wife.

She was, he told me, of a very antique Athenian family, which by constant
effort had preserved its purity of blood; and it was while moving through
Greece in a world weary mood that, on reaching one night the village of Cas
tri, there, on the site of the ancient Delphi, in the centre of an angry throng of
Greeks and Turks, who threatened to rend her to fragments, he first saw An
dromeda his wife. "This incredible courage," he said, "this vast originality was
hers, to take upon herself the part of a modern Hypatia—to venture upon the
task of the bringing back of the gods, in the midst of fanatics, at the latter end
of a century like the present. The crowd from which I rescued her was howling
round her in the vestibule of a just completed temple to Apollo, whose cult she
was then and there attempting to set up."

The love of the woman fastened upon her preserver with passionate fer
vour, and Huguenin, constrained by the vigour of a will not to be resisted,
came at her bidding to live in the grey building of her creation at Delos: in
which solitude, under which shadow, the man and the woman faced each
other. Ere many weeks it was revealed to the husband that he had married a

seer of visions and a dreamer of dreams. And visions of what tinge! and dreams of what madness! He confessed to me that he was awed by her, and with this awe was blended a feeling which, if it was not fear, was akin to fear. That he loved her not at all he now knew, while the extravagance of her passion for him he grew to regard as gruesome. Yet his mind took on the hue of hers; he drank in her doctrines, followed her as a satellite. When for days she hid herself from him, he would wander desolate and full of search over his pathless home. Finding that she habitually yielded her body to the delights of certain seeds that grew on Delos, he found the courage to frown, but ended by himself becoming a bond-slave to the drowsy *ganja* of Hindustan. So, too, with the most strange fascination which she exercised over the animal world: he disliked it—dreaded it; regarded it as excessive and unnatural; but looked on only with the furtive eye of suspicion, and said nothing. When she walked she was accompanied by a magnetised *queue* of living things, felines in particular, and birds of large size; while dogs, on the contrary, shunned her, bristling. She had brought with her from the continent a throng of these followers, of which Huguenin had never beheld the half, since they were imprisoned in unknown nooks of the building; and anon she would vanish, to reappear with new companions. Her kindness to these creatures should, no doubt, have been sufficient to account for her power over them; but Huguenin's mind, already grown morbid, probed darkly after other explanation. The primary *motif* of this unquietness doubtless lay in his wife's fanaticism on the matter of the Pythagorean dogma of the transmigration of souls. On this theme Andromeda, it was clear, was outrageously deranged. She would stand, he declared, with her arm outstretched, her eyes wild-staring, her body rigid, and in a rapid recitative—like the rapt Pythoness—prophesy of the mutations prepared for the spirit of man, dwelling, above all, with contempt, on the paucity of animal forms in the world, and insisting that the spirit of an original man, disembodied, *should and must* re-embody itself in a correspondingly original form. "And," she would often add, "such forms exist, but the God, willing to save the race from frenzy, hides them from the eyes of common men."

It was long, however, before I could get Huguenin to describe the final catastrophe of his wedded life. He related it in these words:—

"You now know that Andromeda was among the great painters—you have gloated upon her portrait of herself. Well, one day, after dilating, as was her wont, on the paucity of forms, she said, 'But you, too, shall be of the initiated: come, you shall see *something*.' She then went swiftly, beckoning, looking back often to smile on me a fond patronage, and I followed, till she stopped before a lately finished painting, pointing. I will not attempt—the attempt would be folly—to tell you what thing I saw before me on the canvas; nor can I explain in words the tempest of anger, of loathing and disgust, that stirred within me at the sight; but at that blasphemy of her fancy, I raised my hand to strike her head; and to this moment I know not if I struck her. My hand, it is true, felt the sensation of contact with something soft; but the blow, if blow there was, was hardly hard enough to harm a creature far feebler than man.

Yet she fell; the film of death spread over her upbraiding eye; one last thing only she spoke, pointing to the uncleanness: 'You may yet see it in the flesh'; and so, still pointing, sped away.

"I bore her body, embalmed in the Greek manner by an artist of Corinth, to one of the smaller apartments on the roof, and saw, as I moved to leave her in her gloom, the mortal smile on her lip within the open coffin. Two weeks later I went again to visit her. My friend, she had vanished—but for the bones; and from the coffin, above that skull, two eyes—living—the very eyes of Andromeda, but full of a newborn brightness—the eyes, too, of the horror she had painted, whose form I now made out in the darkness—looked out upon me. After I had slammed the door, I fainted on the stair."

"The suggestion," I said to him, "which you seem to wish to convey is that of a transition of forms, from man to animal; but, surely, the explanation that the monster, brought by your wife into the house, or born in it, imprisoned unawares by you with the dead, and maddened by famine, fed on the body, is, if not less horrible, yet less improbable."

He looked doubtingly at me a moment, and then coldly said: "There was no monster imprisoned with the dead."

But at least, I pleaded, he would see the necessity of flying from that place. He replied with the avowal that it was no longer doubtful to him, from the effect which any neglect to minister to the monster's wants had upon his own health, that his life was bound up with the life of the being he stayed to maintain; that with the *second* murder which he should perpetrate—nay, with the attempt to perpetrate it, as by flight from the island—his life would be forfeited.

I accordingly formed the idea to effect the deliverance of my friend in spite of himself. Two months had now passed; the end of my visit was drawing near; yet his maladies of brain and body were not relieved: and it pained me to think of leaving him once more alone, a prey to his manias.

That very day, then, while he slept his damp trances, I started the tramp on the track of the scarlet thread. So far it hauled out its length, and the halls through which it passed were of such uniformity, and its path so wound about, that I could not doubt but that the clue once snapped at any point, the voyage along its route could be accomplished only by the most improbable chance. I followed the thread to its end, where it stopped at the foot of a ladder-stair. This I ascended to a door at its top, a door with a hole in it close to the bottom, big enough to admit a plate; but, as I placed my foot on the uppermost step, a whine, complaining low, with a wild likeness to a woman's wail, sent me skipping, sick, whence I came.

But, some little distance from the steps, I broke the thread, and, gathering it up in my hand as I ran, again broke it near the region of the mansion which we occupied.

"In this way," I said, as I held the mass of thread to the flame of a lamp, "shall a man be saved."

I watched him afterwards through my half-shut eyes, as he departed, haggard and shuddering, hugging himself, on his nightly errand; and my heart galloped in an agony of disquiet while I awaited his coming again.

He was long. But when he came, he came swiftly, softly into my chamber and shook me by the shoulder. On his face was a look of unusual coolness, of dignity, of mystery.

"Wake up," he said: "I wish you to leave me to-night."

"But tell me—"

"I will take no refusal. Trust me this once, and go. There is a danger here. Two of the fisher-folk of the harbour will convey you over to Rhenea before the morning."

"But danger!" I said—"from what?"

"I cannot tell you: from the destiny, whatever it be, which awaits me. The thread on which my life depends is *snapped*."

"But suppose I tell you—"

"Ah! . . . you hear that?"

He held up his hand and hearkened: it was a sound of howling round the house.

"It is the wind rising," I muttered, starting up.

"But that—which followed: didn't you *feel* it?"

I made him no answer.

He now clasped with his arms a marble column upon which he rested his forehead, while with one foot he kept on patting the floor; in which posture, quite demoralised and craven, he remained for some time, while the wind continued to rise; and suddenly he span towards me with a scream in a rapture of fear.

"Now at least—*you feel it!*"

I could not deny: it was as if the island had rocked a little to and fro on a pivot.

Now thoroughly demoralised myself, I now caught Huguenin's arm, and sought to draw him from the column which, muttering low, he was again hugging. But he would not stir; and I, determined in any event to stay by him, stood hearing the earthquake's increase while he seemed to take no further note of anything, motionless but for the motion of his foot. In this way an hour went by: at the end of which interval the rocking had become strong, rapid and continuous.

There came a second, when captured by a new panic, I sprang to shake him, understanding that some lamp had been dashed down in that passion of the mansion's agitation.

"Why, man!" I cried, "have you parted with every sense? Can't you feel that the house is in flames?"

On this his eyes, which had become dazed and dull, blazed up with a new lunacy.

"Then," he suddenly shouted in a passion of loudness, "I say she *shall* be saved! *The feathered cheetah!*"

Before I could lay hold of the now foaming maniac, he had dashed past me into a passage. I followed in hot pursuit through rooms and corridors that seemed to reel in a furious dream of heat and reek, hoping that he, weak of lung, would fall choked and exhausted. But some energy seemed to lend him strength—he rushed onward like the hurricane; some mysterious feeling seemed to lead him—never once did he hesitate.

And after all the long chase, which ever swayed at the rocking of the land, but never stopped, I saw that the intuitions of insanity had not failed the madman—he got to the goal he gasped after. I saw him fly up the ladder, whose foot was in a pool of fire, saw him fly to the door of the tomb of Andromeda, already flagrant and drag it open. But, as he dragged it, there broke out of the room—above the roaring of the conflagration, and of the gale, and of that thousandfold growling of the ground—a shriek, shrill, yet ugly with gutturalness, which congealed me in that heat; and immediately I saw proceeding from the interior a creature whose obscenity and vileness language has no vocabulary to describe. For if I say that it was a cat—of great size—its eyes glaring like a conflagration—its fat frame wrapped in a mass of feathers, grey, vermilion-tipped—with a similitude of miniature wings on it—with a width of tail vast, down-turned, like the tails of birds-of-paradise—how by such words can I express half of all the retching of my nausea, the shame, the hate . . . The fire had ere this reached the thing, and on fire I could spy it fly rather than spring at Huguenin's heart; then its fangs like grapnels buried in his breast, the gluttony of its gums that met on his gullet, I saw through a fog of feathers raining, he tottering, tearing at the feathery horror, as backward he toppled from the landing over the spot where a moment before the ladder had stood.

By blessed luck, as I rapidly ran thence, I stumbled upon some exit, to find outside the night quite cloudless, star-lit, though a whirl of all the winds of the world were whistling within the vault of sky that night. In descending, too, to the level, I remarked a rather scorched aspect of some of the leafage, and at one spot saw a series of conical openings in the ground with greenish scoriæ round their edges. Lower still, I stood on a bluff, and looking over the sea, witnessed a sight sublime to wildness: for the sea, too hurried to show billow, to show ripple, and lit up deep within its depth with a sheen of phosphoresence, was speeding as if after the steeds of Diomedes with the fleetest meaning towards Delos. Delos, indeed, seemed to "float," to be swimming like a little doomed fowl counter to the swoop of the boundless. With the morning's light I passed away from this mysterious shrine of Grecian piety, the final sight that greeted my gaze being the still rising reek of Huguenin's grave.

THE HOUSE of SOUNDS

"E caddi come l'uom cui sonno piglia."—DANTE.

A good many years ago, when a young man, a student in Paris, I knew the great Carot, and witnessed by his side many of those cases of mind-malady, in the analysis of which he was such a master. I remember one little maid of the Marais who, until the age of nine, did not differ from her play-mates; but one night, lying abed she whispered into her mother's ear: "Mama, can you not hear *the sound of the world?*" It appears that her geography had just taught her that our globe reels with an enormous velocity on an orbit about the sun; and this *sound of the world* of hers was merely a murmur in the ear, heard in the silence of night. Within six months she was as mad as a March-hare.

I mentioned the case to my friend, Haco Harfager, then occupying with me an old mansion in St Germain, shut in by a wall and jungle of shrubbery. He listened with singular interest, and during a good while sat wrapped in gloom.

Another case which I gave made a great impression upon my friend: A young man, a toy-maker of St Antoine, suffering from consumption—but so-ber, industrious—returning one gloaming to his garret, happened to purchase one of those factious journals which circulate by lamplight over the Boule-vards. This simple act was the beginning of his doom. He had never been a reader: knew little of the reel and turmoil of the world. But the next night he purchased another journal. Soon he acquired a knowledge of politics, the huge movements, the tumult of life. And this interest grew absorbing. Till late into the night, every night, he lay poring over the roar of action, the printed pas-sion. He would awake sick, but brisk in spirit—and bought a morning paper. And the more his teeth gnashed, the less they ate. He grew negligent, irregular at work, turning on his bed through the day. Rags overtook him. As the grand interest grew upon his frail soul, so every lesser interest failed in him. There came a day when he no more cared for his own life; and another day when he tore the hairs from his head.

As to this man the great Carot said to me:

"Really, one does not know whether to chuckle or to weep over such a business. Observe, for one thing, how diversely men are made! There are minds precisely so sensitive as a thread of melted lead: *every* breath will fret and trouble them: and how about the hurricane? For such this scheme of things is clearly no fit habitation, but a Machine of Death, a baleful Immense. *Too* cruel to some is the rushing shriek of Being—they *cannot* stand the world. Let each look well to his own little shred of existence, I say, and leave the monstrous Automaton alone! Here in this poor toy-maker you have a case of the ear: it is only the neurosis, Oxyecoia. Grand was that Greek myth of 'the Harpies'—by *them* was this creature snatched away—or say, caught by a limb in the wheels of the universe, and so perished. It is quite a ravishing exit—translation in a chariot of flame! Only remember that the member first seized was *the pinna*—he bent *ear* to the howl of the world, and ended by himself howling. Between chaos and our shoes swings, I assure you, the thinnest film! I knew a man who had this aural peculiarity: that every sound brought him some knowledge of the matter causing the sound: a rod for instance, of mixed copper and tin striking upon a rod of mixed iron and lead, conveyed to him not merely the proportion of each metal in each rod, but some knowledge of the essential meaning and spirit, as it were, of copper, of tin, of iron and of lead. Him also did the Harpies snatch aloft!"

I have mentioned that I related some of these cases to my friend, Harfager: and I was astonished at the obvious pains which he gave himself to hide his interest, his gaping nostrils. . . .

From first days when we happened to attend the same seminary in Stockholm an intimacy had sprung up between us. But it was not an intimacy accompanied by the ordinary signs of friendship. Harfager was the shyest, most isolated, of beings. Though our joint housekeeping (brought about by a chance meeting at a midnight *séance*) had now lasted some months, I knew nothing of his plans. Through the day we read together, he rapt back into the past, I engrossed with the present; late at night we reclined on sofas within the vast cave of a hearthplace *Louis Onze*, and smoked over the dying fire in silence. Occasionally a *soirée* or lecture might draw me from the house; except once, I never understood that Harfager left it. On that occasion I was hurrying through the Rue St Honoré, where a rush of traffic rattles over the old pavers retained there, when I came upon him. In this tumult he stood in a listening attitude; and for a moment did not know me.

Even as a boy I had seen in my friend the genuine patrician—not that his personality gave any impression of loftiness or opulence: on the contrary. He did, however, suggest an incalculable *ancientness*; and I have known no nobleman who so bore in his expression the assurance of the essential Prince, whose pale blossom is of yesterday, and will perish to-morrow, but whose root shoots through the ages. This much I knew of Harfager; also that on one or other of his islands north of Zetland lived his mother and an aunt; that he was somewhat deaf; but liable to a thousand torments or delights at certain sounds, the whine of a door, the note of a bird. . . .

He was somewhat under the middle height; and inclined to portliness. His nose rose highly aquiline from that sort of brow called "the musical"—that is, with temples which incline *outward* to the cheek-bones, making breadth for the base of the brain; while the direction of the heavy-lidded eyes and of the eyebrows was a downward *droop* from the nose of their outer ends. He wore a thin chin-beard. But the feature of his face were the ears, which were nearly circular, very small and flat, without that outer curve called "the helix." I came to understand that this had long been a trait of his race. Over the whole wan face of my friend was engraved an air of woeful inability, utter gravity of sorrow: one said "Sardanapalus," frail last of the race of Nimrod.

After a year I found it necessary to mention to Harfager my intention of leaving Paris, as we reclined one night in our nooks within the fireplace. He replied to my tidings with a polite "Indeed!" and continued to gloat over the grate: but after an hour turned to me and observed: "Well, it seems to be a hard world."

Truisms uttered in just such a tone of discovery I occasionally heard from him; but his earnest gaze, his despondency now, astonished me.

"Apropos of what?" I asked.

"My friend, do not leave me!" He spread his arms.

I learned that he was the object of a devilish malice; that he was the prey of a horrible temptation. That a lure, a becking hand, a lurking lust, which it was the effort of his life to escape (and to which he was especially liable in solitude) perpetually enticed him; and that so it had been almost from the day when, at the age of five, he had been sent by his father from his desolate home in the ocean.

And whose was this malice?

He told me his mother's and aunt's.

And what was this temptation?

He said it was the temptation to go back—to hurry with the very frenzy of hunger—back to that home.

I demanded with what motives, and in what way, the malice of his mother and aunt manifested itself. He answered that there was, he fancied, no definite motive, but only a fated malevolence; and that the respect in which it manifested itself was the prayers and commands with which they plagued him to go again to the hold of his ancestors.

All this I could not understand, and said so. In what consisted this magnetism, and this peril, of his home? To this Harfager did not reply, but rising from his seat, disappeared behind the hearth-curtains, and left the apartment. When he returned, it was with a quarto tome bound in hide, which proved to be Hugh Gascoigne's "Chronicle of Norse Families" in English black-letter. The passage to which he pointed I read as follows:

> "Now of these two brothers the older, Harold, being of seemly personage and prowess, did go a pilgrimage into Danemark, wherefrom he repaired again home to Hjaltland (Zetland), and with him fetched the amiable Thronda for his wife, who was a daughter of the sank (blood) royal of Danemark. And his younger brother, Sweyn, that was sad and debonair, but far surpassed the other in cunning, received him with all good cheer.
>
> "But eftsoons (soon after) fell Sweyn sick for all his love that he had of Thronda, his brother's wife. And while the worthy Harold ministered about the bed where Sweyn lay sick, lo, Sweyn fastened on him a violent stroke with a sword, and with no longer tarrying enclosed his hands in

bonds, and cast him in the bottom of a deep hold. And because Harold would not deprive himself of the governance of Thronda his wife, Sweyn cut off both his ear[s], and put out one of his eyes, and after divers such torments was ready to slay him. But on a day the valliant Harold, breaking his bonds, and embracing his adversary, did by the sleight of wrestling overthrow him, and escaped. Notwithstanding, he faltered when he came to the Somburg Head, not far from the Castle, and, albeit that he was swift-foot, could no farther run, by reason that he was faint with the long plagues of his brother. And whilst he there lay in a swoon, did Sweyn come upon him, and when he had stricken him with a dart, cast him from Somburg Head into the sea.

"Not long hereafterward did the lady Thronda (though she knew not the manner of her lord's death, nor, verily, if he was dead or alive) receive Sweyn into favour, and with great gaudying and blowing of beamous (trumpets) did become his wife. And right soon they two went thence to sojourn in far parts.

Now, it befell that Sweyn was minded by a dream to have built a great mansion in Hjaltland for the home-coming of the lady Thronda; wherefore he called to him a cunning Master-workman, and sent him to England to gather men for the building of this lusty House, while he himself remained with his lady at Rome. Then came this Architect to London, but passing thence to Hjaltland was drowned, he and his feers (mates), all and some.

And after two years, which was the time assigned, Sweyn Harfager sent a letter to Hjaltland to understand how his great House did: for he knew not of the drowning of the Architect: and soon after he received answer that the House *did well*, and was building on the Isle of Rayba. But that was not the Isle where Sweyn had appointed the building to be: and he was afeard, and near fell down dead for dread, because, in the letter, he saw before him the manner of writing of his brother Harold. And he said in this form: 'Surely Harold is alive, else be this letter writ with ghostly hand.' And he was wo many days, seeing that this was a deadly stroke.

"Thereafter he took himself back to Hjaltland to know how the matter was, and there the old Castle on Somburg Head was break down to the earth. Then Sweyn was wode-wroth, and cried: 'Jhesu mercy, where is all the great house of my fathers gone? alas! this wicked day of destiny!' And one of the people told him that a host of workmen from far parts had break it down. And he said: 'Who hath bid them?' but that could none answer. Then he said again: 'nis (is not) my brother Harold alive? for I have behold his writing': and that, too, could none answer. So he went to Rayba, and saw there a great House stand, and when he looked on it, he said: 'This, sooth, was y-built by my brother Harold, be he dead or be he on-live.' And there he dwelt, and his lady, and his sons' sons until now: for that the House is ruthless and without pity; wherefore 'tis said that upon all who dwell there falleth a wicked madness and a lecherous anguish; and

that by way of the ears do they drinck the cup of the furie of the earless
Harold, till the time of the House be ended."

After I had read the narrative half-aloud, I smiled, saying: "This, Harfager,
is very tolerable romance on the part of the good Gascoigne, but has the look
of indifferent history."

"It is, nevertheless, *history*," he replied.

"You believe that?"

"The house stands solidly on Rayba."

"But you believe that mediæval ghosts superintended the building of their
family mansions?"

"Gascoigne nowhere says that," he answered: "for to be 'stricken with a
darte,' is not necessarily to die; nor, if he did say it, have I any knowledge on
the subject."

"And what, Harfager, is the nature of that 'wicked madness,' that 'lecherous anguish,' of which Gascoigne speaks?"

"Do you ask me?"—he spread his arms—"what do I know? I know noth-
ing! I was banished from the place at the age of five. Yet the cry of it still rings
in my mind. And have I not *told* you of anguishes—even in myself—of inherited longing and loathing. . . ."

Anyway, I *had* to go to Heidelberg just then: so I said I would compromise
by making my absence short, and rejoin him in a few weeks. I took his moody
silence to mean assent; and soon afterwards left him.

But I was detained: and when I got back to our old house found it empty.
Harfager was gone.

It was only after twelve years that a letter was forwarded me—a rather
wild letter, an awfully long one—in the writing of my friend. It was dated at
Rayba. From the writing I understood that it had been dashed off *with furious
haste*, so that I was the more astonished at the very trivial nature of the contents. On the first half page he spoke of our old friendship, and asked if I would
see his mother, who was dying; the rest of the epistle consisted of an analysis of
his mother's family-tree, the apparent aim being to show that she was a genuine Harfager, and a distant cousin of his father. He then went on to comment
on the great prolificness of his race, stating that since the fourteenth century
over *four millions* of its members had lived; three only of them, he believed, being now left. This settled, the letter ended.

Influenced by this, I travelled northward; reached Caithness; passed the
stormy Orkneys; reached Lerwick; and from Unst, the most bleak and northerly of the Zetlands, contrived, by dint of bribes, to pit the weather-worthiness
of a lug-sailed "sixern" (identical with the "lang-schips" of the Vikings) against
a flowing sea and an ugly sky. The trip, I was told, was at such a season of some
risk. It was the sombre December of those seas; and the weather, they said, although never cold, is seldom other than tempestuous. A mist now lay over the
billows, enclosing our boat in a dome of doleful gloaming; and there was a
ghostly something in the look of the silent sea and brooding sky which pro-

duced upon my nerves the mood of a journey out of nature, a cruise beyond the world. Occasionally, however, we ran past one of those "skerries," or sea-stacks, whose craggy sea-walls, disintegrated by the struggles of the Gulf Stream with the North Sea, had a look of awful ruin and havoc. But I only noticed three of these: for before the dun day had well run half its course, sudden darkness was upon us; and with it one of those storms of which the winter of this semi-Arctic sea is one succession. During the haggard glimpses of the following day the rain did not stop; but before darkness had quite fallen, my skipper (who talked continuously to a mate of seal-maidens, and water-horses, and *grüles*), paused to point me out a mound of gloomier grey on the weather-bow, which, he said, should be Rayba.

Rayba, he said, was the centre of quite a nest of those *rösts* (eddies) and cross-currents which the tidal wave hurls with complicated swirlings among all the islands: but at Rayba they ran with more than usual angriness, owing to the row of sea-crags which garrisoned the land around: approach was therefore at all times difficult, and at night foolhardy. With a running sea, however, we came sufficiently close to see the mane of foam which railed round the coast-wall. Its shock, according to the captain, had often more than all the efficiency of artillery, tossing tons of rock to heights of six hundred feet upon the island.

When the sun next pried above the horizon, we had closely approached the coast; and it was then that for the first time the impression of some *spinning* motion of the island (due probably to the swirling movements of the water) was produced upon me. We affected a landing at a *voe*, or sea-arm, on the west coast—the east, though the point of my aim, was out of the question on account of the swell. Here I found in two *skeoes* (or sheds), thatched with feal, five or six seamen, who gained a livelihood by trading for the groceries of the great house on the east; and, taking one of them for a guide, I began the climb of the island.

Now, during the night in the boat, I had been aware of a booming in the ears for which even the roar of the sea round the coast seemed insufficient to account; and this now, as we went on, became immensely augmented—and with it, once more, that conviction within me of *spinning* motions. Rayba I found to be a land of precipices of granite and flaggy gneiss; at about the centre, however, we came upon a tableland, sloping from west to east, and covered by a lot of lochs, which sullenly flowed into one another. I could see no shore eastward to this chain of waters, and by dint of shouting to my leader, and bending ear to his shoutings, I came to know that there *was* no such shore—I say *shout*, for nothing less could have sounded through the steady bellowing as of ten thousand bisons that now resounded on every side. A certain trembling, too, of the earth became distinct. In vain, meantime, did the eye in its dreary survey seek a tree or shrub—for no kind of vegetation, save peat, could brave for a day the perennial tempest of this benighted island. Darkness, half an hour after noon, commenced to fall upon us: and it was soon afterwards that my guide, pointing down a defile near the east coast, hurriedly started back upon the way he had come. I bawled a question after him, as he went: but at this point the voice of mortals had ceased to be in the least audible.

Down this defile, with a sinking of the heart, and a singular sickness of giddiness, I passed; and, on reaching its end, emerged upon a ledge of rock which shuddered to the immediate onsets of the sea—though all this part of the island was, besides, in the grip of an ague not due to the great guns of the sea. Hugging a crag of cliff for steadiness from the gusts, I gazed forth upon a scene not less eerily dismal than some drear district of the dreams of Dante. Three "skerries," flanked by stacks as fantastic and twisted as a witch's finger, and giving a home to hosts of osprey and scart, seal and walrus, lay at some fathoms distance; and from its rush among them, the sea in blanched, tumultuous, but inaudible wrath, like an army with banners, ranted toward the land. Letting go my crag, I staggered some distance to the left: and now all at once an amphitheatre opened before me, and there broke upon my view a panorama of such appalling majesty as had never entered my heart to fancy.

"An amphitheatre," I said: but it was rather the form of a Norman door that I saw. Fancy such a door, half a mile wide, flat on the ground, the rounded part farthest from the sea; and all round it let a wall of rock tower perpendicular forty yards: and now down this rounded door-shape, and *over its whole extent,* let a roaring ocean roll its tonnage in hoary fury—and the stupor with which I looked, and then the shrinking, and then the instinct of flight, will find comprehension.

This was the disemboguement of the lochs of Rayba.

And within the curve of this Norman cataract, robed in the world of its smokes and far-excursive surfs, stood a fabric of brass.

The last beam of the day had now nearly passed; but I could still see through the mist which bleakly nimbused it as in tears, that the building was low in proportion to the hugeness of its circumference; that it was roofed with a dome; and that round it ran two rows of Norman windows, the upper smaller than the lower. Certain indications led me to infer that the house had been founded upon a bed of rock which lay, circular and detached, within the curve of the cataract; but this nowhere emerged above the flood: for the whole floor which I had before me dashed one reeking deep river to the beachless sea— passage to the mansion being made possible by a massive causeway-bridge, with arches, all bearded with sea-weed.

Descending from my ledge, I passed along it, now drenched in spray; and, as I came nearer, could see that the house, too, was to half its height more thickly bearded than an old hull with barnacles and every variety of bright seaweed; also—what was very surprising—that from many spots near the top of the brazen wall ponderous chains, dropping beards, reached out in rays: so that the fabric had the aspect of a many-anchored ark. But without pausing to look closely, I pushed forward, and rushing through the smooth waterfall which poured all around from the roof, by one of its many porches I entered the dwelling.

Darkness now was around me—and sound. I seemed to stand in the centre of some yelling planet, the row resembling the resounding of many thousands of cannon, punctuated by strange crashing and breaking uproars. And a madness descended on me; I was near to tears. "Here," I said, "is the place of weeping; not elsewhere is the vale of sighing." However, I passed forward through a succession of halls, and was wondering where to go next, when a hideous figure, with a lamp in his hand, stamped towards me. I shrank from him! It seemed the skeleton of a lank man wrapped in a winding-sheet, till the light of one tiny eye, and a film of skin over a portion of the face reassured one. Of ears he showed no sign. His name, I afterwards learned, was Aith; and his appearance was explained by his pretence (true or false) that he had once suffered *burning*, almost to the cinder-stage, but had somehow recovered. With an expression of malice, and agitated gestures, he led the way to a chamber on the upper stage, where, having struck light to a taper, he made signs toward a spread table, and left me.

For a long time I sat in solitude, conscious of the shaking of the mansion, though every sense was swallowed up and confounded in the one impression of sound. Water, water, was the world—a nightmare on my breast, a desire to gasp for breath, a tingling on my nerves, a sense of being infinitely drowned and buried in boundless deluges; and when the feeling of giddiness, too, increased, I sprang up and paced—but suddenly stopped, angry, I scarce knew why, with myself. I had, in fact, caught myself walking with a certain *hurry*, not usual with me, not natural to me. So I forced myself to stand and take note of the hall. It was large, and damp with mists, so that its tattered, but rich, furniture looked lost in it, its centre occupied by a tomb bearing the name of a Harfager of the fourteenth century, and its walls old panels of oak. Having drearily seen these things, I waited on with an intolerable consciousness of solitude; but a little after midnight the tapestry parted, and Harfager with a rapid stalk walked in.

In twelve years my friend had grown old. He showed, it is true, a tendency to portliness: yet, to a knowing eye he was in reality tabid, ill-nourished. And his neck stuck forward from his chest; and the lower part of his back had quite a forward bend of age; and his hair floated about his face and shoulders in a wildness of awful whiteness, while a white chin-beard hung to his chest. His dress was a robe of bauge, which, as he went, waved aflaunt from his bare and hairy shins; and he was shod in those soft slippers called *rivlins*.

To my astonishment, he spoke. When I passionately shouted that I could gather no fragment of sound from his moving mouth, he clapped both his palms to his ears, and then anew besieged mine: but again without result: and now, with an angry throw of the hand, he caught up his taper, and walked from the apartment.

There was something strikingly unnatural in his manner—something which reminded me of the skeleton, Aith: an excess of zeal, a fever, a rage, a *loudness*, an eagerness of gait, a great extravagance of gesture. His hand constantly dashed wiffs of hair from a face which, though of the saffron of death, had red eyes—thick-lidded eyes, fixed in a downward and sideward gaze. When he came back to me, it was with a leaf of ivory, and a piece of graphite, hanging from the cord tied round his garment; and he rapidly wrote a petition that, if not too tired, I would take part with him in the funeral of his mother.

I shouted assent.

Once more he clapped his palms to his ears; then wrote: "Do not shout: no whisper in any part of the building is inaudible to me."

I remembered that in early life he had been slightly *deaf.*

We passed together through many apartments, he shading the taper with his hand—a necessary action, for, as I quickly discovered, in no nook of the quivering building was the air in a state of rest, but was for ever commoved by a curious agitation, a faint windiness, like an echo of tempests, which communicated a universal nervousness to the curtains. Everywhere I met the same past grandeur, present raggedness and decay. In many of the rooms were tombs; one was a museum thronged with bronzes, but broken, grown with fungoids, dripping with moisture—it was as if the mansion, in ardour of travail, sweated; and a miasma of decomposition tainted all the air.

I followed Harfager through the maze of his way with some difficulty, for he went headlong—only once stopping, when with a face ungainly wild over the glare of the light, he tossed up his fingers, and gave out a single word: from the form of his lips I guessed the word "*Hark!*"

Presently we entered a very long chamber, in which, on chairs beside a bed, lay a coffin flanked by a file of candles. The coffin was very deep, and had this singularity—that the foot-piece was absent, so that the soles of the corpse could be seen as we approached. I saw, too, three upright rods secured to a side of the coffin, each rod fitted at its top with a little silver bell of the sort called *morrice*, pendent from a flexible spring. And at the head of the bed, Aith, with an air of irascibility, was stamping to and fro within a narrow area.

Harfager deposited the taper upon a stone table, and stood poring with a crazy intentness over the body. I, too, stood and looked at death so grim and rigorous as I think I never saw. The coffin looked angrily full of tangled grey locks, the lady being of great age, bony and hook-nosed; and her face shook with solemn constancy to the quivering of the building. I noticed that over the body had been fixed three bridges, like the bridge of a violin, their sides fitting into grooves in the coffin's sides, and their tops of a shape to fit the slope of the two coffin-lids when closed. One of these bridges passed over the knees of the dead lady; another bridged her stomach; the third her neck. In each of them was a hole, and across each of the three holes passed a string from the morrice-bell above it—the three holes being thus divided by the three tight strings into six semi-circles. Before I could guess the significance of all this, Harfager closed the folding coffin-lids, which had little holes for the passage of the three strings. He then turned the key in the lock, and uttered a word which I took to be "come."

Aith now took hold of the handle at the coffin's head; and out of the dark parts of the hall a lady in black walked forward. She was tall, pallid, of imposing aspect; and from the curvature of her nose, and her circular ears, I guessed her the lady Swertha, aunt of Harfager. Her eyes were quite red—if with crying I could not tell.

Harfager and I taking each a handle near the coffin-foot, and the lady bearing before us one of the black candlesticks, the obsequies began. When I got to the doorway, I noticed in a corner there two more coffins, engraved with the names Harfager and his aunt. Thence we wound our way down a wide stairway winding to a lower floor; and descending thence still lower by narrow brass steps, came to a portal of metal, where the lady, depositing the candlestick, left us.

The chamber of death into which we now bore the body had for its outer wall the brazen outer wall of the whole house at a spot where this closely approached the cataract, and was no doubt profoundly drowned in the world of surge without: so that the earthquake there was urgent. On every side the place was piled with coffins, ranged high and wide upon shelves; and the huge rush and scampering which ensued on our entrance proved it the paradise of troops of rats. As it was inconceivable that these could have eaten a way through sixteen brazen feet—for even the floor here was brazen—I assumed that some fruitful pair must have found in the house, on its building, an ark from the waters. Even this guess, though, seemed wild; and Harfager afterwards confided to me his suspicion that they had for some reason been *placed* there by the original builder.

We deposited our load upon a stone bench in the centre; whereupon Aith made haste to be away. Harfager then repeatedly walked from end to end of the place, scrutinising with many a stoop and peer and upward stretch, the shelves and their props. Could he, I was led to wonder, have any doubts as to their soundness? Damp, in fact, and decay pervaded everything. A bit of timber which I touched crumbled to dust under my thumb.

He presently beckoned to me, and, with yet one halt and *"Hark!"* from him, we passed through the house to my chamber; where, left alone, I paced about, agitated with a vague anger; then tumbled to an agony of slumber.

In the far interior of the mansion even the bleared day of this land of bleakness never rose upon our gloom; but I was able to regulate my gettings-up by a clock which stood in my chamber; or I was called by Harfager, with whom in a short time I renewed more than all our former friendship. That I should say *more* is curious: but so it *was:* and this was proved by the fact that we grew to take, and to excuse, freedoms of speech and of manner which, as two persons of more than usual reserve, we had once never dreamed of permitting to ourselves in respect of each other. Once, for example, in our pacings of aimless haste down passages that vanished in shadow and length of perspective remoteness, he wrote that my step was very slow. I replied that it was just such a step as suited my then mood. He wrote: "You have developed a tendency to *fret.*" I was very offended, and said: "Certainly, there are more fingers than one in the world which *that* ring will fit!"

Another day he was no less than rude to me for seeking to reveal to him the secret of the unhuman keenness of his hearing—and of mine! For I, too, to my dismay, began, as time passed, to catch hints of shouted sounds. The cause might be found, I asserted, in a fervour of the auditory nerve, which, if the cataract were absent, the roar of the ocean, and the row of the perpetual tempest round us, might by themselves be sufficient to bring about; his own ear-- interior, I said, must be inflamed to an exquisite pitch of fever; and I named the disease to him as the "Paracusis Wilisü." When he frowned dissent, I, quite undeterred, proceeded to relate the case (that had occurred within my own experience) of a very deaf lady who could hear the drop of a pin in a railway-train[*]; and now he made me the reply: "Of ignorant people I am accustomed to consider the mere scientist the most ignorant!"

But I, for my part, regarded it as merely far-fetched that he should pretend to be in the dark as to the morbid state of his hearing! He himself, indeed, confessed to me his own, Aith's, and the lady Swertha's proneness to paroxysms of *vertigo*. I was startled! for I had myself shortly previously been roused out of sleep by feelings of reeling and nausea, and an assurance that the room furiously flew round with me. The impression passed away, and I attributed it, perhaps hastily, to some disturbance in the nerve-endings of "the labyrinth," or inner ear. In Harfager, however, the conviction of whirling motions in the house, in the world, got to so horrible a degree of certainty, that its effects sometimes resembled those of lunacy or energumenal possession. Never, he said, was the sensation of giddiness altogether dead in him; seldom the sensation that he gazed with stretched-out arms over the brink of abysms which wooed his half-consenting foot. Once, as we walked, he was hurled as by unearthly powers to the ground, and there for an hour sprawled, bathed in sweat, with distraught bedazzlement and amaze in his stare, which watched the racing walls. He was constantly racked, moreover, with the consciousness of sounds so peculiar in their character, that I could account for them on no other supposition than that of a *tinnitùs* infinitely sick. Through the roar there sometimes visited him, he told me, the lullaby of some bird, from the burden of whose song he had the consciousness that she derived from a very remote country, was of the whiteness of foam, and crested with a comb of mauve. Or else he knew of accumulated human tones, distant, yet articulate, busily contending in volubility, and in the end melting into a medley of musical movements. Or, anon, he was shocked by an infinite and imminent crashing, like the monstrous racket of the crackling of a cosmos of crockery round his ears. He told me, moreover, that he could frequently see, rather than hear, the parti-coloured wheels of a mazy sphere-music deep, deep within the black dark of the cataract's roar. These impressions, which I protested *must* be merely entotic, had sometimes a pleasing effect upon him, and he would stand long to

---

[*]Such cases are known to many medical men. The concussion on the deaf nerve is the cause of the acquired sensitiveness; nor is there any limit to that sensitiveness when the tumult is immensely augmented.

listen with a lifted hand to their seduction: others again inflamed him to a mad anger. I guessed that they were the cause of those *"Harks!"* that at intervals of about an hour did not fail to break from him. But in this I was wrong: and it was with a thrill of dismay that I soon came to know the truth.

For, as we were once passing by an iron door on the lower floor, he stopped, and for some minutes stood listening with a leer most keen and cunning. Presently the cry *"Hark!"* escaped him; and he then turned to me and wrote on the tablet: "Did you not hear?" I had heard nothing but the roar; and he howled into my ear in sounds now audible to me as an echo caught far off in dreams: "You shall see."

He took up the candlestick; produced from the pocket of his robe a key; unlocked the iron door; and we passed into a room very loftily domed in proportion to its area, and empty, save that a pair of steps lay against its wall, and that in the centre of its marble floor was a pool, like a Roman "impluvium," only round like the room—a pool evidently profound in depth, full of a thick and inky fluid. I was very perturbed by its present aspect, for as the candle burned upon its surface, I observed that this had been quite recently *disturbed*, in a style for which the shivering of the house could not account, since *ripples* of slime were now rounding out from its middle to its brink. When I glanced at Harfager for explanation, he gave me a signal to wait; and now for about an hour, with his hands behind his back, paced the chamber; but then paused, and we two stood together by the pool's margin, gazing into the water. Suddenly his clutch tightened on my arm, and I saw, with a touch of horror, a tiny ball, probably of lead, but daubed blood-red by some chemical, fall from the roof, and sink into the middle of the pool. It hissed on contact with the water a whiff of mist.

"In the name of all that is sinister," I whispered, "what thing is this?"

Again he made me a busy and confident signal to wait, moved the ladder-steps toward the pool, handed me the taper. When I had mounted, holding high the light, I saw hanging out of the fogs in the dome a globe of old copper, lengthened into balloon-shape by a neck, at the end of which I could spy a tiny hole. Painted over the globe was barely visible in red print-letters :

"HARFAGER-HOUS: 1388–188."

I was down quicker than I went up!

"But the meaning?" I panted.

"Did you see the writing?"

"Yes. The meaning?"

He wrote: "By comparing Gascoigne with Thrunster, I find that the house was *built* about 1389."

"But the last figures?"

"After the last 8," he replied, "there is another figure not quite obliterated by a tarnish-spot."

"What figure?" I asked.

"It cannot be read but may be surmised. As the year 1888 is now all but passed, it can only be the figure 9."

"Oh, you are depraved in mind!" I cried, very irritated: "you assume—you *state*—in a manner which no mind trained to base its conclusions on facts can bear with patience."

"And you are irrational," he wrote. "You know, I suppose, the formula of Archimedes by which, the diameter of a globe being known, its volume also is known? Now, the diameter of that globe in the dome I know to be four and a half feet; and the diameter of the leaden balls about the third of an inch. Supposing, then, that 1389 was the year in which the globe was full of balls, you may readily calculate that not many fellows of the four million and odd which have since dropped at the rate of one an hour are now left within. The fall of the balls *cannot* persist another year. The figure 9 is therefore forced upon us."

"But you assume, Harfager!" I cried: "Oh, believe me, my friend, this is the very wantonness of wickedness! By what algebra of despair do you know that each ball represents one of the scions of your house, or that the last date was intended to correspond with the stoppage of the horologe. And, even if so, what is the significance of it? It can have *no significance!*"

"Do you want to madden me?" he shouted. Then furiously writing: "I swear that I know nothing of its significance! But it is not evident to you that the thing is a big hour-glass, intended to count the hours, not of a day, but of a cycle; and of a cycle of five hundred years?"

"But the whole contrivance," I passionately cried, "is a baleful phantasm of our brains! How is the fall of the balls regulated? Ah, my friend, you wander—your mind is debauched in this brawl of waters."

"I have not ascertained," he replied, "by what internal works, or clammy medium, or spiral coil, dependent probably for its action upon the vibration of the mansion, the balls are retarded in their fall: that was a matter well within the skill of the mediæval mechanic, the inventor of the clock; but this at least is clear, that one element of their retardation is the smallness of the aperture through which they have to pass; that this element, by known laws of statics, will cease to operate when no more than three balls remain; and that, consequently, the last three will fall at almost the same instant."

"In Heaven's name!" I exclaimed, careless now what folly I poured out, "but your mother is dead, Harfager! Do you deny that there remain but you and the Lady Swertha?"

A glance of disdain was all the answer he then gave me as to this.

But he confessed to me a day later that the leaden drops were a constant sorrow to his ears; that from hour to hour his life was a keen waiting for their fall; that even from his brief sleeps he infallibly started awake at each descent; that in whatever region of the mansion he chanced to be, they found him out with a crashing *loudness*; and that each crash tweaked him with a twinge of anguish within the ear. I was therefore shocked at his declaration that these droppings had now become as the life of life to him; had acquired an entwining so close with the tone of his mind, that their ceasing might even mean for him the reeling of Reason: at which confession he sobbed, with his face buried, as he leant upon a column. When this paroxysm was past, I asked him if it was out of the question that he should once for all cast off the fascination of the horologe, and escape with me from the place. He wrote in mysterious reply: "A *three*-fold cord is not easily broken." I started, asking—"How three-fold?" He wrote with a bitter smile: "To be in love with pain—to pine after aching—is not that a wicked madness?" I stood astonished that he had unconsciously quoted Gascoigne! "a wicked madness!" "a lecherous anguish!" "You have seen my aunt's face," he proceeded; "your eyes were dim if you did not see in it an impious calm, the glee of a blasphemous patience, a grin behind her daring smile." He then spoke of a prospect at the terror of which his whole soul trembled, yet which sometimes laughed in his heart in the form of a *hope*. It was the prospect of any considerable increase in the volume of sound about his ears. At *that*, he said, the brain must totter. On the night of my arrival the noise of my boots, and, since then, my voice occasionally raised, had produced acute pain in him. To such an ear, I understood him to say, the luxury of torture involved in a large sound-increase around was an allurement from which no human virtue could turn: and when I said that I could not even conceive such an increase, much less the means by which it could be effected, he brought out from the archives of the mansion some annals kept by the heads of the family. From these it appeared that the tempests that ever lacerated the latitude of Rayba did not fail to give place, at intervals of some years, to one mammoth madness, one Samson among the merry men, and Sirius among the suns. At such periods the rains descended—and the floods came—even as in the first world-deluge; those *rösts*, or eddies, which ever encircled Rayba, spurning then the bands of lateral space, burst aloft into a whirl of water-spouts, to dance about the little land, upon which, converging, some of them discharged their waters: and the locks which flowed to the cataract thus redoubled their volume, and crashed with redoubled roar. Harfager said it was miraculous that for eighteen years no such grand event had transacted itself at Rayba.

"And what," I asked, "in addition the dropping balls, and the prospect of an increase of sound, is the third strand of that 'three-fold cord' of which you have spoken?"

For answer he led me to a circular hall which, he said, he had ascertained to be the centre of the circular mansion. It was a very large hall—so large as I think I never saw—so large that the amount of wall lighted at one time by the candle seemed nearly flat: and nearly the whole of its area, from floor to roof, was occupied by a column of brass, the space between the wall and column being only such as to admit of a stretched-out arm.

"This column," Harfager wrote, "goes up to the dome and passes beyond it; it goes down to the lower floor, and passes through that; it goes down thence to the brazen flooring of the vaults and *passes through that* into the bedrock. Under each floor it spreads out, helping to support the floor. What is the precise quality of the impression which I have made upon your mind by this description?"

"I do not know," I answered, turning from him: "ask me none of your enigmas, Harfager: I feel a giddiness. . . ."

"But answer me," he said: "consider *the strangeness* of that brazen lowest floor, which I have discovered to be some six feet thick, and whose under-surface, I have reason to think, is somewhat *above* the bed-rock; remember that the fabric is at no point *fastened* to the column; think of the *chains* which ray out from the outer wall, apparently *anchoring* the house to the ground. Tell me, what impression have I *now* made?"

"And is it for *this* you wait?" I cried. "Yet there may have been no malevolent intention! You jump at conclusions! Any fixed building in such a land and spot as this would at any time be liable to be broken up by some sovereign tempest! What if it was the intention of the builder that in such a case the chains should break, and the building, by yielding, be saved?"

"You have no lack of charity at least," he replied; and we then went back to the book we were reading together.

He had not wholly lost the old habit of study, although he could no longer get himself to *sit* to read; so with a volume (often tossed down) he would stamp about within the region of the lamplight; or I, unconscious of my voice, might read to him. By a whim of his mood the few books which now lay within the limits of his patience had all for their motive something of the *picaresque*, or the foppishly speculative: Quevedo's "Tacaño;" or the system of Tycho Brahe; above all, George Hakewill's "Power and Providence of God." One day, however, as I read, he interrupted me with the sentence, *à propos* of nothing: "What I cannot understand is that you, a scientist, should believe that life ceases with the ceasing of breathing"—and from that moment the tone of our reading changed. For he led me to the crypts of the library in the lowest part of the building, and hour after hour, with a *furore* of triumph overwhelmed me with books proving the length of life after "death." What, he asked, was my opinion of Baron Verulam's account of the dead man who was heard to utter words of prayer? or of the bounding bowels of the dead convict? On my expressing unbelief, he seemed surprised, and reminded me of the writhings of dead cobras, of the long beating of a frog's heart after "death." "She is not dead," he quoted, "but *sleepeth*." The idea of Bacon and Paracelsus that the principle of life resides in a spirit or fluid was proof to him that such fluid could not, from its very nature, undergo any *sudden* annihilation, while the organs which it pervades remain. When I asked what limit he, then, set to the persistence of "life" in the "dead," he answered that when decay had so far advanced that the nerves could no longer be called nerves, or when the brain had been disconnected at the neck from the body, as by rats gnawing, then the king of terrors was king verily. With an indiscretion strange to me before my residence at Rayba, I now blurted out the question whether in all this he could be referring to his mother? For a while he stood thoughtful, then wrote: "Even if I had not had reason to believe that my own and Swertha's life in some way hung upon the final cessation of hers, I should still have taken precautions to ascertain the march of the destroyer on her frame: as it is, I shall not lack even the exactest information." He then explained that the rats which ran riot in the place of death would in time do their full work upon her; but would be unable to reach to the region of the throat without first gnawing their way through the three strings stretched across the holes of the bridges within the coffin, and thus, one by one, liberating the three morrisco-bells to tinklings.

The winter solstice had gone; another year began. I was sleeping a deep sleep by night when Harfager came into my chamber, and shook me. His face was ghastly in the taper's glare. A change within a short time had taken place upon him. He was hardly the same. He was like some poor wight into whose surprised eyes in the night have pried the eyes of Affright.

He said that he was aware of strainings and creakings, which gave him the feeling of being suspended in airy spaces by a thread which must break to his weight; and he begged me, for God's sake, to accompany him to the coffins. We passed together through the house, he craven, haggard, his gait now laggard, into the chamber of the dead, where he stole to and fro examining the shelves. Out of the footless coffin of the dowager trembling on its bench I saw a water-rat crawl; and as Harfager passed beneath one of the shortest of the shelves which bore one coffin, it suddenly dropped from a height to dust at his feet. He screamed the cry of a frighted creature; tottered to my support; and I bore him back to the upper parts of the palace.

He sat, with his face buried, in a corner of a small chamber, doddering, overtaken, as it were, with the extremity of age, no longer marking with his "Hark!" the fall of the leaden drops. To my remonstrances he responded only with the moan, "so soon!" Whenever I looked for him, I found him there, his manhood now collapsed in an ague. I do not think that during this time he slept.

On the second night, as I was approaching him, he sprang suddenly upright with the outcry: "The first bell is tinkling!"

And he had scarcely screamed it when, from some long way off, a faint wail, which at its origin must have been a fierce shriek, reached my now feverish ears. Harfager, for his part, clapped his palms to his ears, and dashed from his place, I following in hot chase through the black breadth of the mansion: till we came to a chamber containing a candelabrum, and arrased in faded red. On the floor in swoon lay the lady Swertha, her dark-grey hair in disarray wrapping her like an angry sea; tufts of it scattered, torn from the roots; and on her throat prints of strangling fingers. We bore her to her bed in an alcove; and, having discovered some tincture in a cabinet, I administered it between her fixed teeth. In her rapt countenance I saw that death was not; and, as I found something appalling in her aspect, shortly afterwards left her to Harfager.

When I next saw him his manner had undergone a kind of change which I can only describe as gruesome. It resembled the officious self-importance seen in a person of weak intellect who spurs himself with the thought, "to business! the time is short!" while his walk sickened me with a hint of *ataxie locomotrice*. When I asked him as to his aunt, as to the meaning of the marks of violence on her body, bending ear to his deep and unctuous tones, I could hear: "An attempt has been made upon her life by the skeleton, Aith."

He seemed not to share my astonishment at this thing! nor could give me any clear answer as to his reason for retaining such a servant, or as to the origin of Aith's service. Aith, he told me, had been admitted into the palace during the period of his own absence in youth, and he knew little of him beyond the fact that he was extraordinarily strong. *Whence* he had come, or how, no person except the lady Swertha was aware: and she, it seems, feared, or at least persistently flinched from admitting him into the mystery. He added that, as a matter of fact, the lady, from the day of his coming back to Rayba, had with some object imposed upon herself a dumbness on all subjects, which he had never once known her to break through, except by an occasional note.

With an ataxic strenuousness, with the airs of a drunken man constraining himself to ordered action, Harfager now set himself to the doing of a host of trivial things: he collected chronicles and arranged them in order of date; he docketed or ticketed packets of documents; he insisted upon my assistance in turning the faces of paintings to the wall. He was, however, now constantly stopped by bursts of vertigo, six times in a single hour being hurled to the ground, while blood frequently guttered from his ears. He complained to me in a tone of piteous wail of the wooing of a silver *piccolo* that continually seduced him. As he bent, sweating, over his momentous nothings, his hands fluttered like aspen. I noted the movements of his whimpering lips, the rheum of his sunken eyes: sudden doting had come upon his youth.

On a day he threw it utterly off, and was young anew. He entered my room; roused me from dreams; I observed the lunacy of bliss in his eyes, heard his hiss in my ear:

"Up! *The storm!*"

Ah! I had known it—in the nightmare of the night. I felt it in the air of the room. It had come. I saw it lurid by the lamplight on the hell of Harfager's face.

A glee burst at once into birth within me, as I sprang from my couch, glancing at the clock: it was eight—in the morning. Harfager, with the naked stalk of some maniac prophet, had already taken himself away; and I started out after him. A deepening was clearly felt in the quivering of the edifice; anon for a second it stopped still, as if, breathlessly, to listen; its air was troubled with a vague gustiness. Occasionally there came to me as it were the noising of some far-off lamentation and voice in Ramah, but whether this was in my ear or the screaming of the gale I could not tell; or again I could hear one clear chord of an organ's vaunt. About noon I spied Harfager, lamp in hand, running along a corridor, with naked soles. As we met he looked at me, but hardly with recognition, and passed by; stopped, however, and ran back to howl into my ear the question: "Would you *see?*" He then beckoned before me, and I followed to a very small opening in the outer wall, closed with a slab of brass. As he lifted the latch, the slab dashed inward with instant impetuosity and tossed him a long way, while the breath of the tempest, braying through the brazen tube with a brutal bravura, caught and pinned me upon a corner of a wall, and all down the corridor a long crashing racket of crowds of pictures and couches followed. I nevertheless managed to push my way on the belly to the opening. Hence the sea should have been visible; but my senses were met by nothing but a vision of tumbled tenebrousness, and a general impression of the letter O. The sun of Rayba had gone out. In a moment of opportunity our two forces got the shutter shut again.

"Come!"—he had obtained a fresh glimmer, and beckoned before me— "let's go see how the dead fare in the great desolation:" and we ran, but had hardly got to the middle of the stairway, when I was thrilled by the consciousness of some great shock, the bass of a dull thud, which nothing save the thumping to the floor of the whole lump of the coffins could have caused. I looked for Harfager, and for a moment only saw his heels skedaddling, panic-hounded, his ears stopped, his mouth round! Then, indeed, fear reached me— a tremor in the audacity of my heart, a thought that now at any rate I must desert him in his extremity, and work out my own salvation. Yet it was with hesitancy that I turned to search for him for the last farewell—a hesitancy which I felt to be not unselfish, but selfish, and unhealthy. I rambled through the night, seeking light, and having happened upon a lamp, proceeded to seek for Harfager. Several hours went by in this way, during which I could not doubt from the state of the air in the house that the violence about me was being wildly heightened. Sounds as of screams—unreal, like the shriekings of demons—now reached my ears. As the time of night came on, I began to detect in the greatly augmented baritone of the cataract a fresh character—a shrillness—the whistle of rapture—a malice—the menace of a rabies blind and deaf. It must have been at about the hour of six that I found Harfager. He sat in an obscure room, with his brow bowed down, his hands on his knees, his face covered with hair, and with blood from the ears. The right sleeve of his robe had been rent away in some renewed attempt, I imagined, to manage a window; and the rather crushed arm hung lank from the shoulder. For some time I stood and eyed him mouthing his mumblings; but now that I had found him uttered nothing as to my departure. Presently he looked sharply up with the call "Hark!"—then with impatience, "Hark! Hark!"—then with a shout, "The second bell!" And *again*, in immediate sequence upon his shout, there sounded a wail, vague yet real, through the house. Harfager at the instant dropped reeling with giddiness; but I, snatching up a lamp, dashed out, shivering but eager. For some while the wild wailing went on (either actually, or by reflex action of my ear); and as I ran for the lady's apartment, I saw opposite to it the open door of an armoury, into which I passed, caught up a battle-axe, and was now about to dart in to her aid, when Aith, with a blazing eye, shied out of her chamber. I cast up my axe, and, shouting, dashed forward to down him: but by some chance the lamp fell from me, and before I knew anything more, the axe sprang from my grasp, and I was cast far backward by some most grim vigour. There was, however, enough light shining out of the chamber to show that the skeleton had darted into a door of the armoury, so I instantly slammed and locked the door near me by which I had procured the axe, and hurrying to the other, secured it, too. Aith was thus a prisoner. I then entered the lady's chamber. She lay over the bed in the alcove, and to my bent ear grossly croaked the ruckle of death. A glance at her mangled throat convincing me that her last moments were come, I settled her on the bed, curtained her within the loosened festoons of the hangings of black, and turned from the cursedness of her aspect. On an *escritoire* near I noticed a note, intended apparently for Harfager: "I mean to defy, and fly; not from fear, but for the delight of the defiance itself. *Can* you come?" Taking a flame from the candelabrum, I left her to her loneliness, and throes of her death.

I had passed some way backward when I was startled by a queer sound—a crash—resembling the crash of a tamboureen; and as I could hear it pretty clearly, and from a distance, this meant some prodigious energy. In two minutes it again broke out; and thenceforth at regular intervals—with an effect of pain upon me; and the conviction grew gradually within me that Aith had unhung two of the old brass shields from their pegs, and holding them by their handles, and dashing them viciously together, thus expressed the frenzy that had now overtaken him. When I found my way back to Harfager, very anguish was now stamping in him about the chamber; he shook his head like a tormented horse, brushing and barring from his hearing each crash of the brass shields. "Ah, when—when—" he hoarsely groaned into my ear, "will that ruckle cease in her throat? I will myself, I tell you—*with my own hand*—oh God. . . ." Since the morning his auditory fever (as indeed my own also) appeared to have increased in steady proportion with the roaring and screeching chaos round; and the death-struggle in the lady's throat bitterly filled for him the intervals of the grisly cymbaling of Aith. He presently sent twinkling fingers into the air, and, with his arms cast out, darted into the darkness.

And again I sought him, and long again in vain. As the hours passed, and the day deepened toward its baleful midnight, the cry of the now redoubled cataract, mixed with the mass and majesty of the now climatic tempest, took on too intentional a *shriek* to be longer tolerable to any reason. My own mind escaped my sway, and went its way: for here in the hot-bed of fever I was fevered. I wandered from chamber to chamber, precipitate, dizzy on the upbuoyance of a joy. "As a man upon whom sleep seizes," so I had fallen. Even yet, as I passed near the region of the armoury, the rapturous shields of Aith did not fail to smash faintly upon my ear. Harfager I did not see, for he, too, was doubtless roaming a hurtling Ahasuerus round the world of the house. However, at about midnight, observing light shining from a door on the lower stage, I entered and saw him there—the chamber of the dropping horologe. He sat hugging himself on the ladder-steps, gazing at the gloomy pool. The final lights of the riot of the day seemed dying in his eyes; and he gave me no glance as I ran in. His hands, his bare arm, were all washed with new-shed blood; but of this, too, he looked unconscious; his mouth was hanging open to his pantings. As I eyed him, he suddenly leapt high, smiting his hands with the yell, "The last bell tinkling!" and ran out raving. He therefore did not see (though he may have understood by hearing) the thing which, with cowering awe, I now saw: for a ball slipped from the horologe with a hiss and mist of smoke into the pool; and while the clock once ticked another: and while the clock yet ticked, another! and the smoke of the first had not perfectly thinned, when the smoke of the third, mixing with it, floated toward the dome. Understanding that the sands of the mansion were run, I, too, throwing up my arm, rushed from the spot; but was suddenly stopped in my flight by the sense of some stupendous destiny emptying its vials upon the edifice; and was made aware by a crackling racket, like musketry, above, and the downpour of a world of waters, that some water-spout, in the waltz and whirl, had hurled its broken summit upon us, and burst through the dome. At that moment I beheld Harfager running toward me, his hands buried in his hair; and, as he raced past, I caught him, crying: "Harfager, save yourself! the very fountains, Harfager—by the grand God, man"—I hissed it into his inmost ear—"*the very fountains of the Great Deep . . .!*" He glared at me, and went on his way, while I, whisking myself into a room, closed the door. Here for some time with weak knees I waited; but the eagerness of my frenzy pressed me, and I again stepped out, to find the corridors everywhere thigh-deep with water; while rags of the storm, bragging through the hole in the dome, were now blustering about the house. My light was at once puffed out; but I was surprised by the presence of *another* light—most ghostly, gloomy, blu-ish—mild, yet wild—which now gloated everywhere through the house. I was standing in wonder at this when a gust of auguster passion galloped up the mansion; and, with it, I was made aware of the *snap* of something somewhere. There was a minute's infinite waiting—and then—quick—ever quicker—came the throb, snap, pop, in spacious succession, of the anchoring chains of the mansion before the hurried shoulder of the hurricane. And *again* a second of breathless stillness—and then—deliberately—its hour came—the house moved. My flesh worked like the flesh of worms which squirm. Slowly moved, and stopped—then there was a sweep—and a swirl—and a pause! then a swirl—and a sweep—and a pause! then steady labour on the brazen axis as the labourer tramps by the harrow; then a heightening of zest—then intensity—then the final light liveliness of flight. And now once again, as, staggering and plunging, I spun, the notion of escape for a moment came to me, but this time I shook an impious fist. "No, but, God, no, no," I gasped, "I will no more go from here: there let me waltzing pass in this carnival of the vortices, anarchy of the thunders!"—and I ran staggering. But memory gropes in a greyer gloaming as to all that followed. I struggled up the stairway, now flowing a river, and for a good while ran staggering and plunging, full of wild rantings, about, amid the downfall of roofs, and the ruins of walls. The air was thick with splashes, the whole roof now, save three rafters, having been snatched by the wind away; and in the blush of that bluish moonshine the tapestries were flapping and trailing wildly out after the flying place, like the streaming hair of some ranting fakir stung reeling by the tarantulas of distraction. At one point, where the largest of the porticoes protruded, the mansion began at every revolution to bump with grum shudderings against some obstruction: it bumped, and while the lips said one-two-three it three times bumped again. It was the mænadism of mass! Swift—still swifter—in an ague of flurry it raced, every portico a sail to the gale, racking its great frame to fragments. I, running by the door of a room littered with the ruins of a wall, saw through that livid moonlight Harfager sitting on a tomb—a drum by him, upon which, with a club in his bloody fist, he feebly, but persistingly, beat. The speed of the leaning house had now attained the *sleeping* stage, that last pitch of the spinning-top; and now all at once Harfager dashed away the mat of hair which wrapped his face, sprang, stretched his arms, and began to spin—giddily—in the same direction as the mansion—nor less sleep-embathed, with lifted hair, with quivering cheeks. . . . From such a sight I shied with retching; and, staggering, plunging, presently found myself on the lower floor opposite a porch, where an outer door chancing to crash before me, the breath of the tempest smote freshly upon me. On this an impulse, partly of madness, more of sanity, spurred in my soul; and I spurted out of the doorway, to be whirled far out into the limbo without.

The river at once rushed me deep-drenched toward the sea—though even there, in the depth of whirlpool, a shrill din, like the splitting of a world, reached my ears. It had hardly passed when my body butted in its course upon one of the arches, cushioned with seaweed, of the not all demolished causeway. Nor had I utterly lost consciousness. A clutch freed my head from the drench; and in the end I heaved myself to the level of the summit. Hence to the ledge of rock by which I had come, the bridge being intact, I rowed myself on my face under the thumps of the wind, and under a rushing of rain, like a shimmering of silk through the air. Noticing the same wild shining about me which had blushed through the broken dome into the mansion, I glanced backward—and saw that the dwelling of the Harfagers was a memory of the past; then upward—and the whole north heaven, to the zenith, shone one ocean of variegated glories—the *aurora borealis*, which was being fairily brushed and flustered by the gale. At the augustness of which sight, I was touched to a gush of tears. And with them the dream broke! the infatuation passed! a palm seemed to skin back from my brain the films and media of delusion; and on my knees I threw my hands to heaven in thankfulness for the marvel of my rescue from all the temptation, the tribulation, and the breakage, of Rayba.

THE GREAT KING

"Belphegor was no ordinary devil."—MACHIAVELLI.

Y ou never," said my Uncle Quintus, "heard the story of the Great King? Well, that, perhaps, goes without saying, for you are unable to read cuneiform writing, and I only, and one other learned man, have as yet deciphered the history."

My Uncle Quintus—the indefatigable man—had but lately returned from digging and delving among the ruin-heaps of Nimroud and Khosabad, and where the village of Hillah stands to-day, where Babylon was. It was a wild night, rags of gusts tormented the tapestries, the flicker only of the fire lighted us. We made it the centre of a mumping semicircle, while my Uncle Quintus puffed from a petty pipette the smoke of some preparation of *cannabis*, which had followed him from the East.

"What you have already heard about the King," he said, "is that he went mad with pride; but even then you have no notion of the man's intensities— Nero, Sardanapalus, were innocents. And with all this he was a coward, too."

The queen was Nicotris from Ionia, her Western name Moira, she having the straight nose, the bulging chin, of the daughters of the Greeks. Intercourse between East and West was not yet very close, and it is not known by what providence she was drawn to Babylon, but the King saw, and in his greed for the novel, loved her. And now was seen a spectacle: the Ionic woman was observed to acquire an altogether singular power over the mind of Nebuchadnezzar—a Chaldean king—the embodied majesty—the splendour of the heavens revealed in garments of flesh. And when Nicotris, from being loved, grew to be *feared*, all marvelled. Yet she was the mildest of women: the mighty men called her "the suave" Queen Nicotris.

A wasting malady fell upon this lady. She lay as dead—cold in the blackstone coffin—and her maidens, with dole and plaint, anointed her lips with oil, and through the nights wailed round her their wild *nenia* for the soul flown from life, thrumming the dulcimer and ten-stringed psaltery to chaunts starry, strange, lamenting in melody many days. But when the wardens of the necropolis, followed in procession by the horned archpriests of Astarté, came to bear her from the palace to the tomb, Nicotris, starting from catalepsy, opened her blue eyes, and awoke once more to life. The like was not known before, this dual habiting of earth and the land of shadows. From that day the King ceased to love his queen.

The great stature of Nicotris, her emaciation, the pallor of her face, wrought strongly on the fancy of the King. She would pass lightly as a shadow, the diadem on her head, through the banqueting-chamber, where the King, bright with wine, sat at midnight with his ministers; and as she so passed, she would hold up, mildly smiling, a thin, forewarning finger. Then the silence of a minute, and a frown on the King's brow.

The mystery of her "awaking from the dead" freed her from all compulsion. None could tell what dark secrets she hid within her brain, brought back from those deep, pale kingdoms into which her venturesome spirit had strayed, on what sights of terror her wide eyes had rested in all the trance of that far travel! Was she, indeed, a woman amongst women, or a true visitant from the grave? The King no longer companied with her: nard and cassia and musk could not overcome that odour of the tomb which, in his fantasy, she bore about with her; he shunned the calm of her smile; he fled the embrace of her fleshless breast; first awe, then hate, filled the heart of the King for the suave Queen Nicotris.

Yet Nicotris loved the King, though, knowing all his weaknesses, his pride, she constantly sought to curb him. Often she would draw him, in spite of himself, from the revelry of wine to the moon-lit garden-paradise of the palace, they forming then a great contrast, she tall a head above him, the King obese, swart, with thick lips, and flowing beard. Often, too, she would constrain him to follow her to the top of that tremendous temple of Bel—pyramidal, seven-terraced, to symbolise the planets—where stood the observatory of the astrologers. And here, on this height, when in the dark morning Pleiades sloped steeply in the skies, the Queen would wax ecstatic, and with her scarlet-robed arm, would sweep from azimuth to azimuth the starry deeps, prophesying with authority of one Highest of All—asking who caused the horned horse of Astarté to haunt the earth, and whose hand hurled "the crooked serpent" across the vault. From all this the King would turn with loathing.

But her will was law in the Court. When, for instance, the remnants of Nineveh rebelled, and it was decided that they should all be slain, the Queen walked calmly into the council-hall, and with warning, with persuasiveness, prayed for their preservation; whereupon the King dashed his sceptre down, and stalked from the hall; the Ministers passed out in silence after him: while Nicotris, left alone, bending to the big black baboon from the crags of Ararat, which ever accompanied her steps, said with her placid smile: "You see, Pul, my friend, how these men receive the admonitions of wisdom!" Yet that day the irresistibleness of her will prevailed, and the conquered were spared.

The King was returning from hunting the lion on the plain of Dura, and passing slowly in his chariot through the labyrinth of Babylon when suddenly at a corner he saw a maiden whose beauty overcame his soul. She was daintily shod in badger's skin, and shimmered like a daughter of shahs in fine linen, and silk, and broidered work—blue and purple and vermilion—an emerald raying merrily from her forehead. Her veil being lifted, for a moment the King saw fully the vision, and then the damsel span and vanished down a shadowy alley. The King ordered two of his lords to follow, who thought they saw her enter a house, and into this they ran—the dwellings being all constructed pyramid-wise, with a terrace on the flat roof of each story, on which grew the palms, and cedars, and vines of the famed pleasure-gardens. In a nook, perhaps, of one of these the maiden hid; the people of the house did not know her; the officers tremulously sought her everywhere; but she had vanished. They questioned themselves: was this, then, a creature of air sent by destiny to trouble the brain of the King—a warning from the gods? The nervosity of Nebuchadnezzar, his terror of death, of the sight of death, of the world of spirits, had infected all his Court.

When the King reached the steps of the palace, "Where is Nicotris, the Queen?" he asked of the cup-bearer, who presented to him, while yet in the street, a goblet of spiced wine.

"She lies ill in the forecourt of the women's quarter," answered Vajezatha.

Many times that day did the King inquire of the state of Nicotris. An impatience possessed him as to whether she would fall again into the unnatural death-life—the hateful death without its decay, the unholy life without its pulse—perhaps to wake again? The thing, he thought, must end—*he* would end it. And he remembered the vision of brightness and grace in the street of the city.

He visited her in person at dawn, a fiendish intent born in his brain, the harem being a series of chambers grouped round one of the courts of the palace, and the palace itself a low structure, placed on the top of an immense platform of glazed bricks. The King passed through the gloom of a vault, guarded on each hand by winged cherubim, which formed the entrance to the harem and found Nicotris reclining on an ivory couch in one of the "galleries," her only guard the old ape, the faithful Pul, garrulous by her side. The King gazed long at her, a paleness on his face; he had sworn to end it—with his own secret hand. But though Nicotris could not speak, as if she divined the evil of his thoughts, as if she had heard of the meeting in the street, she lifted up a thin finger. Nebuchadnezzar turned away.

Late that same day a message came to the King declaring that Queen Nicotris had, to all appearance, entered the state of death.

She was carried by her damsels in an uncovered coffin of black marble to a corner of the paradise, if haply the breezes from the plain might again revive her, the paradise occupying a court at a corner of the platform on which the palace stood, abutting the city walls, and enclosed on two sides by the alabaster parapet of the platform, and on the other two by columns connected by curtains of silk. Here many a fountain plashed on crocus and daphne and ixia; gourd, melon, and fig; the love-apple and the henna-tree; and at one end stood a pigmy ebon temple to the God Nisroch, guarded by winged bulls. Before the steps of this the Queen was laid.

The King stepped from the banquet at midnight and walked in the garden, his brain brave with the bright wine of Iran, exultation filling him that he was free at last—for ever—from the awesome Nicotris. She should be promptly entombed, he said; no re-awaking this time! He did not dream how near the queen's body lay.

All suddenly—before the temple steps—he saw. Marble she slumbered below the moon. The King sprang backwards, groaning in pain. Panic seized him, then tumultuous rage. How came she here? It was a fate's mockery, and with the eyeballs of the striped hyena of Shinar shining in his head, like the ounce before it springs he crouched, and just so sinuously crept toward the coffin, drawing with horrid furtiveness a pigmy scimitar from his girdle. He struck. Only *once* has the hand of a man committed an infamy so mephitic. The gash slashed the integuments which ligament the hinges of the jaw together—the mouth howled agape. The King saw the redness—and saw no more.

As he ran, a sob in his throat, two eyes, questioning, upbraiding, from behind a pillar, met his own. He knew the eyes of Pul, the ape, and dashed forward to fell the beast with a stroke, but Pul vanished.

The manner of the Assyrians was to sepulchre in caves without a city, cut out of the rock, or built of painted bricks, each coffin being placed within a rock-chamber of its own, the coffin itself of stone, and the lid of a vitreous material, similar to the modern glass. In such fashion, followed by the mourning Pul, was the good Queen Nicotris, on being found mysteriously disfigured— and *now* at least supposed to be really dead—borne to her rest on the following day, the seventh of the month Adar.

Thus had the King cast off from him the coils of Nicotris. But as he passed at night-fall of that day to the halls of the harem through the now vacant bed-chamber of the Queen, a new wretchedness befel him. It was dark; the curtains of the galleries were drawn; he was alone. In the obscurity—a sighing. Peering, he was aware of a something—an outline. The King turned and fled.

The distemper of the restless mind possessed the King in those days. He would leap from sleep with distraught eye and drenched hair, like a man haunted. A night-sound, the human shape of a drapery, had power to dismay him. He hated solitude. No longer did the banquet of wine work its magic of forgetfulness.

He sent in secret for the chief of the soothsayer-priestesses, who served day and night in the temple of Astarté, and she, coming in the darkest hour before the day, had conference with the King in an inner gallery of the palace, the King sitting on the edge of his couch in disarray, she doddering before him, bent with age, dry of face, with tiny bright eyes full of knowing.

"Two things," he said, "you shall do, or die: you shall lay the spirit that infests me; and you shall tell me the name and abode of a maiden whom, on the first of Adar, I saw in the streets of Babylon."

"I can do even more—I can *show* the King the maiden," answered the hag.

"How?"

"In vision first. If the King will come to an appointed spot to-morrow at midnight, alone—I will show the King this thing."

"I will come."

When the sibyl descended the stairway in the wall, the King rose and walked to and fro in the gallery. He looked over the endlessness of Babylon, on which the moon shone, on the pyramids, temples, the three days' journey of the city walls. From that station he could see on the plain the colossal golden image which he himself had set up. And he stamped with his foot; he brandished his arm, challenging. The thought swelled within him: "Is not this great Babylon . . .?"

And while the King was so thinking, arms from behind involved him, and the touch of a hand lay on his throat. He fell faint . . .

All the next day he wandered from court to court, unkinglike, with ragged head, with foam-flecked beard, and the flight of a dagger from his hand ended in the breast of a cup-bearer who approached with wine.

As night fell his brow grew gloomier, he sitting on the throne of the audience-hall, his head drooping to his knees, the majesty all gone. At midnight he dismissed all; and, looking this way and that, crouched secretly down the great stairway to the south-west gate over against the palace.

Here Zeresh, the sorceress, awaited him. They passed together over the plain, the wind soughing across the desert; and there was a threatening of thunder. But the moon shone bright.

The King stalked, Zeresh struggling to keep by him. Presently he stopped.

"Whither would you lead me?"

"To the city of tombs, O King."

"The *what?*"

"It is there only that I have power to show the King the vision."

The King moved onward more slowly.

"I will tell you something," he said, abruptly, "and let your science unravel it. The Queen Nicotris is dead: yet, as I passed through her apartment by night, a form seemed to stand before me."

Zeresh smiled.

"I know not," she answered, "but if the form was of nothing human, might it not have been that of the favoured Pul, which doubtless still haunts his mistress's chambers?"

"Yet I had ordered that the ape should be hunted from the palace. But what say you to hands, cold like the hands of Nicotris, laid on my flesh in the morning watch?"

Zeresh showed a tooth.

"Without doubt the hands of the playful Pul, oh, King, returned from banishment by climbing the palace platform."

They had come to the ruins of Hur, where the brool of the lion, the whine of the wild cat, stalking amid the fallen walls, caught the ear. On the right the Euphrates; piled round, "whatsoe'er of strange sculptured on alabaster obelisk, or jasper tomb, or mutilated sphinx," outlived the wreck of the erections of the world's first cities. The desolation here was complete.

"Tell me," the King said, "what is the nature of the vision which waits for me."

"The King will first enter the ante-chamber of a tomb."

Nebuchadnezzar shuddered.

"Here heaven will descend to wanton with the nostrils of my lord."

The sibyl had, in fact, commanded two damsels to be in waiting in the darkness, with censers exhaling vapours.

"The King," she continued, "will now advance, draw aside a tapestry, descend three steps, and enter the second hall of the dead; immediately a swarm of spheres will wawl sweetness to his ear."

She had similarly secreted to this room cunning lutists with flute and dulcimer.

"Once more the King will advance, draw aside a curtain and now, before him, he shall see—"

"Her?"

"In a nimbus."

She had stationed in this third hall the most lovely of her acolytes, robed in cloth of silver; directly in front of whom a cauldron over a fire, containing a combination of natron, bitumen and sulphur, was to send up a smoke, through the obscure of which the vision should loom: and the King's eye having rested upon her, the young priestess was to vanish into one of the side-chambers.

The wind had risen, and splashes of rain began to fall accompanied by thunderclaps.

An eagle flew low athwart their way.

"That," Zeresh said, in the strain of the animistic anthropomorphism of the East,* "is the Eagle. He gazes into the sun's heart. How strong his wing! See him preen for flight! He is the emblem of pride."

The King glanced distrustfully at her.

They came to a tarn, by which, on one leg, stood a bittern, in the hurricane which now swept the plain.

"See," said Zeresh, "the bittern: he broods by the lonesome pool; gloomy he is: the emblem of the sullen mood, ever ungrateful, never content."

The King frowned at this.

They had nearly reached the outermost bounds of the city of the dead, when a bison bounded bellowing across their way.

"Look!" Zeresh cried, "the wild ox! He eats the grass of the earth, yet spurns the earth with his foot. Who can tame him? He tosses his head in his strength. He is the emblem of the unbridled spirit—what they of Ionia call 'atasthalia,' the undisciplined soul."

"Cease, hag!" the King cried.

Zeresh covered her mouth with her hand.

They had now come to the entrance to the tombs, when all at once both stopped as if struck to stone, the gold of the hag's face growing a ghastlier hue, a new terror weakening the King's knees. A darkness had fallen upon the earth. The moon brooded a lurid ruby.

"Astarté veils her face!" rattled Zeresh's throat: "there is wrath!"

But when the earth's shadow began to journey from the girdle of the satellite, the hag asked, "Will the King advance?"

The King was leaning on a rock. His lips quivered, but could not speak.

---

*See Job.

"Let us proceed," urged the witch, "or the King's chance of seeing the vision may pass."

With effort he raised himself, to walk now with steps all inconsequent through rows of mausoleums, till Zeresh stopped before an open portal.

"If my lord has courage to enter, the revelation will not fail; all will be as I said—the odours, the music, the vision."

"But the tomb is black as doom; I dare not pass through it!"

"The gloom is necessary," Zeresh answered; "there is nothing for my lord to dread."

The King trembled through the portal into a passage, at the end of which, pushing aside a curtain, he entered the first chamber, lost in the darkness, hearing behind him, down the corridor, the coronachs of the breezes sighing. He waited stationary, that the promised fragrances might gratify him: his nostrils were assailed by the smell of death exhaled by the sarcophagi.

Uttering a grunt of disgust, he groped onward, and drawing aside a tapestry, descended three long steps to the second apartment.

Instantly he was aware of another presence in the apartment, a being rushing like the wind from end to end, which presently in brushing briskly past, touched him. A spirit riving in his pangs! So, too, had thought the maidens secreted there by Zeresh, who had fled with shrieks from the cave before the spectre, not knowing that Pul, since he had followed his mistress to the tombs, had become a denizen of their solitudes.

But the music! With all of sense that remained to him—with a despairing *hope*—the King listened, straining every dazed faculty to catch the strains, while to and fro swept the breath of Pul. And now, indeed, there came a sound—but loud, heart-madding—a sound of clash and clangour, like the crackling of glass, like the battering apart by the dead of the bars of the prison house of death.

The King's flesh crept, and with all sense of direction lost, casting up his arms, he ran. Thus he came to the third drapery, which parted before his flight.

And now at last there was light. The cauldron of Zeresh burning over a pan containing embers, sent up its pharos of vapour, in the midst of which the King's eye lighted on a form at whose horror his brain tottered: a form tall, wrapped from head to foot in the cerements of the grave, her arms outspread, her brow bound about with a napkin. He saw the straight nose—the bulging chin—the risen Nicotris! And, as he looked, the face-cloth, knotted loosely above the poll, slowly unravelled itself, and dropped; the gashed jaws, held together by a single ligament, dropped agape.

. . . From her throat there broke an outcry . . .

King Nebuchadnezzar stood with his eyes staring before him—the muscles of his face rigid—his thick lips parted. So passed a full minute. Then he drew his fingers across his forehead with a look of lunacy; but this, too, soon passed; and now he was calm, as his mouth sidled and settled into the smile of idiotcy.

And he was driven from men; and his dwelling was with the beasts of the field; and his hairs were grown like bird's feathers, as the eagle's; and his nails like bird's claws, as the bittern's; and he did eat grass as the wild ox.

And his body was wet with the dew of heaven.

The Bride

"He shall not see the rivers, the floods, the brooks of honey and butter."
—JOB.

They met at Krupp and Mason's, musical-instrument-makers, of Little Britain, E.C., where Walter had been employed two years, and then came Annie to typewrite, and be serviceable. They began to "go out" together after six o'clock; and when Mrs Evans, Annie's mamma, lost her lodger, Annie mentioned it, and Walter went to live with them at No. 13 Culford Road, N.; by which time Annie and Walter might almost be said to have been engaged. His salary, however, was only thirty shillings a week.

He was the thorough Cockney, Walter; a well-set-up person of thirty, strong-shouldered, with a square brow, a moustache, and black acne-specks in his nose and pale face.

It was on the night of his arrival at No. 13, that he for the first time saw Rachel, Annie's younger sister. Both girls, in fact, were named "Rachel"—after a much-mourned mother of Mrs Evans'; but Annie Rachel was called "Annie," and Mary Rachel was called "Rachel." Rachel helped Walter at the handle of his box to the top-back room, and here, in the lamplight, he was able to see that she was a tallish girl, with hair almost black, and with a sprinkling of freckles on her very white, thin nose, on the tip of which stood collected, usually, some little sweats. She was thin-faced, and her top teeth projected a little so that her lips only closed with effort, she not so pretty as pink-and-white little Annie, though one could guess, at a glance, that she was a person more to be respected.

"What do you think of him?" said Annie, meeting Rachel as she came down.

"He seems a nice fellow," Rachel said: "rather good-looking. And strong in the back, you bet."

Walter spent that evening with them in the area front-room, smoking a foul bulldog pipe, which slushed and gurgled to his suction; and at once Mrs Evans, a dark old lady without waist, all sighs and lack of breath, decided that he was "a gentlemanly, decent fellow." When bedtime came he made the proposal to lead them in prayer; and to this they submitted, Annie having forewarned them that he was "a Christian." As he climbed to his room, the devoted girl found an excuse to slip out after him, and in the passage of the first floor there was a little kiss.

"Only one," she said, with an uplifted finger.

"And what about his little brother, then?" he chuckled—a chuckle with which all his jokes were accompanied: a kind of guttural chuckle, which seemed to descend or stick straining in the throat, instead of rising to the lips.

"You go on," she said playfully, tapped his cheek, and ran down. So Walter slept for the first night at Mrs Evans'.

On the whole, as time passed, he had a good deal of the society of the women: for the theatre was a thing abominable to him, and in the evenings he stayed in the underground parlour, sharing the bread-and-cheese supper, and growing familiar with the sighs of Mrs Evans over her once estate in the world. Rachel, the silent, sewed; Annie, whose relation with Walter was still unannounced, though perhaps guessed, could play hymn-tunes on the old piano, and she played. Last of all, Walter laid down the inveterate wet pipe, led them in prayer, and went to bed. Most mornings he and Annie set out together for Little Britain.

There came a day when he confided to her his intention to ask for a rise of "screw," and when this was actually promised by His Terror, the Boss, there was joy in heaven, and radiance in futurity, and secret talks of rings, a wedding, "a Home." Annie felt herself not far from the kingdom of Hymen, and rejoiced. But nothing, as yet, was said at No. 13: for to Mrs Evans' past grandeurs thirty shillings a week was felt to be inappropriate.

The next Sunday, however, soon after dinner, this strangeness occurred: Rachel, the silent, disappeared. Mrs Evans called for her, Annie called, but it was found that she was not in the house, though the putting away of the dinner-things, her usual task, was only half accomplished. Not till tea-time did Rachel return. She was then cold, and somewhat sullen, and somewhat pale, her lips closing firmly over her projecting teeth. When timidly questioned—for her resentment was greatly feared—she replied that she had just been looking in upon Alice Soulsby, a few squares away, for a little chat: and this was the truth.

It was not, however, the whole truth; she had also looked in at the Church Lane Sunday School on her way: and this fact she guiltily concealed. For half an hour she had sat darkly at the end of the building in a corner, listening to the "address." This address was delivered by Walter. To this school every Sunday, after dinner, he put down the beloved pipe to go. He was, in fact, its "superintendent."

After this, the tone and temper of the little household rapidly changed, and a true element of hell was introduced into its platitude. It became, first of all, a question whether or not Rachel could be "experiencing religion," a thing which her mother and Annie had never dreamt of expecting of her. Praying people, and the Salvationist, had always been the contempt of her strong and callous mind. But on Sunday nights she was now observed to go out alone, and "chapel" was the explanation which she coolly gave. Which chapel she did not specify: but, in reality, it was the Newton Street Hall, at which Walter frequently exhorted and "prayed." In the Church Lane schoolroom there was prayer-meeting on Thursday evenings; and twice within one month Rachel sallied forth on Thursday evening—soon after Walter. The secret disease which preyed upon the poor girl could hardly now be concealed. At first she suffered bitter, solitary shame; sobbed in a hundred paroxysms; hoped to draw a veil over her infirmity. But her gash was too glaring. In the long Sabbath evenings of summer he preached at street corners, and sometimes secretly, sometimes openly, Rachel would attend these meetings, singing meekly with the rest the undivine hymns of the modern evangelist. In his presence, in the parlour, on other nights, she quietly sewed, hardly speaking. When, at seven p.m., she heard his key in the front door her heart darted toward its master; when in the morning he flew away to business her universe was cinders.

"It's a wonder to me what's coming to our Rachel lately," said Annie in the train, coming home; "you're doing her soul good, or something, aren't you?"

He chuckled, with slushy suction-sounds about the back of the tongue and molars.

"Oh, that be jiggered for a tale!" he said: "*she's* all right."

"I know her better than you, you see. She's quite changed—since you've come. Looks to me as if she's having a touch of the blues, or something."

"Poor thing! She wants looking after, don't she?"

Annie laughed, too: but less brutally, more uneasily.

Walter said: "But she *oughtn't* to have the blues, if she's giving her heart to the Lord! People seem to think a Christian must be this and that. A Christian, if it comes to that, ought to be the jolliest fellow going!"

This was on a Thursday, the night of the Church Lane prayer-meeting, and Walter had only time to rush in at No. 13, wash his face, snatch his Bible, and be off. Rachel, for her part, must verily now have been badly bitten with the rabies of love, or she would have felt that to follow to-night, for the third time lately, could not fail to incur remark. But this consideration never even entered a mind now completely blinded and entranced by the personality of Walter. Through the day her work about the house had been rushed forward with this very object, and at the moment when he banged the door after him she was before her glass, dressing in blanched, intense and trembling flurry, and casting, as she bent to give the last touches to her fringe, a look of bitterest hate at the projection of her lip above the teeth.

This night, for the first time, she waited in the chapel till the end of the service, and walked slowly homeward on the way which she knew that Walter would take; and he came striding presently, that morocco Bible in his hand, nearly every passage in which was neatly under-ruled in black and red inks.

"What, is that you?" he said, taking into his a hand cold with sweat.

"It is," she answered, in a hard, formal tone.

"You don't mean to say you've been to the meeting?"

"I do."

"Why, where were my eyes? *I* didn't see you."

"It isn't likely that you would want to, Mr Teeger."

"Go on—drop that! What do you take me for? I'm only too glad! And I tell you what it is, Miss Rachel, I say to you as the Lord Jesus said to the young man: 'Thou art not far from the kingdom of heaven.'"

She was *in* it!—near him, alone, in a darkling square, yet suffering, too, in the flames of a passion such as perhaps consumes only the strongest natures.

She caught for support at his unoffered arm; and when he bent his steps straight homeward, she said, trembling violently: "I don't wish to go home as yet. I wish to have a little walk. Do you mind, Mr Teeger?"

"Mind, no. Come along, then," and they went walking among an intricacy of streets and squares, he talking of "the Work," and of common subjects. After half an hour, she was saying: "I often wish I was a man. A man can say and do what he likes; but with a girl it's different. There's you, now, Mr Teeger, always out and about, having people listening to you, and that. I often wish I was only a man."

"Oh, well, it all depends how you look at it," he said. "And, look here, you may as well call me Walter and be done."

"Oh, I shouldn't think of *that*," she replied. "Not till—"

Her hand trembled on his arm.

"Well, out with it, why don't you?"

"Till—till we know something more definite about you—and Annie."

He chuckled slushily, she now leading him fleetly round and round a square.

"Ah, you girls again!" he cried, "been blabbing again like all the girls! It takes a bright man to hide much from them, don't it?"

"But there isn't much to hide in this case, as far as I can see—*is* there?"

Always Walter laughed, straining deep in the throat. He said: "Oh, come—that would be telling, wouldn't it?"

After a minute's stillness, this treacherous phrase came from Rachel: "Annie doesn't care for anyone, Mr Teeger."

"Oh, come—that's rather a tall order, *any* one. *She's* all right."

"But she *doesn't*. Of course, most girls are silly, and that, and like to get married—"

"Well, that's only nature, ain't it?"

This was a joke; and downward the laugh strained in his throat, like struggling phlegm.

"Yes, but they don't understand what love is," said Rachel. "They haven't an idea. They like to be married women, and have a husband, and that. But they don't know what love is—believe me! The men don't either."

How she trembled!—her body, her dying voice—she pressing heavily upon him, while the moon triumphed now through cloud glaring a moment white on the lunacy of her ghostly face.

"Well, I don't know—I think *I* understand, lass, what it is," he said.

"You don't, Mr Teeger!"

"How's that, then?"

"Because, when it takes you, it makes you—"

"Well, let's have it. You seem to know all about it."

Now Rachel commenced to tell him what "it" was—in frenzied definitions, and a power of expression strange for her. *It* was a lunacy, its name was Legion, it was possession by the furies; it was a spasm in the throat, and a sickness of the limbs, and a yearning of the eye-whites, and a fire in the marrow; it

was catalepsy, trance, apocalypse; it was high as the galaxy, it was addicted to
the gutter; it was Vesuvius, borealis, the sunset; it was the rainbow in a cess-
pool, St John plus Heliogabalus, Beatrice plus Messalina; it was a transfigura-
tion, and a leprosy, and a metempsychosis, and a neurosis; it was the dance of
the mænads, and the bite of the tarantula, and baptism in a sun: out poured
the wild definition in simple words, but with the strife of one fighting for life.
And she had not half done when he understood her fully; and he had no
sooner understood her, than he was subdued, and succumbed.

"You don't mean to say—" he faltered.

"Ah, Mr Teeger," she answered, "there's none so blind as those who will
not see."

His arm stole round her shuddering body.

Everyone is said to have his failing; and this man, Walter, in no respect a
man of strong mind, was certainly on his amatory side, most sudden, promiscu-
ous, and infirm. And this tendency was, if anything, heightened by the quite sincere strain of his mind in the direction of "spiritual things": for, under sudden
temptation, back rushed his being, with the greater rigour, into its natural channel. On the whole had he not been a Puritan, he would have been a Don Juan.

In an instant Rachel's weight was hanging upon his neck, he kissing her
with passion.

After this she said to him: "But you are only doing this out of pity, Walter.
Tell the truth, you are in love with Annie?"

He, like Peter, tumbled at once into a fib. "That's what *you* say!"

"You are," she insisted, filled with the bliss of the fib.

"Bah! I'm not. Never was. *You* are the girl for me."

When they went home, they entered the house at different times, she
first, he waiting twenty minutes in the street.

The house was small, so the sisters slept together in the second-floor front
room; Walter in the second-floor back; Mrs Evans in the first-floor back, the
first-floor front being "the drawing-room." The girls, therefore, generally went
to bed together: and that night, as they undressed, there was a row.

First, a long silence. Then Rachel, to say something, pointed to some new
gloves of Annie's, asking: "How much did you give for those?"

"Money and kind words," replied Annie.

This was the beginning.

"Well, there's no need to be rude about it," said Rachel. She was happy, in
paradise, despised Annie that night.

"Still," said Annie, after a silence of ten minutes before the glass, "*still*, I
should never run after a man like that. I'd die first."

"I haven't the least idea what you're talking about," replied Rachel.

"You have. I should be *ashamed* of myself, if I were you."

"Talk away. You're a little fool."

"It's *you*. Throwing yourself at the head of a man who doesn't care for you.
What *can* you call yourself?"

Rachel laughed—happily, yet dangerously.

"Don't bother yourself, my girl," she said.

"Think of going out every night to meet a man in that way: look here, it's too disgusting of you, girl!"

"Is it?"

"You can't deny that you were with Mr Teeger to-night?"

"That I wasn't."

"It's false! Anyone can see it by the joy in your face."

"Well, suppose I was, what about it?"

"But a woman should be decent, I think; a woman should be able to command her feelings, and not expose herself like that. Believe me, it gives me the creeps all over to think of."

"Never mind, don't be jealous, my girl."

The gentle Annie flamed!

"Jealous! of *you!*"

"There isn't any need, you know—not *yet.*"

"But I'm *not!* There never *will* be need! Do you take Mr Teeger for a raving lunatic? I should go and have some false teeth put in first if I were you!"

Thus did Annie drop to the rock-bed of vulgarity; but she knew it to be necessary in order to touch Rachel, as with a white-hot wire, on her very nerve of anguish, and, in fact, at these words Rachel's face resembled white iron, while she cried out, "Never mind my teeth! It isn't the teeth a man looks at! A man knows a finely built woman when he sees her—not like a little dumpy podge!"

"Thank you. You are very polite," replied Annie, browbeaten by an intensity fiercer than her own. "But still, it's nonsense, Rachel, to talk of my being jealous of *you.* I knew Mr Teeger six months before you. And you won't know him much longer either, for I don't want to have mother disgraced here, and this is no fit place for him to lodge in. I can easily make him leave it soon—"

At this thing Rachel flew, with minatory palm over Annie's cheek, ready to strike. "You *dare* do anything to make him go away! I'll tear your little—"

Annie winked, flinched, uttered a sob, no more fight left in her.

So for two weeks the situation lasted. Only, after that night, so intense grew the bitterness between the sisters, that Annie moved down to the first-floor back, sleeping now with Mrs Evans who dimly wondered. As for Walter, meanwhile, his heart was divided within him. He loved Annie; he was fascinated and mesmerised by Rachel. In another age and country he would have married both. Every day he came to a different resolve, not knowing what to do. One thing was evident—a wedding-ring would be necessary, and he purchased one, uncertain for which of the girls.

"Look here, lass," he said to Annie in the train, coming home, "let us put a stop to this. The boss doesn't seem to be in a hurry about that rise of screw, so suppose we get spliced, and be done?"

"Privately?"

"Rather. Your ma and sister mustn't know,—not just yet a while."

"And you will still keep on living at the house?"

"Well, of course, for the time being."

She looked up into his face and smiled. It was settled.

But two nights afterwards he met Rachel on his way home from prayer-meeting; at first was honest and distant; but then committed the incredible weakness of going with her for a walk among the squares, and ended by winning from her an easily granted promise of marriage, on the same terms as those arranged with Annie.

When, the next day at lunch-time, he put his foot on the threshold of the Registrar's office to give notice, he was still in a state of agonised indecision as to the name which he should couple with his own.

When the official said, "Now the name of the other party?" Walter hesitated, shuffled with his feet, then answered:

"Rachel Evans."

Not till he was again in the street did he remember that Rachel was the name of both the girls, and that liberty of choice between them still remained to him.

Now, from the day of "notice" to the day of wedlock an interval of twenty-one clear days must, by law, elapse, and Walter, though weak enough to inform both the sisters of the step he had taken, was careful to give them only a vague idea of the date fixed. His once clear conscience, meanwhile, was grievously troubled, his feet in a net; he feared to look within himself; he feared to speak to God; and went drifting like flotsam on the river of chance.

And chance alone it was which at last cast him upon the land. The fifth day before the marriage was a Bank Holiday, and he had arranged with Rachel to go out with her that day to Hyde Park, she to wait for him at an arranged spot at two o'clock. At two, then, at a street-corner, stood Rachel waiting, twirling her parasol, walking a little, returning. Walter, however, did not appear, and what could have happened was beyond her divination. Had he misunderstood or missed her? Though incredible, it was the only thing to think. To Hyde Park, at any rate, she went alone, feeling desolate and *ennuyée*, in the vague hope of there meeting him.

What had happened was this: Walter had been half-way toward the rendezvous with Rachel, when he was met in the street by Annie, who had gone to spend the day with a married friend at Stroud Green, but had returned, owing to the husband's illness. Seeing Walter, her face lit up with smiles.

"Harry's down with the influenza," she said, "so I couldn't stay and bore poor Ethel. Where are you going?"

For the first time since his "conversion" twelve years before, Walter, with a high flush, now consciously lied.

"Only to the schoolroom," he said, "to hunt for something."

"Well, I am open to be taken out, if any kind friend will be so kind," she said fondly.

Now, he had that morning vowed to himself to wed Rachel; and by this vow he now again vowed to be bound. All the more reason why, for the last time, he should "take out" Annie.

"Come along, then, old girl," he gaily said: "where shall we go?"

"Let us go to Hyde Park," said Annie. And to Hyde Park they went, Walter, ever and anon, stabbed by the bitter memory of waiting Rachel.

At five o'clock the two were walking along the north bank of the Serpentine westward toward a two-arched bridge, which is also pierced by a third narrow arch over the bank: to this narrow arch, since it was drizzling, they were making for shelter, when Rachel, a person of the keenest vision, sighted them from the south bank. She was frantic at once. Annie, who was supposed to be at Stroud Green! *What treachery!* This, then, was why . . . She ran panting along the bank, toward the bridge, then over it, northward, and now heard the two under the arch, who stood there talking—of the wedding. Unfortunately, just here is a block of masonry, which prevented Rachel from leaning directly over the arch to listen. Yet the necessity to hear was absolute: so she ran back clear of the masonry, and bent far over the parapet, outwards and sidewards toward the arch, straining neck, body, ears, and anyone looking into those staring eyes *then* would have comprehended the doctrine of the Ferine Soul. But she was at a disadvantage, heard only murmurs, and—was that a kiss? Further and further forth she strained. And now suddenly, with a cry, she is in the water, where it is shallow near the bank. In the fall her head struck upon a stone in the mud.

For three days she screamed continuously the name of Walter, filling the street with it, calling him hers only. On the third night, in the midst of a frightful crisis of cries, she suddenly died.

"Oh, Rachel, don't say you are dead!" cried Annie over her.

The death occurred two days before the marriage-day, and on the next, Walter, well wounded, said to Annie: "This knocks our little affair on the head, of course."

Annie was silent. Then, with a pout, she said: "I don't see why. After all, it was her own fault entirely. Why should *we* suffer?"

For the feud between the sisters had become cruel as death; and it outlasted death: Annie, on the subject of Rachel and Walter, being no longer a gentle girl, but marble, without respect or pity.

And so, in spite of the trepidations and hesitancy of Walter, the marriage took place, even while Rachel lay stretched on the bed in the second-floor front of No. 13.

The ceremony did not, however transpire without hitch and omen. It was necessary, first of all, for Walter to forewarn Annie that he had given notice of her to the Registrar by her second name of "Rachel"—a mad-looking proceeding that was almost the cause of a rupture which nothing but Walter's most ardent pleadings could steer him clear of. At any rate it was to "Rachel," and not to "Annie" that he was, as a matter of fact, after all married.

After the ceremony, performed in their lunchtime, they returned to business together in Little Britain.

At ten o'clock the same night, as he was going up to bed, she ran after him, and in the passage there was a long, furtive kiss—their last on earth.

"Twelve o'clock?" he whispered intensely.

She held up her forefinger. "One!"

"Oh, say twelve!"

She did not answer, but drew her palm playfully across his cheek, meaning consent, for Mrs Evans was an inveterately heavy sleeper. He went up. And, careful to leave his door a little ajar, he extinguished his candle, and went to bed. In the apartment near by lay stark in the dark—with learned, eternal eyelids and drowsy brow—the dead.

Walter could not but think of this presence close at hand. "Well, poor girl!" he sighed. "Poor Rachel! Well, well. His way is in the sea, after all, and His path in the Great Deep, and His footsteps are not known." Then he thought of Annie—the little wife! But instead of Annie, there was Rachel. The two women fought vehemently for his thought—and ever the dead was stronger than the living. . . . Instead of Annie there was Rachel—and again Rachel.

At last he could hear twelve strike from a steeple, and sat up in bed, listening eagerly for the door to open, or a footfall on the floor.

A little American clock ticked in the room; and in the flue of the chimney was a sough and chaunt just audible.

Suddenly she was intensely with him, filling the chamber—from nowhere. He had heard no footstep, no opening of the door: yet certainly, she was with him *now*, all suddenly, close to him, over him, talking breathlessly to him.

His first sensation was a shuddering which strongly shook him from head to foot, like the shuddering of Russian cold. She held him down by the shoulders; was stretched at length on the bed, over him; and the room seemed full of a rustling and rushing, very strange, like starched muslins rushing out in stormy agitation. She was speaking, too, to him, *in breathless haste*, whimpering a secret gibberish which whimpered like a pup for passion—about love and its definition, and about the soul, and the worm, and Eternity, and the passion of death, and the nuptials of the tomb, and the lust and hollowness of the void. And he, too, was speaking, whispering through his pattering teeth, saying: "Sh-h-h, Rachel—Annie, I mean—sh-h-h, my girl—your ma will hear! Rachel, don't—sh-h-h, now!" But even while he kept up this "sh-h-h, dear-sh-h-h, now," he was conscious of the invasion of a strange rage, of such a strength as if energy was being vehemently pumped into him from some behemoth omnipotence. The form above him he could hardly discern, the room was so dark, but he felt that her garment was flowing forth from her neck in a continuous flutter, with the rustling of the starch of a thousand shrouds, like the outflow of a pennant in wind; and the quivering gauze seemed now to swell and fill the chamber, and now to sink again to the size of woman. And ever the rhapsody of love and death went on, mixed with the chattered "Sh-h-h, Rachel—Annie, I mean," of Walter; till, suddenly, he was involved in an embrace *so* horrible, felt himself encompassed by a might so intolerable, that his soul fainted within him. He sank back; thought span and failed in darkness beneath the spell of that lullaby; he muttered, "Receive my spirit. . . ."

After two days Walter, still unconscious, died. His disfigured body they placed in a grave not far from Rachel's.

The Purple Cloud

ἔσται καὶ Σάμος ἄμμος ἐσεῖται Δῆλος ἄδηλος
Sibylline Prophecy

Introduction

A bout three months ago—that is to say, toward the end of May of this year
of 1900—the writer whose name appears on the title page received as
noteworthy a letter, and packet of papers, as it has been his lot to examine.
They came from a very good friend of mine, whose name there is no reason
that I should now conceal—Dr. Arthur Lister Browne, M.A. (Oxon.), F.R.C.P.
It happened that for two years I had been spending most of my time in France,
and as Browne had a Norfolk practice, I had not seen him during my visits to
London. Moreover, though our friendship was of the most intimate kind, we
were both atrocious correspondents: so that only two notes passed between us
during those years.

Till, last May, there reached me the letter—and the packet—to which I
refer. The packet consisted of four note books, quite crowded throughout with
those giddy shapes of Pitman's shorthand, whose *ensemble* resembles startled
swarms hovering in flighty poses on the wing. They were scribbled in pencil,
with little distinction between thick and thin strokes, few vowels: so that their
deciphering, I can assure the reader, has been no holiday. The letter also was
pencilled in shorthand; and this letter, together with the second of the note
books which I have deciphered (it was marked "III."), I now publish.

[I must say, however, that in some five instances there will occur sen
tences rather crutched by my own guess work; and in two instances the char
acters were so impossibly mystical, that I had to abandon the passage with a
head ache. But all this will be found immaterial to the general narrative.]

The following is Browne's letter:

"DEAR OLD SHIEL,—I have just been lying thinking of you, wishing that
you were here to give one a last squeeze of the hand before I——'go': for, by all
appearance, 'going' I am. Four days ago, I felt a soreness in the throat, and
passing by old Johnson's surgery at Selbridge, went in and asked him to have a
look at me. He muttered something about membranous laryngitis which made
me smile, but by the time I reached home I was hoarse, and not smiling: before
night I had dyspnœa and laryngeal stridor. I at once telegraphed to London for
Morgan, and, between him and Johnson, they have been opening my trachea,
and burning my inside with chromic acid and the galvanic cautery. The diffi
culty as to breathing has subsided, and it is wonderful how little I suffer: but I
am much too old a hand not to know what's what: the bronchi are involved—

too far involved—and as a matter of absolute fact, there isn't any hope. Morgan is still, I believe, fondly dwelling upon the possibility of adding me to his successful-tracheotomy statistics, but prognosis was always my strong point, and I say No. The very small consolation of my death will be the beating of a specialist in his own line. So we shall see.

"I have been arranging some of my affairs this morning, and remembered these note-books. I intended letting you have them months ago, but you know my habit of putting things off, and the fact that the lady was alive from whom I took down the words, prevented me. Now she is dead, and as a literary man, and a student of life, you should be interested, if you can manage to read them. You may even find them valuable.

"I am under a little morphia at present, propped up in a nice little state of languor, and as I am able to write without much effort, I will tell you in the old Pitman's something about her. Her name was Miss Mary Wilson; she was about thirty when I met her, forty-five when she died, and I knew her intimately all those fifteen years. Do you know anything about the philosophy of the hypnotic trance? Well, that was the relation between us—hypnotist and subject. She had been under another man before my time, but no one was ever so successful with her as I. She suffered from *tic douloureux* of the fifth nerve. She had had most of her teeth drawn before I saw her, and an attempt had been made to wrench out the nerve on the left side by external scission. But it had made no difference: all the clocks of hell tick-tacked in that poor woman's jaw, and it was the mercy of Providence that ever she came across *me*. My organisation was found to have almost complete, and quite easy, control over hers, and with a few passes I could expel her Legion.

"Well, you never saw anyone so singular in personal appearance as my friend, Miss Wilson. Medicine-man as I am, I could never behold her suddenly without a sensation of shock: she suggested so inevitably what we call 'the *other* world,' one detecting about her some odour of the worm, with the feeling that here was rather ghost than woman. And yet I can hardly convey to you the why of this, except by dry details as to the contours of her lofty brow, meagre lips, pointed chin, and ashen cheeks. She was tall and deplorably emaciated, her whole skeleton, except the thigh-bones, being quite visible. Her eyes were of the bluish hue of cigarette smoke, and had in them the strangest, feeble, unearthly gaze; while at thirty-five her paltry wisp of hair was quite white.

"She was well-to-do, and lived alone in old Wooding Manor-house, five miles from Ash Thomas. As you know, I was 'beginning' in these parts at the time, and soon took up my residence at the manor. She insisted that I should devote myself to her alone; and that one patient constituted the most lucrative practice which I ever had.

"Well, I quickly found that, in the state of trance, Miss Wilson possessed very remarkable powers: remarkable, I mean, not, of course, because peculiar to herself in *kind*, but because they were so constant, reliable, exact, and far-reaching, in degree. The veriest fledgling in psychical science will now sit and discourse finically to you about the reporting powers of the mind in its trance state—just as though it was something quite new! This simple fact, I assure you, which the Psychical Research Society, only after endless investigation, admits to be scientific, has been perfectly well known to every old crone since the Middle Ages, and, I assume, long previously. What an unnecessary air of discovery! The certainty that someone in trance in Manchester can tell you what is going on in London, or in Pekin, was not, of course, left to the acumen of an office in Fleet Street; and the society, in establishing the fact beyond doubt for the general public, has not gone one step toward explaining it. They have, in fact, revealed nothing that many of us did not, with absolute assurance, know before.

"But talking of poor Miss Wilson, I say that her powers were *remarkable*, because, though not exceptional in *genre*, they were so special in quantity,—so 'constant,' and 'far-reaching.' I believe it to be a fact that, *in general*, the powers of trance manifest themselves more particularly with regard to space, as distinct from time: the spirit roams in the present—it travels over a plain—it does not *usually* attract the interest of observers by great ascents, or by great descents. I fancy that is so. But Miss Wilson's gift was special to this extent, that she travelled in every direction, and easily in all but one, north and south, up and down, in the past, the present, and the future.

"This I discovered, not at once, but gradually. She would emit a stream of sounds in the trance state—I can hardly call it *speech*, so murmurous, yet guttural, was the utterance, mixed with puffy breath-sounds at the languid lips. This state was accompanied by an intense contraction of the pupils, absence of the knee-jerk, considerable rigor, and a rapt and arrant expression. I got into the habit of sitting long hours at her bed-side, quite fascinated by her, trying to catch the import of that opiate and visionary language which came puffing and fluttering in delibate monotone from her lips. Gradually, in the course of months, my ear learned to detect the words; 'the veil was rent' for me also; and I was able to follow somewhat the course of her musing and wandering spirit.

"At the end of six months I heard her one day repeat some words which were familiar to me. They were these: 'Such were the arts by which the Romans extended their conquests, and attained the palm of victory; and the concurring testimony of different authors enables us to describe them with precision . . .' I was startled: they were part of Gibbon's 'Decline and Fall,' which I easily guessed that she had never read.

"I said in a stern voice: 'Where are you?'

"She replied, 'Us are in a room eight hundred and eleven miles above. A man is writing. Us are reading.'

"I may tell you two things: first, that in trance she never spoke of herself as 'I,' nor even as 'we,' but, for some unknown reason, in the *objective* way, as '*us*': 'us are,' she would say—'us will,' 'us went'; though, of course, she was an educated lady, and I don't think ever lived in the West of England, where they say 'us' in that way; secondly, when wandering in the past, she always represented herself as being '*above*' (the earth?), and higher the further back in time she went; in describing present events she felt herself *on* (the earth); while, as regards the future, she invariably declared that '*us*' were so many miles 'within' (the earth).

"To her excursions in this last direction, however, there seemed to exist certain fixed limits: I say seemed, for I cannot be sure, and only mean that, in spite of my efforts, she never, in fact, went far in this direction. Three, four thousand 'miles' were common figures on her lips in describing her distance 'above'; but her distance 'within' never got beyond sixty-three. Usually, she would say twenty, twenty-five. She appeared, in relation to the future, to re-semble a diver in the deep sea, who, the deeper he strives, finds a more resis-tant pressure, till, at no great depth, resistance becomes prohibition, and he can no further strive.

"I am afraid I can't go on: though I had a good deal to tell you about this lady. During fifteen years, off and on, I sat listening by her dim bed-side to her murmuring trances! At last my expert ear could detect the sense of her faintest sigh. I heard the 'Decline and Fall' from beginning to end. Some of her reports were the most frivolous nonsense: over others I have hung in a horror of inter-est. Certainly, my friend, I have heard some amazing words proceed from those wan lips of Mary Wilson. Sometimes I could hitch her repeatedly to any scene or subject that I chose by the mere exercise of my will; at others, the flighty waywardness of her spirit eluded and baffled me: she resisted—she disobeyed: otherwise I might have sent you, not four note-books, but twenty, or forty. About the fifth year it struck me that it would be well to jot down her more connected utterances, since I knew shorthand. The note-book marked 'I.',* which seems to me the most curious, belongs to the seventh year. Its history, like those of the other three, is this: I heard her one afternoon murmuring in the intonation used when *reading*; the matter interested me; I asked her where she was. She replied: 'Us are forty-eight miles within: us read, and another writes'; from which I concluded that she was some fifteen to thirty years in the future, perusing an as yet unpublished work. After that, during some weeks, I managed to keep her to the same subject, and finally, I fancy, won pretty well the whole work. I believe you would find it striking, and hope you will be able to read my notes.

"But no more of Mary Wilson now. Rather let us think a little of A. L. Browne, F.R.C.P.!—with a breathing-tube in his trachea, and Eternity under his pillow. . . ." [Dr. Browne's letter then continues on a subject of no interest here.]

[The present writer may add that Dr. Browne's prognosis of his own case proved correct, for he passed away two days after writing the above. My tran-scription of the shorthand book marked "III." I now proceed to give without comment, merely reminding the reader that the words form the substance of a book or document to be written, or to be motived (according to Miss Wilson) in that Future, which, no less than the Past, substantially exists in the Pre-sent—though, like the Past, we see it not. I need only add that the title, divi-

---

*This I intend to publish under the title of "The Last Miracle"; "II." will bear that of "The Lord of the Sea"; the present book is marked "III." The perusal of "IV." I have not yet finished, but so far do not consider it suitable for publication.

sion into paragraphs, &c., have been arbitrarily contrived by myself for the sake of form and convenience.]

(*Here begins the note-book marked "III."*)

THE PURPLE CLOUD

Well, the memory seems to be getting rather impaired now, rather weak. What, for instance, was the name of that parson who preached, just before the *Boreal* set out, about the wrongness of any further attempt to reach the North Pole? I have forgotten! Yet four years ago it was as familiar to me as my own name.

Things which took place before the voyage seem to be getting a little cloudy in the memory now. I have sat here, in the loggia of this Cornish villa, to write down some sort of account of what has happened—God knows why, since no eye can ever read it—and at the very beginning I cannot remember the parson's name.

He was a strange sort of man surely, Scotchman from Ayrshire, big and gaunt, with tawny hair. He used to go about London streets in shough and rough-spun clothes, a plaid flung from one shoulder. Once I saw him in Holborn with his rather wild stalk, frowning and muttering to himself. He had no sooner come to London, and opened chapel (I think in Fetter Lane), than the little room began to be crowded; and when, some years afterwards, he moved to a big establishment in Kensington, all sorts of men, even from America and Australia, flocked to hear the thunder-storms that he talked, though certainly it was not an age apt to fly into enthusiasms over that species of pulpit prophets and prophecies. But this particular man undoubtedly did wake the strong dark feelings that sleep in the heart: his eyes were very singular and powerful; his voice from a whisper ran gathering, like snow-balls, and crashed, as I have heard the pack-ice in commotion far yonder in the North; while his gestures were as uncouth and gawky as some wild man's of the primitive ages.

Well, this man—what *was* his name?—Macintosh? Mackay? I think—yes, that was it! *Mackay*. Mackay saw fit to take offence at the fresh attempt to reach the Pole in the *Boreal*; and for three Sundays, when the preparations were nearing completion, stormed against it at Kensington.

The excitement of the world with regard to the North Pole had at this date reached a pitch which can only be described as *fevered*, though that word hardly expresses the strange ecstasy and unrest which prevailed: for the abstract interest which mankind, in mere desire for Knowledge, had always felt in this unknown region was now, suddenly, a thousand and a thousand times intensified by a new, concrete interest—a tremendous *money* interest.

And the new zeal had ceased to be healthy in its tone as the old zeal was: for now the fierce demon Mammon was making his voice heard in this matter.

Within the ten years preceding the *Boreal* expedition, no less than twenty-seven expeditions had set out, and failed.

The secret of this new rage lay in the last will and testament of Mr. Charles P. Stickney of Chicago, that king of faddists, supposed to be the richest individual who ever lived: he, just ten years before the *Boreal* undertaking, had died, bequeathing 175 million dollars to the man, of whatever nationality, who first reached the Pole.

Such was the actual wording of the will—"*the man who first reached*": and from this loose method of designating the person meant had immediately burst forth a prolonged heat of controversy in Europe and America as to whether or no the testator meant *the Chief* of the first expedition which reached: but it was finally decided, on the highest legal authority, that, in any case, the actual wording of the document held good: and that it was the individual, whatever his station in the expedition, whose foot first reached the 90th degree of north latitude, who would have title to the fortune.

At all events, the public ferment had risen, as I say, to a pitch of positive fever; and as to the *Boreal* in particular, the daily progress of her preparations was minutely discussed in the newspapers, everyone was an authority on her fitting, and she was in every mouth a bet, a hope, a jest, or a sneer: for now, at last, it was felt that success was probable. So this Mackay had an acutely interested audience, if a somewhat startled, and a somewhat cynical, one.

A truly lion-hearted man this must have been, after all, to dare proclaim a point-of-view so at variance with the spirit of his age! One against four hundred millions, they bent one way, he the opposite, saying that they were wrong, all wrong! People used to call him "John the Baptist Redivivus": and without doubt he did suggest something of that sort. I suppose that at the time when he had the face to denounce the *Boreal* there was not a sovereign on any throne in Europe who, but for shame, would have been glad of a subordinate post on board.

On the third Sunday night of his denunciation I was there in that Kensington chapel, and I heard him. And the wild talk he talked! He seemed like a man delirious with inspiration.

The people sat quite spell-bound, while Mackay's prophesying voice ranged up and down through all the modulations of thunder, from the hurrying mutter to the reverberant shock and climax: and those who came to scoff remained to wonder.

Put simply, what he said was this: That there was some sort of Fate, or Doom, connected with the Poles of the earth in reference to the human race: that man's continued failure, in spite of continual efforts, to reach them proved this; and that this failure constituted a lesson—*and a warning*—which the race disregarded at its peril.

The North Pole, he said, was not so very far away, and the difficulties in the way of reaching it were not, on the face of them, so very great: human ingenuity had achieved a thousand things a thousand times more difficult; yet in spite of over half-a-dozen well-planned efforts in the nineteenth century, and thirty-one in the twentieth, man had never reached: always he had been baulked, baulked, by some seeming chance—some restraining Hand: and herein lay the lesson—*herein the warning.* Wonderfully—really *wonderfully*—

like the Tree of Knowledge in Eden, he said, was that Pole: all the rest of earth lying open and offered to man—but *That* persistently veiled and "forbidden." It was as when a father lays a hand upon his son, with: "Not here, my child; wheresoever you will—but not here."

But human beings, he said, were free agents, with power to stop their ears, and turn a callous consciousness to the whispers and warning indications of Heaven; and he believed, he said, that the time was now come when man would find it absolutely in his power to stand on that 90th of latitude, and plant an impious right foot on the head of the earth—just as it had been given into the absolute power of Adam to stretch an impious right hand, and pluck of the Fruit of Knowledge; but, said he—his voice pealing now into one long proclamation of awful augury—just as the abuse of that power had been followed in the one case by catastrophe swift and universal, so, in the other, he warned the entire race to look out thenceforth for nothing from God but a lowering sky, and thundery weather.

The man's frantic ernestness, authoritative voice, and savage gestures, could not but have their effect upon all; as for me, I declare, I sat as though a messenger from Heaven addressed me. But I believe that I had not yet reached home, when the whole impression of the discourse had passed from me like water from a duck's back. The Prophet in the twentieth century was not a success. John Baptist himself, camel-skin and all, would have met with only tolerant shrugs. I dismissed Mackay from my mind with the thought: "He is behind his age, I suppose."

But haven't I thought differently of Mackay since, my God . . .?

*   *   *   *   *

Three weeks—it was about that—before that Sunday night discourse, I was visited by Clark, the chief of the coming expedition—a mere visit of friendship. I had then been established a year at No. 11, Harley Street, and, though under twenty-five, had, I suppose, as *élite* a practice as any doctor in Europe.

Élite—but small. I was able to maintain my state, and move among the great: but now and again I would feel the secret pinch of moneylessness. Just about that time, in fact, I was only saved from considerable embarrassment by the success of my book, "Applications of Science to the Arts."

In the course of conversation that afternoon Clark said to me in his haphazard way:

"Do you know what I dreamed about you last night, Adam Jeffson? I dreamed that you were with us on the expedition."

I think he must have seen my start: on the same night I had myself dreamed the same thing; but not a word said I about it now. There was a stammer in my tongue when I answered:

"Who? I?—on the expedition?—I would not go, if I were asked."

"Oh, you would."

"I wouldn't. You forget that I am about to be married."

"Well, we need not discuss the point, as Peters is not going to die," said he. "Still, if anything did happen to him, it is you I should come straight to, Adam Jeffson."

"Clark, you jest," I said: "I know really very little of astronomy, or magnetic phenomena. Besides, I am about to be married. . . ."

"But what about your botany, my friend? *There's* what we should be wanting of you: and as for nautical astronomy, poh, a man with your scientific habit would pick all that up in no time."

"You discuss the matter as gravely as though it were a possibility, Clark," I said, smiling. "Such a thought would never enter my head: there is, first of all, my *fiancée*—"

"Ah, the all-important Countess, eh?—Well, but she, as far as I know the lady, would be the first to force you to go. The chance of stamping one's foot on the North Pole does not occur to a man every day, my son."

"Do talk of something else!" I said. "There is Peters. . . ."

"Well, of course, there is Peters. But, believe me, the dream I had was so clear—"

"Let me alone with your dreams, and your Poles!" I laughed.

Yes, I remember: pretended to laugh loud! But my secret heart knew, even *then,* that one of those crises was occurring in my life which, from my youth, has made it the most extraordinary which any creature of earth ever lived. And I knew that this was so, firstly, because of the two dreams, and secondly, because, when Clark was gone, and I was drawing on my gloves to go to see my *fiancée,* I heard distinctly the old two Voices talk within me: and One said: "Go not to see her now!" and the Other: "Yes, go, go!"

The two Voices of my life! An ordinary person reading my words would undoubtedly imagine that I mean only two ordinary contradictory impulses— or else that I rave: for what modern man could comprehend how real-seeming were those voices, how loud, and how, ever and again, I heard them contend within me, with a nearness "nearer than breathing," as it says in the poem, and "closer than hands and feet."

About the age of seven it happened first to me. I playing one summer evening in a pine-wood of my father's; half a mile away a quarry-cliff; and as I played, it suddenly seemed as if someone said to me, inside of me: "Just take a walk toward the cliff"; and as if someone else said: "Don't go that way at all!"—mere whispers then, which gradually, as I grew up, seemed to swell into cries of wrathful contention! I did go toward the cliff: it was steep, thirty feet high, and I fell. Some weeks later, on recovering speech, I told my astonished mother that "someone had pushed me" over the edge, and that someone else "had caught me" at the bottom!

One night, soon after my eleventh birthday, lying in bed, the thought struck me that my life must be of great importance to some thing or things which I could not see; that two Powers, which hated each other, must be continually after me, one wishing for some reason to kill me, the other for some reason to keep me alive, one wishing me to do so and so, the other to do the opposite; that I was not a boy like other boys, but a creature separate, special, marked for—something. Already I had notions, touches of mood, passing instincts, as occult and primitive, I verily believe, as those of the first man that stepped; so that such Biblical expressions as "The Lord spake to So-and-so, saying" have hardly ever suggested any question in my mind as to how the Voice was *heard:* I did not find it so very difficult to comprehend that originally man had more ears than two; nor should I have been surprised to know that I, in these latter days, more or less resemble those primeval ones.

But not a creature, except perhaps my mother, has ever dreamed me what I here state that I was. I seemed the ordinary youth of my time, bow in my 'Varsity eight, cramming for exams., dawdling in clubs. When I had to decide as to a profession, who could have suspected the conflict that transacted itself in my soul, while my brain was indifferent to the matter—that agony of strife with which the brawling voices shouted, the one: "Be a scientist—a doctor," and the other: "Be a lawyer, an engineer, an artist—be *anything* but a doctor!"

A doctor I became, and went to what had grown into the greatest of medical schools—Cambridge; and there it was that I came across a man, named Scotland, who had a rather odd view of the world. He had rooms, I remember, in the New Court at Trinity, and a set of us were generally there. He was always talking about certain "Black" and "White" Powers, till it became absurd, and the men used to call him "black-and-white-mystery-man," because, one day, when someone said something about "the black mystery of the universe," Scotland interrupted him with the words: "the black-and-white mystery."

Quite well I remember Scotland now—the sweetest, gentle soul he was, with a passion for cats, and Sappho, and the Anthology, very short in stature, with a Roman nose, continually making the effort to keep his neck straight, and draw his paunch in. He used to say that the universe was being frantically contended for by two Powers: a White and a Black; that the White was the stronger, but did not find the conditions on our particular planet very favourable to his success; that he had got the best of it up to the Middle Ages in Europe, but since then had been slowly and stubbornly giving way before the Black; and that finally the Black would win—not everywhere perhaps, but *here*—and would carry off, if no other earth, at least *this* one, for his prize.

This was Scotland's doctrine, which he never tired of repeating; and while others heard him with mere toleration, little could they divine with what agony of inward interest, I, cynically smiling there, drank in his words. Most profound, most profound, was the impression they made upon me.

*   *   *   *   *

But I was saying that when Clark left me, I was drawing on my gloves to go to see my *fiancée,* the Countess Clodagh, when I heard the two voices most clearly.

Sometimes the urgency of one or the other impulse is so overpowering, that there is no resisting it: and it was now with the one that bid me go.

I had to traverse the distance between Harley Street and Hanover Square, and all the time it was as though something shoulted at my physical ear: "Since you go, breathe no word of the *Boreal*, and Clark's visit"; and another shout: "Tell, tell, hide nothing!"

It seemed to last a month: yet it was only some minutes before I was in Hanover Square, and Clodagh in my arms.

She was, in my opinion, the most superb of creatures, Clodagh—that haughty neck which seemed always scorning something just behind her left shoulder. Superb! but ah—I know it now—a godless woman, Clodagh, a bitter heart.

Clodagh once confessed to me that her favourite character in history was Lucrezia Borgia, and when she saw my horror, immediately added: "Well, no, I am only joking!" Such was her duplicity: for I see now that she lived in the constant effort to hide her heinous heart from me. Yet, now I think of it, how completely did Clodagh enthral me!

Our proposed marriage was opposed by both my family and hers: by mine, because her father and grandfather had died in lunatic asylums; and by hers, because, forsooth, I was neither a rich nor a noble match. A sister of hers, much older than herself, had married a common country doctor, Peters of Taunton, and this so-called *mésalliance* made the so-called *mésalliance* with me doubly detestable to her relatives. But Clodagh's extraordinary passion for me was to be stemmed neither by their threats nor prayers. What a flame, after all, was Clodagh! Sometimes she frightened me.

She was at this date no longer young, being by five years my senior, as also, by five years, the senior of her nephew, born from the marriage of her sister with Peters of Taunton. This nephew was Peter Peters, who was to accompany the *Boreal* expedition as doctor, botanist, and meteorological assistant.

On that day of Clark's visit to me I had not been seated five minutes with Clodagh, when I said:

"Dr. Clark—ha! ha! ha!—has been talking to me about the Expedition. He says that if anything happened to Peters, I should be the first man he would run to. He has had an absurd dream. . . ."

The consciousness that filled me as I uttered these words was the *wickedness* of me—the crooked wickedness. But I could no more help it than I could fly.

Clodagh was standing at a window holding a rose at her face. For quite a minute she made no reply. I saw her sharp-cut, florid face in profile, steadily bent and smelling. She said presently in her cold, rapid way:

"The man who first plants his foot on the North Pole will certainly be ennobled. I say nothing of the many millions . . . I only wish that I was a man!"

"I don't know that I have any special ambition that way," I rejoined. "I am happy in my warm Eden with my Clodagh. I don't like the outer Cold."

"Don't let me think little of you!" she answered pettishly.

"Why should you, Clodagh? I am not bound to desire to go to the North Pole, am I?"

"But you *would* go, I suppose, if you could?"

"I might—I—doubt it. There is our marriage . . ."

"Marriage indeed! It is the one thing to transform our marriage from a sneaking difficulty to a ten times triumphant event."

"You mean if *I* personally were the first to stand at the Pole. But there are many in an expedition. It is very unlikely that I, personally—"

"For *me* you will, Adam—" she began.

"'*Will*,' Clodagh?" I cried. "You say '*will*'? there is not the even the slightest shadow of a probability—!"

"But why? There are still three weeks before the start. They say . . ."

She stopped, she stopped.

"They say what?"

Her voice dropped:

"That Peter takes atropine."

Ah, I started then. She moved from the window, sat in a rocking-chair, and turned the leaves of a book, without reading. We were silent, she and I; I standing, looking at her, she drawing the thumb across the leaf-edges, and beginning again, contemplatively. Then she laughed dryly a little—a dry, mad laugh.

"Why did you start when I said that?" she asked, reading now at random.

"*I!* I did not start, Clodagh! What made you think that I started? I did not start! Who told you, Clodagh, that Peters takes atropine?"

"He is my nephew: I should know. But don't look dumbfounded in that absurd fashion: I have no intention of poisoning him in order to see you a multimillionaire, and a Peer of the Realm. . . ."

"My dearest Clodagh!"

"I easily might, however. He will be here presently. He is bringing Mr. Wilson for the evening." (Wilson was going as electrician of the expedition.)

"Clodagh," I said, "believe me, you jest in a manner which does not please me."

"Do I really?" she answered with that haughty, stiff half-turn of her throat: "then I must be more exquisite. But, thank Heaven, it is only a jest. Women are no longer admired for doing such things."

"Ha! ha! ha!—no—no longer admired, Clodagh! Oh, my good Lord! let us change this talk. . . ."

But now she could talk of nothing else. She got from me that afternoon the history of all the Polar expeditions of late years, how far they had reached, by what aids, and why they failed. Her eyes shone; she listened eagerly. Before this time, indeed, she had been interested in the *Boreal*, knew the details of her outfitting, was acquainted with several members of the expedition. But now, suddenly, her mind seemed wholly possessed, my mention of Clark's visit apparently setting her well a-burn with the Pole-fever.

The passion of her kiss as I tore myself from her embrace that day I shall never forget. I went home with a pretty heavy heart.

The house of Dr. Peter Peters was three doors from mine, on the opposite side of the street. Toward one that night, his footman ran to knock me up with the news that Peters was very ill. I hurried to his bed-side, and knew by the first glance at his deliriums and his staring pupils that he was poisoned with atropine.

Wilson, the electrician, who had passed the evening with him at Clodagh's in Hanover Square, was there.

"What on earth is the matter?" he said to me.

"Poisoned," I answered.

"Good God! with what?"

"Atropine."

"Good Heavens!"

"Don't be frightened: I think he will recover."

"Is that certain?"

"Yes, I think—that is, if he leaves off taking the drug, Wilson."

"What! it is he who has poisoned himself?"

I hesitated, I hesitated. But I said:

"He is in the habit of taking atropine, Wilson."

Three hours I remained there, and, God knows, toiled hard for his life: and when I left him in the dark of the fore-day, my mind was at rest: he would recover.

I slept till 11 A.M., and then hurried over again to Peters. In the room were my two nurses, and Clodagh.

My beloved put her forefinger to her lips, whispering:

"Sh-h-h! he is asleep . . ."

She came closer to my ear, saying:

"I heard the news early. I am come to stay with him, till—the last. . . ."

We looked at each other some time—eye to eye, steadily, she and I: but mine dropped before Clodagh's. A word was on my mouth to say, but I said nothing.

The recovery of Peters was not so steady as I had expected. At the end of the first week he was still prostrate. It was then that I said to Clodagh:

"Clodagh, your presence at the bed-side here somehow does not please me. It is so unnecessary."

"Unnecessary certainly," she replied: "but I always had a genius for nursing, and a passion for watching the battles of the body. Since no one objects, why should you?"

"Ah! . . . I don't know. This is a case that I dislike. I have half a mind to throw it to the devil."

"Then do so."

"And you, too—go home, go home, Clodagh!"

"But why?—if one does no harm. In these days of 'the corruption of the upper classes,' and Roman decadence of everything, shouldn't every innocent whim be encouraged by you upright ones who strive against the tide? Whims are the brakes of crimes: and this is mine. I find a sensuous pleasure, almost a sensual, in dabbling in delicate drugs—like Helen, for that matter, and Medea, and Calypso, and the great antique women, who were all excellent chymists. To study the human ship in a gale, and the slow drama of its foundering—isn't that a quite thrilling distraction? And I want you to acquire the habit of letting me have my little way—"

Now she touched my hair with a lofty playfulness that soothed me: but even then I looked upon the rumpled bed, and saw that the man there was really very sick.

I have still a nausea to write about it! Lucrezia Borgia in her own age may have been heroic: but Lucrezia in this late century! One could retch up the heart . . .

The man grew sick on that bed, I say. The second week passed, and only ten days remained before the start of the expedition.

At the end of that second week, Wilson, the electrician, was one evening sitting by Peters' bed-side when I entered.

At that moment, Clodagh was about to administer a dose to Peters; but seeing me, she put down the medicine-glass on the night table, and came toward me; and as she came, I saw a sight which stabbed me: for Wilson took up the deposited medicine-glass, elevated it, looked at it, smelled into it: and he did it with a kind of hurried, light-fingered stealth; and he did it with an under-look, and a meaningness of expression, which, I thought, proved mistrust. . . .

Meantime, Clark came each day. He had himself a medical degree, and about this time I called him in professionally, together with Alleyne of Cavendish Square, to consultation over Peters. The patient lay in a semi-coma broken by passionate vomitings, and his condition puzzled us all. I formally stated that he took atropine—had been originally poisoned by atropine: but we saw that his present symptoms were not atropine symptoms, but, it almost seemed, of some other vegetable poison, which we could not precisely name.

"Mysterious thing," said Clark to me, when we were alone.

"I don't understand it," I said.

"Who are the two nurses?"

"Oh, highly recommended people of my own."

"At any rate, my dream about you comes true, Jeffson. It is clear that Peters is out of the running now."

I shrugged.

"I now formally invite you to join the expedition," said Clark: "do you consent?"

I shrugged again.

"Well, if that means consent," he said, "let me remind you that you have only eight days, and all the world to do in them."

This conversation occurred in the dining-room of Peters' house: and as we passed through the door, I saw Clodagh gliding down the passage outside—rapidly—away from us.

Not a word I said to her that day about Clark's invitation. Yet I asked myself repeatedly: Did she not know of it? Had she not *listened*, and heard?

However that was, about midnight, to my great surprise, Peters opened his eyes, and smiled. By noon the next day, his fine vitality, which so fitted him for an Arctic expedition, had re-asserted itself. He was then leaning on an elbow, talking to Wilson, and except his pallor, and strong stomach-pains, there was now hardly a trace of his late approach to death. For the pains I prescribed some quarter-grain tablets of sulphate of morphia, and went away.

Now, David Wilson and I never greatly loved each other, and that very day he brought about a painful situation as between Peters and me, by telling Peters that I had taken his place in the expedition.

Peters, a touchy fellow, at once dictated a letter of protest to Clark; and Clark sent Peters' letter to me, marked with a big note of interrogation in blue pencil.

Now, all Peters' preparations were made, mine not; and he had six days in which to recover himself. I therefore wrote to Clark, saying that the changed circumstances of course annulled my acceptance of his offer, though I had already incurred the inconvenience of negotiating with a *locum tenens*.

This decided it: Peters was to go, I stay. The fifth day before the departure dawned. It was a Friday, the 15th June. Peters was now in an arm-chair. He was cheerful, but with a fevered pulse, and still the stomach-pains. I was giving him three quarter-grains of morphia a day. That Friday night, at 11 P.M., I visited him, and found Clodagh there, talking to him. Peters was smoking a cigar.

"Ah," Clodagh said, "I was waiting for you, Adam. I didn't know whether I was to inject anything to-night. Is it Yes or No?"

"What do you think, Peters?" I said: "any more pains?"

"Well, perhaps you had better give us another quarter," he answered: "there's still some trouble in the tummy off and on."

"A quarter-grain, then, Clodagh," I said.

As she opened the syringe-box, she remarked with a pout:

"Our patient has been naughty! He has taken some more atropine."

I got angry at once.

"Peters," I cried, "you know you have no right to be doing things like that without consulting me! Do that once more, and I swear I have nothing further to do with you!"

"Rubbish," says Peters: "why all this unnecessary heat? It was a mere flea-bite. I felt that I needed it."

"He injected it with his own hand . . ." remarked Clodagh.

She was now standing at the mantel-piece, having lifted the syringe-box from the night-table, taken from its velvet lining both the syringe and the vial containing the morphia tablets, and gone to the mantel-piece to melt one of the tablets in a little of the distilled water there. Her back was turned upon us, and she was a long time. I was standing; Peters in his arm-chair, smoking. Clodagh then began talking about a Charity Bazaar which she had visited that afternoon.

She was long, she was long. The crazy thought passed through some dim region of my soul: "Why is she so *long?*"

"Ah, that was a pain!" Peters said: "never mind the bazaar, aunt—think of the morphia."

Suddenly an irresistible impulse seized me—to rush upon her, to dash syringe, tablets, glass, and all, from her hands. I *must* have obeyed it—I was on the tip-top point of obeying—my body already leant prone: but in that moment a voice at the opened door behind me said:

"Well, how is everything?"

It was Wilson, the electrician, who stood there. With lightning swiftness I remembered an under-look of mistrust which I had once seen on his face. Oh, well, I would not, and could not!—she was my love—I stood like marble . . .

Clodagh went to meet Wilson with frank right hand, in the left being the fragile glass containing the injection. My eyes were fastened on her face: it was full of reassurance, of free innocence. I said to myself: "I must surely be mad!"

An ordinary chat began, while Clodagh turned up Peters' sleeve, and, kneeling there, injected his fore-arm. As she rose, laughing at something said by Wilson, the drug-glass dropped from her hand, and her heel, by an apparent accident, trod on it. She put the syringe among a number of others on the mantel-piece.

"Your friend has been naughty, Mr. Wilson," she said again with that same pout: "he has been taking more atropine."

"Not really?" said Wilson.

"Let me alone, the whole of you," answered Peters: "I ain't a child."

These were the last intelligible words he ever spoke. He died shortly before 1 A.M. He had been poisoned by a powerful dose of atropine.

From that moment to the moment when the *Boreal* bore me down the Thames, all the world was a mere tumbling nightmare to me, of which hardly any detail remains in my memory. Only I remember the inquest, and how I was called upon to prove that Peters had himself injected himself with atropine. This was corroborated by Wilson, and by Clodagh: and the verdict was in accordance.

And in all that chaotic hurry of preparation, three other things only, but those with clear distinctness now, I remember.

The first—and chief—is that tempest of words which I heard at Kensington from that big-mouthed Mackay on the Sunday night. What was it that led me, busy as I was, to that chapel that night? Well, perhaps I know.

There I sat, and heard him: and most strangely have those words of his peroration planted themselves in my brain, when, rising to a passion of prophecy, he shouted: "And as in the one case, transgression was followed by catastrophe swift and universal, so, in the other, I warn the entire race to look out thenceforth for nothing from God but a lowering sky, and thundery weather."

And this second thing I remember: that on reaching home, I walked into my disordered library (for I had had to hunt out some books), where I met my housekeeper in the act of rearranging things. She had apparently lifted an old Bible by the front cover to fling it on the table, for as I threw myself into a chair my eye fell upon the open print near the beginning. The print was very large, and a shaded lamp cast a light upon it. I had been hearing Mackay's wild comparison of the Pole with the tree of Eden, and that no doubt was the reason why such a start convulsed me: for my listless eyes had chanced to rest upon some words.

"The woman gave me of the tree, and I did eat. . . ."

And a third thing I remember in all that turmoil of doubt and flurry: that as the ship moved down with the afternoon tide a telegram was put into my hand; it was a last word from Clodagh; and she said only this:

"Be first—for Me."

*   *   *   *   *

The *Boreal* left St. Katherine's Docks in beautiful weather on the afternoon of the 19th June, full of good hope, bound for the Pole.

All about the docks was one region of heads stretched out in innumerable vagueness, and down the river to Woolwich a continuous dull roar and murmur of bees droned from both banks to cheer our departure.

The expedition was partly a national affair, subvented by Government: and if ever ship was well-found it was the *Boreal*. She had a frame tougher far than any battle-ship's, capable of ramming some ten yards of drift-ice; and she was stuffed with sufficient pemmican, cod-roe, fish-meal, and so on, to last us not less than six years.

We were seventeen, all told, the five Heads (so to speak) of the undertaking being Clark (our Chief), John Mew (commander), Aubrey Maitland (meteorologist), Wilson (electrician), and myself (doctor, botanist, and assistant meteorologist).

The idea was to get as far east as the 100°, or the 120°, of longitude; to catch there the northern current; to push and drift our way northward; and when the ship could no further penetrate, to leave her (either three, or else four, of us, on ski), and with sledges drawn by dogs and reindeer make a dash for the Pole.

This had also been the plan of the last expedition—that of the *Nix*—and of several others. The *Boreal* only differed from the *Nix*, and others, in that she was a thing of nicer design, of more exquisite forethought.

Our voyage was without incident up to the end of July, when we encountered a drift of ice-floes. On the 1st August we were at Kabarova, where we met our coal-ship, and took in a little coal for emergency, liquid air being our proper motor; also forty-three dogs, four reindeer, and a quantity of reindeer-moss; and two days later we turned our bows finally northward and eastward, passing through heavy "slack" ice under sail and liquid air in crisp weather, till, on the 27th August, we lay moored to a floe off the desolate island of Taimur.

The first thing which we saw here was a bear on the shore, watching for young whitefish: and promptly Clark, Mew, and Lamburn (engineer) went on shore in the launch, I and Maitland following in the pram, each party with three dogs.

It was while climbing away inland that Maitland said to me:

"When Clark leaves the ship for the dash to the Pole, it is three, not two, of us, after all, that he is going to take with him, making a party of four."

I: "Is that so? Who knows?"

Maitland: "Wilson does. Clark has let it out in conversation with Wilson."

I: "Well, the more the merrier. Who will be the three?"

Maitland: "Wilson is sure to be in it, and there may be Mew, making the third. As to the fourth, I suppose *I* shall get left out in the cold."

I: "More likely I."

Maitland: "Well, the race is between us four: Wilson, Mew, you and I. It is a question of physical fitness combined with special knowledge. You are too lucky a dog to get left out, Jeffson."

I: "Well, what does it matter, so long as the expedition as a whole is a success? That is the main thing."

Maitland: "Oh, yes, that's all very fine talk, Jeffson! But is it quite sincere? Isn't it rather a pose to affect to despise $175,000,000? I want to be in at the death, and mean to be, if I can. We are all more or less self-interested."

"*Look,*" I whispered—"a bear."

It was a mother and cub: and with a determined trudge she came wagging her low head, having no doubt smelled the dogs. We separated on the instant, doubling different ways behind ice-boulders, wanting her to go on nearer the shore, before killing; but, passing close, she spied, and bore down at a trot upon me. I fired into her neck, and at once, with a roar, she turned tail, making now straight in Maitland's direction. I saw him run out from cover some hundred yards away, aiming his long-gun: but no report followed: and in half a minute he was under her fore-paws, she striking out slaps at the barking, shrinking dogs. Maitland roared for my help: and at that moment, I, poor wretch, in far worse plight than he, stood shivering in an ague: for suddenly one of those wrangles of the voices of my destiny was filling my bosom with loud commotion, one urging me fly to Maitland's aid, one passionately commanding me be still. But it lasted, I believe, some seconds only: I ran and got a shot into the bear's brain, and Maitland leapt up with a rent down his face.

But singular destiny! Whatever I did—if I did evil, if I did good—the result was the same: tragedy dark and sinister! Poor Maitland was doomed that voyage, and my rescue of him was the means employed to make his death the more certain.

I think that I have already written, some pages back, about a man called Scotland, whom I met at Cambridge. He was always talking about certain "Black" and "White" beings, and their contention for the earth. We others used to call him the black-and-white mystery-man, because, one day—but that is no matter now. Well, with regard to all that, I have a fancy, a whim of the mind—quite wide of the truth, no doubt—but I have it here in my brain, and I will write it down now. It is this: that there may have been some sort of arrangement, or understanding, between Black and White, as in the case of Adam and the fruit, that, should mankind force his way to the Pole and the old forbidden secret biding there, then some mishap should not fail to overtake the race of man; that the White, being kindly disposed to mankind, did not wish this to occur, and intended, for the sake of the race, to destroy our entire expedition before it reached; and that the Black, knowing that the White designed to do this, and by what means, used me—*me!*—to outwit this design, first of all working that I should be one of the party of four to leave the ship on ski.

But the childish attempt, my God, to read the immense riddle of the world! I could laugh at myself, and at poor Black-and-White Scotland, too. The thing can't be so simple.

Well, we left Taimur the same day, and good-bye now to both land and open sea. Till we passed the latitude of Cape Chelyuskin (which we did not sight), it was one succession of ice-belts, with Mew in the crow's-nest tormenting the electric bell to the engine-room, the anchor hanging ready to drop, and Clark taking soundings. Progress was slow, and the Polar night gathered round us apace, as we stole still onward and onward into that blue and glimmering land of eternal frore. We now left off bed-coverings of reindeer-skin and took to sleeping-bags. Eight of the dogs had died by the 25th September, when we were experiencing 19° of frost. In the darkest part of our night, the Northern Light spread its silent solemn banner over us, quivering round the heavens in a million fickle gauds.

The relations between the members of our little crew were excellent—with one exception: David Wilson and I were not good friends.

There was a something—a tone—in the evidence which he had given at the inquest on Peters, which made me mad every time I thought of it. He had heard Peters admit just before death that he, Peters, had administered atropine to himself: and he had had to give evidence of that fact. But he had given it in a most half-hearted way, so much so, that the coroner had asked him: "What, sir, are you hiding from me?" Wilson had replied: "Nothing. I have nothing to tell."

And from that day he and I had hardly exchanged ten words, in spite of our constant companionship in the vessel; and one day, standing alone on a floe, I found myself hissing with clenched fist: "If he dared suspect Clodagh of poisoning Peters, I could *kill* him!"

Up to 78° of latitude the weather had been superb, but on the night of the 7th October—well I remember it—we experienced a great storm. Our tub of a ship rolled like a swing, drenching the whimpering dogs at every lurch, and hurling everything on board into confusion. The petroleum-launch was washed from the davits; down at one time to 40° below zero sank the thermometer; while a high aurora was whiffed into a dishevelled chaos of hues, resembling the smeared palette of some turbulent painter of the skies, or mixed battle of long-robed seraphim, and looking the very symbol of tribulation, tempest, wreck, and distraction. I, for the first time, was sick.

It was with a dizzy brain, therefore, that I went off watch to my bunk. Soon, indeed, I fell asleep: but the rolls and shocks of the ship, combined with the heavy Greenland anorak which I had on, and the state of my body, together produced a frightful nightmare, in which I was conscious of a vain struggle to move, a vain fight for breath, for the sleeping-bag turned to an iceberg on my bosom. Of Clodagh was my grasping dream. I dreamed that she let fall, drop by drop, a liquid, coloured like pomegranate-seeds, into a glass of water; and she presented the glass to Peters. The draught, I knew, was poisonous as death: and in a last effort to break the bands of that dark slumber, I was conscious, as I jerked myself upright, of screaming aloud:

"Clodagh! Clodagh! *Spare the man . . .!*"

My eyes, starting with horror, opened to waking; the electric light was shining in the cabin; and there stood David Wilson looking at me.

Wilson was a big man, with a massively-built, long face, made longer by a beard, and he had little nervous contractions of the flesh at the cheek-bones, and plenty of big freckles. His clinging pose, his smile of disgust, his whole air, as he stood crouching and lurching there, I can shut my eyes, and see now.

What he was doing in my cabin I did not know. To think, my good God, that he should have been led there just then! This was one of the four-men starboard berths: *his* was a-port: yet there he was! But he explained at once.

"Sorry to interrupt your innocent dreams," says he: "the mercury in Maitland's thermometer is frozen, and he asked me to hand him his spirits-of-wine one from his bunk . . ."

I did not answer. A hatred was in my heart against this man.

The next day the storm died away, and either three or four days later the slush-ice between the floes froze definitely. The *Boreal's* way was thus blocked. We warped her with ice-anchors and the capstan into the position in which she should lay up for her winter's drift. This was in about 79° 20′ N. The sun had now totally vanished from our bleak sky, not to reappear till the following year.

Well, there was sledging with the dogs, and bear-hunting among the hummocks, as the months, one by one, went by. One day Wilson, by far our best shot, got a walrus-bull; Clark followed the traditional pursuit of a Chief, examining crustacea; Maitland and I were in a relation of close friendship, and I assisted his meteorological observations in a snow-hut built near the ship. Often, through the twenty-four hours, a clear blue moon, very spectral, very fair, imbued all our dim and livid clime.

It was five days before Christmas that Clark made the great announcement: he had determined, he said, if our splendid northward drift continued, to leave the ship about the middle of March for the dash to the Pole. He would take with him the four reindeer, all the dogs, four sledges, four kayaks, and three companions. The companions whom he had decided to invite were: Wilson, Mew, and Maitland.

He said it at dinner; and as he said it, David Wilson glanced at my wan face with a smile of pleased malice: for *I* was left out.

I remember well: the aurora that night was in the sky, and at its edge floated a moon surrounded by a ring, with two mock-moons. But all shone very vaguely and far, and a fog, which had already lasted some days, made the ship's bows indistinct to me, as I paced the bridge on my watch, two hours after Clark's announcement.

For a long time all was very still, save for the occasional whine of a dog. I was alone, and it grew toward the end of my watch, when Maitland would succeed me. My slow tread tolled like a passing-bell, and the mountainous ice lay vague and white around me, its sheeted ghastliness not less dreadfully silent than eternity itself.

Presently several of the dogs began barking together, left off, and began again. I said to myself: "There is a bear about somewhere."

And after some minutes I saw—I thought that I saw—it. The fog had, if anything, thickened; and it was now very near the end of my watch.

It had entered the ship, I concluded, by the boards which slanted from an opening in the port bulwarks down to the ice. Once before, in November, a bear, having smelled the dogs, had ventured on board at midnight: but *then* there had resulted a perfect hubbub among the dogs. *Now*, even in the midst of my excitement, I wondered at their quietness, though some whimpered—with fear, I thought. I saw the creature steal forward from the hatchway toward the kennels a-port; and I ran noiselessly, and seized the watch-gun which stood always loaded by the companionway.

By this time, the form had passed the kennels, reached the bows, and now was making toward me on the starboard side. I took aim. Never, I thought, had I seen so huge a bear—though I made allowance for the magnifying effect of the fog.

My finger was on the trigger: and at that moment a deathly shivering sickness took me, the wrangling voices shouted at me, with "Shoot!" "Shoot not!" "Shoot!" Ah, well, that latter shout was irresistible. I drew the trigger. The report hooted through the Polar night.

The creature dropped; both Wilson and Clark were up at once: and we three hurried to the spot.

But the very first glance showed a singular kind of bear. Wilson put his hand to the head, and a lax skin came away at his touch. . . . It was Aubrey Maitland who was underneath it, and I had shot him dead.

For the past few days he had been cleaning skins, among them the skin of the bear from which I had saved him at Taimur. Now, Maitland was a born pantomimist, continually inventing practical jokes; and perhaps to startle me with a false alarm in the very skin of the old Bruin which had so nearly done for him, he had thrown it round him on finishing its cleaning, and so, in mere wanton fun, had crept on deck at the hour of his watch. The head of the bear-skin, and the fog, must have prevented him from seeing me taking aim.

This tragedy made me ill for weeks. I saw that the hand of Fate was upon me. When I rose from bed, poor Maitland was lying in the ice behind the great camel-shaped hummock near us.

By the end of January we had drifted to 80° 55´; and it was then that Clark, in the presence of Wilson, asked me if I would make the fourth man, in the place of poor Maitland, for the dash in the spring. As I said "Yes, I am will-ing," David Wilson spat with a disgusted emphasis. A minute later he sighed, with "Ah, poor Maitland . . ." and drew in his breath, with *tut! tut!*

God knows, I had an impulse to spring then and there at his throat, and strangle him: but I curbed myself.

There remained now hardly a month before the dash, and all hands set to work with a will, measuring the dogs, making harness and seal-skin shoes for them, overhauling sledges and kayaks, and cutting every possible ounce of weight. But we were not destined, after all, to set out that year. About the 20th February, the ice began to pack, and the ship was subjected to an appalling pressure. We found it necessary to make trumpets of our hands to shout into one another's ears, for the whole ice-continent was crashing, popping, thundering everywhere in terrific upheaval. Expecting every moment to see the *Boreal* crushed to splinters, we had to set about unpacking provisions, and placing sledges, kayaks, dogs and everything in a position for instant flight. It lasted five days, and was accompanied by a tempest from the north, which, by the end of February, had driven us back south into latitude 79° 40´. Clark, of course, then abandoned the thought of the Pole for that summer.

And immediately afterwards we made a startling discovery: our stock of reindeer-moss was found to be somehow ridiculously small. Egan, our second mate, was blamed; but that did not help matters: the sad fact remained. Clark was advised to kill one or two of the deer, but he pig-headedly refused: and by the beginning of summer they were all dead.

Well, our northward drift recommenced. Toward the middle of February we saw a mirage of the coming sun above the horizon; there were flights of Arctic petrels and snow-buntings; and spring was with us. In an ice-pack of big hummocks and narrow lanes we made good progress all the summer.

When the last of the deer died, my heart sank; and when the dogs killed two of their number, and a bear crushed a third, I was fully expecting what came; it was this: Clark announced that he could now take only two companions with him in the spring: and they were Wilson and Mew. So once more I saw David Wilson's pleased smile of malice.

We settled into our second winter-quarters. Again came December, and all our drear sunless gloom, made worse by the fact that the windmill would not work, leaving us without the electric light.

Ah me, none but those who have felt it could dream of one half the mental depression of that long Arctic night; how the soul takes on the hue of the world; and without and within is nothing but gloom, gloom, and the reign of the Power of Darkness.

Not one of us but was in a melancholic, dismal and dire mood; and on the 13th December Lamburn, the engineer, stabbed Cartwright, the old harpooner, in the arm.

Three days before Christmas a bear came close to the ship, then turned tail. Mew, Wilson, I and Meredith (a general hand) set out in pursuit. After a pretty long chase we lost him, and then scattered different ways. It was very dim, and after yet an hour's search, I was returning weary and disgusted to the ship, when I saw some shadow like a bear sailing away on my left, and at the same time sighted a man—I did not know whom—running like a handicapped ghost some little distance to the right. So I shouted out:

"There he is—come on! This way!"

The man quickly joined me, but, as soon as ever he recognised me, stopped dead. The devil must have suddenly got into him, for he said:

"No, thanks, Jeffson: alone with you I am in danger of my life. . . ."

It was Wilson. And I, too, forgetting at once all about the bear, stopped and faced him.

"I see," said I. "But, Wilson, you are going to explain to me *now* what you mean, you hear? What *do* you mean, Wilson?"

"What I say," he answered deliberately, eyeing me up and down: "alone with you I am in danger of my life. Just as poor Maitland was, and just as poor Peters was. Certainly, you are a deadly beast."

Fury leapt, my God, in my heart. Black as the tenebrous Arctic night was my soul.

"Do you mean," said I, "that I want to put you out of the way in order to go in your place to the Pole? Is that your meaning, man?"

"That's about my meaning, Jeffson," says he: "you are a deadly beast, you know."

"Stop!" I said, with a blazing eye. "I am going to kill *you*, Wilson—as sure as God lives: but I want to hear first. Who *told* you that I killed Peters?"

"Your lover killed him—with *your* collusion. Why, I heard you, man, in your beastly sleep, calling the whole thing out. And I was pretty sure of it before, only I had no proofs. By God, I should enjoy putting a bullet into you, Jeffson!"

"You wrong me, you—you, you wrong me!" I shrieked, my eyes staring with ravenous lust for his blood; "and now I am going to pay you well for it. *Look out, you!*"

I aimed my gun for his heart, and I touched the trigger. He held up his left hand.

"Stop," he said, "stop." (He was one of the coolest of men ordinarily.) "There is no gallows on the *Boreal*, but Clark could easily rig one for you. I want to kill you, too, because there are no criminal courts up here, and it would be doing a good action for my country. But not here—not now. Listen to me—don't shoot. Later we can meet, when all is ready, so that no one may be the wiser, and fight it all out."

As he spoke I let the gun drop. It was better so. I knew that he was much the best shot on the ship, and I an indifferent one: but I did not care, I did not care, if I was killed.

It is a dim, inclement land, God knows: and the spirit of darkness and distraction is there.

Twenty hours later we met behind the great saddle-shaped hummock, some six miles to the S.E. of the ship. We had set out at different times, so that no one might suspect. And each brought a ship's-lantern.

Wilson had dug an ice-grave near the hummock, leaving at its edge a heap of brash-ice and snow to fill it. We stood separated by an interval of perhaps seventy yards, the grave between us, each with a lantern at his feet.

Even so we were mere shadowy apparitions one to the other. The air glow-ered very drearily, and present in my inmost soul were the frills of cold. A chill moon, a mere abstraction of light, seemed to hang far outside the universe. The temperature was at 55° below zero, so that we had on wind-clothes over our anoraks, and heavy foot-bandages under our Lap boots. Nothing but a weird morgue seemed the world, haunted with despondent madness; and ex-actly like that world about us were the minds of us two poor men, full of maca-bre, bleak, and funereal feelings.

Between us yawned an early grave for one or other of our bodies.

I heard Wilson cry out:

"Are you ready, Jeffson?"

"Aye, Wilson!" I cried.

"Then here goes!" cries he.

Even as he spoke, he fired. Surely, the man was in deadly earnest to kill me.

But his shot passed harmlessly by me: as indeed was only likely: we were mere shadows to the other.

I fired perhaps ten seconds later than he: but in those ten seconds he stood perfectly revealed to me in clear, lavender light.

An Arctic fire-ball had traversed the sky, showering abroad a sulphurous glamour over the snow-landscape. Before the intenser blue of its momentary shine had passed away, I saw Wilson stagger forward, and drop. And him and his lantern I buried deep there under the rubble ice.

*   *   *   *   *

On the 13th March, nearly three months later, Clark, Mew and I left the *Boreal* in latitude 85° 15´.

We had with us thirty-two dogs, three sledges, three kayaks, human provi-sions for 112 days, and dog provisions for 40. Being now about 340 miles from the Pole, we hoped to reach it in 43 days, then, turning south, and feeding liv-ing dogs with dead, make either Franz Josef Land or Spitzbergen, at which lat-ter place we should very likely come up with a whaler.

Well, during the first days, progress was very slow, the ice being rough and laney, and the dogs behaving most badly, stopping dead at every difficulty, and leaping over the traces. Clark had had the excellent idea of attaching a gold-beater's-skin balloon, with a lifting power of 35 pounds, to each sledge, and we had with us a supply of zinc and sulphuric-acid to repair the hydrogen-waste from the bags; but on the third day Mew over-filled and burst his balloon, and I and Clark had to cut ours loose to equalise weights, for we could neither leave him behind, turn back to the ship, nor mend the bag. So it happened that at the end of the fourth day out, we had made only nineteen miles, and could still from a hummock discern afar the leaning masts of the old *Boreal*. Clark led on ski, captaining a sledge with 400 lbs. of instruments, ammunition, pemmican, aleuronate bread; Mew followed, his sledge containing provisions only; and last came I, with a mixed freight. But on the third day Clark had an attack of snow-blindness, and Mew took his place.

*   *   *   *   *

Pretty soon our sufferings commenced, and they were bitter enough. The sun, though constantly visible day and night, gave no heat. Our sleeping-bags (Clark and Mew slept together in one, I in another) were soaking wet all the night, being thawed by our warmth; and our fingers, under wrappings of senne-grass and wolf-skin, were always bleeding. Sometimes our frail bamboo-cane kay-aks, lying across the sledges, would crash perilously against an ice-ridge—and they were our one hope of reaching land. But the dogs were the great difficulty: we lost six mortal hours a day in harnessing and tending them. On the twelfth day Clark took a single-altitude observation, and found that we were only in lati-tude 86° 45´; but the next day we passed beyond the farthest point yet reached by man, viz. 86° 53´, attained by the *Nix* explorers four years previously.

*   *   *   *   *

Our one secret thought now was food, food—our day-long lust for the eat-ing-time. Mew suffered from "Arctic thirst."

*   *   *   *   *

Under these conditions, man becomes in a few days, not a savage only, but a mere beast, hardly a grade above the bear and walrus. Ah, the ice! A long and sordid nightmare was that, God knows.

*   *   *   *   *

On we pressed, crawling our little way across the Vast, upon whose hoar silence, from Eternity until then, Boötes only, and that Great Bear, had watched.

*   *   *   *   *

After the eleventh day our rate of march improved: all lanes disappeared, and ridges became much less frequent. By the fifteenth day I was leaving behind me the ice-grave of David Wilson at the rate of ten to thirteen miles a day.

Yet, as it were, his arm reached out and touched me, even there.

His disappearance had been explained by a hundred different guesses on the ship—all plausible enough. I had no idea that anyone connected me in any way with his death.

But on our twenty-second day of march, 140 miles from our goal, he caused a conflagration of rage and hate to break out among us three.

It was at the end of a march, when our stomachs were hollow, our frames ready to drop, and our mood ravenous and inflamed. One of Mew's dogs was sick: it was necessary to kill it: he asked me to do it.

"Oh," I said, "you kill your own dog, of course."

"Well, I don't know," he replied, catching fire at once, "you ought to be used to killing, Jeffson."

"How do you mean, Mew?" said I with a mad start, for madness and the flames of Hell were instant and uppermost in us all: "you mean because my profession—"

"Profession! damn it, no," he snarled like a dog: "go and dig up David Wilson—I dare say you know where to find him—and *he* will tell you my meaning, right enough."

I rushed at once to Clark, who was stooping among the dogs, unharnessing: and savagely pushing his shoulder, I exclaimed:

"That beast accuses me of murdering David Wilson!"

"Well?" said Clark.

"I'd split his skull as clean—!"

"Go away, Adam Jeffson, and let me be!" snarled Clark.

"Is that all you've got to say about it, then—you?"

"To the devil with you, man, say I, and let me be!" cried he: "*you know your own conscience best*, I suppose."

Before this insult I stood with grinding teeth, but impotent. However, from that moment a deeper mood of brooding malice occupied my spirit. Indeed the humour of us all was one of dangerous, even murderous, fierceness. In that pursuit of riches into that region of cold, we had become almost like the beasts that perish.

*   *   *   *   *

On the 10th April we passed the 89th parallel of latitude, and though sick to death, both in spirit and body, pressed still on. Like the lower animals, we were stricken now with dumbness, and hardly once a day spoke a word one to the other, but in selfish brutishness on through a real hell of cold we moved. It is a cursed region—beyond doubt cursed—not meant to be penetrated by man: and rapid and awful was the degeneration of our souls. As for me, never could I have conceived that savagery so heinous could brood in a human bosom as now I felt it brood in mine. If men could enter into a country specially set apart for the habitation of devils, and there become possessed of evil, as we were so would they be.

*   *   *   *   *

As we advanced, the ice every day became smoother; so that, from four miles a day, our rate increased to fifteen, and finally (as the sledges lightened) to twenty.

It was now that we began to encounter a succession of strange-looking objects lying scattered over the ice, whose number continually increased as we proceeded. They had the appearance of rocks, or pieces of iron, incrusted with glass-fragments of various colours, and they were of every size. Their incrustations we soon determined to be diamonds, and other precious stones. On our first twenty-mile day Mew picked up a diamond-crystal as large as a child's foot, and such objects soon became common. We thus found the riches which we sought, beyond all dream; but as the bear and the walrus find them: for ourselves we had lost; and it was a loss of riches barren as ashes, for for all those millions we would not have given an ounce of fish-meal. Clark grumbled something about their being meteor-stones, whose ferruginous substance had been lured by the magnetic Pole, and kept from frictional burning in their fall by the frigidity of the air: and they quickly ceased to interest our sluggish minds, except in so far as they obstructed our way.

*   *   *   *   *

We had all along had good weather: till, suddenly, on the morning of the 13th April, we were overtaken by a tempest from the S.W., of such mighty and solemn volume that the heart quailed beneath it. It lasted in its full power only an hour, but during that time snatched two of our sledges long distances, and compelled us to lie face-downward. We had travelled all the sun-lit night, and were gasping with fatigue; so as soon as the wind allowed us to huddle together our scattered things, we crawled into the sleeping-bags, and instantly slept.

We knew that the ice was in awful upheaval around us; we heard, as our eyelids sweetly closed, the slow booming of distant guns, and brittle cracklings of artillery. This may have been a result of the tempest stirring up the ocean beneath the ice. Whatever it was, we did not care: we slept deep.

We were within ten miles of the Pole.

*   *   *   *   *

In my sleep it was as though someone suddenly shook my shoulder with an urgent "*Up! up!*" It was neither Clark nor Mew, but a dream merely: for Clark and Mew, when I started up, I saw lying still in their sleeping-bag.

I suppose it must have been about noon. I sat staring a minute, and my first numb thought was somehow this: that the Countess Clodagh had prayed me "Be first"—for her. Wondrous little now cared I for the Countess Clodagh in her far unreal world of warmth—precious little for the fortune which she coveted: millions on millions of fortunes swarmed unregarded around me. But that thought, *Be first!* was deeply suggested in my brain, as if whispered there. Instinctively, brutishly, as the Gadarean swine rushed down a steep place, I, rubbing my daft eyes, arose.

The first thing which my mind opened to perceive was that, while the tempest was less strong, the ice was now in extraordinary agitation. I looked abroad upon a vast plain, stretched out to a circular, but waving horizon, and varied by hillocks, boulders, and sparkling meteor-stones that everywhere tinselled the blinding white, some big as houses, most small as limbs. And this great plain was now rearranging itself in a widespread drama of havoc, withdrawing in ravines like mutual backing curtsies, then surging to clap together in passionate mountain-peaks, else jostling like the Symplegades, fluent and inconstant as billows of the sea, grinding itself, piling itself, pouring itself in cataracts of powdered ice, while here and there I saw the meteor-stones leap spasmodically, in dusts and heaps, like geysers or spurting froths in a steamer's wake, a tremendous uproar, meantime, filling all the air. As I stood, I plunged and staggered, and I found the dogs sprawling, with whimperings, on the heaving floor.

I did not care. Instinctively, daftly, brutishly, I harnessed ten of them to my sledge; put on Canadian snow-shoes: and was away northward—alone.

The sun shone with a clear, benign, but heatless shining: a ghostly, remote, yet quite limpid light, which seemed designed for the lighting of other planets and systems, and to strike here by happy chance. A great wind from the S.W., meanwhile, sent thin snow-sweepings flying northward past me.

The odometer which I had with me had not yet measured four miles, when I began to notice two things: first that the jewelled meteor-stones were now accumulating beyond all limit, filling my range of vision to the northern horizon with a dazzling glister: in mounds, and parterres, and scattered disconnection they lay, like largesse of autumn leaves, spread out over those Elysian fields and fairy uplands of wealth, trillions of billions, so that I had need to steer my twining way among them. Now, too, I noticed that, but for these stones, all roughness had disappeared, not a trace of the upheaval going on a little further south being here, for the ice lay positively as smooth as a table before me. It is my belief that this stretch of smooth ice has never, never felt one shock, or stir, or throe, and reaches right down to the bottom of the deep.

*   *   *   *   *

And now with a wild hilarity I flew. Gradually, a dizziness, a lunacy, had seized upon me, till finally, up-buoyed on air, and dancing mad, I sped, I spun, with grinning teeth that chattered and gibbered, and eyeballs of distraction: for a Fear, too—most cold and dreadful—had its hand of ice upon my heart, I being so alone in that place, face to face with the Ineffable: but still, with a giddy levity, and a fatal joy, and a blind hilarity, on I sped, I spun.

*   *   *   *   *

The odometer measured nine miles from my start. I was in the immediate neighbourhood of the Pole.

I cannot say when it began, but now I was conscious of a sound in my ears, distinct and near, a steady sound of splashing, or fluttering, resembling the noising of a cascade or brook: and it grew. Forty more steps I took (slide I could not now for the meteorites)—perhaps sixty—perhaps eighty: and now, to my sudden horror, I stood by a circular clean-cut lake.

One minute only, swaying and nodding there, I stood: and then I dropped down flat in swoon.

*   *   *   *   *

In a hundred years, I suppose, I should never succeed in analysing *why* I swooned: but my consciousness still retains the impression of that horrid thrill. I saw nothing distinctly, for my whole being reeled and toppled drunken, like a spinning-top in desperate death-struggle at the moment when it flags, and wobbles dissolutely to fall; but the very instant that my eyes met what lay before me, I knew, I knew, that here was the Sanctity of Sanctities, the old eternal inner secret of the Life of this Earth, which it was a most burning shame for a man to see. The lake, I fancy, must be a mile across, and in its middle is a pillar of ice, very low and broad; and I had the clear impression, or dream, or notion, that there was a name, or word, graven all round in the ice of the pillar in characters which I could never read; and under the name a long date; and the fluid of the lake seemed to me to be wheeling with a shivering ecstasy, splashing and fluttering, round the pillar, always from west to east, in the direction of the spinning of the earth; and it was borne in upon me—I can't at all say how—that this fluid was the substance of a living creature; and I had the distinct fancy, as my senses failed, that it was a creature with many dull and anguished eyes, and that, as it wheeled for ever round in fluttering lust, it kept its eyes always turned upon the name and the date graven in the pillar. But this must be my madness. . . .

                    *   *   *   *   *

It must have been not less than an hour before a sense of life returned to me; and when the thought stabbed my brain that a long, long time I had lain there in the presence of those gloomy orbs, my spirit seemed to groan and die within me.

In some minutes, however, I had scrambled to my feet, clutched at a dog's harness, and without one backward glance, was flying from that place.

Half-way to the halting-place, I waited Clark and Mew, being very sick and doddering, and unable to advance. But they did not come.

Later on, when I gathered force to go further, I found that they had perished in the upheaval of the ice. One only of the sledges, half buried, I saw near the spot of our bivouac.

                    *   *   *   *   *

Alone that same day I began my way southward, and for five days made good progress. On the eighth day I noticed, stretched right across the southeastern horizon, a region of purple vapour which luridly obscured the face of the sun: and day after day I saw it steadily brooding there. But what it could be I did not understand.

                    *   *   *   *   *

Well, onward through the desert I continued my lonely way, with a baleful shrinking terror in my heart; for very stupendous, alas! is the burden of that Arctic solitude upon one poor human soul.

Sometimes on a halt I have lain and listened long to the hollow silence, recoiling, crushed by it, hoping that at least one of the dogs might whine. I have even crept shivering from the thawed sleeping-bag to flog a dog, so that I might hear a sound.

I had started from the Pole with a well-filled sledge, and the sixteen dogs left alive from the ice-packing which buried my comrades. This was on the evening of the 13th April. I had saved from the wreck of our things most of the whey-powder, pemmican, &c., as well as the theodolite, compass, chronometer, train-oil lamp for cooking, and other implements: I was therefore in no doubt as to my course, and had provisions for ninety days. But ten days from the start my supply of dog-food failed, and I had to begin to slaughter my only companions, one by one.

Well, in the third week the ice became horribly rough, and with moil and toil enough to wear a bear to death, I did only five miles a day. After the day's work I would crawl with a dying sigh into the sleeping-bag, clad still in the load of skins which stuck to me a mere filth of grease, to sleep the sleep of a swine, indifferent if I never woke.

Always—day after day—on the south-eastern horizon, brooded sullenly that curious stretched-out region of purple vapour, like the smoke of the conflagration of the world. And I noticed that its length constantly reached out and out, and silently grew.

*   *   *   *   *

Once I had a very pleasant dream. I dreamed that I was in a garden—an Arabian paradise—so sweet was the perfume. All the time, however, I had a sub-consciousness of the gale which was actually blowing from the S.E. over the ice, and, at the moment when I awoke, was half-wittedly droning to myself: "It is a Garden of Peaches; but I am not really in the garden: I am really on the ice; only, the S.E. storm is wafting to me the aroma of this Garden of Peaches."

I opened my eyes—I started—I sprang to my feet! For, of all the miracles!—I could not doubt—an actual aroma like peach-blossom *was* in the algid air about me!

Before I could collect my astonished senses, I began to vomit pretty violently, and at the same time saw some of the dogs, skeletons as they were, vomiting, too. For a long time I lay very sick in a kind of daze, and, on rising, found two of the dogs dead, and all very queer. The wind had now changed to the north.

Well, on I staggered, fighting each inch of my deplorably weary way. This odour of peach-blossom, my sickness, and the death of the two dogs, remained a wonder to me.

Two days later, to my extreme mystification (and joy), I came across a bear and its cub lying dead at the foot of a hummock. I could not believe my eyes. There she lay on her right side, a spot of dirty-white in a disordered patch of snow, with one little eye open, and her fierce-looking mouth also; and the cub lay across her haunch, biting into her rough fur. I set to work upon her, and allowed the dogs a glorious feed on the blubber, while I myself had a great banquet on the fresh meat. I had to leave the greater part of the two carcasses, and I can feel again now the hankering reluctance—quite unnecessary, as it turned out—with which I trudged onwards. Again and again I found myself asking: "Now, what could have killed those two bears?"

With brutish stolidness I plodded ever on, almost like a walking machine, sometimes nodding in sleep, while I helped the dogs, or manœuvred the sledge over an ice-ridge, pushing or pulling. On the 3rd June, a month and a half from my start, I took an observation with the theodolite, and found that I was not yet 400 miles from the Pole, in latitude 84° 50´. It was as though some Will, some Will, was obstructing and retarding me.

However, the intolerable cold was over, and soon my clothes no longer hung stark on me like armour. Pools began to appear in the ice, and presently, what was worse, my God, long lanes, across which, somehow, I had to get the sledge. But about the same time all fear of starvation passed away: for on the 6th June I came across another dead bear, on the 7th three, and thenceforth, in rapidly growing numbers, I met not bears only, but fulmars, guillemots, snipes, Ross's gulls, little awks—all, all, lying dead on the ice. And never any-where a living thing, save me, and the two remaining dogs.

If ever a poor man stood shocked before a mystery, it was I now. I had a big fear on my heart.

On the 2nd July the ice began packing dangerously, and soon another storm broke loose upon me from the S.W. I left off my trek, and put up the silk tent on a five-acre square of ice surrounded by lanes: and *again*—for the sec-ond time—as I lay down, I smelled that delightful strange odour of peach-blossom, a mere whiff of it, and presently afterwards was taken sick. However, it passed off this time in a couple of hours.

Now it was all lanes, lanes, alas! yet no open water, and such was the diffi-culty and woe of my life, that sometimes I would drop flat on the ice, and sob: "Oh, no more, no more, my God: here let me die." The crossing of a lane might occupy ten or twelve entire hours, and then, on the other side I might find another one opening right before me. Moreover, on the 8th July, one of the dogs, after a feed on blubber, suddenly died; and there was left me only "Reinhardt," a white-haired Siberian dog, with little pert up-sticking ears, like a cat's. Him, too, I had to kill on coming to open water.

This did not happen till the 3rd August, nearly four months from the Pole.

I can't think, my God, that any heart of man ever tholed the appalling nightmare and black abysm of sensations in which, during those four long de-sert months, I weltered: for though I was as a brute, I had a man's heart to feel. What I had seen, or dreamed, at the Pole followed and followed me; and if I shut my poor weary eyes to sleep, those others yonder seemed to watch me still with their distraught and gloomy gaze, and in my spinning dark dreams spun that eternal ecstasy of the lake.

However, by the 28th July I knew from the look of the sky, and the ab-sence of fresh-water ice, that the sea could not be far; so I set to work, and spent two days in putting to rights the now battered kayak. This done, I had no sooner resumed my way than I sighted far off a streaky haze, which I knew to be the basalt cliffs of Franz Josef Land; and in a craziness of joy I stood there, waving my ski-staff about my head, with the senile cheers of a very old man.

In four days this land was visibly nearer, sheer basaltic cliffs mixed with glacier, forming apparently a great bay, with two small islands in the mid-distance; and at fore-day of the 3rd August I arrived at the definite edge of the pack-ice in moderate weather at about the freezing-point.

I at once, but with great reluctance, shot Reinhardt, and set to work to get the last of the provisions, and the most necessary of the implements, into the kayak, making haste to put out to the toilless luxury of being borne on water, after all the weary trudge. Within fourteen hours I was coasting, with my little lug-sail spread, along the shore-ice of that land. It was midnight of a calm Sabbath, and low on the horizon smoked the drowsing red sun-ball, as my canvas skiff lightly chopped her little way through this silent sea. Silent, silent: for neither snort of walrus, nor yelp of fox, nor cry of startled kittiwake, did I hear: but all was still as the jet-black shadow of the cliffs and glacier on the tranquil sea: and many bodies of dead things strewed the surface of the water.

*   *   *   *   *

When I found a little fjord, I went up it to the end where stood a stretch of basalt columns, looking like a shattered temple of Antediluvians; and when my foot at last touched land, I sat down there a long, long time in the rubbly snow, and silently wept. My eyes that night were like a fountain of tears. For the firm land is health and sanity, and dear to the life of man; but I say that the great ungenial ice is a nightmare, and a blasphemy, and a madness, and the realm of the Power of Darkness.

*   *   *   *   *

I knew that I was at Franz Josef Land, somewhere or other in the neighbourhood of C. Fligely (about 82° N.), and though it was so late, and getting cold, I still had the hope of reaching Spitzbergen that year, by alternately sailing all open water, and dragging the kayak over the slack drift-ice. All the ice which I saw was good flat fjord-ice, and the plan seemed feasible enough; so after coasting about a little, and then three days' good rest in the tent at the bottom of a ravine of columnar basalt opening upon the shore, I packed some bear and walrus flesh, with what artificial food was left, into the kayak, and set out early in the morning, coasting the shore-ice with sail and paddle. In the afternoon I managed to climb a little way up an iceberg, and made out that I was in a bay whose terminating headlands were invisible. I accordingly determined to make S.W. by W. to cross it, but, in doing so, I was hardly out of sight of land, when a northern storm overtook me toward midnight; before I could think, the little sail was all but whiffed away, and the kayak upset. I only saved it by the happy chance of being near a floe with an ice-foot, which, projecting under the water, gave me foot-hold; and I lay on the floe in a mooning state the whole night under the storm, for I was half drowned.

And at once, on recovering myself, I abandoned all thought of whalers and of Europe for that year. Happily, my instruments, &c., had been saved by the kayak-deck when she capsized.

*   *   *   *   *

A hundred yards inland from the shore-rim, in a circular place where there was some moss and soil, I built myself a semi-subterranean Eskimo den for the long Polar night. The spot was quite surrounded by high sloping walls of basalt, except to the west, where they opened in a three-foot cleft to the shore, and the ground was strewn with slabs and boulders of granite and basalt. I found there a dead she-bear, two well-grown cubs, and a fox, the latter having evidently fallen from the cliffs; in three places the snow was quite red, over-grown with a red lichen, which at first I took for blood. I did not even yet feel secure from possible bears, and took care to make my den fairly tight, a work which occupied me nearly four weeks, for I had no tools, save a hatchet, knife, and metal-shod ski-staff. I dug a passage in the ground two feet wide, two deep, and ten long, with perpendicular sides, and at its north end a circular space, twelve feet across, also with perpendicular sides, which I lined with stones; the whole excavation I covered with inch-thick walrus-hide, skinned during a whole bitter week from four of a number that lay about the shore-ice; for ridge-pole I used a thin pointed rock which I found near, though, even so, the roof remained nearly flat. This, when it was finished, I stocked well, putting in eve-rything, except the kayak, blubber to serve both for fuel and occasional light, and foods of several sorts, which I procured by merely stretching out the hand. The roof of both circular part and passage was soon buried under snow and ice, and hardly distinguishable from the general level of the white-clad ground. Through the passage, if I passed in or out, I crawled flat, on hands and knees: but that was rare: and in the little round interior, mostly sitting in a cowering attitude, I wintered, harkening to the large and windy ravings of darkling De-cember storms above me.

*   *   *   *   *

All those months the burden of a thought bowed me; and an unanswered question, like the slow turning of a mechanism, revolved in my gloomy spirit: for everywhere around me lay bears, walruses, foxes, thousands upon thou-sands of little awks, kittiwakes, snow-owls, eider-ducks, gulls—dead, dead. Almost the only living things which I saw were some walruses on the drift-floes: but very few compared with the number which I expected. It was clear to me that some inconceivable catastrophe had overtaken the island during the summer, destroying all life about it, except some few of the amphibia, cetacea, and crustacea.

On the 5th December, having crept out from the den during a southern storm, I had, for the third time, a distant whiff of that self-same odour of peach-blossom: but now without any after-effects.

*   *   *   *   *

Well, again came Christmas, the New Year—Spring: and on the 22nd May I set out with a well-stocked kayak. The water was fairly open, and the ice so good, that at one place I could sail the kayak over it, the wind sending me sliding at a fine pace. Being on the west coast of Franz Josef Land, I was in as favourable a situation as possible, and I turned my bow southward with much hope, keeping a good many days just in sight of land. Toward the evening of my third day out I noticed a large flat floe, presenting far-off a singular and lovely sight, for it seemed freighted with a profusion of pink and white roses, showing in its clear crystal the empurpled reflection. On getting near I saw it that it was covered with millions of Ross's gulls, all dead, whose pretty rosy bosoms had given it that appearance.

Up to the 29th June I made good progress southward and westward (the weather being mostly excellent), sometimes meeting dead bears, floating away on floes, sometimes dead or living walrus-herds, with troop after troop of dead kittiwakes, glaucus and ivory gulls, skuas, every kind of Arctic fowl. On that last day—the 29th June—I was about to encamp on a floe soon after midnight, when, happening to look toward the sun, my eye fell, far away south across the ocean of floes, upon something—*the masts of a ship*.

A phantom ship, or a real ship: it was all one; real, I must have instantly felt, it could not be: but at a sight so incredible my heart set to beating in my bosom as though I must surely die, and feebly waving the cane oar about my head, I staggered to my knees, and thence with wry mouth toppled flat.

So overpoweringly sweet was the thought of springing once more, like the beasts of Circe, from a walrus into a man. At this time I was tearing my bear's-meat just like a bear; I was washing my hands in walrus-blood to produce a glairy sort of pink cleanliness, in place of the black grease which chronically coated them.

Worn as I was, I made little delay to set out for that ship; and I had not travelled over water and ice four hours when, to my indescribable joy, I made out from the top of a steep floe that she was the *Boreal*. It seemed most strange that she should be anywhere hereabouts: I could only conclude that she must have forced and drifted her way thus far westward out of the ice-block in which our party had left her, and perhaps now was loitering here in the hope of picking us up on our way to Spitzbergen.

In any case, wild was the haste with which I fought my way to be at her, my gasping mouth all the time drawn back in a *rictus* of laughter at the antici-pation of their gladness to see me, their excitement to hear the grand tidings of the Pole attained. Anon I waved the paddle, although I knew that they could not yet see me, and then I dug deep at the whitish water. What astonished me was her main-sail and fore-mast square-sail—set that calm morning; and her screws were still, for she moved not at all. The sun was abroad like a cold spirit of light, touching the ocean-room of floes with dazzling spots, and a tint almost of rose was on the world, as it were of a just-dead bride in her spangles and white array. The *Boreal* was the one little distant jet-black spot in all this pu-rity: and upon her, as though she were Heaven, I paddled, I panted. But she was in a queerish state: by 9 A.M. I could see that. Two of the windmill arms were not there, and half lowered down her starboard beam a boat hung askew;

moreover, soon after 10 I could clearly see that her main-sail had a long rent down the middle.

I could not at all make her out. She was not anchored, though a sheet-anchor hung at the starboard cathead; she was not moored; and two small ice-floes, one on each side, were sluggishly bombarding her bows.

I began now to wave the paddle, battling for my breath, ecstatic, crazy with excitement, each second like a year to me. Very soon I could make out someone at the bows, leaning well over, looking my way. Something put it into my head that it was Sallitt, and I began an impassioned shouting. "Hi! Sallitt! Hallo! Hi!" I called.

I did not see him move: I was still a good way off: but there he stood, leaning steadily over, looking my way. Between me and the ship now was all navigable water among the floes, and the sight of him so visibly near put into me such a shivering eagerness, that I was nothing else but a madman for the time, sending the kayak flying with venomous digs in quick-repeated spurts, and mixing with the diggings my crazy wavings, and with both the daft shoutings of "Hallo! Hi! Bravo! *I have been to the Pole!*"

Well, vanity, vanity. Nearer still I drew: it was broad morning, going on toward noon: I was half a mile away, I was fifty yards. But on board the *Boreal*, though now they *must* have heard me, seen me, I observed no movement of welcome, but all, all was still as death that still Arctic morning, my God. Only, the ragged sail flapped a little, and—one on each side—two ice-floes sluggishly bombarded the bows, with hollow sounds.

I was certain now that Sallitt it was who looked across the ice: but when the ship swung a little round, I noticed that the direction of his gaze was carried with her movement, he no longer looking my way.

"Why, Sallitt!" I shouted reproachfully: "why, Sallitt, man . . .!" I whined.

But even as I shouted and whined, a perfect wild certainty was in my heart: for an aroma like peach, my God, had been suddenly wafted from the ship upon me, and I must have very well known then that that watchful outlook of Sallitt saw nothing, and on the *Boreal* were dead men all; indeed, very soon I saw one of his eyes looking like a glass eye which has slid askew, and glares distraught. And now again my wretched body failed, and my head dropped forward, where I sat, upon the kayak-deck.

*   *   *   *   *

Well, after a long time, I lifted myself to look again at that forlorn and wandering craft. There she lay, quiet, tragic, as it were culpable of the dark secret she bore; and Sallitt, who had been such good friends with me, would not cease his stare. I knew quite well why he was there: he had leant over to vomit, and had leant ever since, his forearms pressed on the bulwark-beam, his left knee against the boards, and his left shoulder propped on the cathead. When I came near, I saw that with every bump of the two floes against the bows, his face shook in response, and nodded a little; strange to say, he had no covering on his head, and I noted the play of the faint breezes in his uncut hair. After a time I would approach no more, for I was afraid; I did not dare, the silence of the ship seemed so sacred and awful; and till late afternoon I sat there, watching the black and massive hull. Above her water-line emerged all round a half-floating fringe of fresh-green sea-weed, proving old neglect; an abortive attempt had apparently been made to lower, or take in, the larch-wood pram, for there she hung by a jammed davit-rope, stern up, bow in the water; the only two arms of the windmill were moved this way and that, through some three degrees, with an *andante* creaking sing-song; some washed clothes, tied on the bow-sprit rigging to dry, were still there; the iron casing round the bluff bows was red and rough with rust; at several points the rigging was in considerable tangle; occasionally the boom moved a little with a tortured skirling cadence; and the sail, rotten, I presume, from exposure—for she had certainly encountered no bad weather—gave out anon a heavy languid flap at a rent down the middle. Besides Sallitt, looking out there where he had jammed himself, I saw no one.

By a paddle-stroke now, and another presently, I had closely approached her about four in the afternoon, though my awe of the ship was complicated by that perfume of hers, whose fearful effects I knew. My tentative approach, however, proved to me, when I remained unaffected, that, here and now, whatever danger there had been was past; and finally, by a hanging rope, with a thumping desperation of heart, I clambered up her beam.

*   *   *   *   *

They had died, it seemed, very suddenly, for nearly all the twelve were in poses of activity. Egan was in the very act of ascending the companion-way; Lamburn was sitting against the chart-room door, apparently cleaning two carbines; Odling at the bottom of the engine-room stair seemed to be drawing on a pair of reindeer komagar; and Cartwright, who was often in liquor, had his arms frozen tight round the neck of Martin, whom he seemed to be kissing, they two lying stark at the foot of the mizzen-mast.

Over all—over men, decks, rope-coils—in the cabin, in the engine-room—between skylight leaves—on every shelf, in every cranny—lay a purplish ash or dust, very impalpably fine. And steadily reigning throughout the ship, like the very spirit of death, was that aroma of peach-blossom.

*   *   *   *   *

Here it had reigned, as I could see from the log-dates, from the rust on the machinery, from the look of the bodies, from a hundred indications, during something over a year. It was, therefore, mainly by the random workings of winds and currents that this fragrant ship of death had been brought hither to me.

And this was the first direct intimation which I had that the Unseen Powers (whoever and whatever they may be), who through the history of the world had been so very, very careful to conceal their Hand from the eyes of men, hardly any longer intended to be at the pains to conceal their Hand from *me*. It was just as though the *Boreal* had been openly presented to me by a spiritual agency, which, though I could not see, I could readily apprehend.

* * * * *

The dust, though very thin and flighty above-decks, lay thickly deposited below, and after having made a tour of investigation throughout the ship, the first thing which I did was to examine that—though I had tasted nothing all day, and was exhausted to death. I found my own microscope where I had left it in the box in my berth to starboard, though I had to lift up Egan to get at it, and to step over Lamburn to enter the chart-room; but there, toward evening, I sat at the table and bent to see if I could make anything of the dust, while it seemed to me as if all the myriad spirits of men that have sojourned on the earth, and angel and devil, and all Time and all Eternity, hung silent round for my decision; and such an ague had me, that for a long time my wandering finger-tips, all ataxic with agitation, eluded every delicate effort which I made, and I could nothing do.

Of course, I know that an odour of peach-blossom in the air, resulting in death, could only be associated with some vaporous effluvium of cyanogen, or of hydrocyanic ("prussic") acid, or of both; so when I at last managed to examine some of the dust under the microscope, I was not therefore surprised to find, among the general mass of purplish ash, a number of bright-yellow particles, which could only be minute crystals of potassic ferrocyanide. What potassic ferrocyanide was doing on board the *Boreal* I did not know, and I had neither the means, nor the force of mind, alas! to dive then further into the mystery; I understood only that by some extraordinary means the air of the region just south of the Polar environ had been impregnated with a vapour which was either cyanogen, or some product of cyanogen; also, that this deadly vapour, which is very soluble, had by now either been dissolved by the sea, or else dispersed into space (probably the latter), leaving only its faint after-perfume; and seeing this, I let my abandoned head drop again on the table, and long hours I sat there staring mad, for I had a suspicion, my God, and a fear, in my breast.

* * * * *

The *Boreal*, I found, contained sufficient provisions, untouched by the dust, in cases, casks, &c., to last me, probably, fifty years. After two days, when I had partially scrubbed and boiled the filth of fifteen months from my skin, and solaced myself with better food, I overhauled her thoroughly, and spent three more days in oiling and cleaning the engine. Then, all being ready, I dragged my twelve dead and laid them together in two rows on the chart-room floor; and I hoisted for love the poor little kayak which had served me through so many tribulations. At nine in the morning of the 6th July, a week from my first sighting of the *Boreal*, I descended to the engine-room to set out.

The screws, like those of most quite modern ships, were driven by a simple contrivance of a constant stream of liquid air, contained in very powerful tanks, exploding through capillary tubes into non-expansion slide-valve chests, much as in the ordinary way with steam: a motor which gave her, in spite of her bluff hulk, a speed of sixteen knots. It is, therefore, the simplest thing for one man to take these ships round the world, since their movement, or stopping, depend upon nothing but the depressing or raising of a steel handle, provided that one does not get blown to the sky meantime, as liquid air, in spite of its thousand advantages, occasionally blows people. At any rate, I had tanks of air sufficient to last me through twelve years' voyaging; and there was the ordinary machine on board for making it, with forty tons of coal, in case of need, in the bunkers, and two excellent Belleville boilers: so I was well supplied with motors at least.

The ice here was quite slack, and I do not think I ever saw Arctic weather so bright and gay, the temperature at 41°. I found that I was midway between Franz Josef and Spitzbergen, in latitude 79° 23′ N. and longitude 39° E.; my way was perfectly clear; and something almost like a mournful hopefulness was in me as the engines slid into their clanking turmoil, and those long-silent screws began to churn the Arctic sea. I ran up with alacrity and took my stand at the wheel; and the bows of my eventful Argo turned southward and westward.

*   *   *   *   *

When I needed food or sleep, the ship slept, too: when I awoke, she continued her way.

Sixteen hours a day sometimes I stood sentinel at that wheel, overlooking the varied monotony of the ice-sea, till my knees would give, and I wondered why a wheel at which one might sit was not contrived, rather delicate steering being often required among the floes and bergs. By now, however, I was less weighted with my ball of Polar clothes, and stood almost slim in a Lap greatcoat, a round Siberian fur cap on my head.

At midnight when I threw myself into my old berth, it was just as though the engines, subsided now into silence, were a dead thing, and had a ghost which haunted me; for I heard them still, and yet not them, but the silence of their ghost.

Sometimes I would startle from sleep, horrified to the heart at some sound of exploding iceberg, or bumping floe, noising far through that white mystery of quietude, where the floes and bergs were as floating tombs, and the world a liquid cemetery. Never could I describe the strange Doom's-day shock with which such a sound would recall me from far depths of chaos to recollection of myself: for often-times, both waking and in nightmare, I did not know on which planet I was, nor in which Age, but felt myself adrift in the great gulf of time and space and circumstance, without bottom for my consciousness to stand upon; and the world was all mirage and a new show to me; and the boundaries of dream and waking lost.

Well, the weather was most fair all the time, and the sea like a pond. During the morning of the fifth day, the 11th July, I entered, and went moving down, an extraordinary long avenue of snow-bergs and floes, most regularly placed, half a mile perhaps across and miles long, like a Titanic double-procession of statues, or the Ming Tombs, but rising and sinking on the ca-

denced swell; many towering high, throwing placid shadows on the aisle between; some being of a lucid emerald tint; and three or four pouring down cascades that gave a far and chaunting sound. The sea between was of a singular
thick bluishness, almost like raw egg-white; while, as always here, some snow-
clouds, white and woolly, floated in the pale sky. Down this avenue, which produced a mysterious impression of Cyclopean cathedrals and odd sequestered-
ness, I had not passed a mile, when I sighted a black object at the end.

I rushed to the shrouds, and very soon made out a whaler.

Again the same panting agitations, mad rage to be at her, at once possessed me; I flew to the indicator, turned the lever to full, then back to give the
wheel a spin, then up the main-mast ratlins, waving a long foot-bandage of
vadmel tweed picked up at random, and by the time I was within five hundred
yards of her, had worked myself to such a pitch, that I was again shouting that
futile madness: "Hullo! Hi! Bravo! *I have been to the Pole!*"

And those twelve dead that I had in the chart-room must have heard me,
and the men on the whaler must have heard me, and smiled their smile.

For, as to that whaler, I should have known better at once, if I had not
been crazy, since she *looked* like a ship of death, her boom slamming to port
and starboard on the gentle heave of the sea, her fore-sail reefed that serene
morning. Only when I was quite near her, and hurrying down to stop the engines, did the real truth, with perfect suddenness, drench my heated brain; and
I almost ran into her, I was so stunned.

However, I stopped the *Boreal* in time, and later on lowered the kayak,
and boarded the other.

This ship had evidently been stricken silent in the midst of a perfect
drama of activity, for I saw not one of her crew of sixty-two who was not busy,
except one boy. I found her a good-sized thing of 500 odd tons, ship-rigged,
with an auxiliary engine of seventy horse-power, and pretty heavily armour-
plated round the bows. There was no part of her which I did not overhaul, and
I could see that they had had a great time with whales, for a great carcass, attached to the outside of the ship by the powerful cant-purchase tackle, had
been in process of flensing and cutting-in, and on the deck two great blankets
of blubber, looking each a ton-weight, surrounded by twenty-seven men in
many attitudes, some terrifying to see, some disgusting, several grotesque, all so
unhuman, the whale dead, and the men dead, too, and death was there, and
the rank-flourishing germs of Inanity, and a mesmerism, and a silence, whose
dominion was established, and its reign was growing old. Four of them, who
had been removing the gums from a mass of stratified whalebone at the mizzen-mast foot, were quite imbedded in whale-flesh; also, in a barrel lashed to
the main top of the main top-gallant masthead was visible the head of a man
with a long pointed beard, looking steadily out over the sea to the S.W., which
made me notice that five only of the probable eight or nine boats were on
board; and after visiting the 'tween-decks, where I saw considerable quantities
of stowed whalebone plates, and fifty or sixty iron oil-tanks, and cut-up blubber; and after visiting cabin, engine-room, fo'cas'le, where I saw a lonely boy of

fourteen with his hand grasping a bottle of rum under all the turned-up clothes in a chest, he, at the moment of death, being evidently intent upon hiding it; and after two hours' search of the ship, I got back to my own, and half an hour later came upon all the three missing whale-boats about a mile apart, and steered zig-zag near to each. They contained five men each and a steerer, and one had the harpoon-gun fired, with the loose line coiled round and round the head and upper part of the stroke line-manager; and in the others hundreds of fathoms of coiled rope, with toggle-irons, whale-lances, hand-harpoons, and dropped heads, and grins, and lazy *abandon*, and eyes that stared, and eyes that dozed, and eyes that winked.

*   *   *   *   *

After this I began to sight ships not infrequently, and used regularly to have the three lights burning all night. On the 12th July I met one, on the 15th two, on the 16th one, on the 17th three, on the 18th two—all Greenlanders, I think: but, of the nine, I boarded only three, the glass quite clearly showing me, when yet far off, that on the others was no life; and on the three which I boarded were dead men; so that that suspicion which I had, and that fear, grew very heavy upon me.

I went on southward, day after day southward, sentinel there at my wheel; clear sunshine by day, when the calm pale sea sometimes seemed mixed with regions of milk, and at night the immense desolation of a world lit by a sun that was long dead, and by a light that was gloom. It was like Night blanched in death then; and wan as the very kingdom of death and Hades I have seen it, most terrifying, that neuter state and limbo of nothingness, when unreal sea and spectral sky, all boundaries lost, mingled in a vast shadowy void of ghastly phantasmagoria, pale to utter huelessness, at whose centre I, as if annihilated, seemed to swoon in immensity of space. Into this disembodied world would come anon waftures of that peachy scent which I knew: and their frequency rapidly grew. But still the *Boreal* moved, traversing, as it were, bottomless Eternity: and I reached latitude 72°, not far now from Northern Europe.

And now, as to that blossomy peach-scent—even while some floes were yet around me—I was just like some fantastic mariner, who, having set out to search for Eden and the Blessed Islands, finds them, and balmy gales from their gardens come out, while he is yet afar, to meet him with their perfumes of almond and champac, cornel and jasmin and lotus. For I had now reached a zone where the peach-aroma was constant; all the world seemed embalmed in its spicy fragrance; and I could easily imagine myself voyaging beyond the world toward some clime of perpetual and enchanting Spring.

*   *   *   *   *

Well, I saw at last what whalers used to call "the blink of the ice"; that is to say, its bright apparition or reflection in the sky when it is left behind, or not yet come-to. By this time I was in a region where a good many craft of various sorts were to be seen; I was continually meeting them; and not one did I omit to in-

vestigate, while many I boarded in the kayak or the larch-wood pram. Just below latitude 70° I came upon a good large fleet of what I believed to be Lafoden
cod and herring fishers, which must have drifted somewhat on a northward current. They had had a great season, for the boats were well laden with curing
fish. I went from one to the other on a zig-zag course, they being widely scattered, some mere dots to the glass on the horizon. The evening was still and
clear with that astral Arctic clearness, the sun just beginning his low-couched
nightly drowse. These sturdy-looking brown boats stood rocking gently there
with slow-creaking noises, as of things whining in slumber, without the least
damage, awaiting the appalling storms of the winter months on that tenebrous
sea, when a dark doom, and a deep grave, would not fail them. The fishers were
braw carles, wearing, many of them, fringes of beard well back from the chin-
point, with hanging woollen caps. In every case I found below-decks a number
of cruses of corn-brandy, marked *aquavit*, two of which I took into the pram. In
one of the smacks an elderly fisher was kneeling in a forward sprawling pose,
clasping the lug-mast with his arms, the two knees wide apart, head thrown
back, and the yellow eye-balls with their islands of grey iris staring straight up
the mast-pole. At another of them, instead of boarding in the pram, I shut off
the *Boreal's* liquid air at such a point that, by delicate steering, she slackened
down to a stoppage just a-beam of the smack, upon whose deck I was thus able
to jump down. After looking around I descended the three steps aft into the
dark and garrety below-decks, and with stooping back went calling in an awful
whisper: "*Anyone? Anyone?*" Nothing answered me; and when I went up again,
the *Boreal* had drifted three yards beyond my reach. There being a dead calm, I
had to plunge into the water, and in that half-minute there a sudden cold
throng of unaccountable terrors beset me, and I can feel again now that abysmal
desolation of loneliness, and sense of a hostile and malign universe bent upon
eating me up: for the ocean seemed to me nothing but a great ghost.

Two mornings later I came upon another school, rather larger boats these,
which I found to be Brittany cod-fishers. Most of these, too, I boarded. In every
below-decks was a wooden or earthenware image of the Virgin, painted in
gaudy faded colours; in one case I found a boy who had been kneeling before
the statue, but was toppled sideways now, his knees still bent, and the cross of
Christ in his hand. These stalwart blue woollen blouses and tarpaulin sou'-
westers lay in every pose of death, every detail of feature and expression still
perfectly preserved. The sloops were all the same, all, all: with sing-song creaks
they rocked a little, nonchalantly; each, as it were, with a certain sub-
consciousness of its own personality, and callous unconsciousness of all the
others round it: yet each a copy of the others: the same hooks and lines, dis-
embowelling-knives, barrels of salt and pickle, piles and casks of opened cod,
kegs of biscuit, and low-creaking rockings, and a bilgy smell, and dead men.
The next day, about eighty miles south of the latitude of Mount Hekla, I
sighted a big ship, which turned out to be the French cruiser *Lazare Tréport*. I
boarded and overhauled her during three hours, her upper, main, and ar-
moured deck, deck by deck, to her lowest depths, even childishly spying up the

tubes of her two big, rusted turret-guns. Three men in the engine-room had been much mangled, after death, I presume, by a burst boiler; floating about 800 yards to the north-east a long-boat of hers, low in the water, crammed with marines, one oar still there, jammed between the row-lock and the rower's forced-back chin; on the ship's starboard deck, in the long stretch of space between the two masts, the blue-jackets had evidently been piped up, for they lay there in a sort of serried disorder, to the number of two hundred and seventy-five. Nothing could be of suggestion more tragic than the wasted and helpless power of this poor wandering vessel, around whose stolid mass myriads of wavelets, busy as aspen-leaves, bickered with a continual weltering splash that was quite loud to hear. I sat a good time that afternoon in one of her steely port main-deck casemates on a gun-carriage, my head sunken on my breast, furtively eyeing the bluish turned-up feet, all shrunk, exsanguined, of a sailor who lay on his back before me; his soles were all that I could see, the rest of him lying head-downwards beyond the steel door-sill.

Drenched in seas of lugubrious reverie I sat, till, with a shuddering start, I awoke, paddled back to the *Boreal,* and, till sleep conquered me, went on ·my way. At ten the next morning, coming on deck, I spied to the west a group of craft, and turned my course upon them. They turned out to be eight Shetland sixerns, which must have drifted north-eastward hither. I examined them well, but they were as the long list of the others: for all the men, and all the boys, and all the dogs on them were dead.

*　　*　　*　　*　　*

I could have come to land a long time before I did: but I would not: I was so afraid. For I was used to the silence of the ice: and I was used to the silence of the sea: but, God knows it, I was afraid of the silence of the land.

*　　*　　*　　*　　*

Once, on the 15th July, I had seen a whale, or thought I did, spouting very remotely afar on the S.E. horizon; and on the 19th I distinctly saw a shoal of porpoises vaulting the sea-surface, in their swift-successive manner, northward: and seeing them, I had said pitifully to myself: "Well, I am not quite alone in the world, then, my good God—not quite alone."

Moreover, some days later, the *Boreal* had found herself in a bank of cod making away northward, millions of fish, for I saw them, and one afternoon caught three, hand-running, with the hook.

So the sea, at least, had its tribes to be my mates.

But if I should find the land as still as the sea, without even the spouting whale, or school of tumbling sea-hogs—*if Paris were dumber than the eternal ice*—what then, I asked myself, should I do?

*　　*　　*　　*　　*

I could have made short work, and landed at Shetland, for I found myself as far westward as longitude 11° 23´ W.: but I would not: I was so afraid. The shrinking within me to face that vague suspicion which I had, turned me first to a foreign land.

I made for Norway, and on the first night of this definite intention, at about nine o'clock, the weather being gusty, the sky lowering, the air sombrous, and the sea hard-looking, dark, and ridged, I was steaming along at a good rate, holding the wheel, my poor port and starboard lights still burning there, when, without the least notice, I received the roughest physical shock of my life, being shot bodily right over the wheel, thence, as from a cannon, twenty feet to the cabin-door, through it head-foremost down the companion-way, and still beyond some six yards along the passage. I had crashed into some dark and dead ship, probably of large size, though I never saw her, nor any sign of her; and all that night, and the next day till four in the afternoon, the *Boreal* went driving alone over the sea whither she would: for I lay unconscious. When I woke, I found that I had received really very small injuries, considering: but I sat there on the floor a long time in a sulky, morose, disgusted, and bitter mood; and when I rose, pettishly stopped the ship's engines, seeing my twelve dead all huddled and disfigured. Now I was afraid to steam by night, and even in the day-time would not go on for three days: for I was childishly angry with I know not what, and inclined to quarrel with Those whom I could not see.

However, on the fourth day, a rough swell which knocked the ship about, and made me very uncomfortable, coaxed me into moving; and I did so with bows turned eastward and southward.

I sighted the Norway coast four days later, in latitude 63° 19′, at noon of the 11th August, and pricked off my course to follow it; but it was with a slow and dawdling reluctance that I went, at much less than half-speed. In some eight hours, as I knew from the chart, I ought to sight the lighthouse light on Smoelen Island; and when quiet night came, the black water being branded with trails of still moonlight, I passed quite close to it, between ten and twelve, almost under the shadow of the mighty hills: but, oh my God, no light was there. And all the way down I marked the rugged sea-board slumber darkling, afar or near, with never, alas! one friendly light.

*   *   *   *   *

Well, on the 15th August I had another of those maniac raptures, whose passing away would have left an elephant racked and prostrate. During four days I had seen not one sign of present life on the Norway coast, only hills, hills, dead and dark, and floating craft, all dead and dark; and my eyes now, I found, had acquired a crazy fixity of stare into the very bottom of the vacant abyss of nothingness, while I remained unconscious of being, save of one point, rainbow-blue, far down in the infinite, which passed slowly from left to right before my consciousness a little way, then vanished, came back, and passed slowly again, from left to right continually; till some prick, or voice, in my brain would startle me into the consciousness that I was staring, whispering the profound confidential warning: *"You must not stare so, or it is over with you!"* Well,

lost in a blank trance of this sort, I was leaning over the wheel during the afternoon of the 15th, when it was as if some instinct or premonition in my soul
leapt up, and said aloud: "If you look yonder, *you will see . . .!*" I started, and in
one instant had surged up from all that depth of reverie to reality: I glanced to
the right: and there, at last, my God, I saw something human which moved,
rapidly moved: at last!—and it came to me.

That sense of recovery, of waking, of new solidity, of the comfortable
usual, a million-fold too intense for words—how sweetly consoling it was!
Again now, as I write, I can fancy and feel it—the rocky solidity, the adamant
ordinary, on which to base the feet, and live. From the day when I stood at the
Pole, and saw there the dizzy thing that made me swoon, there had come into
my way not one sign or trace that other beings like myself were alive on the
earth with me: till now, suddenly, I had the sweet indubitable proof: for on the
south-western sea, not four knots away, I saw a large, swift ship: and her bows,
which were as sharp as a hatchet, were steadily chipping through the smooth
sea at a pretty high pace, throwing out profuse ribbony foams that went wide-
wavering, with outward undulations, far behind her length, as she ran the sea
in haste, straight northward.

At the moment, I was steering about S.E. by S., fifteen miles out from a
shadowy-blue series of Norway mountains; and just giving the wheel one frantic spin to starboard to bring me down upon her, I flew to the bridge, leant my
back on the main-mast, which passed through it, put a foot on the white iron
rail before me, and there at once felt all the mocking devils of distracted revelry possess me, as I caught the cap from my long hairs, and commenced to
wave and wave and wave, red-faced maniac that I was: for at the second nearer
glance, I saw that she was flying an ensign at the main, and a long pennant at
the main-top, and I did not know what she was flying those flags there for: and
I was embittered and driven mad.

With distinct minuteness did she print herself upon my consciousness in
that five minutes' interval: she was painted a dull and cholera yellow, like
many Russian ships, and there was a faded pink space at her bows under the
line where the yellow ceased: the ensign at her main I made out to be the blue-
and-white saltire, and she was clearly a Russian passenger-liner, two-masted,
two-funnelled, though from her funnels came no trace of smoke, and the position of her steam-cones was anywhere. All about her course the sea was spotted with wobbling splendours of the low sun, large coarse blots of glory near
the eye, but lessening to a smaller pattern in the distance, and at the horizon
refined to a homogeneous band of livid silver.

The double speed of the *Boreal* and the other, hastening opposite ways,
must have been thirty-eight or forty knots, and the meeting was accomplished
in certainly less than five minutes: yet into that time I crowded years of life. I
was shouting passionately at her, my eyes starting from my head, my face all inflamed with rage the most prone, loud and urgent. For she did not stop, nor signal, nor make any sign of seeing me, but came furrowing down upon me like
Juggernaut, with steadfast run. I lost reason, thought, memory, purpose, sense of

relation, in that access of delirium which transported me, and can only remember now that in the midst of my shouting, a word, uttered by the fiends who used my throat to express their frenzy, set me laughing high and madly: for I was crying: "Hi! Bravo! Why don't you stop? *Madmen! I have been to the Pole!*"

That moment an odour arose, and came, and struck upon my brain, most detestable, most execrable; and while one might count ten, I was aware of her near-sounding engines, and that cursed charnel went tearing past me on her mænad way, not fifteen yards from my eyes and nostrils. She was a thing, my God, from which the vulture and the jackal, prowling for offal, would fly with shrieks of loathing. I had a glimpse of decks piled thick with her festered dead.

In big black letters on the round retreating yellow stern my eye-corner caught the word *Yaroslav*, as I bent over the rail to retch and cough and vomit at her. She was a horrid thing.

This ship had certainly been pretty far south in tropical or sub-tropical latitudes with her great crowd of dead: for all the bodies which I had seen till then, so far from smelling ill, seemed to give out a certain perfume of the peach. She was evidently one of those many ships of late years which have substituted liquid air for steam, yet retained their old steam-funnels, &c., in case of emergency: for air, I believe, was still looked at askance by several builders, on account of the terrible accidents which it sometimes caused. The *Boreal* herself is a similar instance of both motors. This vessel, the *Yaroslav*, must have been left with working engines when her crew were overtaken by death, and, her air-tanks being still unexhausted, must have been ranging the ocean with impunity ever since, during I knew not how many months, or, it might be, years.

Well, I coasted Norway for nearly a hundred and sixty miles without once going nearer land than two or three miles: for something held me back. But passing the fjord-mouth where I knew that Aadheim was, I suddenly turned the helm to port, almost before I knew that I was doing it, and made for land.

In half an hour I was moving up an opening in the land with mountains on either hand, streaky crags at their summit, umbrageous boscage below; and the whole softened, as it were, by veils woven of the rainbow.

This arm of water lies curved about like a thread which one drops, only the curves are much more pointed, so that every few minutes the scene was changed, though the vessel just crawled her way up, and I could see behind me nothing of what was passed, or only a land-locked gleam like a lake.

I never saw water so polished and glassy, like clarid polished marble, reflecting everything quite clean-cut in its lucid abysm, over which hardly the faintest zephyr breathed that still sun-down; it wimpled about the bluff *Boreal*, which seemed to move as if careful not to bruise it, in rich wrinkles and creases, like glycerine, or dewy-trickling lotus-oil; yet it was only the sea: and the spectacle yonder was only crags, and autumn-foliage and mountain-slope: yet all seemed caught-up and chaste, rapt in a trance of rose and purple, and made of the stuff of dreams and bubbles, of pollen-of-flowers, and rinds of the peach.

I saw it not only with delight, but with complete astonishment: having forgotten, as was too natural in all that long barrenness of ice and sea, that anything could be so ethereally fair: yet homely, too, human, familiar, and consoling. The air here was richly spiced with that peachy scent, and there was a Sabbath and a nepenthe and a charm in that place at that hour, as it were of those gardens of Hesperus, and fields of asphodel, reserved for the spirits of the just.

Alas! but I had the glass at my side, and for me nepenthe was mixed with a despair immense as the vault of heaven, my good God: for anon I would take it up to spy some perched hut of the peasant, or burg of the "bonder," on the peaks: and I saw no one there; and to the left, at the third bend of the fjord, where there is one of those watch-towers that these people used for watching in-coming fish, I spied, lying on a craggy slope just before the tower, a body which looked as if it must surely tumble head-long, but did not. And when I saw that, I felt definitely, for the first time, that shoreless despair which I alone of men have felt, high beyond the stars, and deep as hell; and I fell to staring again that blank stare of Nirvana and the lunacy of Nothingness, wherein Time merges in Eternity, and all being, like one drop of water, flies scattered to fill the bottomless void of space, and is lost.

The *Boreal's* bow walking over a little empty fishing-boat roused me, and a minute later, just before I came to a new promontory and bend, I saw two people. The shore there is some three feet above the water, and edged with boulders of rock, about which grows a fringe of shrubs and small trees: behind this fringe is a path, curving upward through a sombre wooded little gorge; and on the path, near the water, I saw a driver of one of those Norwegian sulkies called karjolers: he, on the high front seat, was dead, lying sideways and backward, with low head resting on the wheel; and on a trunk strapped to a frame on the axle behind was a boy, his head, too, resting sideways on the wheel, near the other's; and the little pony was dead, pitched forward on its head and fore-knees, tilting the shafts downward; and some distance from them on the water floated an empty skiff.

*   *   *   *   *

When I turned the next fore-land, I all at once began see a number of craft, which increased as I advanced, most of them small boats, with some schooners, sloops, and larger craft, the majority a-ground: and suddenly now I was conscious that, mingling with that delicious odour of spring-blossoms— profoundly modifying, yet not destroying it—was another odour, wafted to me on the wings of the very faint land-breeze: and "Man," I said, "is decomposing": for I knew it well: it was the odour of human corruption.

*   *   *   *   *

The fjord opened finally in a somewhat wider basin, shut-in by quite steep, high-towering mountains, which reflected themselves in the water to their last cloudy crag: and, at the end of this I saw ships, a quay, and a modest, homely old town.

Not a sound, not one: only the languidly-working engines of the *Boreal*. Here, it was clear, the Angel of Silence had passed, and his scythe mown.

I ran and stopped the engines, and, without anchoring, got down into an empty boat that lay at the ship's side when she stopped; and I paddled twenty yards toward the little quay. There was a brigantine with her courses set, three jibs, stay-sails, square-sails, main and fore-sails, and gaff-top-sail, looking hanging and listless in that calm place, and wedded to a still copy of herself, mast-downward, in the water; there were three lumber-schooners, a forty-ton steam-boat, a tiny barque, five Norway herring-fishers, and ten or twelve shallops: and the sailing-craft had all fore-and-aft sails set, and about each, as I passed among them, brooded an odour that was both sweet and abhorrent, an odour more suggestive of the very genius of mortality—the inner mind and meaning of Azrael—than aught that I could have conceived: for all, as I soon saw, were crowded with dead.

Well, I went up the old mossed steps, in that strange dazed state in which one notices frivolous things: I remember, for instance, feeling the lightness of my new clothes: for the weather was quite mild, and the day before I had changed to Summer things, having on now only a common undyed woollen shirt, the sleeves rolled up, and cord trousers, with a belt, and a cloth cap over my long hair, and an old pair of yellow shoes, without laces, and without socks. And I stood on the unhewn stones of the edge of the quay, and looked abroad over a largish piece of unpaved ground, which lay between the first house-row and the quay.

What I saw was not only most woeful, but wildly startling: woeful, because a great crowd of people had assembled, and lay dead, there; and wildly startling, because something in their *tout ensemble* told me in one minute why they were there in such number.

They were there in the hope, and with the thought, to fly westward by boat.

And the something which told me this was a certain *foreign* air about that field of the dead as the eye rested on it, something un-northern, southern, Oriental.

Two yards from my feet, as I stepped to the top, lay a group of three: one a Norway peasant-girl in skirt of olive-green, scarlet stomacher, embroidered bodice, Scotch bonnet trimmed with silver lace, and big silver shoe-buckles; the second was an old Norway man in knee-breeches, and eighteenth-century small-clothes, and red worsted cap; and the third was, I decided, an old Jew of the Polish Pale, in gaberdine and skull-cap, with ear-locks.

I went nearer to where they lay thick as reaped stubble between the quay and a little stone fountain in the middle of the space, and I saw among those northern dead two dark-skinned women in costly dress, either Spanish or Italian, and the yellower mortality of a Mongolian, probably a Magyar, and a big negro in zouave dress, and some twenty-five obvious French, and two Morocco fezes, and the green turban of a shereef, and the white of an Ulema.

And I asked myself this question: "How came these foreign stragglers here in this obscure northern town?"

And my wild heart answered: "There has been an impassioned stampede, northward and westward, of all the tribes of Man. And this that I, Adam Jeffson, here see is but the far-tossed spray of that monstrous, infuriate flood."

*   *   *   *   *

Well, I passed up a street before me, careful, careful where I trod. It was not utterly silent, nor was the quay-square, but haunted by a pretty dense cloud of mosquitoes, and dreamy twinges of music, like the drawing of the violin-bow in elf-land. The street was narrow, pavered, steep, and dark; and the sensations with which I, poor bent man, passed through that dead town, only Atlas, fabled to bear the burden of this Earth, could divine.

*   *   *   *   *

I thought to myself: If now a wave from the Deep has washed over this planetary ship of earth, and I, who alone happened to be in the extreme bows, am the sole survivor of that crew? . . . What then, my God, shall I do?

*   *   *   *   *

I felt, I felt, that in this townlet, save the water-gnats of Norway, was no living thing; that the hum and the savour of Eternity filled, and wrapped, and embalmed it.

The houses are mostly of wood, some of them large, with a *porte-cochère* leading into a semi-circular yard, round which the building stands, very steep-roofed, and shingled, in view of the heavy snow-masses of winter. Glancing into one open casement near the ground, I saw an aged woman, stout and capped, lie on her face before a very large porcelain stove; but I paced on without stoppage, traversed several streets, and came out, as it became dark, upon a piece of grass-land leading downward to a mountain-gorge. It was some distance along this gorge that I found myself sitting the next morning: and how, and in what trance, I passed that whole blank night is obliterated from my consciousness. When I looked about with the return of light I saw majestic fir-grown mountains on either hand, almost meeting overhead at some points, deeply shading the mossy gorge. I rose, and careless of direction, went still onward, and walked and walked for hours, unconscious of hunger; there was a profusion of wild mountain-strawberries, very tiny, which must grow almost into winter, a few of which I ate; there were blue gentianellas, and lilies-of-the-valley, and luxuriance of verdure, and a noise of waters. Occasionally, I saw little cataracts on high, fluttering like white wild rags, for they broke in the mid-fall, and were caught away, and scattered; patches also of reaped hay and barley, hung up, in a singular way, on stakes six feet high, I suppose to dry; there were perched huts, and a seemingly inaccessible small castle or burg, but none of these did I enter: and five bodies only I saw in the gorge, a woman with a babe, and a man with two small oxen.

About three in the afternoon I was startled to find myself there, and turned back. It was dark when I again passed through those gloomy streets of Aadheim, making for the quay, and now I felt both my hunger and a dropping weariness. I had no thought of entering any house, but as I passed by one open *porte-cochère*, something, I know not what, made me turn sharply in, for my mind had become as fluff on the winds, not working of its own action, but the sport of impulses that seemed external. I went across the yard, and ascended a wooden spiral stair by a twilight which just enabled me to pick my way among five or six vague forms fallen there. In that confined place fantastic qualms beset me; I mounted to the first landing, and tried the door, but it was locked; I mounted to the second: the door was open, and with a chill reluctance I took a step inward where all was pitch darkness, the window-stores being drawn. I hesitated: it was very dark. I tried to utter that word of mine, but it came in a whisper inaudible to my ears: I tried again, and this time heard myself say: "*Anyone?*" At the same time I had made another step forward, and trodden upon a soft abdomen; and at that contact terrors the most cold and ghastly thrilled me through and through, for it was as though I saw in that darkness the sudden eye-balls of Hell and frenzy glare upon me, and with a low gurgle of affright I was gone, helter-skelter down the stairs, treading upon flesh, across the yard, and down the street, with pelting feet, and open arms, and sobbing bosom, for I thought that all Aadheim was after me; nor was my horrid haste appeased till I was on board the *Boreal,* and moving down the fjord.

Out to sea, then, I went again; and within the next few days I visited Bergen, and put in at Stavanger. And I saw that Bergen and Stavanger were dead.

It was then, on the 19th August, that I turned my bow toward my native land.

*   *   *   *   *

From Stavanger I steered a straight course for the Humber.

I had no sooner left behind me the Norway coast than I began to meet the ships, the ships—ship after ship; and by the time I entered the zone of the ordinary alternation of sunny day and sunless night, I was moving through the midst of an incredible number of craft, a mighty and wide-spread fleet.

Over all that great expanse of the North Sea, where, in its most populous days of trade, the sailor might perhaps sight a sail or two, I had now at every moment at least ten or twelve within scope of the glass, oftentimes as many as forty, forty-five.

And very still they lay on a still sea, itself a dead thing, livid as the lips of death; and there was an intensity in the calm that was appalling: for the ocean seemed weighted, and the air drugged.

Extremely slow was my advance, for at first I would not leave any ship, however remotely small, without approaching sufficiently to investigate her, at least with the spy-glass: and a strange multitudinous mixture of species they were, trawlers in hosts, war-ships of every nation, used, it seemed, as passenger-boats, smacks, feluccas, liners, steam-barges, great four-masters with sails,

Channel boats, luggers, a Venetian *burchiello*, colliers, yachts, *remorqueurs*, training ships, dredgers, two *dahabeeahs* with curving gaffs, Marseilles fishers, a Maltese *speronare*, American off-shore sail, Mississippi steam-boats, Sorrento lug-schooners, Rhine punts, yawls, old frigates and three-deckers, called to novel use, Stromboli caiques, Yarmouth tubs, xebecs, Rotterdam flat-bottoms, floats, mere gunwaled rafts—anything from anywhere that could bear a human freight on water had come, and was here: and all, I knew, had been making westward, or northward, or both; and all, I knew, were crowded; and all were tombs, listlessly wandering, my God, on the wandering sea with their dead.

And so fair the world about them, too: the brightest suavest autumn weather; all the still air aromatic with that vernal perfume of peach: yet not so utterly still, but if I passed close to the lee of any floating thing, the spicy stirrings of morning or evening wafted me faint puffs of the odour of mortality over-ripe for the grave.

So abominable and accursed did this become to me, such a plague and a hissing, vague as was the offence, that I began to shun rather than seek the ships, and also I now dropped my twelve, whom I had kept to be my companions all the way from the Far North, one by one, into the sea: for now I had definitely passed into a zone of settled warmth.

I was convinced, however, that the poison, whatever it might be, had some embalming, or antiseptic, effect upon the bodies: at Aadheim, Bergen and Stavanger, for instance, where the temperature permitted me to go without a jacket, only the merest hints and whiffs of the processes of dissolution had troubled me.

* * * * *

Very benign, I say, and pleasant to see, was sky and sea during all that voyage; but it was at sun-set that my sense of the wondrously beautiful was roused and excited, in spite of that great burden which I carried. Certainly, I never saw sun-sets resembling those, nor could have conceived of aught so flamboyant, extravagant, and bewitched; for the whole heaven seemed turned into an arena for warring Hierarchies, warring for the universe, or it was like the wild countenance of God defeated, and flying marred and bloody from His enemies. But many evenings I watched it with unintelligent awe, believing it but a portent of the un-sheathed sword of the Almighty; till, one morning, a thought pricked me like a sword, for I suddenly remembered the great sun-sets of the later nineteenth century, witnessed in Europe, America, and, I believe, over the world, after the eruption of the volcano of Krakatoa.

And whereas I had before said to myself: "If now a wave from the Deep has washed over this planetary ship of earth . . .," I said now: "A wave—but not from the Deep: a wave rather which she had reserved, and has spouted, from her own un-motherly entrails . . ."

* * * * *

I had some knowledge of Morse telegraphy, and of the manipulation of tape-machines, telegraphic typing-machines, and the ordinary wireless transmitter and coherer, as of most little things of that sort which came within the outskirts of the interest of a man of science; I had collaborated with Professor Stanistreet in the production of a text-book called "Applications of Science to the Arts," which had brought us some notoriety; and, on the whole, the *minutiæ* of modern things were still pretty fresh in my memory. I could therefore have wired from Bergen or Stavanger, supposing the batteries not run down, to somewhere: but I would not: I was so afraid; afraid lest for ever from nowhere should come one answering click, or flash, or stirring. . . .

*   *   *   *   *

I could have made short work, and landed at Hull: but I would not: I was so afraid. For I was used to the silence of the ice: and I was used to the silence of the sea: but I was afraid of the silence of England.

*   *   *   *   *

I came in sight of the coast on the morning of the 26th August, somewhere about Hornsea, but did not see any town, for I put the helm to port, and went on further south, no longer bothering with the instruments, but coasting at hap-hazard, now in sight of land, and now in the centre of a circle of sea; not admitting to myself the motive of this loitering slowness, nor thinking at all, but ignoring the deep-buried fear of the to-morrow which I shirked, and instinctively hiding myself in to-day. I passed the Wash, I passed Yarmouth, Felixstowe. By now the things that floated motionless on the sea were beyond numbering, for I could hardly lower my eyes ten minutes and lift them, without seeing yet another there: so that soon after dusk I, too, had to lie still among them all, till morning: for they lay dark, and to move at any pace would have been to drown the already dead.

Well, I came to the Thames-mouth, and lay pretty well in among the Flats and Pan Sands towards eight one evening, not seven miles from Sheppey and the North Kent coast: and I did not see any Nore Light, nor Girdler Light: and all along the coast I had seen no light: but as to that I said not one word to myself, not admitting it, nor letting my heart know what my brain thought, nor my brain know what my heart surmised; but with a daft and mock-mistrustful under-look I would regard the darkling land, holding it a sentient thing that would be playing a prank upon a poor man like me.

And the next morning, when I moved again, my furtive eye-corners were very well aware of the Prince's Channel light-ship, and also the Tongue ship, for there they were: but I would not look at them at all, nor go near them: for I did not wish to have anything to do with whatever might have happened beyond my own ken, and it was better to look straight before, seeing nothing, and concerning one's-self with one's-self.

The next evening, after having gone out to sea again, I was in a little to the E. by S. of the North Foreland: and I saw no light there, nor any Sandhead light; but over the sea vast signs of wreckage, and the coasts were strewn with old wrecked fleets. I turned about S.E., very slowly moving—for anywhere hereabouts hundreds upon hundreds of craft lay dead within a ten-mile circle of sea—and by two in the fore-day had wandered up well in sight of the French cliffs: for I had said: "I will go and see the light-beam of the great revolving-drum on Calais pier that nightly beams half-way over-sea to England." And the moon shone clear in the southern heaven that morning, like a great old dying queen whose Court swarms distantly from around her, diffident, pale, and tremulous, the paler the nearer; and I could see the mountain-shadows on her spotty full-face, and her misty aureole, and her lights on the sea, as it were kisses stolen in the kingdom of sleep; and all among the quiet ships mysterious white trails and powderings of light, like palace-corridors in some fairy-land forlorn, full of breathless wan whispers, scandals, and runnings-to-and-fro, with leers, and agitated last embraces, and flight of the princess, and death-bed of the king; and on the N.E. horizon a bank of brown cloud that seemed to have no relation with the world; and yonder, not far, the white coast-cliffs, not so low as at Calais near, but arranged in masses separated by vales of sward, each with its wreck: but no light of any revolving-drum I saw.

*   *   *   *   *

I could not sleep that night: for all the operations of my mind and body seemed in abeyance. Mechanically I turned the ship westward again; and when the sun came up, there, hardly two miles from me, were the cliffs of Dover; and over the crenulated summit of the Castle I spied the Union Jack hang motionless.

I heard eight, nine, o'clock strike in the cabin, and I was still at sea. But some mad, audacious whisper was at my brain: and at 10.30, the 2nd September, immediately opposite the Cross Wall Custom House, the *Boreal's* anchor-chain, after a voyage of three years, two months, and fourteen days, ran thundering, thundering, through the starboard hawse-hole.

Ah, heaven! but I must have been stark mad to let the anchor go! for the effect upon me of that shocking obstreperous hubbub, breaking in upon all that cemetery repose that blessed morning, and lasting it seemed a year, was most appalling; and at the sudden racket I stood excruciated, with shivering knees and flinching heart, God knows: for not less terrifically uproarious than the clatter of the last Trump it raged and raged, and I thought that all the billion dead could not fail to start, and rise, at alarum so excessive, and question me with their eyes. . . .

*   *   *   *   *

On the top of the Cross Wall near I saw a grey crab fearlessly crawl; at the end where the street begins, I saw a single gas-light palely burn that broad day, and at its foot a black man lay on his face, clad only in a shirt and one boot; the harbour was almost packed with every sort of craft, and on a Calais-Dover boat, eight yards from my stern, which must have left Calais crowded to suffocation, I saw the rotted dead lie heaped, she being unmoored, and continually grinding against an anchored green brig.

And when I saw that, I dropped down upon my knees at the capstan, and my heart sobbed out the frail cry: "Well, Lord God, Thou hast destroyed the work of Thy hand. . . ."

*   *   *   *   *

After a time I got up, went below in a state of somnambulism, took a packet of pemmican cakes, leapt to land, and went following the railway that runs from the Admiralty Pier. In an enclosed passage ten yards long, with railway-masonry on one side, I saw five dead lie, and could not believe that I was in England, for all were dark-skinned people, three gaudily dressed, and two in flowing white robes. It was the same when I turned into a long street, leading northward, for here were a hundred, or more, and never saw I, except in Constantinople, where I once lived eighteen months, so variegated a mixture of races, black, brunette, brown, yellow, white, in all the shades, some emaciated like people dead from hunger, and, over-looking them all, one English boy with a clean Eton collar sitting on a bicycle, supported by a lamp-post which his arms clasped, he proving the extraordinary suddenness of the death which had overtaken them all.

I did not know whither, nor why, I went, nor had I the least idea whether all this was visually seen by me in the world which I had known, or in some other, or was all phantasy of my disembodied spirit—for I had the thought that I, too, might be dead since old ages, and my spirit wandering now through the universe of space, in which there is neither north nor south, nor up nor down, nor measure nor relation, nor aught whatever, save an uneasy consciousness of a dream about bottomlessness. Of grief or pain, I think, I felt nothing; though I have a sort of memory now that some sound, resembling a sob or groan, though it was neither, came at regular clockwork intervals from my bosom during three or four days. Meantime, my brain registered like a tape-machine details the most frivolous, the most ludicrous—the name of a street, Strond Street, Snargate Street; the round fur cap—black fur for the side, white ermine for the top—of a portly Karaite priest on his back, whose robes had been blown up to his spread knees, as if lifted and neatly folded there; a violin-bow gripped between the thick, irregular teeth of a little Spaniard with brushed-back hair and mad-looking eyes; odd shoes on the foot of a French girl, one black, one brown. They lay in the street about as numerous as gunners who fall round their carriage, at intervals of five to ten feet, the majority—as was the case also in Norway, and on the ships—in poses of distraction, with spread arms, or wildly distorted limbs, like men who, in the instant before death, called upon the rocks and hills to cover them.

*   *   *   *   *

On the left I came to an opening in the land, called, I believe, "The Shaft," and into this I turned, climbing a very great number of steps, almost covered at one point with dead: the steps I began to count, but left off, then the dead, and left off. Finally, at the top, which must be even higher than the Castle, I came to a great open space laid out with gravel-walks, and saw fortifications, barracks, a citadel. I did not know the town, except by passings-through, and was surprised at the breadth of view. Between me and the Castle to the east lay the district of crowding houses, brick and ragstone, mixed in the distance with vague azure haze; and to the right the harbour, the sea, with their ships; and visible around me on the heights seven or eight dead, biting the dust; the sun now high and warm, with hardly a cloud in the sky; and yonder a mist, which was the coast of France.

It seemed too big for one poor man.

My head nodded. I sat on a bench, black-painted and hard, the seat and back of horizontal boards, with intervals; and as I looked, I nodded, heavy-headed and weary: for it was too big for me. And as I nodded, with forehead propped on my left hand, and the packet of pemmican cakes in my right, there was in my head, somehow, an old street-song of my childhood: and I groaned it sleepily, like coronachs and drear funereal nenias, dirging; and the packet beat time in my right hand, falling and raising, falling heavily and rising, in time.

I'll buy the ring,
You'll rear the kids:
Servants to wait on our ting, ting, ting.

  •   •   •   •   •
  •   •   •   •   •

Ting, ting,
Won't we be happy?
Ting, ting,
That shall be it:
I'll buy the ring,
You'll rear the kids:
Servants to wait on our ting, ting, ting.

  •   •   •   •   •
  •   •   •   •   •

So maundering, I fell forward upon my face, and for twenty-three hours, the living undistinguished from the dead, I slept there.

     *   *   *   *   *

I was awakened by drizzle, leapt up, looked at a silver chronometer which, attached by a leather to my belt, I carried in my breeches-pocket, saw that it was 10 A.M. The sky was dark, and a moaning wind—almost a new thing now to me—had arisen.

I ate some pemmican, for I had a reluctance—needless as it turned out—to touch any of the thousand luxuries here, sufficient no doubt, in a town like Dover alone, to last me five or six hundred years, if I could live so long; and, having eaten, I descended The Shaft, and spent the whole day, though it rained and blustered continually, in wandering about. Reasoning, in my numb way, from the number of ships on the sea, I expected to find the town over-crowded with dead: but this was not so; and I should say, at a venture, that not a thousand English, nor fifteen thousand foreigners, were in it: for that west-ward rage and stampede must have operated here also, leaving the town empty but for the ever new-coming hosts.

The first thing which I did was to go into an open grocer's shop, which was also a post and telegraph office, with the notion, I suppose, to get a mes-sage through to London. In the shop a single gas-light was burning its last, and this, with that near the pier, were the only two that I saw: and ghastly enough they looked, transparently wannish, as it were ashamed, like blinking night-things overtaken by the glare of day. I conjectured that they had so burned and watched during months, or years: for they were now blazing diminished, with streaks and rays in the flame, as if by effort, and if these were the only two, they must have needed time to all-but exhaust the works. Before the counter lay a fashionably-dressed negro with a number of tied parcels scattered about him, and on the counter an empty till, and behind it a tall thin woman with her face resting sideways in the till, her fingers clutching the outer counter-rim, and such an expression of terror as I never saw. I got over the counter to a table behind a wire-gauze, and, like a numb fool, went over the Morse alphabet in my mind before touching the transmitting key, though I knew no code-words, and there, big enough to be seen, was the A B C dial, and who was to answer my message I did not ask myself: for habit was still strong upon me, and my mind refused to reason from what I saw to what I did not see; but the moment I touched the key, and peered greedily at the galvonometer-needle at my right, I saw that it did not move, for no current was passing; and with a kind of fright, I was up, leapt, and got away from the place, though there was a great number of telegrams about the receiver, which, if I had been in my senses, I would have stopped and read.

Turning the corner of the next street, I saw wide-open the door of a sub-stantial large house, and went in. From bottom to top there was no one there, except one English girl, sitting back in an easy-chair in the drawing-room, which was richly furnished with Valenciennes curtains and azure-satin things. She was a girl of the lowest class, hardly clad in black rags, and there she lay with a hanging jaw, in a very crooked and awkward pose, a jemmy at her feet, in her left hand a roll of bank-notes, in her lap three watches. In fact, the bod-ies which I saw here were, in general, either those of new-come foreigners, or else of the very poor, the very old, or the very young.

But what made me remember this house was that I found there on one of the sofas a newspaper: *The Kent Express;* and sitting unconscious of my dead neighbour, I pored a long while over what was written there.

It said in a passage that I tore out and kept:

"Telegraphic communication with Tilsit, Insterburg, Warsaw, Cracow, Przemysl, Gross Wardein, Karlsburg, and many smaller towns lying immediately eastward of the 21st parallel of longitude has ceased during the night. In some at least of them there must have been operators still at their duty, undrawn into the great westward-rushing torrent: but as all messages from Western Europe have been answered only by that dread mysterious silence which, just three months and two days since, astounded the world in the case of Eastern New Zealand, we can only assume that these towns, too, have been added to the long and mournful list; indeed, after last evening's Paris telegrams we might have prophesied with some certainty, not merely their overthrow, but even the hour of it: for the rate-uniformity of the slow-riding vapour which is touring our globe is no longer doubtful, and has even been definitely fixed by Professor Craven at 100½ miles per day, or 4 miles 330 yards per hour. Its nature, its origin, remains, of course, nothing but matter of conjecture: for it leaves no living thing behind it; nor, God knows, is that of any moment now to us who remain. The rumour that it is associated with an odour of almonds is declared, on high authority, to be improbable; but the morose purple of its impending gloom has been attested by tardy fugitives from the face of its rolling and smoky march.

"Is this the end? We do not, and cannot, believe it. Will the pure sky which we to-day see above us be invaded in nine days, or less, by this smoke of the Pit of Darkness? In spite of the assurances of the scientists, we still doubt. For, if so, to what purpose that long drama of History, in which we seem to see the Hand of the Dramaturgist? Surely, the end of a Fifth Act should be obvious, satisfying to one's sense of the complete: but History, so far, long as it has been, resembles rather a Prologue than a Fifth Act. Can it be that the Manager, utterly dissatisfied, would sweep all off, and 'hang up' the piece for ever? Certainly, the sins of mankind have been as scarlet: and if the fair earth which he has turned into Hell, send forth now upon him the smoke of Hell, little the wonder. But we cannot yet believe. There is a sparing strain in nature, and through the world, as a thread, is spun a silence which smiles, and on the end of events we find placarded large the words: 'Why were ye afraid?' A dignified Hope, therefore—even now, when we cower beneath this world-wide shadow of the wings of the Condor of Death—becomes us: and, indeed, we see such an attitude among some of the humblest of our people, from whose heart arises the cry: 'Though He slay me, yet will I trust in Him.' Hear, therefore, O Lord! O Lord, look down, and save!

"But even as we thus write of hope, Reason, if we would hear her, whispers us 'fool': and inclement is the sky of earth. No more ships can New York Harbour contain, and whereas among us men die weekly of privations by the hundred thousand, yonder across the sea they perish by the million: for where the rich are pinched, how can the poor live? Already 700 out of the 1000 millions of our race have perished, and the empires of civilisation have crumbled like sand-castles in a horror of anarchy. Thousands upon thousands of unburied dead, anticipating the more deliberate doom that comes and smokes, and rides and comes and comes, and does not fail, encumber the streets of London, Manchester, Liverpool. The guides of the nation have fled; the father stabs his child, and the wife her husband, for a morsel of food; the fields lie waste; wanton crowds carouse in our churches, universities, palaces, banks and hospitals; we understand that late last night three territorial regiments, the Munster Fusiliers, and the Lothian and East Lancashire Regiments, riotously disbanded themselves, shooting two officers; infectious diseases, as we all know, have spread beyond limit; in several towns the police seem to have disappeared, and, in nearly all, every vestige of decency; the results following upon the sudden release of the convicts appear to be monstrous in the respective districts; and within three short months Hell seems to have acquired this entire planet, sending forth Horror, like a rabid wolf, and Despair, like a disastrous sky, to devour and confound her. Hear, therefore, O Lord, and forgive our iniquities! O Lord, we beseech Thee! Look down, O Lord, and spare!"

*   *   *   *   *

When I had read this, and the rest of the paper, which had one whole sheet-side blank, I sat a long hour there, eyeing a little patch of the purple ash on a waxed board near the corner where the girl sat with her time-pieces, so useless in her Eternity; and there was not a feeling in me, except a pricking of curiosity, which afterwards became morbid and ravenous, to know something more of that cloud, or smoke, of which this man spoke, of its dates, its origin, its nature, its minute details. Afterwards, I went down, and entered several houses, seeking for more papers, but did not find any; then I found a paper-shop which was open, with boards outside, but either it had been deserted, or printing must have stopped about the date of the paper which I had read, for the only three newspapers there were dated long prior, and I did not read them.

Now it was raining, and a blustering autumn day it was, distributing the odours of the world, and bringing me continual mixed whiffs of flowers and the hateful stench of decay. But I would not mind it much.

I wandered and wandered, till I was tired of spahi and bashi-bazouk, of Greek and Catalan, of Russian "pope" and Coptic abuna, of dragoman and Calmuck, of Egyptian maulawi and Afghan mullah, Neapolitan and sheik, and the nightmare of wild poses, colours, stuffs and garbs, yellow-green kefie of the Bedouin, shawl-turbans of Baghdad, the voluminous rose-silk tob of women, and face-veils, and stark distorted nakedness, and sashes of figured muslin, and the workman's cords, and the red tarboosh. About four, for very weariness, I was sitting on a door-step, bent beneath the rain; but soon was up again, fascinated no doubt by this changing bazaar of sameness, its chance combinations and permutations, its novelty in monotony. About five I was at a station, marked Harbour Station, in and about which lay a considerable crowd, but not one train. I sat again, and rested, rose and roamed again; soon after six I found myself at another station called "Priory"; and here I saw two long trains, both crowded, one on a siding, and one at the up-platform.

I examined both engines, and found them of the old boiler steam-type with manholes, heaters, autoclaves, feed-pump, &c., now rare in western countries, except England. In one there was no water, but in that at the platform, the float-lever, barely tilted toward the float, showed that there was some in the boiler. Of this one I overhauled all the machinery, and found it good, though rusted. There was plenty of fuel, and oil, which I supplemented from a near shop: and during ninety minutes my brain and hands worked with an intelligence as it were automatic, of their own motion. After three journeys across the station and street, I saw the fire blaze well, and the manometer move; when the lever of the safety-valve, whose load I lightened by half an atmosphere, lifted, I jumped down, and tried to disconnect the long string of carriages from the engine: but failed, the coupling being an automatic arrangement new to me; nor did I care. It was now very dark; but there was still some oil for bull's-eye and lantern, and I lit them. I forgot nothing. I rolled driver and stoker—the guard was absent—one to the platform, one upon the rails: and I took their place there. At about 8.30 I ran out from Dover, my throttle-valve pealing high a long falsetto through the bleak and desolate night.

*   *   *   *   *

My aim was London. But even as I set out, my heart smote me: I knew nothing of the metals, their junctions, facing-points, sidings, shuntings, and complexities. Even as to whether I was going toward, or away from, London, I was not sure. But just in proportion as my first timorousness of the engine hardened into familiarity and self-sureness, I quickened speed, wilfully, with an obstinacy deaf and blind.

Finally, from a mere crawl at first, I was flying at a shocking velocity, while something, tongue in cheek, seemed to whisper me: "There must be other trains blocking the lines, at stations, in yards, and everywhere—it is a maniac's ride, a ride of death, and Flying Dutchman's frenzy: remember your dark five-deep brigade of passengers, who rock and bump together, and will suffer in a collision." But with mulish stubbornness I thought: "They wished to go to London"; and on I raged, not wildly exhilarated, so far as I can remember, nor lunatic, but feeling the dull glow of a wicked and morose Unreason urge in my bosom, while I stoked all blackened at the fire, or saw the vague mass of dead horse or cow, running trees and fields, and dark homestead and deep-slumbering farm, flit ghostly athwart the murky air, as the half-blind saw "men like trees walking."

Long, however, it did not last: I could not have been twenty miles from Dover when, on a long reach of straight lines, I made out before me a tarpaulined mass opposite a signal-point: and at once callousness changed to terror within me. But even as I plied the brake, I felt that it was too late: I rushed to the gangway to make a wild leap down an embankment to the right, but was thrown backward by a quick series of rough bumps, caused by eight or ten cattle which lay there across the lines: and when I picked myself up, and leapt, some seconds before the impact, the speed must have considerably slackened, for I received no fracture, but lay in semi-coma in a patch of yellow-flowered whin on level ground, and was even conscious of a fire on the lines forty yards away, and, all the night, of vague thunder sounding from somewhere.

*   *   *   *   *

About five, or half-past, in the morning I was sitting up, rubbing my eyes, in a dim light mixed with drizzle. I could see that the train of my last night's debauch was a huddled-up chaos of fallen carriages and disfigured bodies. A five-barred gate on my left opened into a hedge, and swung with creaks: two yards from my feet lay a shaggy pony with swollen wan abdomen, the very picture of death, and also about me a number of dead wet birds.

I picked myself up, passed through the gate, and walked up a row of trees to a house at their end. I found it to be a little country-tavern with a barn, forming one house, the barn part much larger than the tavern part. I went into the tavern by a small side-door—behind the bar—into a parlour—up a little stair—into two rooms: but no one was there. I then went round into the barn, which was paved with cobble-stones, and there lay a dead mare and foal, some fowls, two cows. A ladder-stair led to a closed trap-door in the floor above. I went up, and in the middle of a wilderness of hay saw nine people—labourers, no doubt—five men and four women, huddled together, and with them a tin-pail containing the last of some spirit; so that these had died merry.

I slept three hours among them, and afterwards went back to the tavern, and had some biscuits of which I opened a new tin, with some ham, jam and apples, of which I made a good meal, for my pemmican was gone.

Afterwards I went following the rail-track on foot, for the engines of both the collided trains were smashed. I knew northward from southward by the position of the sun; and after a good many stoppages at houses, and by railway-banks, I came, at about eleven in the night, to a great and populous town.

By the Dane John and the Cathedral, I immediately recognised it as Canterbury, which I knew well. And I walked up Castle Street to the High Street, conscious for the first time of that regularly-repeated sound, like a sob or groan, which was proceeding from my throat. As there was no visible moon, and these old streets very dim, I had to pick my way, lest I should desecrate the dead with my foot, and they all should rise with hue and cry to hunt me. However, the bodies here were not numerous, most, as before, being foreigners: and these, scattered about this strict old English burg in that mourning dark night, presented such a scene of the baneful wrath of God, and all abomination of desolation, as broke me quite down at one place, where I stood in travail with jeremiads and sore sobbings and lamentations, crying out upon it all, God knows.

Only when I stood at the west entrance of the Cathedral I could discern, spreading up the dark nave, to the lantern, to the choir, a phantasmagorical mass of forms: I went a little inward, and striking three matches, peered nearer: the two transepts, too, seemed crowded—the cloister-doorway was blocked— the south-west porch thronged, so that a great congregation must have flocked hither shortly before their fate overtook them.

Here it was that I became definitely certain that the after-odour of the poison was not simply lingering in the air, but was being more or less given off by the bodies: for the blossomy odour of this church actually overcame that other odour, the whole rather giving the scent of old mouldy linens long embalmed in cedars.

Well, away with stealthy trot I ran from the abysmal silence of that place, and in Palace Street near made one of those sudden immoderate rackets that seemed to outrage the universe, and left me so woefully faint, decrepit, and gasping for life (the noise of the train was different, for there I was flying, but here a captive, and which way I ran was capture). Passing in Palace Street, I saw a little lamp-shop, and wanting a lantern, tried to get in, but the door was locked; so, after going a few steps, and kicking against a policeman's truncheon, I returned to break the window-glass. I knew that it would make a fearful noise, and for some fifteen or twenty minutes stood hesitating: but never could I have dreamed, my good God, of *such* a noise, so passionate, so dominant, so divulgent, and, O Heaven, so long-lasting: for I seemed to have struck upon the weak spot of some planet, which came suddenly tumbling, with protracted racket and *débâcle*, about my ears. It was a good hour before I would climb in; but then quickly found what I wanted, and some big oil-cans; and till one or two in the morning, the innovating flicker of my lantern went peering at random into the gloomy nooks of the town.

Under a deep old Gothic arch that spanned a pavered alley, I saw the little window of a little house of rubble, and between the two diamond-paned sashes rags tightly beaten in, the idea evidently being to make the place air-tight against the poison. When I went in I found the door of that room open, though it, too, had been stuffed at the edges; and on the threshold an old man and woman lay low. I conjectured that, thus protected, they had remained shut in, till hunger, or the lack of oxygen in the used-up air, drove them forth, whereupon the poison, still active, must have instantly ended them. I found afterwards that this expedient of making air-tight had been widely resorted to; and it might well have proved successful, if both the supply of inclosed air, and food, had been anywhere commensurate with the durability of the poisonous state.

Weary, weary as I grew, some morbid persistence sustained me, and I would not rest. About four in the morning I was at a station again, industriously bending, poor wretch, at the sooty task of getting another engine ready for travel. This time, when steam was up, I succeeded in uncoupling the carriages from the engine, and by the time morning broke, I was lightly gliding away over the country, whither I did not know, but making for London.

*   *   *   *   *

Now I went with more intelligence and caution, and got on very well, travelling seven days, never at night, except it was very clear, never at more than twenty or twenty-five miles, and crawling through tunnels. I do not know the maze into which the train took me, for very soon after leaving Canterbury it must have gone down some branch-line, and though the names were marked at stations, that hardly helped me, for of their situation relatively to London I was seldom sure. Moreover, again and again was my progress impeded by trains on the metals, when I would have to run back to a shunting-point or a siding, and, in two instances, these being far behind, changed from my own to the impeding engine. On the first day I travelled unhindered till noon, when I stopped in open country that seemed uninhabited for ages, only that half a mile to the left, on a shaded sward, was a large stone house of artistic design, coated with tinted harling, the roof of red Ruabon tiles, with timbered gables. I walked to it after another row with putting out the fire and arranging for a new one, the day being bright and mild, with great masses of white cloud in the sky. The house had an outer and an inner hall, three reception-rooms, fine oil-paintings, a kind of museum, and a large kitchen. In a bedroom above-stairs I found three women with servants' caps, and a footman, arranged in a strange symmetrical way, head to head, like rays of a star. As I stood looking at them, I could have sworn, my good God, that I heard someone coming up the stairs. But it was some slight creaking of the breeze in the house, augmented a hundred-fold to my inflamed and fevered hearing: for, used for years now to this silence of Eternity, it is as though I hear all sounds through an ear-trumpet. I went down, and after eating, and drinking some clary-water, made of brandy, sugar, cinnamon, and rose-water, which I found in plenty, I lay down on a sofa in the inner hall, and slept a quiet sleep until near midnight.

I went out then, still possessed with the foolish greed to reach London, and after getting the engine to rights, went off under a clear black sky thronged with worlds and far-sown spawn, some of them, I thought, perhaps like this of mine, whelmed and drowned in oceans of silence, with only one inhabitant to see it, and hear its silence. And all the long night I travelled, stopping twice only, once to get the coal from an engine which had impeded me, and once to drink some water, which I took care, as always, should be running water. When I felt my head nod, and my eyes close about 5 A.M., I threw myself, just outside the arch of a tunnel upon a grassy bank, pretty thick with stalks and flowers, the workings of early dawn being then in the east: and there, till near eleven, slept.

On waking, I noticed that the country now seemed more like Surrey than Kent: there was that regular swell and sinking of the land; but, in fact, though it must have been either, it looked like neither, for already all had an aspect of return to a state of wild nature, and I could see that for a year at the least no hand had tended the soil. Near before me was a stretch of lucerne of such extraordinary growth, that I was led during that day and the succeeding one to examine the condition of vegetation with some minuteness, and nearly everywhere I detected a certain hypertrophic tendency in stamens, calycles, pericarps, pistils, in every sort of bulbiferous growth that I looked at, in the rushes, above all, the fronds, mosses, lichens, and all cryptogamia, and in the trefoils, clover especially, and some creepers. Many crop-fields, it was clear, had been prepared, but not sown; some had not been reaped: and in both cases I was struck with their appearance of rankness, as I was also when in Norway, and was all the more surprised that this should be the case at a time when a poison, whose action is the arrest of oxidation, had traversed the earth; I could only conclude that its presence in large volumes in the lower strata of the atmosphere had been more or less temporary, and that the tendency to exuberance which I observed was due to some principle by which Nature acts with freer energy and larger scope in the absence of man.

Two yards from the rails I saw, when I got up, a little rill beside a rotten piece of fence, barely oozing itself onward under masses of foul and stagnant fungoids: and here there was a sudden splash, and life: and I caught sight of the hind legs of a diving young frog. I went and lay on my belly, poring over the clear dulcet little water, and presently saw two tiny bleaks, or ablets, go gliding low among the swaying moss-hair of the bottom-rocks, and thought how gladly would I be one of them, with my home so thatched and shady, and my life drowned in their wide-eyed reverie. At any rate, these little creatures are alive, the batrachians also, and, as I found the next day, pupæ and chrysales of one sort or another, for, to my deep emotion, I saw a little white butterfly staggering in the air over the flower-garden of a rustic station named Butley.

*　　*　　*　　*　　*

It was while I was lying there, poring upon that streamlet, that a thought came into my head: for I said to myself: "If now I be here alone, alone, alone . . . alone, alone . . . one on the earth . . . and my girth have a spread of 25,000 miles . . . what will happen to my mind? Into what kind of creature shall I writhe and change? I may live two years so! What will have happened then? I may live five years—ten! What will have happened after the five? the ten? I may live twenty, thirty, forty . . ."

Already, already, there are things that peep and sprout within me . . .!

*　　*　　*　　*　　*

I wanted food and fresh running water, and walked from the engine half a mile through fields of lucerne whose luxuriance quite hid the foot-paths, and reached my shoulder. After turning the brow of a hill, I came to a park, passing through which I saw some dead deer and three persons, and emerged upon a terraced lawn, at the end of which stood an Early English house of pale brick with copings, plinths, and stringcourses of limestone, and spandrels of carved marble; and some distance from the porch a long table, or series of tables, in the open air, still spread with cloths that were like shrouds after a month of burial; and the table had old foods on it and some lamps; and all around it, and all on the lawn, were dead peasants. I seemed to know the house, probably from some print which I may have seen, but I could not make out the escutcheon, though I saw from its simplicity that it must be very ancient. Right across the façade spread still some of the letters in evergreens of the motto: "Many happy returns of the day," so that someone must have come of age, or something, for inside all was gala, and it was clear that these people had defied a fate which they, of course, foreknew. I went nearly throughout the whole spacious place of thick-carpeted halls, marbles, and famous oils, antlers and arras, and gilt saloons, and placid large bed-chambers: and it took me an hour. There were here not less than a hundred and eighty people. In the first of a vista of three large reception-rooms lay what could only have been a number of quadrille parties, for to the *coup d'œil* they presented a two-and-two appearance, made very repulsive by their jewels and evening-dress. I had to steel my heart to go through this house, for I did not know if these people were looking at me as soon as my back was turned. Once I was on the very point of flying, for I was going up the great central stairway, and there came a pelt of dead leaves against a window-pane in a corridor just above on the first floor, which thrilled me to the inmost soul. But I thought that if I once fled, they would all be at me from behind, and I should be gibbering mad long, long before I reached the outer hall, and so stood my ground, even defiantly advancing. In a small dark bedroom in the north wing on the second floor—that is to say, at the top of the house—I saw a tall young lady and a groom, or wood-man, to judge by his clothes, horribly riveted in an embrace on a settee, she with a light coronet on her head in low-necked dress, and their lipless teeth still fiercely pressed together. I collected in a bag some delicacies from the under-regions of this house, Lyons sausages, salami, mortadel, apples, roes, raisins, artichokes, biscuits, a few wines, bottled fruit, pickles, coffee, and so on, with a gold plate, tin-opener, cork-screw, fork, &c., and dragged them all the long way back to the engine before I could eat.

*   *   *   *   *

My brain was in such a way, that it was several days before the perfectly obvious means of finding my way to London, since I wished to go there, at all occurred to me; and the engine went wandering the intricate railway-system of the south country, I having twice to water her with a coal-bucket from a pool, for the injector was giving no water from the tank under the coals, and I did not know where to find any near tank-sheds. On the fifth evening, instead of into London, I ran into Guildford.

*   *   *   *   *

That night, from eleven till the next day, there was a great storm over England: let me note it down. And ten days later, on the 17th of the month came another; on the 23rd another; and I should be put to it to count the number since. And they do not resemble English storms, but rather Arctic ones, in a certain very suggestive something of personalness, and a carousing malice, and a Tartarus gloom, which I cannot quite describe. That night at Guildford, after wandering about, and becoming very weary, I threw myself upon a cushioned pew in an old Norman church with two east apses, called St. Mary's, using a Bible-cushion for pillow, and placing some distance away a little tin lamp turned low, whose ray served me for *veilleuse* through the night. Happily I had taken care to close up everything, or, I feel sure, the roof must have gone. Only one dead, an old lady in a chapel on the north side of the chancel, whom I rather mistrusted, was there with me: and there I lay listening: for, after all, I could not sleep a wink, while outside vogued the immense tempest. And I communed with myself, thinking: "I, poor man, lost in this conflux of infinitudes and vortex of the world, what can become of me, my God? For dark, ah dark, is the waste void into which from solid ground I am now plunged a million fathoms deep, the sport of all the whirlwinds: and it were better for me to have died with the dead, and never to have seen the wrath and turbulence of the Ineffable, nor to have heard the thrilling bleakness of the winds of Eternity, when they pine, and long, and whimper, and when they vociferate and blaspheme, and when they expostulate and intrigue and implore, and when they despair and die, which ear of man should never hear. For they mean to eat me up, I know, these Titanic darknesses: and soon like whiff I shall pass away, and leave the world to them." So till next morning I lay mumping, with shivers and cowerings: for the shocks of the storm pervaded the locked church to my very heart; and there were thunders that night, my God, like callings and laughs and banterings, exchanged between distant hill-tops in Hell.

*   *   *   *   *

Well, the next morning I went down the steep High Street, and found a young nun at the bottom whom I had left the previous evening with a number of girls in uniform opposite the Guildhall—half-way up the street. She must have been spun down, arm over arm, for the wind was westerly, and whereas I had left her completely dressed to her wimple and beads, she was now nearly stripped, and her flock scattered. And branches of trees, and wrecked houses, and reeling clouds of dead leaves were everywhere that wild morning.

This town of Guildford appeared to be the junction of an extraordinary number of railway-lines, and before again setting out in the afternoon, when the wind had lulled, having got an A B C guide, and a railway-map, I decided upon my line, and upon a new engine, feeling pretty sure now of making London, only thirty miles away. I then set out, and about five o'clock was at Surbiton, near my aim; I kept on, expecting every few minutes to see the great city, till darkness fell, and still, at considerable risk, I went, as I thought, forward: but no London was there. I had, in fact, been on a loop-line, and at Surbiton gone wrong again; for the next evening I found myself at Wokingham, farther away than ever.

I slept on a rug in the passage of an inn called The Rose, for there was a wild, Russian-looking man, with projecting top-teeth, on a bed in the house, whose appearance I did not like, and it was late, and I too tired to walk further; and the next morning pretty early I set out again, and at 10 A.M. was at Reading.

The notion of navigating the land by precisely the same means as the sea, simple and natural as it was, had not at all occurred to me: but at the first accidental sight of a compass in a little shop-window near the river at Reading, my difficulties as to getting to any desired place vanished once and for all: for a good chart or map, the compass, a pair of compasses, and, in the case of longer distances, a quadrant, sextant or theodolite, with a piece of paper and pencil, were all that were necessary to turn an engine into a land-ship, one choosing the lines which ran nearest the direction of one's course, whenever they did not run precisely.

Thus provided, I ran out from Reading about seven in the evening, while there was still some light, having spent there some nine hours. This was the town where I first observed that shocking crush of humanity, which I afterwards met in every large town west of London. Here, I should say, the English were quite equal in number to the foreigners: and there were enough of both, God knows: for London must have poured many here. There were houses, in every room of which, and on the stairs, the dead actually overlay each other, and in the streets before them were points where only on flesh, or under carriages, was it possible to walk. I went into the great County Gaol, from which, as I had read, the prisoners had been released two weeks before-hand, and there I found the same pressed condition, cells occupied by ten or twelve, the galleries continuously rough-paved with faces, heads, and old-clothes-shops of robes; and in the parade-ground, against one wall, a mass of human stuff, like tough grey clay mixed with rags and trickling black gore, where a crush as of hydraulic power must have acted. At a corner between a gate and a wall near the biscuit-factory of this town I saw a boy, whom I believe to have been blind, standing jammed, at his wrist a chain-ring, and, at the end of the chain, a dog; from his hap-hazard posture I conjectured that he, and chain, and dog had been lifted from the street, and placed so, by the storm of the 7th of the month; and what made it very curious was that his right arm pointed a little outward just over the dog, so that, at the moment when I first sighted him, he seemed a drunken fellow setting his dog at me. In fact, all the dead I found much mauled and stripped and huddled: and the earth seemed to be making an abortive effort to sweep her streets.

Well, some little distance from Reading I saw a big flower-seed farm, looking dead in some plots, and in others quite rank: and here again, fluttering quite near the engine, two little winged aurelians in the quiet evening air. I went on, passing a great number of crowded trains on the down-line, two of them in collision, and very broken up, and one exploded engine; even the fields and cuttings on either hand of the line had a rather populous look, as if people, when trains and vehicles failed, had set to trudging westward in caravans and streams. When I came to a long tunnel near Slough, I saw round the foot of the arch an extraordinary quantity of wooden *débris*, and as I went very slowly through, was alarmed by the continuous bumping of the train, which, I knew, was passing over bodies; at the other end were more *débris*; and I easily guessed that a company of desperate people had made the tunnel air-tight at the two arches, and provisioned themselves, with the hope to live there till the day of destiny was passed; whereupon their barricades must have been crashed through by some up-train and themselves crushed, or else, other crowds, mad to share their cave of refuge, had stormed the boardings. This latter, as I afterwards found, was a very usual event.

I should very soon have got to London now, but, as my bad luck would have it, I met a long up-train on the metals, with not one creature in any part of it. There was nothing to do but to tranship, with all my things, to its engine, which I found in good condition with plenty of coal and water, and to set it going, a hateful labour: I being already jet-black from hair to toes. However, by half-past ten I found myself stopped by another train only a quarter of a mile from Paddington, and walked the rest of the way among trains in which the standing dead still stood, propped by their neighbours, and over metals where bodies were as ordinary and cheap as waves on the sea, or twigs in a forest. I believe that wild crowds had given chase on foot to moving trains, or fore-run them in the frenzied hope of inducing them to stop.

I came to the great shed of glass and girders which is the station, the night being perfectly soundless, moonless, starless, and the hour about eleven.

I found later that all the electric generating-stations, or all that I visited, were intact; that is to say, must have been shut down before the arrival of the doom; also that the gas-works had almost certainly been abandoned some time previously: so that this city of dreadful night, in which, at the moment when Silence choked it, not less than forty to sixty millions swarmed and droned, must have more resembled Tartarus and the foul shades of Hell than aught to which my fancy can liken it.

For, coming nearer the platforms, I saw that trains, in order to move at all, must have moved through a slough of bodies pushed from behind, and forming a packed homogeneous mass on the metals: and I knew that they *had* moved. Nor could I now move, unless I decided to wade: for flesh was everywhere, on the roofs of trains, cramming the interval betwixt them, on the platforms, splashing the pillars like spray, piled on trucks and lorries, a carnal quagmire; and outside, it filled the space between a great host of vehicles, carpeting all that region of London. And all here that odour of blossoms, which nowhere yet, save on one vile ship, had failed, was now wholly overcome by another: and the thought was in my head, my God, that if the soul of man had sent up to Heaven the odour which his body gave to me, then it was not strange that things were as they were.

I got out from the station, with ears, God knows, that still awaited the accustomed noising of this accursed town, habituated as I now was to all the dumb and absent void of Soundlessness; and I was overwhelmed in a new awe, and lost in a wilder woesomeness, when, instead of lights and business, I saw the long street which I knew brood darker than Babylons desolate, and in place of its ancient noising, heard, my God, a shocking silence, rising higher than I had ever heard it, and blending with the silence of the inane, eternal stars in heaven.

*   *   *   *   *

I could not get into any vehicle for some time, for all thereabouts was practically a mere block; but near the Park, which I attained by stooping among wheels, and selecting my foul steps, I overhauled a Daimler car, found in it two cylinders of petrol, lit the ignition-lamp, removed with averted abhorrence three bodies, mounted, and broke that populous stillness. And through streets nowhere empty of bodies I went urging eastward my jolting, and spattered, and humming way.

*   *   *   *   *

That I should have persisted, with so much pains, to come to this unbounded catacomb, seems now singular to me: for by that time I could not have been sufficiently daft to expect to find another being like myself on the earth, though I cherished, I remember, the irrational hope of yet somewhere finding dog, or cat, or horse, to be with me, and would anon think bitterly of Reinhardt, my Arctic dog, which my own hand had shot. But, in reality, a morbid curiosity must have been within me all the time to read the real truth of what had happened, so far as it was known, or guessed, and to gloat upon all that drama, and cup of trembling, and pouring out of the vials of the wrath of God, which must have preceded the actual advent of the end of Time. This inquisitiveness had, at every town which I reached, made the search for newspapers uppermost in my mind; but, by bad luck, I had found only four, all of them ante-dated to the one which I had read at Dover, though their dates gave me some idea of the period when printing must have ceased, viz. soon after the 17th July—about three months subsequent to my arrival at the Pole—for none I found later than this date; and these contained nothing scientific, but only orisons and despairings. On arriving, therefore, at London, I made straight for the office of the *Times,* only stopping at a chemist's in Oxford Street for a bottle of antiseptic to hold near my nose, though, having once left the neighbourhood of Paddington, I had hardly much need of this.

I made my way to the square where the paper was printed, to find that, even there, the ground was closely strewn with calpac and pugaree, black abayeh and fringed praying-shawl, hob-nail and sandal, figured lungi and striped silk, all very muddled and mauled. Through the dark square to the twice-dark building I passed, and found open the door of an advertisement-office; but on striking a match, saw that it had been lighted by electricity, and had therefore to retrace my stumbling steps, till I came to a shop of lamps in a near alley, walking meantime with timid cares that I might hurt no one—for in this enclosed neighborhood I began to feel strange tremors, and kept striking matches, which, so still was the black air, hardly flickered.

When I returned to the building with a little lighted lamp, I at once saw a file on a table, and since there were a number of dead there, and I wished to be alone, I took the heavy mass of paper between my left arm and side, and the lamp in my right hand; passed then behind a counter; and then, to the right, up a stair which led me into a very great building and complexity of wooden steps and corridors, where I went peering, the lamp visibly trembling in my hand, for here also were the dead. Finally, I entered a good-sized carpeted room with a baize-covered table in the middle, and large smooth chairs, and on the table many manuscripts impregnated with purple dust, and around were books in shelves. This room had been locked upon a single man, a tall man in a frock-coat, with a pointed grey beard, who at last moment had decided to fly from it, for he lay at the threshold, apparently fallen dead the moment he opened the door. Him, by drawing his feet aside, I removed, locked the door upon myself, sat at the table before the dusty file, and, with the little light near, began to search.

I searched and read until far into the morning. But God knows, He alone . . .

I had not properly filled the little reservoir with oil, and about three in the fore-day, it began to burn sullenly lower, letting sparks, and turning the glass grey: and in my deepest chilly heart was the question: "Suppose the lamp goes out before the daylight . . ."

I knew the Pole, and cold, I knew them well: but to be frozen by panic, my God! I read, I say, I searched, I would not stop: but I read that night racked by terrors such as have never yet entered into the heart of man to conceive. My flesh moved and crawled like a lake which, here and there, the breeze ruffles. Sometimes for three, four minutes, the profound interest of what I read would fix my mind, and then I would peruse an entire column, or two, without consciousness of the meaning of one single word, my brain all drawn away to the innumerable host of the wan dead that camped about me, pierced with horror lest they should start, and stand, and accuse me: for the grave and the worm was the world; and in the air a sickening stirring of cerements and shrouds; and the taste of the pale and insubstantial grey of ghosts seemed to infect my throat, and faint odours of the loathsome tomb my nostrils, and the toll of deep-toned passing-bells my ears; finally the lamp smouldered very low, and my charnel fancy teemed with the screwing-down of coffins, lych-gates and sextons, and the grating of ropes that lower down the dead, and the first sound of the earth upon the lid of that strait and gloomy home of the mortal; that lethal look of cold dead fingers I seemed to see before me, the insipidness of dead tongues, the pout of the drowned, and the vapid froths that ridge their lips, till my flesh was moist as with the stale washing-waters of morgues and mortuaries, and with such sweats as corpses sweat, and the mawkish tear that lies on dead men's cheeks; for what is one poor insignificant man in his flesh against a whole world of the disembodied, he alone with them, and nowhere, nowhere another of his kind, to whom to appeal against them? I read, and I searched: but God, God knows . . . If a leaf of the paper, which I slowly, warily, stealingly turned, made but one faintest rustle, how did that *reveille* boom in echoes through the vacant and haunted chambers of my poor aching heart, my God! and there was a cough in my throat which for a cruelly long time I would not cough, till it burst in horrid clamour from my lips, sending crinkles of cold through my inmost blood. For with the words which I read were all mixed up visions of crawling hearses, wails, and lugubrious crapes, and piercing shrieks of madness in strange earthy vaults, and all the mournfulness of the black Vale of Death, and the tragedy of corruption. Twice during the ghostly hours of that night the absolute and undeniable certainty that some presence—some most gashly silent being—stood at my right elbow, so thrilled me, that I leapt to my feet to confront it with clenched fists, and hairs that bristled stiff in horror and frenzy. After that second time I must have fainted; for when it was broad day, I found my dropped head over the file of papers, supported on my arms. And I resolved then never again after sunset to remain in any house: for that night was enough to kill a horse, my good God; and that this is a haunted planet I know.

*   *   *   *   *

What I read in the *Times* was not very definite, for how could it be? but in the main it confirmed inferences which I had myself drawn, and fairly satisfied my mind.

There had been a battle royal in the paper between my collaborator Professor Stanistreet and Dr. Martin Rogers, and never could I have conceived such an indecorous piece of business, men like them calling one another "tyro," "dreamer," and in one place "block-head." Stanistreet denied that the perfumed odour of almonds attributed to the advancing cloud could be due to anything but the excited fancy of the reporting fugitives, because, said he, it was unknown that either Cn, HCn, or K_4FeCn_6 had been given out by volcanoes, and the destructiveness to life of the travelling cloud could only be owing to CO and CO_2. To this Rogers, in an article characterised by extraordinary heat, replied that he could not understand how even a "tyro" (!) in chemical and geological phenomena would venture to rush into print with the statement that HCn had not commonly been given out by volcanoes: that it *had* been, he said, was perfectly certain; though whether it had been or not could not affect the decision of a reasoning mind as to whether it was being: for that cyanogen, as a matter of fact, was not rare in nature, though not directly occurring, being one of the products of the common distillation of pit-coal, and found in roots, peaches, almonds, and many tropical flora; also that it had been actually pointed out as probable by more than one thinker that some salt or salts of Cn, the potassic, or the potassic ferrocyanide, or both, must exist in considerable stores in the earth at volcanic depths. In reply to this, Stanistreet in a two-column article used the word "dreamer," and Rogers, when Berlin had been already silenced, finally replied with his amazing "block-head." But, in my opinion, by far the most learned of the scientific dicta was from the rather unexpected source of Sloggett, of the Dublin Science and Art Department: he, without fuss, accepted the statements of the fugitive eye-witnesses, down to the assertion that the cloud, as it rolled travelling, seemed mixed from its base to the clouds with languid tongues of purple flame, rose-coloured at their edges. This, Sloggett explained, was the characteristic flame of both cyanogen and hydrocyanic acid vapour, which, being inflammable, may have become locally ignited in the passage over cities, and only burned in that limited and languid way on account of the ponderous volumes of carbonic anhydride with which they must, of course, be mixed: the dark empurpled colour was due to the presence of large quantities of the scoriæ of the trappean rocks: basalts, green-stone, trachytes, and the various porphyries. This article was most remarkable for its clear divination, because written so early—not long, in fact, after the cessation of telegraphic communication with Australia and China; and at a date so early Sloggett stated that the character of the devastation not only proved an eruption—another, but far greater Krakatoa—probably in some South Sea region, but indicated that its most active product must be, not CO, but potassic ferrocyanide (K_4FeCn_6), which, undergoing distillation with the products of sulphur in the heat of eruption, produced hydrocyanic acid (HCn); and this volatile acid, he said, remaining in a vaporous state in all climates above a temperature of $26.5°$ C., might involve the entire earth, if the eruption proved sufficiently powerful, travelling chiefly in a direction contrary to the earth's west-to-east motion, the only regions which would certainly be exempt being the colder regions of the Arctic circles, where the vapour of the acid would assume the liquid state, and fall as rain. He did not anticipate that vegetation would be permanently affected, unless the eruption were of inconceivable duration and activity, for though the poisonous quality of hydrocyanic acid consisted in its sudden and complete arrest of oxidation, vegetation had two sources of life—the soil as well as the air; with this exception, all life, down to the lowest evolutionary forms, would disappear (here was the one point in which he was somewhat at fault), until the earth reproduced them. For the rest, he fixed the rate of the on-coming cloud at from 100 to 105 miles a day; and the date of eruption, either the 14th, 15th, or 16th of April—which was either one, two, or three days after arrival of the *Boreal* party at the Pole; and he concluded by saying that, if the facts were as he had stated them, then he could suggest no hiding-place for the race of man, unless such places as mines and tunnels could be made air-tight; nor could even they be of use to any considerable number, except in the event of the poisonous state of the air being of very short duration.

*   *   *   *   *

I had thought of mines before: but in a very languid way, till this article, and other things that I read, as it were struck my brain a slap with the notion. For "there," I said, "if anywhere, shall I find a man. . . ."

*   *   *   *   *

I went out from that building that morning feeling like a man bowed down with age, for the depths of unutterable horror into which I had had glimpses during that one night made me very feeble, and my steps tottered, and my brain reeled.

I got out into Farringdon Street, and at the near Circus, where four streets meet, had under my furthest range of vision nothing but four fields of bodies, bodies, clad in a rag-shop of every faded colour, or half-clad, or not clad at all, actually, in some cases, over-lying one another, as I had seen at Reading, but here with a markedly more skeleton appearance: for I saw the swollen-looking shoulders, sharp hips, hollow abdomens, and stiff bony limbs of people dead from famine, the whole having the grotesque air of some *macabre* battle-field of fallen marionettes. Mixed with these was an extraordinary number of vehicles of all sorts, so that I saw that driving among them would be impracticable, whereas the street which I had taken during the night was fairly clear. I thought a minute what I should do: then went by a parallel back-street, and came to a shop in the Strand, where I hoped to find all the information which I needed about the excavations of the country. The shutters were up, and I did not wish to make any noise among these people, though the morning was bright, it being about ten o'clock, and it was easy to effect entrance, for I saw a crowbar in a big covered furniture-van near. I, therefore, went northward, till I came to the British Museum, the cataloguing-system of which I knew well, and passed in. There was no one at the library-door to bid me stop, and in the great round reading-room not a soul, except one old man with a bag of goître hung at his neck, and spectacles, he lying up a book-ladder near the shelves, a "reader" to the last. I got to the printed catalogues, and for an hour was up-stairs among the dim sacred galleries of this still place, and at the sight of certain Greek and Coptic papyri, charters, seals, had such a dream of this ancient earth, my good God, as even an angel's pen could not express on paper. Afterwards, I went away loaded with half a good hundred-weight of Ordnance-maps, which I had stuffed into a bag found in the cloak-room, with three to-pographical books; I then, at an instrument-maker's in Holborn, got a sextant and theodolite, and at a grocer's near the river put into a sack-bag provisions to last me a week or two; at Blackfriars Bridge wharf-station I found a little sharp white steamer of a few tons, which happily was driven by liquid air, so that I had no troublesome fire to light: and by noon I was cutting my solitary way up the Thames, which flowed as before the ancient Britons were born, and saw it, and built mud-huts there amid the primæval forest; and afterwards the Romans came, and saw it, and called it Tamesis, or Thamesis.

                    *   *   *   *   *

   That night, as I lay asleep on the cabin-cushions of my little boat under the lee of an island at Richmond, I had a clear dream, in which something, or someone, came to me, and asked me a question: for it said: "Why do you go seeking another man?—that you may fall upon him, and kiss him? or that you may fall upon him, and murder him?" And I answered sullenly in my dream: "I would not murder him. I do not wish to murder anyone."

                    *   *   *   *   *

   What was essential to me was to know, with certainty, whether I was really alone: for some instinct began to whisper me: "Find that out: be sure, be sure: for without the assurance you can never be—yourself."
   I passed into the great Midland Canal, and went northward, leisurely advancing, for I was in no hurry. The weather remained very warm, and great

part of the country still dressed in autumn leaves. I have written, I think, of the terrific character of the tempests witnessed in England since my return: well, the calms were just as intense and novel. This observation was forced upon me: and I could not but be surprised. There seemed no middle course now: if there was a wind, it was a storm: if there was not a storm, no leaf stirred, not a roughening zephyr ran the water. I was reminded of maniacs that laugh now, and rave now—but never smile, and never sigh.

On the fourth afternoon I passed by Leicester, and the next morning left my pleasant boat, carrying maps and compass, and at a small station took engine, bound for Yorkshire, where I loitered and idled away two foolish months, sometimes travelling by steam-engine, sometimes by automobile, sometimes by bicycle, and sometimes on foot, till the autumn was quite over.

*   *   *   *   *

There were two houses in London to which especially I had thought to go: one in Harley Street, and one in Hanover Square: but when it came to the point, I would not; and there was a little embowered home in Yorkshire, where I was born, to which I thought to go: but I would not, confining myself for many days to the eastern half of the county.

One morning, while passing on foot along the coast-wall from Bridlington to Flambro', on turning my eyes from the sea, I was confronted by a thing which for a moment struck me with the most profound astonishment. I had come to a mansion, surrounded by trees, three hundred yards from the cliffs: and there, on a path at the bottom of the domain, right before me, was a board marked: "Trespassers will be Prosecuted." At once a mad desire—the first which I had had—to laugh, to roar with laughter, to send wild echoes of merriment clapping among the chalk gullies, and abroad on the morning air, seized upon me: but I kept it under, though I could not help smiling at this poor man, with his little delusion that a part of the earth was his.

Here the cliffs are, I should say, seventy feet high, broken by frequent slips in the upper stratum of clay, and, as I proceeded, climbing always, I encountered some rather formidable gullies in the chalk, down and then up which I had to scramble, till I came to a great mound or barrier, stretching right across the great promontory, and backed by a natural ravine, this, no doubt, having been raised as a rampart by some of those old invading pirate-peoples, who had their hot life-scuffle, and are done now, like the rest. Going on, I came to a bay in the cliff, with a great number of boats lodged on the slopes, some quite high, though the declivities are steep; toward the inner slopes is a lime-kiln which I explored, but found no one there. When I came out on the other side, I saw the village, with an old tower at one end, on a bare stretch of land; and thence, after an hour's rest in the kitchen of a little inn, went out to the coast-guard station, and the lighthouse.

Looking across the sea eastward, the light-keepers here must have seen that thick cloud of convolving browns and purples, perhaps mixed with small tongues of fire, slowly walking the water, its roof in the clouds, upon them: for this headland is in precisely the same longitude as London; and, reckoning from the hour when, as told in the *Times*, the cloud was seen from Dover over Calais, London and Flambro' must have been overtaken soon after three o'clock on the Sunday afternoon, the 25th July. At sight in open daylight of a doom so gloomy—prophesied, but perhaps hoped against to the last, and now come—the light-keepers must have fled howling, supposing them to have so long remained faithful to duty: for here was no one, and in the village very few. In this lighthouse, which is a circular white tower, eighty feet high, on the edge of the cliff, is a book for visitors to sign their names: and I will write something down here in black and white: for the secret is between God only, and me: After reading a few of the names, I took my pencil, and I wrote my name there.

*   *   *   *   *

The reef before the Head stretches out a quarter of a mile, looking bold in the dead low-water that then was, and showing to what extent the sea has pushed back this coast, three wrecks impaled on them, and a big steamer quite near, waiting for the first movements of the already strewn sea to perish. All along the cliff-wall to the bluff crowned by Scarborough Castle northward, and to the low vanishing coast of Holderness southward, appeared those cracks and caves which had brought me here, though there seemed no attempts at barricades; however, I got down a rough slope on the south side to a rude wild beach, strewn with wave-worn masses of chalk: and never did I feel so paltry and short a thing as there, with far-outstretched bays of crags about me, their bluffs encrusted at the base with stale old leprosies of shells and barnacles, and crass algæ-beards, and, higher up, the white cliff all stained and weather-spoiled, the rock in some parts looking quite chalky, and elsewhere gleaming hard and dull like dirty marbles, while in the huge withdrawals of the coast yawn darksome gullies and caverns. Here, in that morning's walk, I saw three little hermit-crabs, a limpet, and two ninnycocks in a pool of weeds under a bearded rock. What astonished me here, and, indeed, everywhere, in London even, and other towns, was the incredible number of birds that strewed the ground, at some points resembling a real rain, birds of almost every sort, including tropic specimens: so that I had to conclude that they, too, had fled before the cloud from country to country, till conquered by weariness and grief, and then by death.

By climbing over rocks thick with periwinkles, and splashing through great sloppy stretches of crinkled sea-weed, which give a raw stench of brine, I entered the first of the gullies: a narrow, long, winding one, with sides polished by the sea-wash, the floor rising inwards. In the dark interior I struck matches, able still to hear from outside the ponderous spasmodic rush and jostle of the sea between the crags of the reef, but now quite faintly. Here, I knew, I could meet only dead men, but urged by some curiosity, I searched to the end, wading in the middle through a three-feet depth of sea-weed twine: but there was no one; and only belemnites and fossils in the chalk. I searched several to the south of the headland, and then went northward past it toward another opening and place of perched boats, called in the map North Landing: where, even now, a distinct smell of fish, left by the old crabbers and herring-fishers, was perceptible. A number of coves and bays opened as I proceeded; a faded green turf comes down in curves at some parts on the cliff-brows, like wings of a young soldier's hair, parted in the middle, and plastered on his brow; isolated chalk-masses are numerous, obelisks, top-heavy columns, bastions; at one point no less than eight headlands stretched to the end of the world before me, each pierced by its arch, Norman or Gothic, in whole or in half; and here again caves, in one of which I found a carpet-bag stuffed with a wet pulp like bread, and, stuck to the rock, a Turkish tarboosh; also, under a limestone quarry, five dead asses: but no man. The east coast had evidently been shunned. Finally, in the afternoon I reached Filey, very tired, and there slept.

*   *   *   *   *

I went onward by train-engine all along the coast to a region of iron-ore, alum, and jet-excavations round Whitby and Middlesborough. By by-ways near the small place of Goldsborough I got down to the shore at Kettleness, and reached the middle of a bay in which is a cave called the Hob-Hole, with excavations all around, none of great depth, made by jet-diggers and quarrymen. In the cave lay a small herd of cattle, though for what purpose put there I cannot guess; and in the jet-excavations I found nothing. A little further south is the chief alum-region, as at Sandsend, but as soon as I saw a works, and the great gap in the ground like a crater, where the lias is quarried, containing only heaps of alum-shale, brushwood-stacks, and piles of cement-nodules extracted from the lias, I concluded that here could have been found no hiding; nor did I purposely visit the others, though I saw two later. From round Whitby, and those rough moors, I went on to Darlington, not far now from my home: but I would not continue that way, and after two days' indecisive lounging, started for Richmond and the lead mines about Arkengarth Dale, near Reeth. Here begins a region of mountain, various with glens, fells, screes, scars, swards, becks, passes, villages, river-heads, and dales. Some of the faces which I saw in it almost seemed to speak to me in a broad dialect which I knew. But they were not numerous in proportion: for all this countryside must have had its population multiplied by at least some hundreds; and the villages had rather the air of Danube, Levant, or Spanish villages. In one, named Marrick, I saw that the street had become the scene either of a great battle or a great massacre; and soon I was everywhere coming upon men and women, English and foreign, dead from violence: cracked heads, wounds, unhung jaws, broken limbs, and so on. Instead of going direct to the mines from Reeth, that waywardness which now rules my mind, as squalls an abandoned boat, took me somewhat further south-west to the village of Thwaite, which I actually could not enter, so occupied with dead was every spot on which the eye rested a hundred yards about it. Not far from here I turned up, on foot now, a very steep, stony road to the right, which leads over the Buttertubs Pass into Wensleydale, the day being very warm and bright, with large clouds that looked like lakes of molten silver giving off grey fumes in their centre, casting moody shadows over the swardy

dale, which below Thwaite expands, showing Muker two miles off, the largest
village of Upper Swaledale. Soon, climbing, I could look down upon miles of
Swaledale and the hills beyond, a rustic panorama of glens and grass, river and
cloud-shadow, and there was something of lightness in my step that fair day,
for I had left all my maps and things, except one, at Reeth, to which I meant to
return, and the earth, which is very good, was—mine. The ascent was rough,
and also long: but if I paused and looked behind—I saw, I saw. Man's notion of
a Heaven, a Paradise, reserved for the spirits of the good, clearly arose from
impressions which the earth made upon his mind: for no Paradise can be fairer
than this; just as his notion of a Hell arose from the squalid mess into which his
own foolish habits of thought and action turned this Paradise. At least, so it
struck me then: and, thinking it, there was a hiss in my breath, and as I went
up into what more and more acquired the character of a mountain-pass, with
points of almost Alpine savagery: for after I had skirted the edge of a deep glen
on the left, the slopes changed in character, heather was on the mountain-
sides, a fretting beck sent up its noise, then screes, and scars, and a considerable waterfall, and a landscape of crags; and lastly a broad and rather desolate
summit, palpably nearer the clouds.

*   *   *   *   *

Five days later I was at the mines: and here I first saw that wide-spread
scene of horror with which I have since become familiar. The story of six out of
ten of them all is the same, and short: selfish "owners," an ousted world, an
easy bombardment, and the destruction of all concerned, before the arrival of
the cloud in many cases. About some of the Durham pit-mouths I have been
given the impression that the human race lay collected there; and that the notion of hiding himself in a mine must have occurred to every man alive, and
sent him thither.

In these lead mines, as in most vein-mining, there are more shafts than in
collieries, and hardly any attempt at artificial ventilation, except at rises,
winzes and cul-de-sacs. I found accordingly that, though their depth does not
exceed three hundred feet, suffocation must often have anticipated the other
dreaded death. In nearly every shaft, both up-take and down-take, was a ladder, either of the mine, or of the fugitives, and I was able to descend without
difficulty, having dressed myself in a house at the village in a check flannel
shirt, a pair of two-buttoned trousers with circles of leather at the knees, thick
boots, and a miner's hat, having a leather socket attached to it, into which fitted a straight handle from a cylindrical candlestick; with this light, and also a
Davy-lamp, which I carried about with me for a good many months, I lived for
the most part in the deeps of the earth, searching for the treasure of a life, to
find everywhere, in English duckies and guggs, Pomeranian women in gaudy
stiff cloaks, the Walachian, the Mameluk, the Khirgiz, the Bonze, the Imaum,
and almost every type of man.

*   *   *   *   *

One most brilliant autumn day I walked by the village market-cross at Barnard, come at last, but with a tenderness in my heart, and a reluctance, to where I was born; for I said I would go and see my sister Ada, and—the other old one. I leaned and loitered a long time on the bridge, gazing up to the craggy height, which is heavy with waving wood, and crowned by the Castle-tower, the Tees sweeping round the mountain-base, smooth here and sunlit, but a mile down, where I wished to go, but would not, brawling bedraggled and lacerated, like a sweet strumpet, all shallow among rocks under reaches of shadow—the shadow of Rokeby Woods. I climbed very leisurely up the hillside, having in my hand a bag with a meal, and up the stair in the wall to the top I went, where there is no parapet, but a massiveness of wall that precludes danger; and here in my miner's attire I sat three hours, brooding sleepily upon the scene of lush umbrageous old wood that marks the way the river takes, from Marwood Chase up above, and where the rapid Balder bickers in, down to bowery Rokeby, touched now with autumn; the thickness of trees lessening away toward the uplands, where there are far etherealised stretches of fields within hedgerows, and in the sunny mirage of the farthest azure remoteness hints of lonesome moorland. It was not till near three that I went down along the river, then, near Rokeby, traversing the old meadow, and ascending the old hill: and there, as of old, was the little black square with yellow letters on the gate-wall:

HUNT HILL HOUSE.

No part, no house, I believe, of this countryside was empty of strange corpses: and they were in Hunt Hill, too. I saw three in the weedy plot to the right of the garden-path, where once the hawthorn and lilac tree had grown from well-rollered grass, and in the little bush-wilderness to the left, which was always a wilderness, one more: and in the breakfast-room, to the right of the hall, three; and in the new wooden clinker-built attachment opening upon the breakfast-room, two, half under the billiard-table; and in her room overlooking the porch on the first floor, the long thin form of my mother on her bed, with crushed-in left temple, and at the foot of the bed, face-downward on the floor, black-haired Ada in a night-dress.

Of all the men and women who died, they two alone had burying. For I digged a hole with the stable-spade under the front lilac; and I wound them in the sheets, foot and form and head; and, not without throes and qualms, I bore and buried them there.

*   *   *   *   *

Some time passed after this before the long, multitudinous, and perplexing task of visiting the mine-regions again claimed me. I found myself at a place called Ingleborough, which is a big table-mountain, with a top of fifteen to twenty acres, from which the sea is visible across Lancashire to the west; and in the sides of this strange hill are a number of caves which I searched during

three days, sleeping in a garden-shed at a very rural and flower-embowered village, for every room in it was thronged, a place marked Clapham in the chart,
in Clapdale, which latter is a dale penetrating the slopes of the mountain: and
there I found by far the greatest of the caves which I saw, having ascended a
path from the village to a hollow between two grass slopes, where there is a
beck, and so entering an arch to the left, screened by trees, into the limestone
cliff. The passage narrows pretty rapidly inwards, and I had not proceeded two
yards before I saw the clear traces of a great battle here. All this region had, in
fact, been invaded, for the cave must have been famous, though I did not remember it myself, and for some miles round the dead were pretty frequent,
making the immediate approach to the cave a matter for care, if the foot was to
be saved from pollution. It is clear that there had been an iron gate across the
entrance, that within this a wall had been built across, shutting in I do not
know how many, perhaps one or two, perhaps hundreds: and both gate and
wall had been stormed and broken down, for there still were the sledges and
rocks which, without doubt, had done it. I had a lamp, and at my forehead the
lighted candle, and I went on quickly, seeing it useless now to choose my steps
where there was no choice, through a passage incrusted, roof and sides, with a
scabrous petrified lichen, the roof low for some ninety yards, covered with
down-looking cones, like an inverted forest of children's toy-trees. I then came
to a round hole, apparently artificial, opening through a curtain of stalagmitic
formation into a great cavern beyond, which was quite animated and festal
with flashes, sparkles, and diamond-lustres, hung in their myriads upon a
movement of the eye, these being produced by large numbers of snowy wet stalagmites, very large and high, down the centre of which ran a continuous long
lane of clothes and hats and faces; with hasty reluctant feet I somehow passed
over them, the cave all the time widening, thousands of stalactites appearing
on the roof of every size, from virgin's breast to giant's club, and now everywhere the wet drip, drip, as it were a populous busy bazaar of perspiring brows
and hurrying feet, in which the only business is to drip. Where stalactite meets
stalagmite there are pillars: where stalactite meets stalactite in fissures long or
short there are elegances, flimsy draperies, delicate fantasies; there were also
pools of water in which hung heads and feet, and there were vacant spots at
outlying spaces, where the arched roof, which continually heightened itself,
was reflected in the chill gleam of the floor. Suddenly, the roof came down, the
floor went up, and they seemed to meet before me; but looking, I found a low
opening, through which, drawing myself on the belly over slime for some yards
in repulsive proximity to dead personalities, I came out upon a floor of sand
and pebbles under a long dry tunnel, arched and narrow, grim and dull, without stalactites, suggestive of monks, and catacomb-vaults, and the route to the
grave; and here the dead were much fewer, proving either that the general
mob had not had time to penetrate so far inward, or else that those within, if
they were numerous, had gone out to defend, or to harken to, the storm of
their citadel. This passage led me into an open space, the grandest of all, loftily
vaulted, full of genie riches and buried treasures of light, the million-fold *en-*

semble of lustres dancing schottishe with the eye, as it moved or was still: this place, I should guess, being quite half a mile from the entrance. My prying lantern showed me here only nineteen dead, men of various nations, and at the far end two holes in the floor, large enough to admit the body, through which from below came up a sound of falling water. Both of these holes, I could see, had been filled with cement concrete—wisely, I fancy, for a current of air from somewhere seemed to be now passing through them: and this would have resulted in the death of the hiders. Both, however, of the fillings had been broken through, one partially, the other wholly, by the ignorant, I presume, who thought to hide in a secret place yet beyond, where they may have believed, on seeing the artificial work, that others were. I had my ear a long time at one of these openings, listening to that mysterious chant down below in a darkness most murky and dismal; and afterwards, spurred by the stubborn will which I had to be thorough, I went back, took a number of outer robes from the bodies, tied them well together, then one end round the nearest pillar, and having put my mouth to the hole, calling: "Anyone? Anyone?" let myself down by the rope of garments, the candle at my head: I had not, however, descended far into those mournful shades, when my right foot plunged into water: and instantly the feeling of terror pierced me that all the evil things in the universe were at my leg to drag me down to Hell: and I was up quicker than I went down: nor did my flight cease till, with a sigh of deliverance, I found myself in open air.

*   *   *   *   *

After this, seeing that the autumn warmth was passing away, I set myself with more system to my task, and within the next six months worked with steadfast will, and strenuous assiduity, seeking, not indeed for a man in a mine, but for some evidence of the possibility that a man might be alive, visiting in that time Northumberland and Durham, Fife and Kinross, South Wales and Monmouthshire, Cornwall and the Midlands, the lead mines of Derbyshire, of Allandale and other parts of Northumberland, of Alston Moor and other parts of Cumberland, of Arkendale and other parts of Yorkshire, of the western part of Durham, of Salop, of Cornwall, of the Mendip Hills of Somersetshire, of Flint, Cardigan, and Montgomery, of Lanark and Argyll, of the Isle of Man, of Waterford and Down; I have gone down the 360-ft. Grand Pipe iron ladder of the abandoned graphite-mine at Barrowdale in Cumberland, half-way up a mountain 2,000 feet high; and visited where cobalt and manganese ore is mined in pockets at the Foel Hiraeddog mine near Rhyl in Flintshire, and the lead and copper Newton Stewart workings in Galloway; the Bristol coal-fields, and the mines of South Staffordshire, where, as in Somerset, Gloucester, and Shropshire, the veins are thin, and the mining-system is the "long-wall," whereas in the North, and Wales, the system is the "pillar-and-stall"; I have visited the open workings for iron ores of Northamptonshire, and the underground stone-quarries, and the underground slate-quarries, with their alternate pillars and chambers, in the Festiniog district of North Wales; also the rock-salt workings; the tin, copper and cobalt workings of Cornwall; and where the minerals were brought to the surface on the backs of men, and where they were brought by adit-levels provided with rail-roads, and where, as in old Cornish mines, there are two ladders in the shaft, moved up and down alternately, see-saw, and by skipping from one to the other at right moments you ascended or descended, and where the drawing-up is by a gin or horse-whinn, with vertical drum; the Tisbury and Chilmark quarries in Wiltshire, the Spinkwell and Cliffwood quarries in Yorkshire; and every tunnel, and every recorded hole: for something urged within me, saying: "You must be *sure* first, or you can never be—yourself."

*   *   *   *   *

At the Farnbrook Coal-field, in the Red Colt Pit, my inexperience nearly ended my life: for though I had a minute theoretical knowledge of all British workings, I was, in my practical relation to them, like a man who has learnt seamanship on shore. At this place the dead were accumulated, I think beyond precedent, the dark plain around for at least three miles being as strewn as a reaped field with stacks, and, near the bank, much more strewn than stack-fields, filling the only house within sight of the pit-mouth—the small place provided for the company's officials—and even lying over the great mountain-heap of wark, composed of the shale and *débris* of the working. Here I arrived on the morning of the 15th December, to find that, unlike the others, there was here no rope-ladder or other contrivance fixed by the fugitives in the ventilating-shaft, which, usually, is not very deep, being also the pumping-shaft, containing a plug-rod at one end of the beam-engine which works the pumps; but looking down the shaft, I discerned a vague mass of clothes, and afterwards a thing that could only be a rope-ladder, which a batch of the fugitives, by hanging to it their united weight, must have dragged down upon themselves, to prevent the descent of yet others. My only way of going down, therefore, was by the pit-mouth, and as this was an important place, after some hesitation I decided, very rashly. First I provided for my coming up again by getting a great coil of half-inch rope, which I found in the bailiff's office, probably 130 fathoms long, rope at most mines being so plentiful, that it almost seemed as if each fugitive had provided himself in that way. This length of rope I threw over the beam of the beam-engine in the bite where it sustains the rod, and paid one end down the shaft, till both were at the bottom: in this way I could come up, by tying one rope-end to the rope-ladder, hoisting it, fastening the other end below, and climbing the ladder; and then I set to work to light the pit-mouth engine-fire to effect my descent. This done, I started the engine, and brought up the cage from the bottom, the 300 yards of wire-rope winding with a quaint deliberateness round the drum, reminding me of a camel's nonchalant leisurely obedience. When I saw the four meeting chains of the cage-roof emerge, the pointed roof, and two-sided frame, I stopped the ascent, and next attached to the knock-off gear a long piece of twine which I had provided; carried the other end to the cage, in which I had five companions; lit my hat-candle, which was my test for choke-damp, and the Davy; and without the least reflection, pulled the string. That hole was 900 feet deep. First the cage gave a little up-leap, and then began to descend—quite normally, I thought, though the candle at once went out—nor had I the least fear; a strong current of air, indeed, blew up the shaft: but that happens in shafts. *This* current, however, soon became too vehemently boisterous for anything: I saw the lamp-light struggle, the dead cheeks quiver, I heard the cage-shoes go singing down the wire-rope guides, and quicker we went, and quicker, that facile descent of Avernus, slipping lightly, then raging, with sparks at the shoes and guides, and a hurricane in my ears and eyes and mouth. When we bumped upon the "dogs" at the bottom, I was tossed a foot upwards with the stern-faced others, and then lay among them in the eight-foot space without consciousness.

It was only when I sat, an hour later, disgustedly reflecting on this incident, that I remembered that there was always some "hand-working" of the engine during the cage-descents, an engineman reversing the action by a handle at every stroke of the piston, to prevent bumping. However, the only permanent injury was to the lamp: and I found many others inside.

I got out into the coal-hole, a large black hall 70 feet square by 15 high, the floor paved with iron sheets; there were some little holes round the wall, dug for some purpose which I never could discover, some waggons full of coal and shale standing about, and all among the waggons, and on them, and under them, bodies, clothes. I got a new lamp, pouring in my own oil, and went down a long steep ducky-road, very rough, with numerous rollers, over which ran a rope to the pit-mouth for drawing up the waggons; and in the sides here, at regular intervals, man-holes, within which to rescue one's self from down-tearing waggons; and within these man-holes, here and there, a dead, and in others every sort of food, and at one place on the right a high dead heap, the air here hot at 64 or 65 degrees, and getting hotter with the descent.

The ducky led me down into a standing—a space with a turn-table—of unusual size, which I made my base of operations for exploring. Here was a very considerable number of punt-shaped putts on carriages, and also waggons, such as took the new-mined coal from putt to pit-mouth; and raying out from this open standing, several avenues, some ascending as guggs, some descending as dipples, and the dead here all arranged in groups, the heads of this group pointing up this gugg, of that group down toward that twin-way, of that other down that dipple, and the central space, where weighing was done, almost empty: and the darksome silence of this deep place, with all these multitudes, I found extremely gravitating and hypnotic, drawing me, too, into their great Passion of Silence in which they lay, all, all, so fixed and veteran; and at one time I fell a-staring, nearer perhaps to death and the empty Gulf than I knew; but I said I would be strong, and not sink into their habit of stillness, but let them keep to their own way, and follow their own fashion, and I would keep to my own way, and follow my own fashion, nor yield to them, though I was but one against many; and I roused myself with a shudder; and setting to work, caught hold of the drum-chain of a long gugg, and planting my feet in the chogg-holes in which rested the wheels of the putt-carriages that used to come roaring down the gugg, I got up, stooping under a roof only three feet high, till I came, near the end of the ascent, upon the scene of another battle: for in this gugg about fifteen of the mine-hands had clubbed to wall themselves in, and had done it, and I saw them lie there all by themselves through the broken cement, with their bare feet, trousers, naked bodies all black, visage all fierce and wild, the grime still streaked with sweat-furrows, the candle in their rimless hats, and, outside, their own "getting" mattocks and boring-irons to besiege them. From the bottom of this gugg I went along a very undulating twin-way, into which, every thirty yards or so, opened one of those steep putt-ways which they called topples, the twin-ways having plates of about 2½ ft. gauge for the putts from the headings, or workings, above to come down upon, full of coal and shale: and all about here, in twin-way and topples, were ends and corners, and not one had been left without its walling-in, and only one was then intact, some, I fancied, having been broken open by their own builders at the spur of suffocation, or hunger; and the one intact I broke into with a mattock—it was only a thin cake of plaster, but air-tight—and in a space not seven feet long behind it I found the very ill-smelling corpse of a carting-boy, with guss and tugger at his feet, and the pad which protected his head in pushing the putts, and a great heap of loaves, sardines, and bottled beer against the walls, and five or six mice that suddenly pitched screaming through the opening which I made, greatly startling me, there being of dead mice an extraordinary number in all this mine-region. I went back to the standing, and at one point in the ground, where there was a windlass and chain, lowered myself down a "cut"—a small pit sunk perpendicularly to a lower coal-stratum, and here, almost thinking I could hear the perpetual rat-rat of notice once exchanged between the putt-boys below and the windlass-boys above, I proceeded down a dipple to another place like a standing, for in this mine there were six, or perhaps seven, veins: and there immediately I came upon the acme of the horrible drama of this Tartarus, for all here was not merely crowded, but, at some points, a packed congestion of flesh, giving out a strong smell of the peach, curiously mixed with the stale coal-odour of the pit, for here ventilation must have been limited; and a large number of these masses had been shot down by only three hands, as I found: for through three hermetical holes in a plaster-wall, built across a large gugg, projected a little the muzzles of three rifles, which must have glutted themselves with slaughter; and when, after a horror of disgust, having swum as it were through a dead sea, I got to the wall, I peeped from a small clear space before it through a hole, and made out a man, two youths in their teens, two women, three girls, and piles of cartridges and provisions; the hole had no doubt been broken from within at the spur of suffocation, when the poison must have entered; and I conjectured that here must be the mine-owner, director, manager, or something of that sort, with his family. In another dipple-region, when I had re-ascended to a higher level, I nearly fainted before I could retire from the commencement of a region of after-damp, where there had been an explosion, the bodies lying all hairless, devastated, and grotesque.

But I did not desist from searching every other quarter, no momentary work, for not till near six did I go up by the pumping-shaft rope-ladder.

*   *   *   *   *

One day, standing in that wild region of bare rock and sea, called Corn-wall Point, whence one can see the crags and postillion wild rocks where Land's End dashes out into the sea, and all the wild blue sea between, and not a house in sight, save the chimney of some little mill-like place peeping be-tween the rocks inland—on that day I finished what I may call my official search.

In going away from that place, walking northward, I came upon a lonely house by the sea, a very beautiful house, made, it was clear, by an artist, of the bungalow type, with an exquisitely sea-side expression. I went to it, and found its special feature a spacious loggia or verandah, sheltered by the overhanging upper story. Up to the first floor, the exterior is of stone in rough-hewn blocks with a distinct batter, while extra protection from weather is afforded by green slating above. The roofs, of low pitch, are also covered with green slates, and a feeling of strength and repose is heightened by the very long horizontal lines. At one end of the loggia is a hexagonal turret, opening upon the loggia, con-taining a study or nook. In front, the garden slopes down to the sea, sur-rounded by an architectural sea-wall; and in this place I lived three weeks. It was the house of the poet Machen, whose name, when I saw it, I remembered very well, and he had married a very beautiful young girl of eighteen, obviously Spanish, who lay on the bed in the large bright bedroom to the right of the log-gia, on her left exposed breast being a baby with an india-rubber comforter in its mouth, both mother and child wonderfully preserved, she still quite lovely, white brow under low curves of black hair. The poet, strange to say, had not died with them, but sat in the sitting-room behind the bedroom in a long loose silky-grey jacket, at his desk—actually writing a poem! writing, I could see, fu-riously fast, the place all littered with the written leaves—at three o'clock in the morning, when, as I knew, the cloud overtook this end of Cornwall, and stopped him, and put his head to rest on the desk; and the poor little wife must have got sleepy, waiting for it to come, perhaps sleepless for many long nights before, and gone to bed, he perhaps promising to follow in a minute to die with her, but bent upon finishing that poem, and writing feverishly on, running a race with the cloud, thinking, no doubt, "just two couplets more," till the thing came, and put his head to rest on the desk, poor carle: and I do not know that I ever encountered aught so complimentary to my race as this dead poet Ma-chen, and his race with the cloud: for it is clear now that the better kind of those poet men did not write to please the vague inferior tribes who might read them, but to deliver themselves of the divine warmth that thronged in their bosom; and if all the readers were dead, still they would have written; and for God to read they wrote. At any rate, I was so pleased with these poor people, that I stayed with them three weeks, sleeping under blankets on a couch in the drawing-room, a place full of lovely pictures and faded flowers, like all the

house: for I would not touch the young mother to remove her. And finding on
Machen's desk a big note-book with soft covers, dappled red and yellow, yet
not written in, I took it, and a pencil, and in the little turret-nook wrote day
after day for hours this account of what has happened, nearly as far as it has
now gone. And I think I may continue to write it, for I find in it a strange consolation, and companionship.

*   *   *   *   *

In the Severn Valley, somewhere in the plain between Gloucester and
Cheltenham, in a rather lonely spot, I at that time travelling on a tricycle-
motor, I spied a curious erection, and went to it. I found it of considerable size,
perhaps fifty feet square, and thirty high, made of pressed bricks, the perfectly
flat roof, too, of brick, and not one window, and only one door: this door,
which I found open, was rimmed all round its slanting rims with india-rubber,
and when closed must have been perfectly air-tight. Just inside I came upon
fifteen English people of the dressed class, except two, who were evidently
bricklayers: six ladies, and nine men: and at the further end, two more, men,
who had their throats cut; along one wall, from end to end were provisions;
and I saw a chest full of mixed potassic chlorate and black oxide of manganese,
with an apparatus for heating it, and producing oxygen—a foolish thing, for
additional oxygen could not alter the quantity of breathed carbonic anhydride,
which is a direct narcotic poison. Whether the two with cut throats had sacri-
ficed themselves for the others when breathing difficulties commenced, or been
killed by the others, was not clear. When they could bear it no longer, they
must have finally opened the door, hoping that by then, after the passage of so
many days perhaps, the outer air would be harmless, and so met their death. I
believe that this erection must have been run up by their own hands under the
direction of the two bricklayers, for they could not, I suppose, have got workmen, except on the condition of the workmen's admission: on which condition
they would naturally employ as few as possible.

In general, I observed that the rich must have been more urgent and earnest in seeking escape than the others: for the poor realised only the near and
visible, lived in to-day, and cherished the always-false notion that to-morrow
would be just like to-day. In an out-patients' waiting-room, for instance, in the
Gloucester infirmary, I chanced to see an astonishing thing: five bodies of poor
old women in shawls, come to have their ailments seen-to on the day of doom;
and these, I concluded, had been unable to realise that anything would really
happen to the daily old earth which they knew, and had walked with assurance
on: for if everybody was to die, they must have thought, who would preach in
the Cathedral on Sunday evenings?—so they could not have believed. In an
adjoining room sat an old doctor at a table, the stethoscope-tips still clinging in
his ears: a woman with bared chest before him; and I thought to myself: "Well,
this old man, too, died doing his work. . . ."

In this same infirmary there was one surgical ward—for in a listless mood I
went over it—where the patients had died, not of the poison, nor of suffoca-

tion, but of hunger: for the doctors, or someone, had made the long room air-tight, double-boarding the windows, felting the doors, and then locking them outside; they themselves must have perished before their precations for the imprisoned patients were complete: for I found a heap of maimed shapes, mere skeletons, crowded round the door within. I knew very well that they had not died of the cloud-poison, for the pestilence of the ward was unmixed with that odour of peach which did not fail to have more or less embalming effects upon the bodies which it saturated. I rushed stifling from that place; and thinking it a pity, and a danger, that such a horror should be, I at once set to work to gather combustibles to burn the building to the ground.

It was while I sat in an arm-chair in the street the next afternoon, smoking, and watching the flames of this structure, that something was suddenly born in me, something from the lowest Hell: and I smiled a smile that never yet man smiled. And I said: "I will burn, I will burn: I will return to London. . . ."

*　　*　　*　　*　　*

While I was on this eastward journey, stopping for the night at the town of Swindon, I had a dream: for I dreamed that a little brown bald old man, with a bent back, whose beard ran in one thin streamlet of silver from his chin to trail along the ground, said to me: "You think that you are alone on the earth, its sole Despot: well, have your fling: but as sure as God lives, as God lives, as God lives"—he repeated it six times—"sooner or later, later or sooner, you will meet another. . . ."

And I started from that frightful sleep with the brow of a corpse, wet with sweat. . . .

*　　*　　*　　*　　*

I returned to London on the 29th of March, arriving within a hundred yards of the Northern Station one windy dark evening about eight, where I alighted, and walked to Euston Road, then eastward along it, till I came to a shop which I knew to be a jeweller's, though it was too dark to see any painted words. The door, to my annoyance, was locked, like nearly all the shop-doors in London: I therefore went looking near the ground and into a cart, for something heavy, very soon saw a labourer's ponderous boots, cut one from the shrivelled foot, and set to beat at the glass till it came raining; then knocked away the bottom splinters, and entered.

No horrors now at that clatter of broken glass; no sick qualms; my pulse steady; my head high; my step royal; my eye cold and calm.

*　　*　　*　　*　　*

Eight months previously, I had left London a poor burdened, cowering wight. I could scream with laughter now at that folly! But it did not last long. I returned to it—the Sultan.

*　　*　　*　　*　　*

No private place being near, I was going to that hotel in Bloomsbury: but though I knew that numbers of candlesticks would be there, I was not sure that I should find sufficient: for I had acquired the habit within the past few months of sleeping with at least sixty lighted about me, and their form, pattern, style, age, and material was of no small importance. I selected ten from the broken shop, eight gold and silver, and two of old of ecclesiastical brass, and having made a bundle, went out, found a bicycle at the Metropolitan Station, pumped it, tied my bundle to the handle-bar, and set off riding. But since I was too lazy to walk, I should certainly have procured some other means of travelling, for I had not gone ten jolted and creaking yards, when something went snap—it was a front fork—and I found myself half on the ground, and half across the bare knees of a Highland soldier. I flew with a shower of kicks upon the foolish thing: but that booted nothing; and this was my last attempt in that way in London, the streets being in an unsuitable condition.

All that dismal night it blew great guns: and during nearly three weeks, till London was no more, there was a storm, with hardly a lull, that seemed to be-howl her destruction.

*   *   *   *   *

I slept in a a room on the second-floor of a Bloomsbury hotel that night; and waking the next day at ten, ate with accursed shiverings in the cold banqueting-room; went out then, and under drear low skies walked a long way to the West district, accompanied all the time by a sound of flapping flags—fluttering robes and rags—and grotesquely grim glimpses of decay. It was pretty cold, and though I was warmly clad, the base *bizarrerie* of the European clothes which I wore had become a perpetual offence and mockery in my eyes: at the first moment, therefore, I set out whither I knew that I should find such clothes as a man might wear: to the Turkish Embassy in Bryanston Square.

I found it open, and all the house, like most other houses, almost carpeted with dead forms. I had been acquainted with Redouza Pasha, and cast an eye about for him amid that invasion of veiled hanums, fierce-looking Caucasians in skins of beasts, a Sheik-ul-Islam in green cloak, a khalifa, three emirs in cashmere turbans, two tziganes, their gaudy brown mortality more glaringly abominable than even the Western's. I could recognise no Redouza here: but the stair was fairly clear, and I soon came to one of those boudoirs which sweetly recall the deep-buried inner seclusion and dim sanctity of the Eastern home: a door encrusted with mother-of-pearl, sculptured ceiling, candles clustered in tulips and roses of opal, a brazen brasero, and, all in disarray, the silken chemise, the long winter-cafetan doubled with furs, costly cabinets, sachets of aromas, babooshes, stuffs of silk. When, after two hours, I went from the house, I was bathed, anointed, combed, scented, and robed.

*   *   *   *   *

I have said to myself: "I will ravage and riot in my Kingdoms. I will rage like the Cæsars, and be a withering blight where I pass like Sennacherib, and wallow in soft delights like Sardanapalus. I will build me a palace, vast as a city, in which to strut and parade my Monarchy before the Heavens, with stones of pure molten gold, and rough frontispiece of diamond, and cupola of amethyst, and pillars of pearl. For there were many men to the eye: but there was One only, really: and I was he. And always I knew it:—some faintest secret whisper which whispered me: 'You are the Arch-one, the *motif* of the world, Adam, and the rest of men not much.' And they are gone—all! all!—as no doubt they deserved: and I, as was meet, remain. And there are wines, and opiums, and haschish; and there are oils, and spices, fruits and bivalves, and soft-breathing Cyclades, and scarlet luxurious Orients. I will be restless and turbulent in my territories: and again, I will be languishing and fond. I will say to my soul: 'Be Full.'"

*   *   *   *   *

I watch my mind, as in the old days I would watch a new precipitate in a test-tube, to see into what sediment it would settle.

I am very averse to trouble of any sort, so that the necessity for the simplest manual operations will rouse me to indignation: but if a thing will contribute largely to my ever-growing voluptuousness, I will undergo a considerable amount of labour to accomplish it, though without steady effort, being liable to side-winds and whims, and purposeless relaxations.

In the country I became very irritable at the need which confronted me of occasionally cooking some green vegetable—the only item of food which it was necessary to take some trouble over: for all meats, and many fish, some quite delicious, I find already prepared in forms which will remain good probably a century after my death, should I ever die. In Gloucester, however, I found peas, asparagus, olives, and other greens, already prepared to be eaten without base cares: and these, I now see, exist everywhere in stores so vast comparatively to the needs of a single man, that may be called infinite. Everything, in fact, is infinite compared with my needs. I take my meals, therefore, without more trouble than a man who had to carve his joint, or chicken: though even that little I sometimes find most irksome. There remains the detestable degradation of lighting fires for warmth, which I have occasionally to do: for the fire at the hotel invariably goes out while I sleep. But that is an inconvenience of this vile northern island only, to which I shall soon bid eternal glad farewells.

During the afternoon of my second day in London, I sought out a strong petrol motor in Holborn, overhauled and oiled it a little, and set off over Blackfriars Bridge, making for Woolwich through that other more putrid London on the south river-side. One after the other, I connected, as I came upon them, two drays, a cab, and a private carriage, to my motor in line behind, having cut away the withered horses, and using the reins, chain-harness, &c., as impromptu couplings. And with this novel train, I rumbled eastward.

Half-way I happened to look at my old silver chronometer of *Boreal*-days, which I have kept carefully wound—and how I can be still thrown into these sudden frantic agitations by a nothing, a *nothing*, my good God! I do not know. This time it was only the simple fact that the hands chanced to point to 3.10

P.M., the precise moment at which all the clocks of London had stopped—for each town has its thousand weird fore-fingers, pointing, pointing still, to the moment of doom. In London it was 3.10 on a Sunday afternoon. I first noticed it going up the river on the face of the "Big Ben" of the Parliament-house, and I now find that they all, all, have this 3.10 mania, time-keepers still, but keepers of the end of Time, fixedly noting for ever and ever that one moment. The cloud-mass of fine penetrating *scoriæ* must have instantly stopped their works, and they had fallen silent with man. But in their insistence upon this particular minute I had found something so hideously solemn, yet mock-solemn, personal, and as it were addressed to *me*, that when my own watch dared to point to the same moment, I was thrown into one of those sudden, paroxysmal, panting turmoils of mind, half rage, half horror, which have hardly once visited me since I left the *Boreal*. On the morrow, alas, another awaited me; and again on the second morrow after.

*   *   *   *   *

My train was execrably slow, and not until after five did I arrive at the entrance-gates of the Woolwich Royal Arsenal; and seeing that it was too late to work, I uncoupled the motor, and leaving the others there, turned back; but overtaken by lassitude, I procured candles, stopped at the Greenwich Observatory, and in that old dark pile, remained for the night, listening to a furious storm. But, a-stir by eight the next morning, I got back by ten to the Arsenal, and proceeded to analyse that vast and multiple entity. Many parts of it seemed to have been abandoned in undisciplined haste, and in the Cap Factory, which I first entered, I found tools by which to effect entry into any desired part. My first search was for time-fuses of good type, of which I needed two or three thousand, and after a wearily long time found a great number symmetrically arranged in rows in a range of buildings called the Ordnance Store Department. I then descended, walked back to the wharf, brought up my train, and began to lower the fuses in bag-fulls by ropes through a shoot, letting go each rope as the fuses reached the cart. However, on winding one fuse, I found that the mechanism would not go, choked with scoriæ; and I had to resign myself to the task of opening and dusting every one: a wretched labour in which I spent that day, like a workman. But about four I threw them to the devil, having done two hundred odd, and then hummed back in the motor to London.

*   *   *   *   *

That same evening at six I paid, for the first time, a visit to my old self in Harley Street. It was getting dark, and a bleak storm that hooted like whooping-cough swept the world. At once I saw that even *I* had been invaded: for my door swung open, banging, a lowered catch preventing it from slamming; in the passage the car-lamp shewed me a young man who seemed a Jew, seated as if in sleep with dropped head, a back-tilted silk-hat pressed down upon his head to the ears; and lying on his face, or back, or side, six more, one a girl with Arlesienne head-dress, one a negress, one a Deal lifeboat's-man, and three of uncertain race; the first room—the waiting-room—is much more numerously occupied, though there still, on the table, lies the volume of *Punch*, the *Gentlewoman*, and the book of London views in heliograph. Behind this, descending two steps, is the study and consulting-room, and there, as ever, the revolving-cover oak writing-desk: but on my little shabby-red sofa, a large lady much too big for it, in shimmering brown silk, round her left wrist a *trousseau* of massive gold trinkets, her head dropped right back, almost severed by an infernal gash from the throat. Here were two old silver candle-sticks, which I lit, and went up-stairs: in the drawing-room sat my old house-keeper, placidly dead in a rocking-chair, her left hand pressing down a batch of the open piano-keys, among many strangers. But she was very good: she had locked my bedroom against intrusion; and as the door stands across a corner behind a green-baize curtain, it had not been seen, or, at least, not forced. I did not know where the key might be, but a few thumps with my back drove it open: and there lay my bed intact, and everything tidy. This was a strange coming-back to it, Adam.

But what intensely interested me in that room was a big thing standing at the maroon-and-gold wall between wardrobe and dressing-table—that gilt frame—and that man painted within it there. It was myself in oils, done by—I forget his name now: a towering celebrity he was, and rather a close friend of mine at one time. In a studio in St. John's Wood, I remember, he did it; and many people said that it was quite a great work of art. I suppose I was standing before it quite thirty minutes that night, holding up the bits of candle, lost in wonder, in amused contempt at that thing there. It is I, certainly: that I must admit. There is the high-curving brow—really a King's brow, after all, it strikes me now—and that vacillating look about the eyes and mouth which used to make my sister Ada say: "Adam is weak and luxurious." Yes, that is wonderfully done, the eyes, that dear, vacillating look of mine; for although it is rather a staring look, yet one can almost see the dark pupils stir from side to side: very well done. And there is the longish face; and the rather thin, stuck-out moustache, shewing both lips which pout a bit; and there is the nearly black hair; and there is the rather visible paunch; and there is, oh good Heaven, the neat pink cravat—ah, it must have been *that*—*the cravat*—that made me burst into laughter so loud, mocking, and uncontrollable the moment my eye rested there! "Adam Jeffson," I muttered reproachfully when it was over, "could that poor thing in the frame have been *you?*"

I cannot quite state why the tendency toward Orientalism—Oriental dress—all the manner of an Oriental monarch—has taken full possession of me: but so it is: for surely I am hardly any longer a Western, "modern" mind, but a primitive and Eastern one. Certainly, that cravat in the frame has receded a million, million leagues, ten thousand forgotten æons, from me! Whether this is a result due to my own personality, of old acquainted with Eastern notions, or whether, perhaps, it is the natural accident to any mind wholly freed from trammels, I do not know. But I seem to have gone right back to the very beginnings, and resemblance with man in his first, simple, gaudy conditions. My hair, as I sit here writing, already hangs a black, oiled string down my back; my scented beard sweeps in two opening whisks to my ribs; I have on the *izar*, a pair of drawers of yomani cloth like cotton, but with yellow stripes; over this a soft shirt, or *quamis*, of white silk, reaching to my calves; over this a short vest of gold-embroidered crimson, the *sudeyree*; over this a khaftan of green-striped silk, reaching to the ankles, with wide, long sleeves divided at the wrist, and bound at the waist with a voluminous gaudy shawl of Cashmere for girdle; over this a warm wide-flowing torrent of white drapery, lined with ermine. On my head the skull-cap, covered by a high crimson cap with a deep-blue tassel; and on my feet is a pair of thin yellow-morocco shoes, covered over with thick red-morocco babooshes. My ankles—my ten fingers— my wrists—are heavy with gold and silver ornaments; and in my ears, which, with considerable pain, I bored three days since, are two needle-splinters, to prepare the holes for rings.

                    *   *   *   *   *

O Liberty! I am free. . . .

                    *   *   *   *   *

While I was going to visit my old home in Harley Street that night, at the very moment when I turned north from Oxford Street into Cavendish Square, this thought, fiercely hissed into my ears, was all of a sudden seething in me: "If now I should lift my eyes, and see a man walking yonder—just yonder—*at the corner there*—turning from Harewood Place into Oxford Street—what, my good God, should I do?—I without even a knife to run and plunge into his heart?"

And I turned my eyes—ogling, suspicious eyes of furtive horror— reluctantly, lingeringly turned—and I peered deeply with lowered brows across the murky winds at that same spot: but no man was there.

Horribly frequent is this nonsense now become with me—in streets of towns—in deep nooks of the country: the invincible assurance that, if I but turn the head, and glance just *there*—at a certain fixed spot—I shall surely see—I *must* see—a man. And glance I must, glance I must, though I perish: and when I glance, though my hairs creep and stiffen like stirring amœbæ; yet in my eyes, I know, is monarch indignation against the intruder, and my neck stands stiff as sovereignty itself, and on my brow sits more than all the lordship of Persepolis and Iraz.

To what point of wantonness this arrogance of royalty may lead me, I do not know: I will watch, and see. It is written: "It is not good for man to be alone!" But good or no, the arrangement of One planet, One inhabitant, already seems to me, not merely a natural and proper, but the *only* natural and proper, condition; so much so, that any other arrangement has now, to my mind, a certain improbable, wild, and far-fetched unreality, like the utopian schemes of dreamers and faddists. That the whole world should have been made for *me* alone—that London should have been built in order that *I* might enjoy the vast heroic spectacle of its burning—that all history, and all civilisation should have existed only in order to accumulate for my pleasures its inventions and facilities, its stores of purple and wine, of spices and gold—no more extraordinary does it all seem to me than to some little unreflecting Duke of the my former days seemed the possessing of lands which his remote forefathers seized, and slew the occupiers: nor, in reality, is it even so extraordinary, I being alone. But what sometimes strikes me with some surprise is, not that the present condition of the world, with one sole master, should seem the common-place and natural condition, but that it should have come to seem so common-place and natural—in nine months. The mind of Adam Jeffson is adaptable.

* * * * *

I sat a long time thinking such things by my bed that night, till finally I was disposed to sleep there. But I had no considerable number of candle-sticks, nor was even sure of candles. I remembered, however, that Peter Peters, three doors away on the other side of the street, had had four handsome silver candelabra in his drawing-room, each containing six stems; and I said to myself: "I will search for candles in the kitchen, and if I find any, will go and get Peter Peters' candelabra, and sleep here."

I took then the two lights which I had, my good God; went down to the passage; then down to the basement; and there had no difficulty in finding three packets of large candles, the fact being, I suppose, that the cessation of gas-lighting had compelled everyone to provide themselves in this way, for there were a great many wherever I looked. With these I re-ascended, went into a little alcove on the second-floor where I had kept some drugs, got a bottle of carbolic oil, and for ten minutes went dashing all the corpses in the house. I then left the two lighted bits of candle on the waiting-room table, and, with the car-lamp, passed along the passage to the front-door, which was very violently banging. I stepped out to find that the storm had increased to a mighty turbulence (though it was dry), which at once caught my clothes, and whirled them into a flapping cloud about and above me; also, I had not crossed the street when my lamp was out. I persisted, however, half blinded, to Peters' door. It was locked: but immediately near the pavement was a window, the lower sash up, into which, with little trouble, I lifted myself and passed. My foot, as I lowered it, stood on a body: and this made me angry and restless. I hissed a curse, and passed on, scraping the carpet with my soles, that I might hurt no one: for I did not wish to hurt any one. Even in the almost darkness of the room I recognised Peters' furniture, as I expected: for the house was his on a long lease, and I knew that his mother had had the intention to occupy it after his death. But as I passed out into the passage, all was mere blank darkness, and I, depending upon the lamp, had left the matches in the other house. I groped my way to the stairs, and had my foot on the first step, when I was stopped by a vicious shaking of the front-door, which someone seemed to be at with hustlings and the most urgent poundings: I stood with peering stern brows two or three minutes, for I knew that if I once yielded to the flinching at my heart, no mercy would be shown me in this house of tragedy, and thrilling shrieks would of themselves arise and ring through its haunted chambers. The rattling continued an inordinate time, and so instant and imperative, that it seemed as if it could not fail to force the door. But, though horrified, I whispered to my heart that it could only be the storm which was struggling at it as with the grasp of a man, and after a time went on, feeling my way by the broad rail, in my brain somehow the thought of a dream which I had had in the *Boreal* of the woman Clodagh, how she let drop a fluid like pomegranate-seeds into water, and tendered it to Peter Peters: and it was a mortal purging-draught; but I would not stop, but step by step went up, though I suffered very much, my brows peering at the utter darkness, and my heart shocked at its own rashness. I got to the first landing, and as I turned to ascend the second part of the stair, my left hand touched something icily cold: I made some quick instinctive movement of terror, and, doing so, my foot struck against something, and I stumbled, half falling over what seemed a small table there. Immediately a horrible row followed, for something fell to the ground: and in that instant, ah, I heard something—a voice—a human voice, which uttered words close to my ear—the voice of Clodagh, for I knew it: yet not the voice of Clodagh in the flesh, but her voice clogged with clay and worms, and full of effort, and thick-tongued: and in that ghastly speech of the grave I distinctly heard the words:

"*Things being as they are in the matter of the death of Peter . . .*"

And there it stopped dead, leaving me so sick, my God, so sick, that I could hardly snatch my robes about me to fly, fly, fly, soft-footed, murmuring in pain, down the steps, down like a sneaking thief, but quick, snatching myself away, then wrestling with the cruel catch of the door which she would not let me open, feeling her all the time behind me, watching me. And when I did get out, I was away up the length of the street, trailing my long *jubbah,* glancing backward, panting, for I thought that she might dare to follow, with her daring evil will. And all that night I lay on a common bench in the wind-tossed and dismal Park.

*   *   *   *   *

The first thing which I did when the sun was up was to return to that place: and I returned with a hard and masterful brow.

Approaching Peters' house I saw now, what the darkness had hidden from me, that on his balcony was someone—quite alone there. The balcony is a slight open-work wrought-iron structure, connected to a small roof by three slender voluted pillars, two at the ends, one in the middle: and at the middle one I saw someone, a woman—kneeling—her arms clasped tight about the pillar, and her face rather upward-looking. Never did I see aught more horrid: there were the gracious curves of the woman's bust and hips still well preserved in a clinging dress of red cloth, very faded now; and her reddish hair floated loose in a large flimsy cloud about her; but her face, in that exposed position, had been quite eaten away by the winds to a noseless skeleton, which grinned from ear to ear, with slightly-dropped under-jaw—most horrid in contrast with the body, and frame of hair. I meditated upon her a long time that morning from the opposite pavement. An oval locket at her throat contained, I knew, my likeness: for eight years previously I had given it to her. It was Clodagh, the poisoner.

I thought that I would go into that house, and walk through it from top to bottom, and sit in it, and spit in it, and stamp in it, in spite of any one: for the sun was now high. I accordingly went in again, and up the stairs to the spot where I had been frightened, and had heard the words. And here a great rage took me, for I at once saw that I had been made the dupe of the malign wills that beset me, and the laughing-stock of Those for whom I care not a fig. From a little mahogany table there I had knocked sideways to the ground, in my stumble, a small phonograph with a great 25-inch japanned-tin horn, which, the moment that I now noticed it, I took and flung with a great racket down the stairs: for that this it was which had addressed me I did not doubt; it being indeed evident that its clock-work mechanism had been stopped by the volcanic scoriæ in the midst of the delivery of a record, but had been started into a few fresh oscillations by the shock of the fall, making it utter those thirteen words, and stop. I was sufficiently indignant at the moment, but have since been glad, for I was thereby put upon the notion of collecting a number of cylinders with records, and have been touched with indescribable sensations, sometimes thrilled, at hearing the silence of this Eternity broken by those singing and speaking voices, so life-like, yet most ghostly, of the old dead.

*   *   *   *   *

Well, the most of that same day I spent in a high chamber at Woolwich, dusting out, and sometimes oiling, time-fuses: a work in which I acquired such facility in some hours, that each finally occupied me no more than ninety to a hundred seconds, so that by evening I had, with the previous day's work, close on 600. The construction of these little things is very simple, and, I believe, effective, so that I should have no difficulty in making them myself in large numbers, if it were necessary. Most contain a tiny dry battery, which sends a current along a bell of copper wire at the running-down moment, the clocks being contrived to be set for so many days, hours, and minutes, while others ignite by striking. I arranged in rows in the covered van those which I had prepared, and passed the night in an inn near the Barracks. I had brought candlesticks from London in the morning, and arranged the furniture—a settee, chest-of-drawers, basin-stand, table, and a number of chairs—in three-quarter circle round the bed, so getting a triple-row altar of lights, mixed with vases of the house containing small palms and evergreens; with this I mingled a smell of ambergris from the scattered contents of some Turkish sachets which I had; in the bed a bottle of sweet Chypre-wine, with *bonbons*, nuts, and Havannas. As I lay me down, I could not but reflect, with a smile which I knew to be evil, upon that steady, strong, smouldering lust within me which was urging me through all those pains at the Arsenal, I who shirked every labour as unkingly. So, however, it was: and the next morning I was at it again after an early breakfast, my fingers at first quite stiff with cold, for it blew a keen and January gale. By nine I had 820 fuses; and judging those sufficient to commence with, got into the motor, and took it round to a place called the East Laboratory, a series of detached buildings, where I knew that I should find whatever I wanted: and I prepared my mind for a day's labour. In this place I found incredible stores: mountains of percussion-caps, more chambers of fuses, small-arm cartridges, shells, and all those murderous explosive mixtures, a-making and made, with which modern savagery occupied its leisure in exterminating itself: or, at least, savagery civilised in its top-story only: for civilisation was apparently from the head downwards, and never once grew below the neck in all those centuries, those people being certainly much more mental than cordial, though I doubt if they were genuinely mental either—reminding one rather of that composite image of Nebuchadnezzar, head of gold, breast brazen, feet of clay—head man-like, heart cannibal, feet bestial—like aegipeds, and mermaids, and puzzling undeveloped births. However, it is of no importance: and perhaps I am not much better than the rest, for I, too, after all, am of them. At any rate, their lyddites, melanites, cordites, dynamites, powders, jellies, oils, marls, and civilised barbarisms and obiahs, came in very well for their own destruction: for by two o'clock I had so worked, that I had on the first cart the phalanx of fuses; on the second a goodly number of kegs, cartridge-cases and cartridge-boxes, full of powder, explosive cottons and gelatines, and liquid nitro-glycerine, and earthy dynamite, with some bombs, two reels of cordite, two pieces of tarred cloth, a small iron ladle, a shovel, and a crow-bar; the cab came next, containing a considerable quantity of loose coal; and lastly, in the private carriage lay four big cans of common oil. And first, in the Laboratory, I connected a fuse-conductor with a huge tin of blasting-gelatine, and I set the fuse on the ground, timed for the midnight of the twelfth day thence; and after that I visited the Main Factory, the Carriage Department, the Ordnance Store Department, the Royal Artillery Barracks, and the Powder Magazines in the Marshes, traversing, as it seemed to me, miles of building; and in some I laid heaps of oil-saturated coal with an explosive in suitable spots on the ground-floor near wood-work, and in some an explosive alone: and all I timed for ignition at midnight of the twelfth day.

Hot now, and black as ink, I proceeded through the town, stopping with perfect system at every hundredth door: and I laid the faggots of a great burning: and timed them all for ignition at midnight of the twelfth day.

       *   *   *   *   *

Whatever door I found closed against me I drove at it with a maniac malice.

       *   *   *   *   *

Shall I commit the whole dark fact to paper?—that deep, deep secret of the human organism?

As I wrought, I waxed wicked as a demon! And with lowered neck, and forward curve of the lower spine, and the blasphemous strut of tragic play-actors, I went. For here was no harmless burning which I did—but the crime of arson; and a most fiendish, though vague, malevolence, and the rage to burn and raven and riot, was upon me like a dog-madness, and all the mood of Nero, and Nebuchadnezzar: and from my mouth proceeded all the obscenities of the slum and of the gutter, and I sent up such hisses and giggles of challenge to Heaven that day as never yet has man let out. But this way lies a spinning frenzy. . . .

*   *   *   *   *

I have taken a dead girl with wild huggings to my bosom; and I have touched the corrupted lip, and spat upon her face, and tossed her down, and crushed her teeth with my heel, and jumped and jumped upon her breast, like the snake-stamping zebra, mad, mad . . .!

*   *   *   *   *

I was desolated, however, that first day of the faggot-laying, even in the midst of my sense of omnipotence, by one thing, which gave me some kicks to the motor: for it was only crawling, so that a good part of the way I was stalking by its side; and when I came to that hill near the Old Dover Road, the whole thing stopped, and refused to move, the weight of the train being too great for my horse-power traction. I did not know what to do, and stood there in angry impotence a full half-hour, for the notion of setting up an electric station, with or without automatic stoking-gear, presented so hideous a picture of labour to me, that I would not entertain it. After a time, however, I thought that I re-membered that there was a comparatively new power-station in St. Pancras driven by turbines: and at once, I uncoupled the motor, covered the drays with the tarpaulins, and went driving at singing speed, choosing the emptier by-streets, and not caring whom I crushed. After some trouble I found, in fact, the station in an obscure by-street made of two long walls, and went in by a win-dow, a rage upon me to have my will quickly accomplished. I ran up some stairs, across two rooms, into a gallery containing a switch-board, and in the room below saw the works, all very neat-looking, but, as I soon found, very dusty. I went down, and fixed upon a generating set—there were three—that would give a decent load, and then saw that the switch-gear belonging to this particular generator was in order. I then got some cloths and thoroughly cleaned the dust off the commutators; ran next—for I was in a strange fierce haste—and turned the water into the turbines, and away went the engine; I hurried to set the lubricators running on the bearings, and in a couple of min-utes had adjusted the speed, and the brushes of the generators, and switched the current on the line. By this time, however, I saw that it was getting dark, and feared that little could be done that day; still, I hurried out, the station still running, got into the car, and was off to look for a good electric one, of which there are hosts in the streets, in order at least to clean up and adjust the motor that night. I drove down three by-streets, till I turned into Euston Road: but I had no sooner reached it than I pulled up—with sudden jerk—with a shout of astonishment.

The cursed street was all lighted up and gay! and three shimmering electric globes, not far apart, illuminated every feature of a ghastly battle-field of dead.

And there was a thing there, the grinning impression of which I shall carry to my grave: a thing which spelled and spelled at me, and ceased, and began again, and ceased, and spelled at me. For, above a shop which faced me was a flag, a red flag with white letters, fluttering on the gale with the words: "Metcalfe's Stores"; and beneath the flag, stretched right across the house, was the thing which spelled, letter by letter, in letters of light: and it spelled two words, deliberately, coming to the end, and going back to recommence:

Drink
Roboral.

And that was the last word of civilised Man to me, Adam Jeffson—its final gospel and message—to *me*, my good God! *Drink Roboral!*

I was put into such a passion of rage by this blatant ribaldry, which affected me like the laughter of a skeleton, that I rushed from the car, with the intention, I believe, of seeking stones to stone it: but no stones were there: and I had to stand impotently enduring that rape of my eyes, its victoriously-dogged iteration, its taunting leer, its Drink Roboral—D,R,I,N,K R,O,B,O,R,A,L.

It was one of those electrical spelling-advertisements, worked by a small motor commutator driven by a works-motor, and I had now set it going: for on some night before that Sabbath of doom the chemist must have set it to work, but finding the works abandoned, had not troubled to shut it down again. At any rate, this thing stopped my work for that day, for when I went to shut down the works it was night; so I drove to the place which I had made my home in sullen and weary mood: for I knew that Roboral would not cure the least of all my sores.

* * * * *

The next morning I awoke in quite another frame of mind, disposed to idle, and let things go. After rising, dressing, washing in cold diluted rose-water, and descending to the *salle-à-manger*, where I had laid my morning-meal the previous evening, I promenaded an hour the only one of these long sombrous tufted corridors in which were not more than two dead, though behind the doors on either hand, all of which I had locked, I knew that they lay in plenty. When I was warmed, I again went down, looked into my motor, got three cylinders from one of a number of motors standing near, lit up, and drove away—to Woolwich, as I thought at first: but instead of crossing the river by Blackfriars, I went more eastward; and having passed from Holborn into Cheapside, which was impassable, unless I crawled, was about to turn, when I noticed a phonograph-shop: into this I got by a side-door, suddenly seized by quite a curiosity to hear what I might hear. I took a good one with microphone diaphragm, and a number of record-cylinders in a brass-handled box, and I put them into the car, for there was still a very strong peach-odour in this closed shop, which displeased me. I then proceeded southward and westward through by-streets, seeking some probable house into which to go from the rough cold winds, when I saw the Parliament-house, and thither, turning river-ward by Westminster Hall to Palace Yard, I went, and with my two parcels, one weighting each arm, walked into this old place along a line of purple-dusted busts; I deposited my boxes on a table beside a massive brass thing lying there, which, I suppose, must be what they called the Mace; and I sat to hear.

Unfortunately, the phonograph was a clockwork one, and when I wound it, it would not go: so that I got very angry at my absurdity in not bringing an electric mechanism, as I could with much less trouble have put in a chemical than cleaned the clock-work; and this thing put me into such a rage, that I nearly tore it to pieces, and was half for kicking it: but there was a man sitting in an old straight-backed chair quite near me, which they called the Speaker's Chair, who was in such a pose, that he had, every time I glanced suddenly at him, precisely the air of bending forward with interest to watch what I was doing, a Mohrgrabim kind of man, almost black, with Jewish nose, crinkled hair, keffie, and flowing robe, probably, I should say, an Abyssinian Galla; with him were five or six people about the benches, mostly leaning forward with rested head, so that this place had quite a void sequestered mood. At all events, this Galla, or Bedouin, with his grotesque interest in my doings, restrained my hands: and, finally, by dint of peering, poking, dusting, and adjusting, in an hour's time I got the phonograph to go very well.

And all that morning, and far into late afternoon, forgetful of food, and of the cold which gradually possessed me, I sat there listening, musing—cylinder after cylinder: frivolous songs, orchestras, voices of famous men whom I had spoken with, and shaken their solid hands, speaking again to me, but thick-tongued, with hoarse effort and gurgles, from out the vague void beyond the grave: most strange, most strange. And the third cylinder that I put on, ah, I knew, with a fearful start, that voice of thunder, I knew it well: it was the preacher, Mackay's; and many, many times over I heard those words of his that day, originally spoken, it seems, when the cloud had just passed the longitude of Vienna; and in all that torrent of speech not one single word of "I told you so": but he cries:

". . . praise Him, O Earth, for He is He: and if He slay me, I will laugh raillery at His Sword, and banter Him to His face: for His Sword is sharp Mercy, and His poisons kill my death. Fear not, therefore, little flock of Man! but take my comfort to your heart to-night, and my sweets to your tongue: for though ye have sinned, and hardened yourselves as brass, and gone far, far astray in these latter wildernesses, yet He is infinitely greater than your sin, and will lead you back. Break not, break not, poor broken heart of Earth: for from Him I run herald to thee this night with the sweet and secret message, that of old He chose thee, and once mixed conjugally with thee in an ancient sleep, O Afflicted: and He is thou, and thou art He, flesh of His flesh, and bone of His bone; and if thou perish utterly, it is that He has perished utterly, too: for thou art He. Hope, therefore, most, and cheeriest smile, at the very apsis and black nadir of Despair: for He is nimble as a weasel, and He twists like Proteus, and His solstices and equinoxes, His tropics and turning-points and recurrences are innate in Being, and when He falls He falls like harlequin and shuttle-cocks, shivering plumb to His feet, and each third day, lo, He is risen again, and His defeats are but the stepping-stones and rough scaffolding from which He builds His Parthenons, and from the densest basalt gush His rills, and the last end of this Earth shall be no poison-cloud, I say to you, but Carnival and Harvest-home . . . though ye have sinned, poor hearts . . ."

*   *   *   *   *

So Mackay, with thick-tongued metallic effort. I found this brown room of the Commons-house, with its green benches, and grilled galleries, so agreeable to my mood, that I went again the next morning, and listened to more records, till they tired me: for what I had was a prurient itch to hear secret scandals, and revelations of the festering heart, but these cylinders, gathered from a shop, divulged nothing. I then went out to make for Woolwich, but in the car saw the poet's note-book in which I had written: and I took it, went back, and was writing an hour, till I was tired of that, too; and judging it too late for Woolwich that day, wandered about the dusty committee-rooms and recesses of this considerable place. In one room another foolishness suddenly seized upon me, shewing how my slightest whim has become more imperious within me than all the laws of the Medes and Persians: for in that room, Committee Room No. 15, I found an apparently young policeman lying flat on his back, who pleased me: his helmet tilted under his head, and near one white-gloved hand a blue official envelope; the air of that stagnant quiet room was still perceptibly peach-scented, and he gave not the slightest odour that I could detect, though he had been corporal and stalwart, his face now the colour of dark ashes, in each hollow cheek a ragged hole about the size of a sixpence, the flimsy vaulted eye-lids well embedded in their caverns, from under whose fringe of eye-lash was whispered the word: "*Eternity.*" His hair seemed very long for a policeman, or perhaps it had grown since death; but what interested me about him, was the envelope at his hand: for "what," I asked myself, "was this fellow doing here with an envelope at three o'clock on a Sunday afternoon?" This made me look closer, and then I saw by a mark at the left temple that he had been shot, or felled; whereupon I was thrown into quite a great rage, for I thought that this poor man was killed in the execution of his duty, when many of his kind perhaps, and many higher than he, had fled their post to pray or riot. So, after looking at him a long time, I said to him: "Well, D. 47, you sleep very well: and you did well, dying so: I am pleased with you, and to mark my favour, I decree that you shall neither rot in the common air, nor burn in the common flames: for by my own hand shall you be distinguished with burial."

And this wind so possessed me, that I at once went out: with the crow-bar from the car I broke the window of a near iron-monger's in Parliament Street, got a spade, and went into Westminster Abbey. I soon prised up a grave-slab of some famous man in the north transept, and commenced to shovel: but, I do not know how, by the time I had digged a foot the whole impulse passed from me: I left off the work, promising to resume it: but nothing was ever done, for the next day I was at Woolwich, and busy enough about other matters.

*   *   *   *   *

During the next nine days I worked with a fever on me, and a map of London before me.

There were places in that city!—secrets, vastnesses, horrors! In the wine-vaults at London Docks was a vat which must certainly have contained twenty and thirty thousand gallons: and with dancing heart I laid a train there; the to-bacco-warehouse must have covered eighty acres: and there I laid a fuse. In a house near Regent's Park, standing in a garden, and shut in from the street by a high wall, I saw a thing . . .! and what shapes a great city hid I now first know.

*   *   *   *   *

I left no quarter unremembered, taking a train, no longer of four, but of eight, vehicles, drawn by an electric motor which I re-charged every morning, mostly from the turbine station at St. Pancras, once from a steam-station with very small engine and dynamo, found in the Palace Theatre, which gave little trouble, and once from a similar little station in a Strand hotel. With these I visited West Ham and Kew, Finchley and Clapham, Dalston and Marylebone; I exhausted London; I deposited piles in the Guildhall, in Holloway Gaol, in the new pillared Justice-hall of Newgate, in the Tower, in the Parliament-house, in St. Giles' Workhouse, in the Crypt and under the organ of St. Paul's, in the South Kensington Museum, in the Royal Agricultural Society, in Whiteley's place, in the Trinity House, in Liverpool Street, in the Office of Works, in the secret recesses of the British Museum; in a hundred inflammable warehouses, in five hundred shops, in a thousand private dwellings. And I timed them all for ignition at midnight of the 23rd April.

By five in the afternoon of the 22nd, when I left my train in Maida Vale, and drove alone to the solitary house on high ground near Hampstead Heath which I had chosen, the thing was well finished.

*   *   *   *   *

The great morning dawned, and I was early astir: for I had much to do that day.

I intended to make for the sea-shore the next morning, so had therefore to choose a good petrol motor, store it, and have it in a place of safety: I had also to drag another vehicle after me, stored with trunks of time-fuses, books, clothes, and other little things.

My first journey was to Woolwich, whence I took all that I might ever re-quire in the way of mechanism; thence to the National Gallery, where I cut from their frames the "Vision of St. Helena," Murillo's "Boy Drinking," and "Christ at the Column"; and thence to the Embassy to bathe, anoint myself, and dress.

As I had anticipated, and hoped, a blustering spring gale was blowing from the north.

Even as I set out from Hampstead, about 9 A.M., I had been able to guess that some of my fuses had somehow anticipated the appointed hour: for I saw three red hazes at various points in the air, was heard the far vague booming of an occasional explosion; and by 11 A.M. I felt sure that a large region of north-eastern London must be in flames. With the solemn feelings of bridegrooms and marriage-mornings—with a flinching, a flinching heart, God knows, yet a heart up-buoyed on thrilling joys—I went on making preparations for the Gargantuan orgy of the night.

*   *   *   *   *

The house at Hampstead, which no doubt still stands, is of rather pleasing design in quite a stone and rural style, with good breadths of wall-surface, two plain coped gables, mullioned windows, and oversailing slate verge-roofs, but, rather spoiling it, a high square three-storied tower at the south-east angle, on the topmost floor of which I had slept the previous night. There I had provided myself with a jar of pale tobacco mixed with rose-leaves and opium, found in a foreign house in Seymour Street, also a genuine Saloniki hookah, together with the best wines, nuts, and so on, and a gold harp of the musician Krasinski, stamped with his name, taken from his house in Portland Street.

But so much did I find to do that day, so many odd things turned up which I thought that I would take with me, that it was not till near six that I drove finally northward through Camden Town. And now an ineffable awe possessed my soul at the solemn noise which everywhere encompassed me, an ineffable awe, a blissful terror. Never, never could I have dreamed of aught so great and potent. All above my head there rushed southward with wide-spread wing of haste a sparkling smoke; and mixed with the immense roaring I heard mysterious hubbubs of tumblings and rumblings, which I could not at all comprehend, like the moving-about of furniture in the houses of Titans; while pervading all the air was a most weird and tearful sound, as it were threnody, and a wild wail of pain, and dying swan-songs, and all lamentations and tribulations of the world. Yet I was aware that, at an hour so early, the flames must be far from general; in fact, they had not well commenced.

*   *   *   *   *

As I had left a good semicircular region of houses, with a radius of four hundred yards, without combustibles to the south of the isolated house which I was to occupy, and as the wind was so strongly from the north, I simply left my two vehicles at the door of the house, without fear of any injury: nor did any occur. I then went up to the top of the tower, lit the candles, and ate voraciously of the dinner which I had left ready, for since the morning I had taken nothing; and then, with hands and heart that quivered, I arranged the clothes of the low spring-bed upon which to throw my frame in the morning hours. Opposite the wall, where lay the bed, was a Gothic window, pretty large, with low sill, hung with poppy-figured muslin, and looking diectly south, so that I could recline at ease in the red-velvet easy-chair, and see. It had evidently been a young lady's room: for on the toilette were cut-glass bottles, a plait of brown hair, powders, *rouge-aux-lèvres*, one little bronze slipper, and knick-knacks, and I loved her and hated her, though I did not see her anywhere. About half-past eight I sat at the window to watch, all being arranged and ready at my right hand, the candles extinguished in the red room: for the theatre was opened, was opened: and the atmosphere of this earth seemed turned into Hell, and Hell was in my soul.

*   *   *   *   *

Soon after midnight there was a sudden and very visible increase in the conflagration. On all hands I began to see blazing structures soar, with grand hurrahs, on high. In fives and tens, in twenties and thirties, all between me and the remote limit of my vision, they leapt, they lingered long, they fell. My spirit more and more felt, and danced—deeper mysteries of sensation, sweeter thrills. I sipped exquisitely, I drew out enjoyment leisurely. Anon, when some more expansive angel of flame would arise from the Pit with steady aspiration, and linger with outspread arms, and burst, I would lift a little from the chair, leaning forward to clap, as at some famous acting; or I would call to them in shouts of cheer, giving them the names of Woman. For now I seemed to see nothing but some bellowing pandemonic universe through crimson glasses, and the air was wildly hot, and my eye-balls like theirs that walk staring in the inner midst of burning fiery furnaces, and my skin itched with a fierce and prickly itch. Anon I touched the chords of the harp to the air of Wagner's "Walküren-ritt."

Near three in the morning, I reached the climax of my guilty sweets. My drunken eyelids closed in a luxury of pleasure, and my lips lay stretched in a smile that dribbled; a sensation of dear peace, of almighty power, consoled me: for now the whole area which through streaming tears I surveyed, mustering its ten thousand thunders, and brawling beyond the stars the voice of its south-ward-rushing torment, billowed to the horizon one grand Atlantic of smokeless and flushing flame; and in it sported and washed themselves all the fiends of Hell, with laughter, shouts, wild flights, and holiday; and I—first of my race—had flashed a signal to the nearer planets. . . .

*   *   *   *   *

*   *   *   *   *

Those words: "signal to the nearer planets" I wrote nearly fourteen months ago, some days after the destruction of London, I being then on board the old *Boreal*, making for the coast of France: for the night was dark, though calm, and I was afraid of running into some ship, yet not sleepy, so I wrote to occupy my fingers, the ship lying still. The book in which I wrote has been near me: but no impulse to write anything has visited me, till now I continue; not, however, that I have very much to put down.

I had no intention of wearing out my life in lighting fires every morning to warm myself in the inhospitable island of Britain, and set out to France with the view of seeking some palace in the Riviera, Spain, or perhaps Algiers, there, for the present at least, to make my home.

I started from Calais toward the end of April, taking my things along, the first two days by train, and then determining that I was in no hurry, and a pet-rol motor easier, took one, and maintained a generally southern and somewhat eastern direction, ever-anew astonished at the wildness of the forest vegetation which, within so short a space since the disappearance of man, chokes this pleasant land, even before the definite advent of summer.

After three weeks of slow travelling—for though I know several countries very well, France with her pavered villages, hilly character, vines, forests, and primeval country-manner, is always new and charming to me—after three weeks I came unexpectedly to a valley which had never entered my head; and the moment that I saw it, I said: "Here I will live," though I had no idea what it was, for the monastery which I saw did not look at all like a monastery, accord-ing to my ideas: but when I searched the map, I discovered that it must be La Chartreuse de Vauclaire in Périgord.

It is my belief that this word "Vauclaire" is nothing else than a corruption of the Latin *Vallis Clara*, or Bright Valley, for *l*'s and *u*'s did interchange about in this way, I remember: *cheval* becoming *chevau(x)* in the plural, like "fool" and "fou," and the rest: which proves the dear laziness of French people, for the "l" was too much trouble for them to sing, and when they came to *two* "l's" they quite succumbed, shying that vault, or *voute*, and calling it some *y*. But at any rate, this Vauclaire, or Valclear, was well named: for here, if anywhere, is Paradise, and if anyone knew how and where to build and brew liqueurs, it was those good old monks, who followed their Master with *entrain* in that Cana miracle, and in many other things, I fancy, but æsthetically shirked to say to any mountain: "Be thou removed."

*   *   *   *   *

The general hue of the vale is a deep cerulean, resembling that blue of the robes of Albertinelli's Madonnas; so, at least, it strikes the eye on a clear fore-noon of spring or summer. The monastery consists of an oblong space, or garth, around three sides of which stand sixteen small houses, with regular intervals between, all identical, the cells of the fathers; between the oblong space and the cells come cloisters, with only one opening to the exterior; in the western part of the oblong is a little square of earth under a large cypress-shade, within which, as in a home of peace, it sleeps: and there, straight and slanting, stand little plain black crosses over graves. . . .

To the west of the quadrangle is the church, with the hostelry, and an as-phalted court with some trees and a fountain; and beyond, the entrance-gate.

All this stands on a hill of gentle slope, green as grass; and it is backed close against a steep mountain-side, of which the tree-trunks are conjectural, for I never saw any, the trees resembling rather one continuous leafy tree-top, run out high and far over the extent of the mountain.

*   *   *   *   *

I was there four months, till something drove me away. I do not know what had become of the fathers and brothers, for I only found five, four of whom I took in two journeys in the motor beyond the church of Saint Martial d'Artenset, and left them there; and the fifth remained three weeks with me, for I would not disturb him in his prayer. He was a bearded brother of forty years or thereabouts, who knelt in his cell robed and hooded in all his phantom white: for in no way different from whatever is most phantom, visionary and eerie must a procession of these people have seemed by gloaming, or dark night. This particular brother knelt, I say, in his small chaste room, glaring upward at his Christ, who hung long-armed in a little recess between the side of three narrow book-shelves and a projection of the wall; and under the Christ a gilt and blue Madonna; the books on the three shelves few, leaning different ways. His right elbow rested on a square plain table, at which was a wooden chair; behind him, in a corner, the bed: a bed all enclosed in dark boards, a broad perpendicular board along the foot, reaching the ceiling, a horizontal board at the side over which he got into bed, another narrower one like it at the ceiling for fringe and curtain, and another perpendicular one hiding the pillow, making the clean bed within a very shady and cosy little den, on the wall of this den being another smaller Christ, and a little picture. On the perpendicular board at the foot hung two white garments, and over a second chair at the bed-side another: all very neat and holy. He was a large stern man, blond as corn, but with some red, too, in his hairy beard; and appalling was the significance of those eyes that prayed, and the long-drawn cavity of those saffron cheeks. I cannot explain to myself my reverence for this man; but I had it, certainly. Many of the others, it is clear, had fled: but not he: and to the near-marching cloud he opposed the Cross, holding one real as the other—he alone among many. For Christianity was an *élite* religion, in which all were called, but few chosen, differing from Mohammedanism and Buddhism, which grasped and conquered all within their reach: the effect of Christ rather resembling Plato's and Dante's, it would seem: but Mahomet's more like Homer's and Shakespeare's.

It was my way to plant at the portal the big, carved chair from the chancel on the hot days, and rest my soul, refusing to think of anything, drowsing and smoking for hours. All down there in the plain waved gardens of delicious fruit about the prolonged silver thread of the river Isle, whose course winds loitering quite near the foot of the monastery-slope. This slope dominates a tract of distance that is not only vast, but looks immense, although the horizon is bounded by a semicircle of low hills, rather too stiff and uniform for perfect beauty; the interval of plain being occupied by yellow ploughed lands which

were never sown, weedy now, and crossed and recrossed by vividly-green rib-
bons of vine, with stretches of pale-green lucerne, orchards and the white village of Monpont near the railway, all embowered, the Isle drawing its mercurial
streams through the village-meadow, which is dark with shades of oaks: and to
have played there a boy, and used it familiarly from birth as one's own hand or
foot, must have been very sweet and homely; after this, the river divides, and
takes the shape of a heart; and very far away are visible the grey banks of the
Gironde. On the semicircle of hills, when there was little distance-mist, I saw
the ruins of some seigneurial château, for the siegneurs, too, knew where to
build; and to my left, between a clump of oaks and an avenue of poplars, the
bell-tower of the village-church of Saint Martial d'Artenset—a very ancient
type of tower, I believe, and common in France, rather ponderous, consisting
of a square mass with a smaller square mass stuck on, the latter having large
Gothic windows; and behind me the west face of the monastery-church, over
the door being the statue of Saint Bruno.

Well, one morning after four months, I opened my eyes in my cell to the
piercing consciousness that I had burned Monpont over-night: and so overcome was I with regret for this poor inoffensive little place, that for two days,
hardly eating, I paced between the oak and walnut pews of the nave, massive
stalls they are, separated by grooved Corinthian pilasters, wondering what was
to become of me, and if I was not already mad; and there are some little angels
with extraordinarily human Greuze-like faces, supporting the nerves of the
apse, which, after a time, every time I passed them, seemed conscious of me
and my existence there; and the wood-work which ornaments the length of the
nave, and of the choir also, elaborate with carved marguerites and roses, here
and there took in my eyes significant forms from certain points of view; and
there is a partition—for the nave is divided into two chapels, one for the
brothers and one for the fathers, I conclude—and in this partition a massive
door, which yet looks quite light and graceful, carved with oak and acanthus
leaves, and every time I passed through I had the impression that the door was
a sentient thing, subconscious of me; and the delicate Italian-Renaissance
brick vault which springs from the vast nave seemed to look upon me with a
gloomy knowledge of me, and of the heart within me; and at about four in the
afternoon of the second day, after pacing the church for hours, I fell down at
one of the two altars near that carved door of the screen, praying God to have
mercy upon my soul; and in the very midst of my praying, I was up and away,
the devil in me, and I got into the motor, and did not come back to Vauclaire
for another month, and came leaving great tracts of burned desolation behind
me, towns and forests, Bordeaux burned, Lebourne burned, Bergerac burned.

*   *   *   *   *

I returned to Vauclaire, for it seemed now my home; and there I experienced a true, a deep repentance; and I humbled myself before my Maker. And
while in this state, sitting one bright day in front of the monastery-gate, something said to me: "You will never be a good man, nor permanently escape Hell

and Frenzy, unless you have an aim in life, devoting yourself heart and soul to some great work, which will exact all your science, your thought, your ingenuity, your knowledge of modern things, your strength of body and will, your skill of head and hand: otherwise you are bound to succumb. Do this, therefore, beginning, not to-morrow nor this afternoon, but now: for though no man will see your work, there is still the Almighty God, who is also something, in His way: and He will see how you strive, and try, and groan: and perhaps, seeing, He may have mercy upon you."

*   *   *   *   *

In this way arose the idea of the Palace—an idea, indeed, which had entered my brain before, but merely as a bombastic and visionary outcome of my raving moods: now, however, in a very different way, soberly, and soon concerning itself with details, difficulties, means, limitations, and every kind of practical matter-of-fact; and every obstruction which, one by one, I foresaw was, one by one, as the days passed, over-borne by the vigour with which that thought, rapidly becoming a mania, possessed me. After a week of incessant meditation, I decided Yes: and I said: I will build a palace, which shall be both a palace and a temple: the first human temple worthy the King of Heaven, and the only human palace worthy the King of Earth.

*   *   *   *   *

After this decision I remained at Vauclaire another week, a very different man to the lounger it had seen, strenuous, converted, humble, making plans of this and of that, of the detail, and of the whole, drawing, multiplying, adding, conic sections and the rule-of-three, totting up the period of building, which came out at a little over twelve years, estimating the quantities of material, weight and bulk, my nights full of nightmare as to the *sort*, deciding as to the size and structure of the crane, forge, and work-shop, and the necessarily-limited weights of their component parts, making a list of over 2,400 objects, and finally, up to the third week after my departure from Vauclaire, skimming through the topography of nearly the whole earth, before fixing upon the island of Imbros for my site.

*   *   *   *   *

I returned to England, and, once more, to the hollow windows and strewn streets of black, burned-out and desolate London: for its bank-vaults, etc., contained the necessary complement of the gold brought from Paris, and then lying in the *Speranza* at Dover; nor had I sufficient familiarity with French industries and methods to find, even with the help of *Bottins*, one half of the 4,000 odd objects which I had now catalogued. My ship was the *Speranza*, which had brought me from Havre; for at Calais, to which I first went, I could find nothing suitable for all purposes, the *Speranza* being an American yacht, very palatially fitted, three-masted, air-driven, with a carrying capacity of 2,000 tons, Tobin-bronzed, in good condition, containing sixteen interacting tanks, with a five-block pulley-arrangement amid-ships that enables me to lift very

considerable weights without the aid of the hoisting air-engine, high in the water, sharp, handsome, containing a few tons only of sand-ballast, and needing
when I found her only three days' work at the water-line and engines to make
her decent and fit. I threw out her dead, backed her from the Outer to the Inner Basin to my train on the quai, took in the twenty-three hundred-weight
bags of gold, and the half-ton of amber, and with this alone went to Dover,
thence to Canterbury by motor, and thence in a long train, with a store of dynamite from the Castle for blasting possible obstructions, to London: meaning
to make Dover my *dépôt*, and the London rails my thoroughfare from all parts
of the country.

But instead of three months, as I had calculated, it kept me nine: a har-
rowing slavery. I had to blast no less than forty-three trains from the path of
my loaded wagons, several times blasting away the metals as well, and then
having to travel hundreds of yards without metals: for the labour of kindling
the obstructing engines, to shunt them down sidings perhaps distant, was a
thing which I would not undertake. However, all's well that ends well, though
if I had it to go through again, certainly I should not. The *Speranza* is now lying
nine miles off Cape Roca, a heavy mist on the still water, this being the 19th of
June at 10 in the night: no wind, no moon: cabin full of mist: and I pretty listless and disappointed, wondering in my heart why I was such a fool as to take
all that trouble, nine long servile months, my good God, and now seriously
thinking of throwing the whole vile thing to the devil; she pretty deep in the
water, pregnant with the palace. When the thirty-three . . .

```
        *       *       *       *       *

        *       *       *       *       *

        *       *       *       *       *

        *       *       *       *       *

        *       *       *       *       *
```

Those words: "when the thirty-three" were written by me over seventeen
years since—long years—seventeen in number, nor have I now any idea to
what they refer. The book in which I wrote I had lost in the cabin of the *Speranza*, and yesterday, returning to Imbros from an hour's aimless cruise, discovered it there behind a chest.

I find now considerable difficulty in guiding the pencil, and these few lines
now written have quite an odd look, like the handwriting of a man not very
proficient in the art: it is seventeen years, seventeen, seventeen . . . ah! And
the expression of my ideas is not fluent either: I have to think for the word a
minute, and I should not be surprised if the spelling of some of them is queer.
My brain has been thinking inarticulately perhaps, all these years: and the English words and letters, as they now stand written, have rather an improbable
and foreign air to me, as a Greek or Russian book might look to a man who has
not so long been learning those languages as to forget the impossibly foreign

impression received from them on the first day of tackling them. Or perhaps it is only my fancy: for that I have fancies I know.

But what to write? The history of those seventeen years could not be put down, my good God: at least, it would take seventeen more to do it. If I were to detail the building of the palace alone, and how it killed me nearly, and how I twice fled from it, and had to return, and became its bounden slave, and dreamed of it, and grovelled before it, and prayed, and raved, and rolled; and how I forgot to make provision in the west side for the contraction and expansion of the gold in the colder weather and the heats of summer, and had to break down nine months' work, and how I cursed Thee, how I cursed Thee; and how the lake of wine evaporated faster than the conduits replenished it, and the three journeys which I had to take to Constantinople for shiploads of wine, and my frothing despairs, till I had the thought of placing the reservoir in the platform; and how I had then to break down the south side of the platform to the very bottom, and the month-long nightmare of terror that I had lest the south side of the palace would undergo subsidence; and how the petrol failed, and of the three-weeks' search for petrol along the coast; and how, after list-rubbing all the jet, I found that I had forgotten the necessary rouge for polishing; and how, in the third year, I found the fluate, which I had for waterproofing the pores of the platform-stone, nearly all leaked away in the *Speranza's* hold, and I had to get silicate of soda at Gallipoli; and how, after two years' observation, I had to come to the conclusion that the lake was leaking, and discovered that this Imbros sand was not suitable for mixing with the skin of Portland cement which covered the cement concrete, and had to substitute sheet-bitumen in three places; and how I did all, all for the sake of God, thinking: "I will work, and be a good man, and cast Hell from me: and when I see it stand finished, it will be an Altar and a Testimony to me, and I shall find peace, and be well": and how I have been cheated—seventeen years, long years of my life—for there is no God; and how my plasterers'-hair failed me, and I had to use flock, hessian, scrym, wadding, wood-street paving-blocks, and whatever I could find, for filling the interspaces between the platform cross-walls; and of the espagnolette bolts, how a number of them mysteriously disappeared, as if snatched to Hell by harpies, and I had to make them; and how the crane-chain would not reach two of the silver-panel castings when they were finished, and they were too heavy for me to lift, and the wringing of the hands of my despair, and my biting of the earth, and the transport of my fury; and how, for a whole wild week, I searched in vain for the text-book which describes the ambering process; and how, when all was nearly over, in the blasting away of the forge and crane with dynamite, a long crack appeared down the gold of the east platform-steps, and how I would not be consoled, but mourned and mourned; and how, in spite of all my tribulations, it was sweetly interesting to watch my power slowly grow from the first feeble beginnings of the landing of materials and unloading them from the motor, a hundredweight at a time, till I could swing four tons—see the solid metals flow—enjoy the gliding sounds of the handle, crank-shaft, and system of levers, forcing inwards the mould-end, and the upper and lower plungers, for pressing the material—built at ease in a travelling-cage—and watch from my hut-door through sleepless hours, under the electric moon-light of this land, the three piles of gold stones, the silver panels, the two-foot squares of jet, and be comforted; and how the putty-wash—but it is past, it is past: and not to live over again that vulgar nightmare of means and ends have I taken to this writing again—but to put down something else, if I dare.

Seventeen years, my good God, of that delusion! I could write down no sort of explanation for all those groans and griefs, at which a reasoning being would not shriek with laughter. I should have lived at ease in some palace of the Middle-Orient, and burned my cities: but no, I must be "a good man"—vain thought. The words of a wild madman, that preaching man in England who prophesied what happened, were with me, where he says: "the defeat of Man is *His* defeat"; and I said to myself: "Well, the last man shall not be quite a fiend, just to spite That Other." And I worked and groaned, saying: "I will be a good man, and burn nothing, nor utter aught unseemly, nor debauch myself, but choke back the blasphemies that Those Others shriek through my throat, and build and build, with moils and groans." And it was Vanity: though I do love the house, too, I love it well, for it is my home on the waste earth.

I had calculated to finish it in twelve years, and I should have finished it in fourteen, instead of in sixteen and seven months, but one day, when the south, north, and east platform-steps were already finished—it was in the July of the third year, and near sunset—as I left off work, instead of going to the tent where my dinner lay ready, I walked down to the ship—most strangely—in a daft, mechanical sort of way, without saying a word to myself, an evil-meaning smile of malice on my lips; and at midnight I was lying off Mitylene, thirty miles to the south, having bid, as I thought, a last farewell to all those toils. I was going to burn Athens.

I did not, however: but kept on my way westward round Cape Matapan, intending to destroy the forests and towns of Sicily, if I found there a suitable motor for travelling, for I had not been at the pains to take the motor on board at Imbros; otherwise I would ravage parts of southern Italy. But when I came thereabouts, I was confronted with an awful horror: for no southern Italy was there, and no Sicily was there, unless a small new island, probably not five miles long, was Sicily; and nothing else I saw, save the still-smoking crater of Stromboli. I cruised northward, searching for land, and for a long time would not believe the evidence of the instruments, thinking that they wilfully misled me, or I stark mad. But no: no Italy was there, till I came to the latitude of Naples, it, too, having disappeared, engulfed, engulfed, all that stretch. From this monstrous thing I received so solemn a shock and mood of awe, that the evil mind in me was quite chilled and quelled; for it was, and is, my belief that a widespread re-arrangement of the earth's surface is being purposed, and in all that drama, O my God, how shall I be found?

However, I went on my way, but more leisurely, not daring for a long time to do anything, lest I might offend anyone; and, in this foolish cowering mind, coasted all the western coast of Spain and France during five weeks, in that prolonged intensity of calm weather which now alternates with storms that transcend all thought, till I came again to Calais: and there, for the first time, landed.

Here I would no longer contain myself, but burned; and that magnificent stretch of forest between Agincourt and Abbéville, covering five square miles, I burned; and Abbéville I burned; and Amiens I burned; and three forests between Amiens and Paris I burned; and Paris I burned; burning and burning during four months, leaving behind me smoking districts, a long tract of ravage, like some being of the Pit that blights where pass his flaming wings.

     *   *   *   *   *

This of city-burning has now become a habit with me more enchanting—and infinitely more debased—than ever was opium to the smoker, or alcohol to the drunkard. I count it among the prime necessaries of my life: it is my brandy, my bacchanal, my secret sin. I have burned Calcutta, Pekin, and San Francisco. In spite of the restraining influence of this palace, I have burned and burned. I have burned two hundred cities and countrysides. Like Leviathan disporting himself in the sea, so I have rioted in this earth.

     *   *   *   *   *

After an absence of six months, I returned to Imbros: for I was for looking again upon the work which I had done, that I might mock myself for all that unkingly groveling: and when I saw it, standing there as I had left it, frustrate and forlorn, and waiting its maker's hand, some pity and instinct to build took me—for something of God was in Man—and fell upon my knees, and spread my arms to God, and was converted, promising to finish the palace, with prayers that as I built so He would build my soul, and save the last man from the enemy. And I set to work that day to list-rub the last few dalles of the jet.

     *   *   *   *   *

I did not leave Imbros after that during four years, except for occasional brief trips to the coast—to Kilid-Bahr, Gallipoli, Lapsaki, Gamos, Rodosto, Erdek, Erekli, or even once to Constantinople and Scutari—if I happened to want anything, or if I was tired of work: but without once doing the least harm to anything, but containing my humours, and fearing my Maker. And full of peaceful charm were those little cruises through this Levantic world, which, truly, is rather like a light sketch in water-colours done by an angel than like the dun real earth; and full of self-satisfaction and pious contentment would I return to Imbros, approved of my conscience, for that I had surmounted temptation, and lived tame and stainless.

I had set up the southern of the two closed-lotus pillars, and the platform-top was already looking as lovely as heaven, with its alternate two-foot squares of pellucid gold and pellucid jet, when I noticed one morning that the *Speranza's* bottom was really now too foul, and the whim took me then and there to leave all, and clean her as far as I could. I at once went on board, descended to the hold, threw off my sudeyrie, and began to shift the ballast over to starboard, so as to tilt up her port bottom to the scraper. This was wearying labour, and about noon I was sitting on a bag, resting in the almost darkness, when something seemed to whisper to me these words: "*You dreamed last night that there is an old Chinaman alive in Pekin.*" Horridly I started: I *had* dreamed something of the sort, but, from the moment of waking, till then, I had forgotten it: and I leapt livid to my feet.

I cleaned no *Speranza* that day, nor for four days did I anything, but sat on the cabin-house and mused, my supporting palm among the hairy draperies of my chin: for the thought of such a thing, if it could by any possibility be true, was detestable as death to me, changing the colour of the sun, and the whole aspect of the world: and anon, at the outrage of that thing, my brow would flush with wrath, and my eyes blaze: till in the fourth afternoon, I said to myself: "That old Chinaman in Pekin is likely to get burned to death, I think, or blown to the clouds!"

So, a second time, on the 4th March, the poor palace was left to build itself. For, after a short trip to Gallipoli, where I got some young lime-twigs in boxes of earth, and some preserved limes and ginger, I set out for a long voyage to the East, passing through the Suez Canal, and visiting Bombay, where I was three weeks, and then destroyed it.

*　　*　　*　　*　　*

I had the thought of going across Hindostan by engine, but did not like to leave my ship, to which I was very attached, not sure of finding anything so suitable and good at Calcutta; and, moreover, I was afraid to abandon my petrol motor, which I had taken on board with the air-windlass, since I was going to uncivilised land. I therefore went down western Hindostan.

All that northern shore of the Arabian Sea has at the present time an odour which it wafts far over the water, resembling odours of happy vague dream-lands, sweet to smell in the early mornings as if the earth were nothing but a perfume, and life an inhalation.

On that voyage, however, I had, from beginning to end, twenty-seven fearful storms, or, if I count that one near the Carolines, then twenty-eight. But I do not wish to write of these rages: they were too inhuman: and how I came alive through them against all my wildest hope, Someone, or Something, only knows.

I will write down here a thing: it is this, my God—something which I have observed: a definite obstreperousness in the mood of the elements now, when once roused, which grows, which grows continually. Tempests have become very far more wrathful, the sea more truculent and unbounded in its insolence; when it thunders, it thunders with a venom new to me, cracking as though it would split the firmament, and bawling through the heaven of heavens, as if roaring to devour all things; in Bombay once, and in China thrice, I was shaken by earthquakes, the second and third marked by a certain extravagance of agitation, that might turn a man grey. Why should this be, my God? I remember reading very long ago that on the American prairies, which from time immemorial had been swept by great storms, the storms gradually subsided when man went to reside permanently there. If this be true, it would seem that the mere presence of man had a certain subduing or mesmerising effect upon the native turbulence of Nature, and his absence now may have removed the curb. It is my belief that within fifty years from now the huge forces of the earth will be let fully loose to tumble as they will; and this planet will become one of the undisputed playgrounds of Hell, and the theatre of commotions stupendous as those witnessed on the face of Saturn.

*   *   *   *   *

The Earth is all on my brain, on my brain, O dark-minded Mother, with thy passionate cravings after the Infinite, thy regrets, and mighty griefs, and co-matose sleeps, and sinister coming doom, O Earth: and I, poor man, though a king, sole witness of thy bleak tremendous woes. Upon her I brood, and do not cease, but brood and brood—the habit, if I remember right, first becoming fixed and fated during that long voyage eastward: for what is in store for her God only knows, and I have seen in my broodings long visions of her future, which, if a man should see with the eye of flesh, he would spread the arms, and wheel and wheel through the mazes of a hiccuping giggling frenzy, for the vision only is the very verge of madness. If I might cease but for one hour that perpetual brooding upon her! But I am her child, and my mind grows and grows to her like the off-shoots of the banyan-tree, that take root downward, and she sucks and draws it, as she draws my feet by gravitation, and I cannot take wing from her: for she is greater than I, and there is no escaping her; and at the last, I know, my soul will dash itself to ruin, like erring sea-fowl upon pharos-lights, against her wild and mighty bosom. Often a whole night through I lie open-eyed in the dark, with bursting brain, thinking of that hollow Gulf of Mexico, how identical in shape and size with the protuberance of Africa just opposite, and how the protuberance of the Venezuelan and Brazilian coast fits in with the in-curve of Africa: so that it is obvious to me—it is quite *obvious*—that they once were one; and one night rushed so far apart; and the wild Atlantic knew that thing, and ran gladly, hasting in between: and how if eye of flesh had been there to see, and ear to hear that cruel thundering, my God, my God—what horror! And if now they meet again, so long apart . . . but that way fury lies. Yet one cannot but think: I lie awake and think, for she fills my soul, and absorbs it, with all her moods and ways. She has meanings, secrets, plans. Strange, strange, for instance, that simi-larity between the scheme of Europe and the scheme of Asia: each with three southern peninsulas pointing south: Spain corresponding with Arabia, Italy with India, the Morea and Greece, divided by the Gulf of Corinth, corresponding with the Malay Peninsula and Annam, divided by the Gulf of Siam; each with two northern peninsulas pointing south, Sweden and Norway, Korea and Kam-schatka; each with two great islands similarly placed, Britain and Ireland, and the Japanese Hondo and Yezo; the Old World and the New has each a penin-sula pointing north—Denmark and Yucatan: a forefinger with long nail—and a thumb—pointing to the Pole. What does she mean? What can she mean, O Ye that made her? Is she herself a living being, with a will and a fate, as sailors said that ships were living entities? And that thing that wheeled at the Pole, wheels it still yonder, yonder, in its dark ecstasy? Strange that volcanoes are all near the sea: I don't know why; I don't think that anyone ever knew. This fact, in connection with submarine explosions, used to be cited in support of the chemical theory of volcanoes, which supposed the infiltration of the sea into ravines containing the materials which form the fuel of eruptions: but God knows if that is true. The lofty ones are intermittent—a century, two, ten, of still waiting, and then their talk silenced for ever some poor district; the low ones are constant in action. Who could know the dark way of the world? Sometimes they form a linear system, consisting of several vents which extend in one direction, near together, like chimneys of some long foundry beneath. In mountains, a series of serrated peaks denotes the presence of dolomites; rounded heads mean calcareous rocks; and needles, crystalline schists. The preponderance of land in the northern hemisphere denotes the greater intensity there of the causes of elevation at a remote geologic epoch: that is all that one can say about it: but whence that greater intensity? I have some knowledge of the earth for only ten miles down: but she has eight thousand miles: and whether through all that depth she is flame or fluid, hard or soft, I do not know, I do not know. Her method of forming coal, geysers and hot sulphur-springs, and the jewels, and the atols and coral reefs; the metamorphic rocks of sedimentary origin, like gneiss, the plutonic and volcanic rocks, rocks of fusion, and the unstratified masses which constitute the basis of the crust; and harvests, the burning flame of flowers, and the passage from the vegetable to the animal: I do not know them, but they are of her, and they are like me, molten in the same furnace of her fiery heart. She is dark and moody, sudden and ill-fated, and rends her young like a cannibal lioness; and she is old and wise, and remembers Hur of the Chaldees which Uruk built, and that Temple of Bel which rose in seven pyramids to symbolise the planets, and Birs-i-Nimrud, and Haran, and she bears still, as a thing of yesterday, old Persepolis and the tomb of Cyrus, and those cloister-like vihârah-temples of the ancient Buddhists, cut from the Himalayan rock; and returning from the Far East, I stopped at Ismailia, and so to Cairo, and saw where Memphis was, and stood one bright midnight before that great pyramid of Shafra, and that dumb Sphynx, and, seated in a well of one of the rock-tombs, looked till tears of pity streamed down my cheeks: for great is the earth, and her Ages, but man "passeth away." These tombs have columns extremely like the two palace-pillars, only that these are round, and mine are square: for I chose it so: but the same band near the top, then over this the closed lotus-flower, then the small square plinth, which separates them from the architrave, only mine have no architrave; the tombs consist of a little outer temple or court, then comes a well, and inside another chamber, where, I suppose, the dead were, a ribbon-like astragal surrounding the walls, which are crowned with boldly-projecting cornices, surmounted by an abacus. And here, till the pressing want of food drove me back, I remained: for more and more the earth over-grows me, woos me, assimilates me; so that I ask myself this question: "Must I not, in time, cease to be a man, and become a small earth, precisely her copy, extravagantly weird and fierce, half-demoniac, half-ferine, wholly mystic—morose and turbulent—fitful, and deranged, and sad—like her?"

*   *   *   *   *

A whole month of that voyage, from May the 15th to June the 13th, I wasted at the Andaman Islands near Malay: for that any old Chinaman should be alive in Pekin began, after some time, to seem the most quixotic notion that ever entered a human brain; and these jungled islands, to which I came after a shocking vast orgy one night at Calcutta, when I fired not only the city but the river, pleased my fancy to such an extent, that at one time I intended to abide there. I was at the one called in the chart "Saddle Hill," the smallest of them, I think: and seldom have I had such sensations of peace as I lay a whole burning day in a rising vale, deeply-shaded in palm and tropical ranknesses, watching thence the *Speranza* at anchor: for there was a little offing here at the shore whence the valley arose, and I could see one of its long peaks lined with cocoanut-trees, and all cloud burned out of the sky except the flimsiest lawn-figments, and the sea as absolutely calm as a lake roughened with breezes, yet making a considerable noise in its breaking on the shore, as I have noticed in these sorts of places: I do not know why. These poor Andaman people seem to have been quite savage, for I met a number of them in roaming the island, nearly skeletons, yet with limbs and vertebræ still, in general, cohering, and in some cases dry-skinned and mummified relics of flesh, and never anywhere a sign of clothes: a very singular thing, considering their nearness to high old civilisations all about them. They looked small and black, or almost; and I never found a man without finding on or near him a spear and other weapons: so that they were eager folk, and the wayward dark earth was in them, too, as she should be in her children. They had in many cases some reddish discoloration, which may have been the traces of betel-nut stains: for betel-nuts abound there. And I was so pleased with these people, that I took on board with the gig one of their little tree-canoes: which was my foolishness: for gig and canoe were only three days later washed from the decks into the middle of the sea.

*   *   *   *   *

I passed down the Straits of Malacca, and in that short distance between the Andaman Islands and the S.W. corner of Borneo I was thrice so mauled, that at times it seemed out of the question that anything built by man could escape such unfettered cataclysms, and I resigned myself, but with bitter re-proaches, to perish darkly. The effect of the third upon me, when it was over, was the unloosening afresh of all my evil passion: for I said: "Since they mean to slay me, death shall find me rebellious"; and for weeks I did not sight some specially happy village, or umbrageous spread of woodland, that I did not stop the ship, and land the materials for their destruction; so that nearly all those spicy lands about the north of Australia will bear the traces of my hand for

many a year: for more and more my voyage became dawdling and zigzaged, as
the merest whim directed it, or the movement of the pointer on the chart; and
I thought of eating the lotus of surcease and nepenthe in some enchanted nook
of this bowering summer, where from my hut-door I could see through the
pearl-hues of opium the sea-lagoon slaver lazily upon the old coral atol, and
the cocoanut-tree would droop like slumber, and the bread-fruit tree would
moan in sweet and weary dream, and I should watch the *Speranza* lie anchored
in the pale atol-lake, year after year, and wonder what she was, and whence,
and why she dozed so deep for ever, and after an age of melancholy peace and
burdened bliss, I should note that sun and moon had ceased revolving, and
hung inert, opening anon a heavy lid to doze and drowse again, and God would
sigh "Enough," and nod, and Being would swoon to sleep: for that any old
Chinaman should be alive in Pekin was a thing so fantastically maniac, as to
draw from me at times sudden fits of wild red laughter that left me faint.

During a space of four months, from the 18th June to the 23rd October, I
visited the Fijis, where I saw skulls still surrounded with remnants of extraordinary haloes of stiff hair, women clad in girdles made of thongs fixed in a belt,
and, in Samoa near, bodies crowned with coronets of nautilus-shell, and traces
of turmeric-paint and tattooing, and in one townlet a great assemblage of carcasses, suggesting by their look some festival, or dance: so that I believe that
these people were overthrown without the least foreknowledge of anything.
The women of the Maoris wore an abundance of green-jade ornaments, and I
found a peculiar kind of shell-trumpet, one of which I have now, also a tattooing chisel, and a nicely-carved wooden bowl. The people of New Caledonia, on
the other hand, went, I should think, naked, confining their attention to the
hair, and in this resembling the Fijians, for they seemed to wear an artificial
hair made of the fur of some creature like a bat, and also they wore wooden
masks, and great rings—for the ear, no doubt—which must have fallen to the
shoulders: for the earth was in them all, and made them wild, perverse and
various like herself. I went from one to the other without any system whatever,
searching for the ideal resting-place, and often thinking that I had found it: but
only wearying of it at the thought that there was a yet deeper and dreamier in
the world. But in this search I received a check, my God, which chilled me to
the marrow, and set me flying from these places.

*   *   *   *   *

One evening, the 29th November, I dined rather late—at eight—sitting,
as was my custom in calm weather, cross-legged on the cabin-rug at the port
aft corner, a small semicircle of *Speranza* gold-plate before me, and near above
me the red-shaded lamp with green conical reservoir, whose creakings never
cease in the stillest mid-sea, and beyond the plates the array of preserved
soups, meat-extracts, meats, fruit, sweets, wines, nuts, liqueurs, coffee on the
silver spirit-tripod, glasses, cruet, and so on, which it was always my first care to
select from the store-room, open, and lay out once for all in the morning on
rising. I was late, seven being my hour: for on that day I had been engaged in

the occasionally necessary, but always deferred, task of overhauling the ship, brushing here a rope with tar, there a board with paint, there a crank with oil, rubbing a door-handle, a brass-fitting, filling the three cabin-lamps, dusting mirrors and furniture, dashing the great neck-joinered plains of deck with bucketfulls, or, high in the air, chopping loose with its rigging the mizzen top-mast, which since a month was sprained at the clamps, all this in cotton draw-ers under loose *quamis*, bare-footed, my beard knotted up, the sun a-blaze, the sea smooth and pale with the smooth pallor of strong currents, the ship still enough, no land in sight, yet great tracts of sea-weed making eastward—I working from 11 A.M. till near 7, when sudden darkness interrupted: for I wished to have it all over in one obnoxious day. I was therefore very tired when I went down, lit the central chain-lever lamp and my own two, washed and dressed in my bedroom, and sat to dinner in the dining-hall corner. I ate vora-ciously, with sweat, as usual, pouring down my eager brow, using knife or spoon in the right hand, but never the Western fork, licking the plates clean in the Mohammedan manner, and drinking pretty freely. Still I was tired, and went upon deck, where I had the threadbare blue-velvet easy-chair with the broken left arm before the wheel, and in it sat smoking cigar after cigar from the In-dian D box, half-asleep, yet conscious. The moon came up into a pretty cloud-less sky, and she was bright, but not bright enough to out-shine the enlightened flight of the ocean, which that night was one continuous swamp of Jack-o'-lantern phosphorescence, a wild but faint luminosity mingled with stars and flashes of brilliance, the whole trooping unanimously eastward, as if in haste with elfin momentous purpose, a boundless congregation, in the sweep of a strong oceanic current. I could hear it, in my slumbrous lassitude, struggling and gurgling at the tied rudder, and making wet sloppy noises under the sheer of the poop; and I was aware that the *Speranza* was gliding along pretty fast, drawn into that procession at the rate of four to six knots: but I did not care, knowing very well that no land was within two hundred miles of my bows, for I was in longitude 173°, in the latitude of Fiji and the Society Islands, between those two: and after a time the cigar drooped and dropped from my mouth, and sleep overcame me, and I slept there, in the lap of the Infinite.

*   *   *   *   *

So that something preserves me, Something, Someone: *and for what? . . .* If I had slept in the cabin, I must most certainly have perished: for lying there on the poop, I dreamed a dream which once I had dreamed on the ice, far, far yonder in the forgotten hyperborean North: that I was in an Arabian paradise, a Garden of Peaches; and I had a very long vision of it, for I walked among the trees, and picked the fruit, and pressed the blossoms to my nostrils with breath-less inhalations of love: till a horrible sickness woke me: and when I opened my eyes, the night was black, the moon gone down, everything wet with dew, the sky arrayed with most glorious stars like a thronged bazaar of tiaraed rajahs and begums with spangled trains, and all the air fragrant with that mortal scent; and high and wide uplifted before me—stretching from the northern to the

southern limit—a row of eight or nine inflamed smokes, as from the chimneys
of some Cyclopean foundry a-work all night, most solemn, most great and
dreadful in the solemn night: eight or nine, I should say, or it might be seven,
or it might be ten, for I did not count them; and from those craters puffed up
gusts of encrimsoned material, here a gust and there a gust, with tinselled
fumes that convolved upon themselves, and sparks and flashes, all veiled in a
garish haze of light: for the foundry worked, though languidly; and upon a
rocky land four miles ahead, which no chart had ever marked, the *Speranza*
drove straight with the current of the phosphorus sea.

As I rose, I fell flat: and what I did thereafter I did in a state of existence
whose acts, to the waking mind, appear unreal as dream. I must at once, I think,
have been conscious that here was the cause of the destruction of mankind; that
it still surrounded its own neighbourbood with poisonous fumes; and that I was
approaching it. I must have somehow crawled, or dragged myself forward. There
is an impression on my mind that it was a purple land of pure porphyry; there is
some faint memory, or dream, of hearing a long-drawn booming of waves upon
its crags: I do not know whence I have them. I think that I remember retching
with desperate jerks of my travailing intestines; also that I was on my face as I
moved the regulator in the engine-room: but any recollection of going down the
stairs, or of coming up again, I have not. Happily, the wheel was tied, the rudder
hard to port, and as the ship moved, she must, therefore, have turned; and I
must have been back to untie the wheel in good time, for when my senses came,
I was lying there, my head against the under gimbal, one foot on a spoke of the
wheel, no land in sight, and morning breaking.

This made me so sick, that for either two or three days I lay without eating
in the chair near the wheel, only rarely waking to sufficient sense to see to it
that she was making westward from that place; and on the morning when I finally roused myself I did not know whether it was the second or the third
morning: so that my calendar, so scrupulously kept, may be a day out, for to
this day I have never been at the pains to ascertain whether I am here writing
now on the 5th or the 6th of June.

*   *   *   *   *

Well, on the fourth, or the fifth, evening after this, as the sun was sinking
beyond the rim of the sea, I happened to look where he hung motionless on
the starboard bow: and there I saw a clean-cut black-green spot against his
red—a most unusual sight here and now—a ship: a poor thing, as it turned out
when I got near her, without any sign of mast, heavily water-logged, some relics
of old rigging hanging over, even her bowsprit broken in the middle (though I
could not see it), and she nothing more than a hirsute green mass of old weeds
and sea-things from bowsprit-tip to poop, and from bulwarks to water-line,
stout as a hedgehog, only awaiting there the next high sea to founder.

It being near my dinner-hour and night's rest, I stopped the *Speranza* some
fifteen yards from her, and commenced to pace my spacious poop, as usual, before eating; and as I paced, I would glance at her, wondering at her destiny,

and who were the human men that had lived on her, their Christian names, and family names, their age, and thought, and way of life, and beards; till the desire arose within me to go to her, and see; and I threw off my outer garments, uncovered and unroped the cedar cutter—the only boat, except the air-pinnace, left to me intact—and got her down by the mizzen five-block pulley-system. But it was a ridiculous nonsense, for having paddled to her, I was thrown into paroxysms of rage by repeated failures to scale her bulwarks, low as they were; my hands, indeed, could reach, but I found no hold upon the slimy mass, and three rope-ends which I caught were also untenably slippery: so that I jerked always back into the boat, my clothes a mass of filth, and the only thought in my blazing brain a twenty-pound charge of guncotton, of which I had plenty, to blow her to uttermost Hell. I had to return to the *Speranza*, get a half-inch rope, then back to the other, for I would not be baulked in such a way, though now the dark was come, only slightly tempered by a half-moon, and I getting hungry, and from minute to minute more fiendishly ferocious. Finally, by dint of throwing, I got the rope-loop round a mast-stump, drew myself up, and made fast the boat, my left hand cut by some cursed shell: and all for what? the imperiousness of a whim. The faint moonshine shewed an ample tract of deck, invisible in most parts under rolled beds of putrid seaweed, and no bodies, and nothing but a concave, large esplanade of seaweed. She was a ship of probably 1,500 tons, three-masted, and a sailer. I got aft (for I had on thick outer babooshes), and saw that only four of the companion-steps remained; by a small leap, however, I could descend into that desolation, where the stale sea-stench seemed concentrated into a very essence of rankness. Here I experienced a singular ghostly awe and timorousness, lest she should sink with me, or something: but striking matches, I saw an ordinary cabin, with some fungoids, skulls, bones and rags, but not one cohering skeleton. In the second starboard berth was a small table, and on the floor a thick round ink-pot, whose continual rolling on its side made me look down; and there I saw a flat square book with black covers, which curved half-open of itself, for it had been wet and stained. This I took, and went back to the *Speranza*: for that ship was nothing but an emptiness, and a stench of the crude elements of life, nearly assimilated now to the rank deep to which she was wedded, and soon to be absorbed into its nature and being, to become a sea in little, as I, in time, my God, shall be nothing but an earth in little.

During dinner, and after, I read the book, with some difficulty, for it was pen-written in French, and discoloured, and it turned out to be the journal of someone, a passenger and voyager, I imagine, who called himself Albert Tissu, and the ship the *Marie Meyer*. There was nothing remarkable in the narrative that I could see—commonplace descriptions of South Sea scenes, records of weather, cargoes, and the like—till I came to the last written page: and that was remarkable enough. It was dated the 13th of April—strange thing, my good God, incredibly strange—that same day, twenty long years ago, when I reached the Pole; and the writing on that page was quite different from the neat look of the rest, proving immoderate excitement, wildest haste; and he heads it "*Cinq Heures*,"—I suppose in the evening, for he does not say: and he writes: "Monstrous event! phenomenon without likeness! the witnesses of which must for ever live immortalised in the annals of the universe, an event which will make even Mama, Henri and Juliette admit that I was justified in undertaking this most eventful voyage. Talking with Captain Tombarel on the poop, when a sudden exclamation from him—'*Mon Dieu!*' His visage whitens! I follow the direction of his gaze to eastward! I behold! eight *kilomètres* perhaps away—*ten monstrous waterspouts*, reaching up, up, high enough—all apparently in one straight line, with intervals of nine hundred *mètres*, very regularly placed. They do not wander, dance, nor waver, as waterspouts do; nor are they at all lily-shaped, like waterspouts: but ten hewn pillars of water, with uniform diameter from top to bottom, only a little twisted here and there, and, as I divine, fifty *mètres* in girth. Five, ten, stupendous minutes we look, while Captain Tombarel mechanically repeating and repeating under his breath '*Mon Dieu!*' '*Mon Dieu!*' the whole crew now on the poop, I agitated, but collected, watch in hand. And suddenly, all is blotted out: the pillars of water, doubtless still there, can no more be seen: for the ocean all about them is steaming, hissing higher still than the pillars a dense white vapour, vast in extent, whose venomous sibilation we at this distance can quite distinctly hear. It is affrighting, it is intolerable! the eyes can hardly bear to watch, the ears to hear! it seems unholy travail, monstrous birth! But it lasts not long: all at once the *Marie Meyer* commences to pitch and roll violently, and the sea, a moment since calm, is now rough! and at the same time, through the white vapour, we see a dark shadow slowly rising—the shadow of a mighty back, a new-born land, bearing upwards flames of fire, slowly, steadily, out of the sea, into the clouds. At the moment when that sublime emergence ceases, or seems to cease, the grand thought that smites me is this: 'I, Albert Tissu, am immortalised: my name shall never perish from among men!' I rush down, I write it. The latitude is 16° 21′ 13″ South; the longitude 176° 58′ 19″ West.* There is a great deal of running about on the decks—they are descending. There is surely a strange odour of almonds—I only hope—it is so dark, *mon D*—"

So the Frenchman, Tissu.

*　　*　　*　　*　　*

With all that region I would have no more to do: for all here, it used to be said, lies a great sunken continent; and I thought it would be rising and shewing itself to my eyes, and driving me stark mad: for the earth is full of these contortions, sudden monstrous grimaces and apparitions, which are like the face of Medusa, affrighting a man into spinning stone; and nothing could be more appallingly insecure than living on a planet.

I did not stop till I had got so far northward as the Philippine Islands, where I was two weeks—exuberant, odorous places, but so hilly and rude, that at one place I abandoned all attempt at travelling in the motor, and left it in a

---

*This must be French reckoning, from meridian of Paris.

valley by a broad, shallow, noisy river, full of mossy stones: for I said: "Here I will live, and be at peace"; and then I had a fright, for during three days I could not re-discover the river and the motor, and I was in the greatest despair, thinking: "When shall I find my way out of these jungles and vastnesses?" For I was where no paths were, and had lost myself in deeps where the lure of the earth is too strong and rank for a single man, since in such places, I suppose, a man would rapidly be transformed into a tree, or a snake, or a tiger. At last, however, I found the place, to my great joy, but I would not shew that I was glad, and, to hide it, fell upon a front wheel of the car with some kicks. I could not make out who the people were that lived here: for the relics of some seemed quite black, like New Zealand races, and I could still detect the traces of tattooing, while others suggested Mongolian types, and some looked like pigmies, and some like whites. But I cannot detail the two-years' incidents of that voyage: for it is past, and like a dream: and not to write of that—of all that—have I taken this pencil in hand after seventeen long, long years.

*   *   *   *   *

Singular my reluctance to put it on paper.

I will write rather of the voyage to China, and how I landed the motor on the wharf at Tientsin, and went up the river through a maize and rice-land most charming in spite of intense cold, I thick with clothes as an Arctic traveller; and of the three dreadful earthquakes within two weeks; and how the only map which I had of the city gave no indication of the whereabouts of its military depositories, and I had to seek for them; and of the three days' effort to enter them, for every gate was solid and closed; and how I burned it, but had to observe its flames, without deep pleasure, from beyond the walls to the south, the whole place being one cursed plain; yet how, at one moment, I cried aloud with wild banterings and glad laughters of Tophet to that old Chinaman still alive within it; and how I coasted, and saw the hairy Ainus, man and woman hairy alike; and how, lying one midnight awake in my cabin, the *Speranza* being in a still glassy water under a cliff overhung by drooping trees—it was the harbour of Chemulpo—to me lying awake came the thought: "Suppose now you should hear a step walking to and fro, leisurely, on the poop above you—*just suppose*"; and the night of horrors which I had, for I could not help supposing, and at one time really thought that I heard it: and how the sweat rolled and poured from my brow; and how I went to Nagasaki, and burned it; and how I crossed over the great Pacific deep to San Francisco, for I knew that Chinamen had been there, too, and one of them might be alive; and how, one calm day, the 15th or the 16th April, I, sitting by the wheel in the mid-Pacific, suddenly saw a great white hole that ran and wheeled, and wheeled and ran, in the sea, coming toward me, and I was aware of the hot breath of a reeling wind, and then of the hot wind itself, which deep-groaned the sound of the letter V, humming like a billion spinning-tops, and the *Speranza* was on her side, sea pouring over her port-bulwarks, and myself in the corner between deck and taffrail, drowning fast, but unable to stir; but all was soon past and the white hole in the sea, and the hot spinning-top of wind, ran wheeling beyond, to the southern horizon, and the *Speranza* righted herself: so that it was clear that someone wished to destroy me, for that a typhoon of such vehemence ever blew before I cannot think; and how I came to San Francisco, and how I burned it, and had my sweets: for it was mine; and how I thought to pass over the great trans-continental railway to New York, but would not, fearing to leave the *Speranza*, lest all the ships in the harbour there should be wrecked, or rusted, and buried under sea-weed, and turned unto the sea; and how I went back, my mind all given up now to musings upon the earth and her ways, and a thought in my soul that I would return to those deep places of the Filipinas, and become an autochthone—a tree, or a snake, or a man with snake-limbs, like the old autochthones: but I would not: for Heaven was in man, too: Earth and Heaven; and how as I steamed round west again, another winter come, and I now in a mood of dismal despondencies, on the very brink of the inane abyss and smiling idiotcy, I saw in the island of Java a great temple of Boro Budor: and like a tornado, or volcanic event, my soul was changed: for my recent studies in the architecture of the human race recurred to me with interest, and three nights I slept in the temple, examining it by day. It is vast, with that look of solid massiveness which above all characterises the Japanese and Chinese building, my measurement of its widdth being 529 feet, and it rises terrace-like in six stories to a height of about 120 or 130 feet: here Buddhist and Brahmin forms are combined into a most richly-developed whole, with a voluptuousness of tracery that is simply intoxicating, each of the five off-sets being divided into an innumerable series of external niches, containing each a statue of the sitting Boodh, all surmounted by a number of cupolas, and the whole crowned by a magnificent dagop: and when I saw this, I had the impulse to return to my home after so long wandering, and to finish the temple of temples, and the palace of palaces; and I said: "I will return, and build it as a testimony to God."

*　　*　　*　　*　　*

Save for a time, near Cairo, I did not once stop on that homeward voyage, but turned into the little harbour at Imbros at a tranquil sunset on the 7th of March (as I reckon), and I moored the *Speranza* to the ring in the little quay, and I raised the battered motor from the hold with the middle air-engine (battered by the typhoon in the mid-Pacific, which had broken it from its rope-fastenings and tumbled it head-over-heels to port), and I went through the windowless village-street, and up through the plantains and cypresses which I knew, and the Nile mimosas, and mulberries, and Trebizond palms, and pines, and acacias, and fig-trees, till the thicket stopped me, and I had to alight: for in those two years the path had finally disappeared; and on, on foot, I made my way, till I came to the board-bridge, and leant there, and looked at the rill; and thence climbed the steep path in the sward toward that rolling table-land where I had built with many a groan; and half-way up, I saw the tip of the crane-arm, then the blazing top of the south pillar, then the shed-roof, then the platform, a blinking blotch of glory to the watery eyes under the setting sun. But the tent, and nearly all that it contained, was gone.

*   *   *   *   *

For two days I would do nothing, simply lying and watching, shirking a load so huge: but on the fifth morning I languidly began something: and I had not worked an hour, when a fever took me—to finish it, to finish it—and it lasted upon me, with only three brief intervals, nearly seven years; nor would the end have been so long in coming, but for the unexpected difficulty of getting the four flat roofs water-tight, for I had to take down half the east one. Finally, I made them of gold slabs one-and-a-quarter inch thick, smooth on both sides, on each beam double gutters being fixed along each side of the top flange to catch any leakage at the joints, which are filled with slaters'-cement. The slabs are clamped to the top flanges by steel clips, having bolts set with plaster-of-Paris in holes drilled in the slabs. These clips are 1½ in. by 3/17 in., and are 17 in. apart. The roofs are slightly pitched to the front edges, where they drain into gold-plated copper-gutters on plated wrought-iron brackets, with one side flashed up over the blocks, which raise the slabs from the beam-tops, to clear the joint gutters. . . . But now I babble again of that base servitude, which I would forget, but cannot: for every measurement, bolt, ring, is in my brain, like a burden; but it is past—and it was vanity.

*   *   *   *   *

Six months ago to-day it was finished: six months more protracted, desolate, burdened, than all those sixteen years in which I built.

I wonder what a man—another man—some Shah, or Tsar, of that far-off past, would say now of me, if an eye could rest upon me! With awe would he certainly shrink before the wild majesty of these eyes; and though I am not lunatic—for I am not, I am not—how he would fly from me with the exclamation: "There is the lunacy of Pride!"

For there would seem to him—it must be so—in myself, in all about me, something extravagantly royal, touched with terror. My body has fattened, and my girth now fills out to a portly roundness its broad Babylonish girdle of crimson cloth, minutely gold-embroidered, and hung with silver, copper and gold coins of the Orient; my beard, still black, sweeps in two divergent sheaves to my hips, flustered by every wind; as I walk through this palace, the amber-and-silver floor reflects in its depths my low-necked, short-armed robe of purple, blue, and scarlet, a-glow with luminous stones. I am ten times crowned Lord and Emperor; I sit a hundred times enthroned in confirmed, obese old Majesty. Challenge me who will—challenge me who dare! Among those myriad worlds upon which I nightly pore, I may have my Peers and Compeers and Fellow-denizens . . . but *here* I am Sole; Earth acknowledges my ancient sway and hereditary sceptre: for though she draws me, not yet, not yet, am I hers, but she is mine. It seems to me not less than a million million æons since other beings, more or less resembling me, walked impudently in the open sunlight on this planet, which is rightly mine—I can indeed no longer picture to myself, nor even credit, that such a state of things—so fantastic, so far-fetched, so infinitely droll—could have existed: though, at bottom, I suppose, I know that it must have been really so. Up to ten years ago, in fact, I used frequently to dream that there were others. I would see them walk in the streets like ghosts, and be troubled, and start awake: but never now could such a thing, I think, occur to me in sleep: for the wildness of the circumstance would certainly strike my consciousness, and immediately I should know that the dream was a dream. For now, at least, I am sole, I am lord. The golden walls of this palace which I have built look down, enamoured of their reflection, into a lake of the choicest, purplest wine.

Not that I made it of wine because wine is rare; nor the walls of gold because gold is rare: that would have been too childish: but because I would match for beauty a human work with the works of those Others: and because it happens, by some persistent freak of the earth, that precisely things most rare and costly are generally the most beautiful.

The vision of glorious loveliness which is this palace now risen before my eyes cannot be described by pen on paper, though there *may* be words in the lexicons of language which, if I sought for them with inspired wit for sixteen years, as I have built for sixteen years, might as vividly express my thought on paper, as the stones-of-gold, so grouped and built, express it to the eye: but, failing such labours and skill, I suppose I could not give, if there were another man, and I tried to give, the faintest conception of its celestial charm.

It is a structure positively as clear as the sun, and as fair as the moon—the sole great human work in the making of which no restraining thought of cost has played a part: one of its steps alone being of more cost than all the temples, mosques and besestins, the palaces, pagodas and cathedrals, built between the ages of the Nimrods and the Napoleons.

The house itself is very small—only 40 ft. long, by 35 broad, by 27 high: yet the structure as a whole is sufficiently enormous, high uplifted: the rest of the bulk being occupied by the platform, on which the house stands, each side of this measuring at its base 480 ft., its height from top to bottom 130 ft., and its top 48 ft. square, the elevation of the steps being just nearly 30 degrees, and the top reached from each of the four points of the compass by 183 low long steps, very massively overlaid with smooth molten gold—not forming a continuous flight, but broken into threes and fives, sixes and nines, with landings between the series, these from the top looking like a great terraced parterre of gold. It is thus an Assyrian palace in scheme: only that the platform has steps on all sides, instead of one. The platform-top, from its edge to the golden walls of the house, is a mosaic consisting of squares of the glassiest clarified gold, and squares and of the glassiest jet, corner to corner, each square 2 ft. wide. Around the edge of the platform on top run 48 square plain gold pilasters, 12 on each side, 2 ft. high, tapering upwards, and topped by a knob of solid gold, pierced with a hole through which passes a lax inch-and-a-half silver chain, hung with little silver balls which strike together in the breeze. The mansion consists of an outer court, facing east toward the sea, and the house proper, which encloses an inner court. The outer court is a hollow oblong 32 ft. wide by 8 ft. long, the summit of its three walls being battlemented; they are 18½ ft. in height, or 8½ ft. lower than the house; around their gold sides, on inside and outside, 3 ft. from the top, runs a plain flat band of silver, 1 ft. wide, projecting 2/3 in., and at the gate, which is a plain Egyptian entrance, facing eastwards, 2½ ft. narrower at top than at bottom, stand the two great square pillars of massive plain gold, tapering upwards, 45 ft. high, with their capital of band, closed lotus, and thin plinth; in the outer court, immediately opposite the gate, is an oblong well, 12 ft. by 3 ft., reproducing in little the shape of the court, its sides, which are gold-lined, tapering downward to near the bottom of the platform, where a conduit of 1/8 in. diameter automatically replenishes the ascertained mean evaporation of the lake during the year, the well containing 105,360 litres when nearly full, and the lake occupying a circle round the platform of 980 ft. diameter, with a depth of 3½ ft. Round the well run pilasters connected by silver chains with little balls, and it communicates by a 1/8 in. conduit with a pool of wine let into the inner court, this being fed from eight tall and narrow golden tanks, tapering upwards, which surround it, each containing a different red wine, sufficient to last for all purposes during my lifetime. The ground of the outer court is also a mosaic of jet and gold: but thenceforth the jet-squares give place throughout to squares of silver, and the gold-squares to squares of clear amber, clear as solidified oil. The entrance is by an Egyptian doorway 7 ft. high, with folding-doors of gold-plated cedar, opening inwards, surrounded by a very large projecting coping of plain silver, 3½ ft. wide, severe simplicity of line throughout enormously multiplying the effect of richness of material. The interior resembles, I believe, rather a Homeric, than an Assyrian or Egyptian house—except for the "galleries," which are purely Babylonish and Old Hebrew. The inner court, with its wine-pool and tanks, is a small oblong 8 ft. by 9 ft., upon which open four silver-latticed window-oblongs in the same proportion, and two doors, before and behind, oblongs in the same proportion. Round this run the eight walls of the house proper, the inner being 10 ft. from the outer, each parallel two forming a single long corridor-like chamber, except the front (east) two, which are divided into three apartments; in each side of the house are six panels of massive plain silver, half-an-inch thinner in their central space, where are affixed paintings, 22 or else 21 taken at the burning of Paris from a place called "The Louvre," and 2 or else 3 from a place in England: so that the panels having the look of frames, and are surrounded by oval garlands of the palest amethyst, topaz, sapphire, and turquoise which I could find, each garland being of only one kind of stone, a mere oval ring two feet wide at the sides and narrowing to an inch at the top and bottom, without designs. The galleries are five separate recesses in the outer walls under the roofs, two in the east façade, and one in the north, south, and west, hung with pavilions of purple, blue, rose and white silk on rings and rods of gold, with gold pilasters and banisters, each entered by four steps from its roof, to which lead, north and south, two spiral stairs of cedar. On the east roof stands the kiosk, under which is the little lunar telescope; and from that height, and from the galleries, I can watch under the bright moonlight of this climate, which is very like lime-light, the for-ever silent blue hills of Macedonia, and where the islands of Samothraki, Lemnos, Tenedos slumber like purplish fairies on the Ægean Sea: for, usually, I sleep during the day, and keep a night-long vigil, often at midnight descending to bathe my coloured baths in the lake, and to disport myself in that strange intoxication of nostrils, eyes, and pores, dreaming long wide-eyed dreams at the bottom, to return dazed, and weak, and drunken. Or again—*twice* within these last void and idle six months—I have suddenly run, bawling out, from this temple of luxury, tearing off my gaudy rags, to hide in a hut by the shore, smitten for one intense moment with realisation of the past of this earth, and moaning: "alone, alone . . . all alone, alone, alone . . . alone, alone. . . ." For events precisely resembling eruptions take place in my brain; and one spangled midnight—ah, how spangled!—I may kneel on the roof with streaming, up-lifted face, with out-spread arms, and awe-struck heart, adoring the Eternal: the next, I may strut like a cock, wanton as sin, lusting to burn a city, to wallow in filth, and, like the Babylonian maniac, calling myself the equal of Heaven.

*   *   *   *   *

But it was not to write of this—of all this—!

Of the furnishing of the palace I have written nothing. . . . But why I hesitate to admit to myself what I *know*, is not clear. If They speak to me, I may surely write of Them: for I do not fear Them, but am Their peer.

Of the island I have written nothing: its size, climate, form, vegetation. . . . There are two winds: a north and a south wind; the north is cool, and the south is warm; and the south blows during the winter months, so that sometimes on Christmas-day it is quite hot; and the north, which is cool, blows from May to September, so that the summer is hardly ever oppressive, and the climate was made for a king. The mangal-stove in the south hall I have never once lit.

The length, I should say, is 19 miles; the breadth 10, or thereabouts; and the highest mountains should reach a height of some 2,000 ft., though I have not been all over it. It is very densely wooded in most parts, and I have seen large growths of wheat and barley, obviously degenerate now, with currants, figs, valonia, tobacco, vines in rank abundance, and two marble quarries. From the palace, which lies on a sunny plateau of beautifully-sloping swards, dotted with the circular shadows thrown by fifteen huge cedars, and seven planes, I can see on all sides an edge of forest, with the gleam of a lake to the north, and in the hollow to the east the rivulet with its little bridge, and a few clumps and beds of flowers. I can spy right through—

*   *   *   *   *

It shall be written now:

I have this day heard within me the contention of the Voices.

*   *   *   *   *

I had thought that they were done with me! That all, all, all, was ended! I have not heard them for twenty years!

But to-day—distinctly—breaking in with brawling impassioned suddenness upon my consciousness . . . I heard.

This late *far niente* and vacuous inaction here have been undermining my spirit; this inert brooding upon the earth; this empty life, and bursting brain! Immediately after eating at noon to-day, I said to myself:

"I have been duped by the palace: for I have wasted myself in building, hoping for peace, and there is no peace. Therefore now I shall fly from it, to another, sweeter work—not of building, but of destroying—not of Heaven, but of Hell—not of self-denial, but of reddest orgy. Constantinople—beware!" I tossed the chair aside, and with a stamp was on my feet: and as I stood—again, again—I heard: the startlingly sudden wrangle, the fierce, vulgar outbreak and voluble controversy, till my consciousness could not hear its ears: and one urged: "Go! go!" and the other: "Not there! . . . where you like, . . . but not there! . . . for your life!"

I did not—for I could not—go: I was so overcome. I fell upon the couch shivering.

These Voices, or impulses, plainly as I felt them of old, quarrel within me now with an openness new to them. Lately, influenced by my long scientific habit of thought, I have occasionally wondered whether what I used to call "the two Voices" were not in reality two strong instinctive movements, such as most men may have felt, though with less force. But to-day doubt is past, doubt is past: nor, unless I be very mad, can I ever doubt again.

*   *   *   *   *

I have been thinking, thinking of my life: there is a something which I cannot understand.

There was a man whom I met once in that dark backward and abysm of time, when I must have been very young—I fancy at some college or school in England, and his name now is far enough beyond scope of my memory, lost in the vast limbo of past things. But he used to talk continually about certain "Black" and "White" Powers, and of their strife for this world. He was a short man with a Roman nose, and lived in fear of growing a paunch. His forehead a-top, in profile, was more prominent than the nose-end, he parted his hair in the middle, and had the theory that the male form was more beautiful than the female. I forget what his name was—the dim clear-obscure being. Very profound was the effect of his words upon me, though, I think, I used to make a point of slighting them. This man always declared that "the Black" would carry off the victory in the end: and so he has, so he has.

But assuming the existence of this "Black" and this "White" being—and supposing it to be a fact that my reaching the Pole had any connection with the destruction of my race, according to the notions of that extraordinary

Scotch parson—then it must have been the power of *"the Black"* which carried me, in spite of all obstacles, to the Pole. So far I can understand.

But *after* I had reached the Pole, what further use had either White or Black for me? Which was it—White or Black—that preserved my life through my long return on the ice—and *why?* It could not have been "the Black"! For I readily divine that from the moment when I touched the Pole, the only purpose of the Black, which had previously preserved, must have been to destroy me, with the rest. It must have been "the White," then, that led me back, retarding me long, so that I should not enter the poison-cloud, and then openly presenting me the *Boreal* to bring me home to Europe. But his motive? And the significance of these recommencing wrangles, after such a silence? This I do not understand!

Curse Them, curse Them, with their mad tangles! I care nothing for Them! Are there any White Idiots and Black Idiots—*at all?* Or are these Voices that I hear nothing but the cries of my own strained nerves, and I all mad and morbid, morbid and mad, mad, my good God?

This inertia here is *not good* for me! This stalking about the palace! and long thinkings about Earth and Heaven, Black and White, White and Black, and things beyond the stars! My brain is like bursting through the walls of my poor head.

To-morrow, then, to Constantinople.

*   *   *   *   *

Descending to go to the ship, I had almost reached the middle of the east platform-steps, when my foot slipped on the smooth gold: and the fall, though I was not walking carelessly, had, I swear, all the violence of a fall caused by a push. I struck my head, and, as I rolled downward, swooned. When I came to myself, I was lying on the very bottom step, which is thinly washed by the wine-waves: another roll and I suppose I must have drowned. I sat there an hour, lost in amazement, then crossed the causeway, came down to the *Speranza* with the motor, went through her, spent the day in work, slept on her, worked again to-day, till four, at both ship and time-fuses (I with only 700 fuses left, and in Stamboul alone must be 8,000 houses, without counting Galata, Tophana, Kassim-pacha, Scutari, and the rest), started out at 5.30, and am now at 11 P.M. lying motionless two miles off the north coast of the island of Marmora, with moonlight gloating on the water, a faint north breeze, and the little pale land looking immensely stretched-out, solemn and great, as if that were the world, and there were nothing else; and the tiny island at its end immense, and the *Speranza* vast, and I only little. To-morrow at 11 A.M. I will moor the *Speranza* in the Golden Horn at the spot where there is that low damp nook of the bagnio behind the naval magazines and that hill where the palace of the Capitan Pacha is.

*   *   *   *   *

I found that great tangle of ships in the Golden Horn wonderfully preserved, many with hardly any moss-growths. Thus must be due, I suppose, to the little Ali-Bey and Kezat-Hanah, which flow into the Horn at the top, and made no doubt a constant current.

Ah, I remember the place: long ago I lived here some months, or, it may be, years. It is the fairest of cities—and the greatest. I believe that London in England was larger; but no city, surely, ever *seemed* so large. But it is flimsy, and will burn like tinder. The houses are made of light timber, with interstices filled by earth and bricks, and some of them look ruinous already, with their lovely faded tints of green and gold and red and blue and yellow, like the hues of withered flowers: for it is a city of paints and trees, and all in the little winding streets, as I write, are volatile almond-blossoms, mixed with maple-blossoms, white with purple. Even the most splendid of the Sultan's palaces are built in this combustible way: for I believe that they had a notion that stone-building was presumptuous, though I have seen some very thick stone-houses in Galata. Thus place, I remember, lived in a constant state of sensation on account of nightly flares-up; and I have come across several tracts already devastated by fires. The ministers-of-state used to attend them, and if the fire would not go out, the Sultan himself was obliged to be there, in order to encourage the firemen. Now it will burn still better.

But I have been here six weeks, and still no burning: for the place seems to plead with me, it is so ravishing, so that I do not know why I did not live here, and spare my toils during those sixteen nightmare years; for two whole weeks the impulse to burn was quieted; and since then there has been an irritating whisper at my ear which said: "It is not really like the great King that you are, this burning, but like a foolish child, or a savage, who liked to see fireworks; or least, if you must burn, do not burn poor Constantinople, which is so charming, and so very old, with its balsamic perfumes, and the blossomy trees of white and light-purple peeping over the walls of the cloistered painted houses, and all those lichened tombs—those granite menhirs and regions of ancient marble tombs between the quarters, Greek tombs, Byzantine, Jew, Mussulman tombs, with their strange and sacred inscriptions—overwaved by their cypresses and their vast plane-trees." And for weeks I would do nothing: but roamed about, with two minds in me, under the tropic brilliance of the sky by day, and the vast dreamy nights of this place that are like nights seen through azure-tinted glasses, and in each of them is not one night, but the thousand-and-one long crowded nights of glamour and fancy: for I would sit on the immense esplanade of the Seraskierat, or the mighty grey stones of the porch of the mosque of Mehmed-fatih, dominating from its great steps all Stamboul, and watch the moon for hours and hours, so passionately bright she soared through clear and cloud, till I would be smitten with doubt of my own identity, for whether I were she, or the earth, or myself, or some other thing or man, I did not know, all being so silent alike, and all, except myself, so vast, the Seraskierat, and the Suleimanieh, and Stamboul, and the Marmora Sea, and the earth, and those argent fields of the moon, all large alike compared with me, and measure and space were lost, and I with them.

*   *   *   *   *

These proud Turks died stolidly, many of them. In streets of Kassim-pacha, in crowded Taxim on the heights of Pera, and under the long Moorish arcades of Sultan-Selim, I have seen the open-air barber's razor with his bones, and with him the half-shaved skull of the faithful, and the long two-hours' nar-ghile with traces of burnt tembaki and haschish still in the bowl. Ashes now are they all, and dry yellow bone; but in the houses of Phanar and noisy old Galata, and in the Jew quarter of Pri-pacha, the black shoe and head-dress of the Greek is still distinguishable from the Hebrew blue. It was a mixed ritual of colours here in boot and hat: yellow for Mussulman, red boots, black calpac for Armenian, for the Effendi a white turban, for the Greek a black. The Tartar skull shines from under a high taper calpac, the Nizain-djid's from a melon-shaped head-piece; the Imam's and Dervish's from a grey conical felt; and there is here and there a Frank in European rags. I have seen the towering tur-ban of the Bashi-bazouk, and his long sword, and some softas in the domes on the great wall of Stamboul, and the beggar, and the street-merchant with large tray of water-melons, sweetmeats, raisins, sherbet, and the bear-shewer, and the Barbary organ, and the night-watchman who evermore cried "Fire!" with his long lantern, two pistols, dirk, and wooden javelin. Strange how all that old life has come back to my fancy now, pretty vividly, and for the first time, though I have been here several times lately. I have gone out to those plains beyond the walls with their view of rather barren mountain-peaks, the city looking nothing but minarets shooting through black cypress-tops, and I seemed to see the wild muezzin at some summit, crying the midday prayer: "*Mohammed Resoul Allah!*"—the wild man; and from that great avenue of cy-presses which traverses the cemetery of Scutari, the walled city of Stamboul lay spread entire up to Phanar and Eyoub in their cypress-woods before me, the whole embowered now in trees, all that complexity of ways and dark alleys with overhanging balconies of old Byzantine houses, beneath which a rider had to stoop the head, where old Turks would lose their way in mazes of the pictur-esque; and on the shaded Bosphorus coast, to Foundoucli and beyond, some peeping yali, snow-white palace, or old Armenian cot; and the Seraglio by the sea, a town within a town; and southward the sea of Marmora, blue-and-white, and vast, and fresh as a sea just born, rejoicing at its birth and at the jovial sun, all brisk, alert, to the shadowy islands afar: and as I looked, I suddenly said aloud a wild, mad thing, my God, a wild and maniac thing, a shrieking maniac thing for Hell to laugh at: for something said with my tongue: "*This city is not quite dead.*"

*   *   *   *   *

*   *   *   *   *

Three nights I slept in Stamboul itself at the palace of some sanjak-bey or emir, or rather dozed, with one slumbrous eye that would open to watch my visitors Sinbad, and Ali Baba, and old Haroun, to see how they slumbered and dozed: for it was in the small luxurious chamber where the bey received those speechless all-night visits of the Turks, long rosy hours of perfumed romance, and drunkenness of the fancy, and visionary languor, sinking toward morning into the yet deeper peace of dreamless sleep; and there, still, were the white *yatags* for the guests to sit cross-legged on for the waking dream, and to fall upon for the final swoon, and the copper brazier still scenting of essence-of-rose, and the cushions, rugs, hangings, the monsters on the wall, the haschish-chibouques, narghiles, hookahs, and drugged pale cigarettes, and a secret-looking lattice beyond the door, painted with trees and birds; and the air narcotic and grey with the pastilles which I had burned, and the scented smokes which I had smoked; and I all drugged and mumbling, my left eye suspicious of Ali there, and Sinbad, and old Haroun, who dozed. And when I had slept, and rose to wash in a room near the overhanging latticed balcony of the façade, before me to the north lay Galata in sunshine, and that steep large street mounting to Pera, once full at every night-fall of divans on which grave dervishes smoked narghiles, and there was no space for passage, for all was divans, lounges, almond-trees, heaven-high hum, chibouques in forests, the dervish, and the innumerable porter, the horse-hirer with his horse from Tophana, and arsenal-men from Kassim, and traders from Galata, and artillery-workmen from Tophana; and on the other side of the house, the south end, a covered bridge led across a street, which consisted mostly of two immense blind walls, into a great tangled wilderness of flowers, which was the harem-garden, where I passed some hours; and here I might have remained many days, many weeks perhaps, but that, dozing one fore-day with those fancied others, it was as if there occurred a laugh somewhere, and a thing said: "But this city is not quite dead!" waking me from deeps of peace to startled wakefulness. And I thought to myself: "If it be not quite dead, it *will* be soon—and with some suddenness!" And that morning I was at the Arsenal.

*　　*　　*　　*　　*

It is long since I have so deeply enjoyed, even to the marrow. It may be "the White" who has the guardianship of my life: but assuredly it is "the Black" who reigns in my soul.

Grandly did old Stamboul, Galata, Tophana, Kassim, right out beyond the walls of Phanar and Eyoub, blaze and burn. The whole place, except one little region of Galata, was like so much tinder, and in the five hours between 8 P.M. and 1 A.M. all was over. I saw the tops of those vast masses of cemetery-cypresses round the tombs of the Osmanlis outside the walls, and those in the cemetery of Kassim, and those round the mosque of Eyoub, shrivel away instantaneously, like flimsy hair caught by a flame; I saw the Genoese tower of Galata go heading obliquely on an upward curve, like Sir Roger de Coverley and wild rockets, and burst high, high, with a report; in pairs, and threes, and fours, I saw the blue cupolas of the twelve or fourteen great mosques give in and subside, or soar and rain, and the great minarets nod the head, and topple; and I saw the flames reach out and out across the empty breadth of the Etmei-dan—three hundred yards—to the six minarets of the Mosque of Achmet, wrapping the red Egyptian-granite obelisk in the centre; and across the breadth of the Serai-Meidani it reached to the buildings of the Seraglio and the Sub-lime Porte; and across those vague barren stretches that lie between the houses and the great wall; and across the seventy or eighty great arcaded bazaars, all-enwrapping, it reached; and the spirit of fire grew upon me: for the Golden Horn itself was a tongue of fire, crowded, west of the galley-harbour, with ex-ploding battleships, Turkish frigates, corvettes, brigs—and east, with tens of thousands of feluccas, caiques, gondolas and merchantmen aflame. On my left burned all Scutari; and between six and eight in the evening I had sent out thirty-seven vessels under low horse-powers of air, with trains and fuses laid for 11 P.M., to light with their wandering fires the Sea of Marmora. By midnight I was encompassed in one great furnace and fiery gulf, all the sea and sky in-flamed, and earth a-flare. Not far from me to the left I saw the vast Tophana barracks of the Cannoniers, and the Artillery-works, after long reluctance and delay, take wing together; and three minutes later, down by the water, the bar-rack of the Bombardiers and the Military School together, grandly, grandly; and then, to the right, in the valley of Kassim, the Arsenal: these occupying the sky like smoky suns, and shedding a glaring day over many a mile of sea and land; I saw the two lines of ruddier flaring where the barge-bridge and the raft-bridge over the Golden Horn made haste to burn; and all that vastness burned with haste, quicker and quicker—to fervour—to fury—to unanimous rabies: and when its red roaring stormed the infinite, and the might of its glow-ing heart was Gravitation, Being, Sensation, and I its compliant wife—then my head nodded, and with crooked lips I sighed as it were my last sigh, and tum-bled, weak and drunken, upon my face.

*   *   *   *   *

*   *   *   *   *

O wild Providence! Unfathomable madness of Heaven! that ever I should write what now I write! I will not write it. . . .

*   *   *   *   *

The hissing of it! It is only a crazy dream! a tearing-out of the hair by the roots to scatter upon the raving storms of Saturn! My hand will not write it!

*   *   *   *   *

In God's name—! During four nights after the burning I slept in a house—French as I saw by the books, &c., probably the Ambassador's, for it has very large gardens and a beautiful view over the sea, situated on the rapid east declivity of Pera; it is one of the few large houses which, for my safety, I had left standing round the minaret whence I had watched, this minaret being at the top of the old Mussulman quarter on the heights of Taxim, between Pera proper and Foundoucli. At the bottom, both at the quay of Foundoucli, and at that of Tophana, I had left under shelter two caiques for double safety, one a Sultan's gilt craft, with gold spur at the prow, and one a boat of those zaptias that used to patrol the Golden Horn as water-police: by one or other of these I meant to reach the *Speranza*, she being then safely anchored some distance up the Bosphorus coast. So, on the fifth morning I set out for the Tophana quay; but a light rain had fallen over-night, and this had re-excited the thin grey smoke resembling quenched steam, which, as from some reeking district of Abaddon, still trickled upward over many a square mile of blackened tract, though of flame I could see no sign. I had not accordingly advanced far over every sort of *débris*, when I found my eyes watering, my throat choked, and my way almost blocked by roughness: whereupon I said: "I will turn back, cross the region of tombs and barren waste behind Pera, descend the hill, get the zaptia boat at the Foundoucli quay, and so reach the *Speranza*."

Accordingly, I made my way out of the region of smoke, passed beyond the limits of smouldering ruin and tomb, and soon entered a rich woodland, somewhat scorched at first, but soon green and flourishing as the jungle. This cooled and soothed me, and being in no hurry to reach the ship, I was led on and on, in a somewhat north-western direction, I fancy. Somewhere hereabouts, I thought, was the place they called "The Sweet Waters," and I went on with the vague notion of coming upon them, thinking to pass the day, till afternoon, in the forest. Here nature, in only twenty years, has returned to an exuberant savagery, and all was now the wildest vegetation, dark dells, rills wimpling through deep-brown shade of sensitive mimosa, large pendulous fuchsia, palm, cypress, mulberry, jonquil, narcissus, daffodil, rhododendron, acacia, fig. Once I stumbled upon a cemetery of old gilt tombs, absolutely overgrown and lost, and thrice caught glimpses of little trellised yalis choked in boscage. With slow and listless foot I went, munching an almond or an olive, though I could swear that olives were not formerly indigenous to any soil so northern: yet here they are now, pretty plentiful, though elementary, so that modifications whose end I cannot see are certainly proceeding in everything, some of the cypresses which I met that day being immense beyond anything I ever heard of: and the thought, I remember, was in my head, that if a twig or leaf should change into a bird, or into a fish with wings, and fly before my eyes, what then should I do? and I would eye a branch suspiciously anon. After a long time I penetrated into a very sombre grove. The day outside the wood was brilliant and hot, and very still, the leaves and flowers here all motionless. I seemed, as it were, to hear the vacant silence of the world, and my foot treading on a twig, produced the report of pistols. I presently reached a glade in a thicket, about eight yards across, that had a scent of lime and orange, where the just-sufficient twilight enabled me to see some old bones, three skulls, and the edge of a tam-tam peeping from a tuft of wild corn with corn-flowers, and here and there some golden champac, and all about a profusion of musk-roses. I had stopped—*why* I do not recollect—perhaps thinking that if I was not getting to the Sweet Waters, I should seriously set about finding my way out. And as I stood looking about me, I remember that some cruising insect trawled near my ear its lonely drone.

Suddenly, God knows, I started, I started.

I imagined—I dreamed—that I saw a pressure in a bed of moss and violets, *recently made!* And while I stood gloating upon that impossible thing, I imagined—I dreamed—the lunacy of it!—that I heard a laugh! . . . the laugh, my good God, of a human soul.

Or it seemed half a laugh, and half a sob: and it passed from me in one fleeting instant.

Laughs, and sobs, and idiot hallucinations, I had often heard before, feet walking, sounds behind me: and, even as I had heard them, I had known that they were nothing. But brief as was this impression, it was yet so thrillingly *real*, that my poor heart received, as it were, the very shock of death, and I fell backward into a mass of moss, supported on the right palm, while the left pressed my working bosom; and there, toiling to catch my breath, I lay still, all my soul focussed into my ears. But now I could hear no sound, save only the vast and audible hum of the silence of the universe.

There was, however, the foot-print. If my eye and ear should so conspire against me, that, I thought, was hard.

Still I lay, still, in that same pose, without a stir, sick and dry-mouthed, infirm and languishing, with dying breaths: but keen, keen—and malign.

I would wait, I said to myself, I would be artful as snakes, though so woefully sick and invalid: I would make no sound. . . .

After some minutes I became conscious that my eyes were leering—leering in one fixed direction: and instantly, the mere fact that I had a sense of direction proved to me that I must, *in truth*, have heard something! I strove—I managed—to raise myself: and as I stood upright, feebly swaying there, not the terrors of death alone were in my breast, but the authority of the monarch was on my brow.

I moved: I found the strength.

Slow step by slow step, with daintiest noiselessness, I moved to a thread of moss that from the glade passed into the thicket, and along its winding way I stepped, in the direction of the sound, Now my ears caught the purling noise of a brooklet, and following the moss-path, I was led into a mass of bush only two or three feet higher than my head. Through this, prowling like a stealthy cat, I wheedled my painful way, emerged upon a strip of open long-grass, and was now faced, three yards before me, by a wall of acacia-trees, prickly-pear and pichulas, between which and a forest beyond I spied a gleam of running water.

On my hands and knees I crept toward the acacia-thicket, entered it a little, and leaning far forward, peered. And there—at once—ten yards to my right—I saw.

Singular to say, my agitation, instead of intensifying to the point of apoplexy and death, now, at the actual sight, subsided to something very like calmness. With malign and sullen eye askance I stood, and steadily I watched her there.

* * * * *

She was on her knees, her palms lightly touching the ground, supporting her. At the edge of the streamlet she knelt, and she was looking with a species of startled shy astonishment at the reflexion of her face in the limpid brown water. And I, with sullen eye askance regarded her a good ten minutes' space.

[margin note: like eye in Milton]

* * * * *

I believe that her momentary laugh and sob, which I had heard, was the result of surprise at seeing her own image; and I firmly believe, from the expression of her face, that this was the first time that she had seen it.

* * * * *

Never, I thought, as I stood moodily gazing, had I seen on the earth a creature so fair (though, analysing now at leisure, I can quite conclude that there was nothing at all remarkable about her good looks). Her hair, somewhat lighter than auburn, and frizzy, was a real garment to her nakedness, covering her below the hips, some strings of it falling, too, into the water: her eyes, a dark blue, were wide in a most silly expression of bewilderment. Even as I eyed and eyed her, she slowly rose: at once I saw in all her manner an air of unfamiliarity with the world, as of one wholly at a loss what to do. Her pupils did not seem accustomed to light; and I could swear that that was the first day in which she had seen a tree or a stream.

Her age appeared eighteen or twenty. I guessed that she was of Circassian blood, or, at least, origin. Her skin was whitey-brown, or old ivory-white.

* * * * *

She stood up motionless, at a loss. She took a lock of her hair, and drew it through her lips. There was some look in her eyes, which I could plainly see now, somehow indicating wild hunger, though the wood was full of food. After letting go her hair, she stood again feckless and imbecile, with sideward-hung head, very pitiable to see I think now, though no faintest pity touched me then. It was clear that she did not at all know what to make of the look of things. Finally, she sat on a moss-bank, reached and took a musk-rose, laid it on her palm, and looked hopelessly at it.

* * * * *

One minute after my actual sight of her my extravagance of agitation, I say, died down to something like calm. The earth was mine by old right: I felt that: and this creature a mere slave upon whom, without heat or haste, I might perform my will: and for some times I stood, coolly enough considering what that will should be.

I had at my girdle the little cangiar, with its silver handle encrusted with coral, and curved blade six inches long, damascened in gold, and sharp as a razor; the blackest and the basest of all the devils of the Pit was whispering in my ear with calm persistence: "Kill, kill—and eat."

Why I should have killed her I do not know. That question I now ask myself. It must be true, true that it is "not good" for man to be alone. There was a religious sect in the Past which called itself "Socialist": and with these must have been the truth, man being at his best and highest when most social, and at his worst and lowest when isolated: for the Earth gets hold of all isolation, and draws it, and makes it fierce, base, and materialistic, like sultans, aristocracies, and the like: but Heaven is where two or three are gathered together. It may be so: I do not know, nor care. But I know that after twenty years of solitude on a planet the human soul is more enamoured of solitude than of life, shrinking like a tender nerve from the rough intrusion of Another into the secret realm of Self: and hence, perhaps, the bitterness with which solitary castes, Brahmins, patricians, aristocracies, always resisted any attempt to invade their slowly-acquired domain of privileges. Also, it may be true, it may, it may, that after twenty years of solitary selfishness, a man becomes, without suspecting it—not at all noticing the slow stages—a real and true beast, a horrible, hideous beast, mad, prowling, like that King of Babylon, his nails like birds' claws, and his hair like eagles' feathers, with instincts all inflamed and fierce, delighting in darkness and crime for their own sake. I do not know, nor care: but I know that, as I drew the cangiar, the basest and the slyest of the devils of the Pit was whispering me, tongue in check: "Kill, kill—and be merry."

With excruciating slowness, like a crawling glacier, tender as a nerve of the touching leaves, I moved, I stole, obliquely toward her through the wall of bush, the knife behind my back. Once only there was a restraint, a check: I felt myself held back: I had to stop: for one of the ends of my divided beard had caught in a limb of prickly-pear.

I set to disentangling it: and it was, I believe, at the moment of succeeding that I first noticed the state of the sky, a strip of which I could see across the rivulet: a minute or so before it had been pretty clear, but now was busy with hurrying clouds. It was a sinister muttering of thunder which had made me glance upward.

When my eyes returned to the sitting figure, she was looking foolishly about the sky with an expression which almost proved that she had never before heard that sound of thunder, or at least had no idea what it could bode. My fixed regard lost not one of her movements, while inch by inch, not breathing, careful as the poise of a balance, I crawled. And suddenly, with a rush, I was out in the open, running her down. . . .

She leapt: perhaps two, perhaps three, paces she fled: then stock still she stood—within some four yards of me—with panting nostrils, with enquiring face.

I saw it all in one instant, and in one instant all was over. I had not checked the impetus of my run at her stoppage, and I was on the point of reaching her with the uplifted knife, when I was checked and smitten by a stupendous violence: a flash of blinding light, attracted by the steel which I held,

she has God's protection

struck tingling through my frame, and at the same time the most passionate crash of thunder that ever shocked a poor human ear felled me to the ground. The cangiar, snatched from my hand, pitched near the girl's foot.

I did not entirely lose consciousness, though, surely, the Powers no longer hide themselves from me, and their close contact is too intolerably rough and vigorous for a poor mortal man. During, I should think, three or four minutes, I lay so astounded under that bullying cry of wrath, that I could not move a finger. When at last I did sit up, the girl was standing near me, with a sort of smile, holding out to me the cangiar in a pouring rain.

I took it from her, and my doddering fingers dropped it into the stream.

* * * * *

Pour, pour came the rain, raining as it can in this place, not long, but a deluge while it lasts, dripping in thick liquidity, like a profuse sweat, through the forest, I seeking to get back by the way I had come, flying, but with difficulty and slowness, and a feeling in me that I was being tracked. And so it proved: for when I struck into more open space, nearly opposite the west walls, but now on the north side of the Golden Horn, where there is a flat grassy ground somewhere between the valley of Kassim and Charkoi, with horror I saw that _protégée_ of Heaven, or of someone, not ten yards behind, following me like a mechanical figure, it being now near three in the afternoon, and the rain drenching me through, and I tired and hungry, and from all the ruins of Constantinople not one whiff of smoke ascending.

I trudged on wearily till I came to the quay of Foundoucli, and the zaptia boat; and there she was with me still, her hair nothing but a thin drowned string down her back.

* * * * *

* * * * *

Not only can she not speak to me in any language that I know: but she can speak in _no_ language: it is my belief that she has _never_ spoken.

She never saw a boat, or water, or the world, till now—I could swear it. She came into the boat with me, and sat astern, clinging for dear life to the gunwale by her finger-nails, and I paddled the eight hundred yards to the _Speranza_, and she came up to the deck after me. When she saw the open water, the boat, the yalis on the coast, and then the ship, astonishment was imprinted on her face. But she appears to know little fear. She smiled like a child, and on the ship touched this and that, as if each were a living thing.

It was only here and there that one could see the ivory-brown of her skin: the rest was covered with dirt, like old bottles long lying in cellars.

By the time we reached the _Speranza_, the rain suddenly stopped: I went down to my cabin to change my clothes, and had to shut the door in her face to keep her out. When I opened it, she was there, and she followed me to the windlass, when I went to set the anchor-engine going. I intended, I suppose, to take her to Imbros, where she might live in one of the broken-down houses of the village. But when the anchor was not yet half up, I stopped the engine, and let the chain run again. For I said, "No, I will be alone, I am not a child."

I knew that she was hungry by the look in her eyes: but I cared nothing for that. I was hungry, too: that was all I cared about.

I would not let her be there with me another instant. I got down into the boat, and when she followed, I rowed her back all the way past Foundoucli and the Tophana quay to where one turns into the Golden Horn by St. Sophia, around the mouth of the Horn being now a vast semicircle of charred wreckage, carried out by the river-currents. I went up the steps on the Galata side before one comes to where the barge-bridge was. When she had followed me on to the embankment, I walked up one of those rising streets, very encumbered now with stone-*débris* and ashes, but still marked by some standing black wall-fragments, it being now not far from night, but the air as clear and washed as the translucency of a great purple diamond with the rain and the afterglow of the sun, and all the west aflame.

When I was about two hundred yards up in this old mixed quarter of Greeks, Turks, Jews, Italians, Albanians, and noise and cafedjis and wine-bibbing, having turned two corners, I suddenly gathered my skirts, spun round, and, as fast as I could, was off at a heavy trot back to the quay. She was after me, but being taken by surprise, I suppose, was distanced a little at first. However, by the time I could scurry myself down into the boat, she was so near, that she only saved herself from the water by a balancing stoppage at the brink, as I pushed off. I then set out to get back to the ship, muttering: "You can have Turkey, if you like, and I will keep the rest of the world."

I rowed sea-ward, my face toward her, but steadily averted, for I would not look her way to see what she was doing. However, as I turned the point of the quay, where the open sea washes quite rough and loud, to go northward and disappear from her, I heard a babbling cry—the first sound which she had uttered. I did look then: and she was still quite near me, for the silly maniac had been running along the embankment, following me.

"Little fool," I cried out across the water, "what are you after now?" And, oh my good God, shall I ever forget that strangeness, that wild strangeness, of my own voice, addressing on this earth another human soul?

There she stood, whimpering like an abandoned dog after me. I turned the boat, rowed, came to the first steps, landed, and struck her two stinging slaps, one on each cheek.

While she cowered, surprised no doubt, I took her by the hand, led her back to the boat, landed on the Stamboul side, and set off, still leading her, my object being to find some sort of possible edifice near by, not hopelessly burned, in which to leave her: for in all Galata there was plainly none, and Pera, I thought, was too far to walk to. But it would have been better if I had gone to Pera, for we had to walk quite three miles from Seraglio Point all along the city battlements to the Seven-towers, she picking her bare-footed way after me through the great Sahara of charred stuff, and night now well arrived, the moon a-drift in the heaven, making the desolate lonesomeness of the ruins tenfold desolate, so that my heart smote me then with bitterness and remorse, and I had a vision of myself that night which I will not put down on paper. At last, however, pretty late in the evening, I spied a large mansion with green lattice-work façade, and a shaknisier, and terrace-roof, which had been hidden from me by the arcades of a bazaar, a vast open space at about the centre of Stamboul, one of the largest of the bazaars, I should think, in the middle of which stood the mansion, probably the home of pasha or vizier: for it had a very distinguished look in that place. It seemed very little hurt, though the vegetation that had apparently choked the great open space was singed to a black fluff, among which lay thousands of calcined bones of man, horse, ass, and camel, for all was distinct in that bright, yet so pensive and forlorn, moonlight, which was that Eastern moonlight of pure astral mystery which illumines Persepolis, and Babylon, and ruined cities of the old Anakim.

The house, I knew, would contain divans, *yatags*, cushions, foods, wines, sherbets, henna, saffron, mastic, raki, haschish, costumes, and a hundred luxuries still good. There was an outer wall, but the foliage over it had been singed away, and the gate all charred. It gave way at a push from my palm. The girl was close behind me. I next threw open a little green lattice-door in the façade under the shaknisier, and entered. Here it was dark, and the moment that she, too, was within, I slipped out quickly, slammed the door in her face, and hooked it upon her by a little hook over the latch.

I now walked out some yards beyond the court, then stopped, listening for her expected cry: but all was still; five minutes—ten—I waited: but no sound. I then continued my morose and melancholy way, hollow with hunger, intending to start that night for Imbros.

But this time I had hardly advanced twenty steps, when I heard a frail and strangled cry, apparently in mid-air behind me, and glancing, saw the creature lying at the gateway, a white thing in black stubble-ashes. She had evidently jumped, well outward, from a small casement of lattice on a level with the little shaknisier grating, through which once peeped bright eyes, thirty feet aloft.

I hardly believe that she was conscious of danger in jumping, for all the laws of life are new to her, and, having sought and found the opening, she may have merely come with blind instinctiveness after me, taking the first way open to her. I walked back, pulled at her arm, and found that she could not stand. Her face was screwed with silent pain—she did not moan. Her left foot, I could see, was bleeding: and by the wounded ankle I took her, and dragged her so through the ashes across the narrow court, and tossed her like a little dog with all my force within the door, cursing her.

Now I would not go back the long way to the ship, but struck a match, and went lighting up girandoles, cressets, candelabra, into a confusion of lights among great numbers of pale-tinted pillars, rose and azure, with verd-antique, olive, and Portoro marble, and serpentine. The mansion was large, I having to traverse quite a desert of embroidered brocade-hangings, slender columns, and Broussa silks, till I saw a stair-case doorway behind a Smyrna *portière*, went up, and wandered some time in a house of gilt-barred windows, with very little furniture, but palatial spaces, solitary huge pieces of *faïence* of inestimable age, and arms, my footfalls quite stifled in the Persian carpeting. I passed through a covered-in hanging-gallery, with one window-grating overlooking an inner court, and by this entered the harem, which declared itself by a greater luxury, bric-à-bracerie, and profusion of manner. Here, descending a short curved stair behind a *portière*, I came into a marble-paved sort of larder, in which was an old negress in blue dress, her hair still adhering, and an infinite supply of sweetmeats, French preserved foods, sherbets, wines, and so on. I put a number of things into a pannier, went up again, found some of those exquisite pale cigarettes which drunken in the hollow of an emerald, also a jewelled two-yard-long chibouque, and tembaki: and with all descended by another stair, and laid them on the steps of a little raised kiosk of green marble in a corner of the court; went up again, and brought down a still-snowy *yatag* to sleep on; and there, by the kiosk-step, ate and passed the night, smoking for several hours in a state of languor. In the centre of the court is a square marble well, looking white through a rankness of wild vine, acacias in flower, weeds, jasmines, and roses, which overgrew it, as well as the kiosk and the whole court, climbing even the four-square arcade of Moorish arches round the open space, under one of which I had deposited a long lantern of crimson silk: for here no breath of the fire had come. About two in the morning I fell to sleep, a deeper peace of shadow now reigning where so long the melancholy silver of the moon had lingered.

*   *   *   *   *

About eight in the morning I rose and made my way to the front, intending that that should be my last night in this ruined place: for all the night, sleeping and waking, the thing which had happened filled my brain, growing from one depth of incredibility to a deeper, so that at last I arrived at a sort of certainty that it could be nothing but a drunken dream: but as I opened my eyes afresh, the deep-cutting realisation of that impossibility smote like a pang of lightning-stroke through my being: and I said: "I will go again to the far Orient, and forget": and I started out from the court, not knowing what had become of her during the night, till, having reached the outer chamber, with a wild start I saw her lying there at the door in the very spot where I had flung her, asleep sideways, head on arm. Softly, softly, I stept over her, got out, went running at a cautious clandestine trot. The morning was in high *fête*, most fresh and pure, and to breathe was to be young, and to see such a sunlight lighten even upon ruin so vast was to be blithe. After running two hundred yards to one of the great bazaar-portals, I looked back to see if I was followed: but all that space was desolately empty. I then walked on past the arch, on which a green oblong, once inscribed, as usual, with some text in gilt hieroglyphs, is still discernible; and, emerging, saw the great panorama of destruction, a few vast standing walls, with hollow Oriental windows framing deep sky beyond, and here and there a pillar, or half-minaret, and down within the walls of the old Seraglio still some leafless, branchless trunks, and in Eyoub and Phanar leafless forests, and on the northern horizon Pera with the steep upper-half of the Iani-Chircha street still there, and on the height the European houses, and all between blackness, stones, a rolling landscape of ravine, like the hilly pack-ice of the North if its snow were ink, and to the right Scutari, black, laid low, with its vast region of tombs, and rare stumps of its forests, and the blithe blue sea, with the widening semicircle of floating *débris*, looking like brown foul scum at some points, congested before the bridgeless Golden Horn: for I stood pretty high in the centre of Stamboul somewhere in the region of the Suleimanieh, or of Sultan-Selim, as I judged, with immense purviews into abstract distances and mirage. And to me it seemed too vast, too lonesome, and after advancing a few hundred yards beyond the bazaar, I turned again.

*   *   *   *   *

I found the girl still asleep at the house-door, and stirring her with my foot, woke her. She leapt up with a start of surprise, and a remarkable sinuous agility, and gazed an astounded moment at me, till, separating reality from dream and habit, she realised me: but immediately subsided to the floor again, being in evident pain. I pulled her up, and made her limp after me through several halls to the inner court, and the well, where I set her upon the weedy margin, took her foot in my lap, examined it, drew water, washed it, and bandaged it with a strip torn from my caftan-hem, now and again speaking gruffly to her, so that she might no more follow me.

After this, I had breakfast by the kiosk-steps, and, when I was finished, put a mass of truffled *foie gras* on a plate, brushed through the thicket to the well, and gave it her. She took it, but looked foolish, not eating. I then, with my fore-finger, put a little into her mouth, whereupon she set hungrily to eat it all. I also gave her some ginger-bread, a handful of bonbons, some Krishnu wine, and some anisette.

I then started out afresh, gruffly bidding her to stay there, and left her seated on the well, her hair hanging down the opening, she peering after me through the bushes. But I had not half reached the ogival bazaar-portal, when looking anxiously back, I saw that she was limping after me. So that this creature tracks me in the manner of a nutshell following about in the wake of a ship.

I turned back with her to the house, for it was necessary that I should plan some further method of eluding her. That was five days ago, and here I have stayed: for the house and court are sufficiently agreeable, and form a museum of real *objets d'art*. It is settled, however, that to-morrow I return to Imbros.

*   *   *   *   *

It seems certain that she never wore, nor knew of, clothes.

I have dressed her, first sousing her thoroughly with sponge and soap in luke-warm rose-water in the silver cistern of the harem-bath, which is a circular marbled apartment with a fountain and the complicated ceilings of these houses, and frescoes, and gilt texts of the Koran on the walls, and pale rose-silk hangings. On the divan I had heaped a number of selected garments, and having shewed her how to towel herself, I made her step into a pair of the trousers called *shinti-*

yan made of yellow-striped white-silk; this, by a running string, I tied loosely round the upper part of her hips; then, drawing up the bottoms to her knees, tied them there, so that their voluminous baggy folds, overhanging still to the ankles, have rather the look of a skirt; over this I put upon her a blue-striped chiffon chemise, or quamis, reaching a little below the hips; I then put on a short jacket or vest of scarlet satin, thickly embroidered in gold and precious stones, reaching somewhat below the waist, and pretty tight-fitting; and, making her lie on the couch, I put upon her little feet little yellow baboosh-slippers, then anklets, on her fingers rings, round her neck a necklace of sequins, finally dyeing her nails, which I cut, with henna. There remained her head, but with this I would have nothing to do, only pointing to the tarboosh which I had brought, to a square kerchief, to some corals, and to the fresco of a woman on the wall, which, if she chose, she might copy. Lastly, I pierced her ears with the slver needles which they used here: and after two hours of it left her.

About an hour afterwards I saw her in the arcade round the court, and, to my great surprise, she had a perfect plait down her back, and over her head a green-silk feredjeh, or hood, precisely as in the picture.

*   *   *   *   *

Here is a question, the answer to which would be interesting to me: Whether or not for twenty years—or say rather twenty centuries, twenty eternal æons—I have been stark mad, a raving maniac; and whether or not I am now suddenly sane, sitting here writing in my right mind, my whole mood and tone changed, or rapidly changing? And whether such change can be due to the presence of only one other being in the world with me?

*   *   *   *   *

This singular being! Where she has lived—and how—is a problem to which not the faintest solution is conceivable. She had, I say, never seen clothes: for when I began to dress her, her perplexity was unbounded; also, during her twenty years, she has never seen almonds, figs, nuts, liqueurs, chocolate, conserves, vegetables, sugar, oil, honey, sweetmeats, orange-sherbet, mastic, salt, raki, tobacco, and many such things: for she showed perplexity at all these, hesitation to eat them: but she has known and tasted *white wine:* I could see that. Here, then, is a mystery.

*   *   *   *   *

I have not gone to Imbros, but remained here some days longer observing her.

I have allowed her to sit in a corner at meal-time, not far from where I eat, and I have given her food.

She is wonderfully clever! I continually find that, after an incredibly short time, she has most completely adapted herself to this or that. Already she wears her outfit as coquettishly as though born to clothes. Without at all seeming observant—for, on the contrary, she gives an impression of great flightiness—she watches me, I am convinced, with pretty exact observation. She knows precisely when I am speaking roughly, bidding her go, bidding her come, tired of her, tolerant of her, scorning her, cursing her. If I wish her to the devil, she quickly divines it by my face, and will disappear. Yesterday I noticed something queer about her, and soon discovered that she had been staining her lids with black kohol, like the *hanums*, so that, having found a box, she must have guessed its use from the pictures. Wonderfully clever!—imitative as a mirror. Two mornings ago I found an old mother-of-pearl kittur, and sitting under the arcade, touched the strings, playing a simple air; I could just see her behind one of the arch-pillars on the opposite side, and she was listening with apparent eagerness, and, I fancied, panting. Well, returning from a walk beyond the Phanar walls in the afternoon, I heard the same air coming out from the house, for she was repeating it pretty faultlessly by ear.

Also, during the forenoon of the previous day, I came upon her—for footsteps make no sound in this house—in the pacha's visitors'-hall: and what was she doing?—copying the poses of three dancing-girls frescoed there! So that she would seem to have a character as light as a butterfly's, and is afraid of nothing.

*   *   *   *   *

Now I know.

I had observed that at the beginning of every meal she seemed to have something on her mind, going toward the door, hesitating as if to see whether I would follow, and then returning. At length yesterday, after sitting to eat, she jumped up, and to my infinite surprise, said her first word: said it with a most quaint, experimental effort of the tongue, as a fledgling trying the air: the word "*Come.*"

That morning, meeting her in the court, I had told her to repeat some words after me: but she had made no attempt, as if shy to break the long silence of her life; and now I felt some sort of foolish pleasure in hearing her utter that word, often no doubt heard from me: and after hurriedly eating, I went with her, saying to myself: "She must be about to shew me the food to which she is accustomed: and perhaps that will solve her origin."

And so it has proved. I have now discovered that to the moment when she saw me, she had tasted only her mother's milk, dates, and that white wine of Ismidt which the Koran permits.

As it was getting dark, I lit and took with me the big red-silk lantern, and we set out, she leading, and walking confoundedly fast, slackening when I swore at her, then getting fast again: and she walks with a certain levity, flightiness, and liberated *furore*, very hard to describe, as though space were a luxury to be revelled in. By what instinctive cleverness, or native vigour of memory, she found her way I cannot tell, but she led me such a walk that night, miles, miles, till I became furious, darkness having soon fallen with only a faint moon obscured by cloud, and a drizzle which haunted the air, she without light climbing and picking her thinly-slippered steps over mounds of *débris* and loosely-strewn masonry with unfailing agility, I occasionally splashing a foot with horror into one of those little ponds which always marked the Stamboul streets. When I was nearer her, I would see her peer across and upward toward Pera, as if that were a remembered land-mark, and would note the perpetual aspen oscillations of the long coral drops in her ears, and the nimble ply of her limbs, wondering with a groan if Pera was our goal.

Our goal was even beyond Pera. When we came to the Golden Horn, she pointed to my caique which lay at the Old Seraglio steps, and over the water we went, she lying quite at ease now, with her face at the level of the water in the centre of the crescent-shape, as familiarly as a *hanum* of old engaged in some escapade through the crowded Babel of Galata and that north side of the Horn.

Through Galata we passed, I already cursing the journey: and, following the line of the coast and that great steep thoroughfare of Pera, we came at last, almost in the country, to a great wall, and the entrance to an immense terraced garden, whose limits were invisible, many of the trees and avenues being still intact.

I knew it at once: I had lain a special fuse-train in the great palace at the top of the terraces: the royal palace, Yildiz.

Up and up we went through the grounds, a few unburned old bodies in rags of uniform still discernible here and there as the lantern swung past them, a musician in sky-blue, a fantassin and officer-of-the-guard in scarlet, forming a cross, with domestics of the palace in red-and-orange.

The palace itself was quite in ruins, together with all its surrounding barracks, mosque, and seraglio, and, as we reached the top of the grounds, presented a picture very like those which I have seen of the ruins of Persepolis, only that here the columns, both standing and fallen, were innumerable, and all more or less blackened; and through doorless doors we passed, down immensely-wide short flights of steps, and up them, and over strewed courtyards, by tottering fragments of arcades, all roofless, and tracts of charcoal between interrupted avenues of pillars, I following, expectant, and she very eager now. Finally, down a flight of twelve or fourteen rather steep and narrow steps, very dislocated, we went to a level which, I thought, must be the floor of the palace vaults: for at the bottom of the steps we stood on a large plain floor of plaster, which bore the marks of the flames; and over this the girl ran a few steps, pointed with excited recognition to a hole in it, ran further, and disappeared down the hole.

When I followed, and lowered the lantern a little, I saw that the drop down was about eight feet, made less than six feet by a heap of stone-rubbish below, the falling of which had caused the hole: and it was by standing on this rubbish-heap, I knew at once, that she must have been enabled to climb out into the world.

I dropped down, and found myself in a low flat-roofed cellar, with a floor of black earth, very fusty and damp, but so very vast in extent that even in the day-time, I suppose, I could not have discerned its boundaries; I fancy, indeed, that it extends beneath the whole palace and its environs—an enormous stretch of space: with the lantern I could only see a very limited portion of its area. She still led me eagerly on, and I presently came upon a whole region of flat boxes, each about two feet square, and nine inches high, made of very thin laths, packed to the roof; and about a-hundred-and-fifty feet from these I saw, where she pointed, another region of bottles, fat-bellied bottles in chemises of wicker-work, stretching away into gloom and total darkness. The boxes, of which a great number lay broken open, as they can be by merely pulling with the fingers at a pliant crack, contain dates; and the bottles, of which many thousands lay empty, contain, I saw, old Ismidt wine. Some fifty or sixty casks, covered with mildew, some old pieces of furniture, and a great cube of rotting, curling parchments, showed that this cellar had been more or less loosely used for the occasional storage of superfluous stores and knick-knacks.

It was also more or less loosely used as a domestic prison. For in the lane between the region of boxes and the region of bottles, near the former, there lay on the ground the skeleton of a woman, the details of whose costume were still appreciable, with thin brass gyves on her wrists: and when I had examined her well, I knew the whole history of the creature standing silent by my side.

She is the daughter of the Sultan, as I assumed when I had once determined that the skeleton is both the skeleton of her mother, and the skeleton of the Sultana.

That the skeleton was her mother is clear: for when the cloud occurred just twenty-one years since, the woman was, of course, at that moment in the prison, which must have been air-tight, and with her the girl: but since the girl is certainly not much more than twenty—she looks younger—she must at that time have been either unborn or a young babe: but a babe would hardly be imprisoned with another than its own mother. I am rather inclined to think that the girl was unborn at the moment of the cloud, and was born in the cellar.

That the mother was the Sultana is clear from her fragments of dress, and the symbolic character of her every ornament, crescent ear-rings, heron-feather, and the blue campaca enamelled in a bracelet. This poor woman, I have thought, may have been the victim of some unbounded fit of imperial passion, incurred by some domestic crime, real or imagined, which may have been pardoned in a day had not death overtaken her master and the world.

There are four steep steps at about the centre of the cellar, leading up to a locked iron trap-door, apparently the only opening into this great hole: and this trap-door must have been so nearly air-tight as to bar the intrusion of the poison in anything like a deadly quantity.

But how rare—how strange—the coincidence of chances here. For, if the trap-door was absolutely air-tight, I cannot think that the supply of oxygen in the cellar, large as it was, would have been sufficient to last the girl twenty years, to say nothing of what her mother used up before death: for I imagine that the woman must have continued to live some time in her dungeon, sufficiently long, at least, to teach her child to procure its food of dates and wine; so that the door must have been only just sufficiently hermetic to bar the poison, yet admit some oxygen; or else, the place may have been absolutely air-tight at the time of the cloud, and some crack, which I have not seen, opened to admit oxygen after the poison was dispersed: in any case—the all-but-infinite rarity of the chance!

Thinking these things I climbed out, and we walked to Pera, where I slept in a great white-stone house in five or six acres of garden overlooking the cemetery of Kassim, having pointed out to the girl another house in which to sleep.

This girl! what a history! After existing twenty years in a sunless world hardly three acres wide, she one day suddenly saw the only sky which she knew collapse at one point! a hole appeared into yet a world beyond! It was *I* who had come, and kindled Constantinople, and set her free.

*   *   *   *   *

Ah, I see something now! I see! it was for this that I was preserved: I to be a sort of new-fangled Adam—and this little creature to be my Eve! That is it! *The White* does not admit defeat: he would recommence the Race again! At the last, the eleventh hour—in spite of all—he would turn defeat into victory, and outwit that Other.

However, if this be so—and I seem to see it quite clearly—then in that White scheme is a singular flaw: at *one* point, it is obvious, that elaborate Fore-thought fails: for I have a free will—and I refuse, I refuse.

Certainly, in this matter I am on the side of the Black: and since it depends absolutely upon me, this time Black wins.

No more men on the earth after me, ye Powers! To *you* the question may be nothing more than a gambling excitement as to the final outcome of your aërial squabble: but to the poor men who had to bear the wrongs, Inquisitions, rack-rents, Waterloos, unspeakable horrors, it was hard earnest, you know! Oh, the wretchedness—the deep, deep pain—of that bungling ant-hill, happily wiped out, my God! My sweetheart Clodagh . . . she was not an ideal being! There was a man called Judas who betrayed the gentle Founder of the Christian Faith, and there was some Roman king named Galba, a horrid dog, and a French devil, Gilles de Raiz: and the rest were all much the same, much the same. Oh no, it was not a good race, that small infantry which called itself Man: and here, falling on my knees before God and Satan as I write, I swear, I swear: Never through me shall it spring and fester again.

*   *   *   *   *

I cannot realise her! Not at all, at all, at all! If she is out of my sight and hearing ten minutes, I fall to doubting her reality. If I lose her for half a day, all the old feelings, resembling certainties, come back, that I have only been dreaming—that this appearance cannot be an actual objective fact of life, since the impossible is impossible.

Seventeen long years, seventeen long years, of madness. . . .

*   *   *   *   *

To-morrow I start for Imbros: and whether this girl chooses to follow me, or whether she stays behind, I will see her from the moment I land no more.

*   *   *   *   *

*   *   *   *   *

She must rise very early. I who am now regularly on the palace-roof at dawn, sometimes from between the pavilion-curtains of the galleries, or from the steps of the telescope-kiosk, may spy her far down below, a dainty microscopic figure, generally running about the sward, or gazing up in wonder at the palace from the lake-edge.

It is now three months since she came with me to Imbros.

I left her the first night in that pale-yellow house with the two green jalousies facing the beach, where there was everything that she would need; but I knew that, like all the houses there now, it leaked profusely, and the next day I went down to the curving stair, cut through the rock at the back and south of the village, climbed, and half a mile beyond found that park and villa with gables, which I had noted from the sea. The villa is almost intact, very strongly built of purplish marble, though small, and very like a Western house, with shingles, and three gables, so that I think it must have been the yali of some Englishman, for it contains a number of English books, though the only body I saw there looked like an Aararat Kurd, with spiral string wound down his turban, yellow ankle-pantaloons, and flung red shoulder-cloak; and all in the heavily-wooded park, and all about the low rock-steps up the hill, profusions of man-dragora; and from the rock-steps to the house a narrow long avenue of acacias, mossy underfoot, that mingle overhead, the house standing about four yards from the edge of the perpendicular sea-cliff, whence one can see the *Speranza's* main top-mast, and broken mizzen-mast-head, in her quiet haven. After examining the place I went down again to the village, and her house: but she was not there: and two hours long I paced about among the weeds of these amateur little alleys and flat-roofed windowless houses (though some have terrace-roofs, and a rare aperture), whose once-raw yellows, greens, and blues look now like sunset tints when the last flush is gone, and they fade dun. When at last she came running with open mouth, I took her up the rock-steps, and into the house, and there she has lived, one of its gable-tips, I now find (that overlooking the sea), being just visible from the north-east corner of the palace-roof, two miles from it.

That night again, when I was leaving her, she made an attempt to follow me. But I was resolved to end it, then: and cutting a sassafras-whip I cut her deep, three times, till she ran, crying.

*   *   *   *   *

So, then, what is my fate henceforth?—to think always, from sun to moon, and from moon to sun, of one only thing—and that thing an object for the microscope?—to become a sneaking Paul Pry to spy upon the silly movements of one little sparrow, like some fatuous motiveless gossip of old, his occupation to peep, his one faculty to scent, his honey and his achievement to unearth the infinitely unimportant? I would kill her first!

*   *   *   *   *

I am convinced that she is no stay-at-home, but roams continually over the island: for thrice, wandering myself, I have come upon her.

The first time she was running with flushed face, intent upon striking down a butterfly with a twig held in the left hand (for both hands she uses with dexterity). It was about nine in the morning, in her park, near the bottom where there are high grass-growths and ferny luxuriance between the close tree-trunks, and shadow, and the broken wall of an old funeral-kiosk sunk aslant under moss, creepers, and wild flowers, behind which I peeped hidden and wet with dew. She has had the assurance to modify the dress I put upon her, and was herself a butterfly, for, instead of the shintiyan, she had on a zouave, hardly reaching to the waist, of saffron satin, no feredjé, but a scarlet fez with violet tassel, and baggy pantaloons of azure silk; down her back the long auburn plait, quite neat, but all her front hair loose and wanton, the fez cocked backward, while I caught glimpses of her fugitive heels lifting out of the dropping slipper-sole. She is pretty clever, but not clever enough, for that butterfly escaped, and in one instant I saw her change into weary and sad, for on this earth is nothing more fickle than that Proteus face, which resembles a landscape swept with cloud-shadows on a bright day. Fast beat my heart that morning, owing to the consciousness that, while I saw, I was unseen, yet might be seen.

Another noontide, three weeks afterwards, I came upon her a good way up yonder to the west of the palace, sleeping on her arm in an alley between overgrown old trellises, where rioting wild vine buried her in gloom: but I had not been peeping through the bushes a minute, when she started up and looked wildly about, her quick consciousness, I imagine, detecting a presence: though I think that I managed to get away unseen. She keeps her face very dirty: all about her mouth was dry-stained with a polychrome of grape, *mûrs*, and other coloured juices, like slobbering *gamins* of old. I could also see that her nose and cheeks are now sprinkled with little freckles.

Four days since I saw her a third time, and then found that the primitive instinct to represent the world in *pictures* has been working in her: for she was drawing. It was down in the middle one of the three east-and-west village streets, for thither I had strolled toward evening, and coming out upon the street from between an old wall and a house, saw her quite near. I pulled up short—and peered. She was lying on her face all among grasses, a piece of yellow board before her, and in her fingers a chalk-splinter: and very intently she drew, her tongue-tip travelling along her short upper-lip from side to side, regularly as a pendulum, her fez tipped far back, and the left foot swinging upward from the knee. She had drawn her yali at the top, and now, as I could see by peering well forward, was drawing underneath the palace—from memory, for where she lay it is all hidden: yet the palace it was, for there were the waving lines meant for the steps, the two slanting pillars, the slanting battlements of the outer court, and before the portal, with turban reaching above the roof, and my two whisks of beard sweeping below the knees—myself.

Something spurred me, and I could not resist shouting a sudden "Hi!" whereupon she scrambled like a spring-bok to her feet, I pointing to the drawing, smiling.

This creature has a way of mincing her pressed lips, while she shakes the head, intensely cooing a fond laugh: and so she did then.

"You are a clever little wretch, you know," said I, she cocking her eye, trying to divine my meaning with vague smile.

"Oh, yes, a clever little wretch," I went on in a gruff voice, "clever as a serpent, no doubt: for in the first case it was the Black who used the serpent, but now it is the White. But it will not do, you know. Do you know what you are to me, you? You are my Eve!—a little fool, a little piebald frog like you. But it will not do at all, at all! A nice race it would be with you for mother, and me for father, wouldn't it?—half-criminal like the father, half-idiot like the mother: just like the last, in short. They used to say, in fact, that the offspring of a brother and sister was always weak-headed; and from such a wedlock certainly came the human race, so no wonder it was what it was: and so it would have to be again now. Well no—unless we have the children, and cut their throats at birth: and *you* would not like that at all, I know, and, on the whole, it would not work, for the White would be striking a poor man dead with His lightning, if I attempted that. No, then: the modern Adam is some eight to twenty thousand years wiser than the first—you see? less instinctive, more rational. The first disobeyed by commission: I shall disobey by omission: only his disobedience was a sin, mine is a heroism. I have not been a particularly ideal sort of beast so far, you know: but in me, Adam Jefferson—I swear it—the human race shall at last attain a true nobility, the nobility of self-extinction. I shall turn out trumps: I shall prove myself stronger than Tendency, World-Genius, Providence, Currents of Fate, White Power, Black Power, or whatever is the name for it. No more Clodaghs, Lucrezia Borgias, Semiramises, Pompadours, Irish Landlords, Hundred-Years' Wars—you see?"

She kept her left eye obliquely cocked like a little fool, wondering, no doubt, what I was saying.

"And talking of Clodagh," I went on, "I shall call you that henceforth, to keep me reminded. So that is your name—not Eve—but Clodagh, who was a Poisoner, you see? She poisoned a poor man who trusted her: and that is your name now—not Eve, but Clodagh—to remind me, you most dangerous little speckled viper! And in order that I may no more see your foolish little pretty face, I decree that, for the future, you wear a *yashmak* to cover up your lips, which, I can see, were meant to be seductive, though dirty; and you can leave the blue eyes, and the little white-skinned freckled nose uncovered, if you like, they being commonplace enough. Meantime, if you care to see how to draw a palace—I will show you."

Before I stretched my hand, she was presenting the board—so that she had guessed something of my meaning! But some hard tone in my talk had wounded her, for she presented it looking very glum, her under-lip pushing a little obliquely out, very pathetically, I must say, as always when she is just ready to cry.

In a few strokes I drew the palace, and herself standing at the portal between the pillars: and now great was her satisfaction, for she pointed to the sketched figure, and to herself, interrogatively: and when I nodded "yes," she went cooing her fond murmurous laugh, pressed and mincing lips: and it is clear that, in spite of my beatings, she is in no way afraid of me.

Before I could move away, I felt some rain-drops, and down in some seconds rushed a shower. I looked, saw that the sky was rapidly darkening, and ran into the nearest of the little cubical houses, leaving her glancing sideways upward, with the quaintest artlessness of interest in the down-pour: for she is not yet quite familiarised with the operations of nature, and seems to regard them with a certain amiable inquisitive seriousness, as though they were living beings, comrades as good as herself. She presently joined me, but even then she stretched her hand out to feel the drops.

Now there came a thunder-clap, the wind was rising, and rain spattering about me: for the panes of these houses, made, I believe, of paper saturated in almond-oil, have long disappeared, and rains, penetrating by roof and rare window, splash the bones of men. I gathered up my skirts to rush toward other shelter, but she was before me, saying in her experimental voice that word of hers: "*Come.*"

She ran in advance, and I, with the outer robe over my head, followed, urging flinching way against the whipped rain-wash. She took the way by the stone horse-pond, through an alley to the left between two blind walls, then down a steep path through wood to the rock-steps, and up we ran, and along the hill, to her yali, which is a mile nearer the village than the palace, though by the time we pelted into its dry shelter we were wet to the skin.

Sudden darkness had come, but she quickly found some matches, lit one, looking at it with a certain meditative air, and applied it to a candle and to a bronze Western lamp on the table, which I had taught her to oil and light. Near a Western fire-place was a Turkish mangal, like one which she had seen me light to warm bath-waters in Constantinople, and when I pointed to it, she ran to the kitchen, returned with some chopped wood, and very cleverly lit it. And there for several hours I sat that night, reading (the first time for many years): it was a book by the poet Milton, found in a glazed book-case on the other side of the fire-place: and most strange, most novel, I found those august words about warring angels that night, while the storm raved: for this man had evidently taken no end of pains with his book, and done it gallantly well, too, making the thing hum: and I could not conceive why he should have been at that trouble— unless it were for the same reason that I built the palace, because some spark bites a man, and he would be like—but that is all vanity, and delusion.

Well, there is a rage in the storms of late which really transcends bounds; I do not remember if I have noted it in these sheets before: but I never could have conceived a turbulence so huge. Hour after hour I sat there that night, smoking a chibouque, reading, and listening to the batteries and lamentations of that haunted air, shrinking from it, fearing even for the *Speranza* by her quay in the sequestered harbour, and for the palace-pillars. But what astonished me was that girl: for, after sitting on the ottoman to my left some time, she fell sideways asleep, not the least fear about her, though I should have thought that nervousness at such a turmoil would be so natural to her: and whence she has this light confidence in the world into which she has so abruptly come I do not know, for it is as though someone inspired her with the mood of nonchalance, saying: "Be of good cheer, and care not a pin about anything: for God is God."

I heard the ocean swing hoarse like heavy ordnance against the cliffs below, where they meet the outer surface of the southern of the two claws of land that form the harbour: and the thought came into my mind: "If now I taught her to speak, to read, I could sometimes make her read to me."

The winds seemed wilfully struggling for the house to snatch and wing it away into the drear Eternities of the night: and I could not but heave a sigh: "Alas for us two poor waifs and castaways of our race, little bits of flotsam and seaweed-hair cast up here a moment, ah me, on this shore of the Ages, soon to be dragged back, O turgid Eternity, into thy abysmal gorge; and upon what strand—who shall say?—shall she next be flung, and I, divided then perhaps by all the stretch of the trillion-distanced astral gulf?" And such a pity, and a wringing of the heart, seemed in things, that a tear fell from my eyes that ominous midnight.

She started up at a gust of more appalling volume, rubbing her eyes, with dishevelled hair (it must have been about midnight), listening a minute, with that demure, droll interest of hers, to the noise of the elements, and then smiled to me; rose then, left the room, and presently returned with a pomegranate and some almonds on a plate, also some delicious old sweet wine in a Samian cruche, and an old silver cup, gilt inside, standing in a zarf. These she placed on the table near me, I murmuring: "Hospitality."

She looked at the book, which I read as I ate, with lowered left eye-lid, seeking to guess its use, I suppose. Most things she understands at once, but this must have baffled her: for to see one looking fixedly at a thing, and not know what one is looking at it for, must be very disconcerting.

I held it up before her, saying:

"Shall I teach you to read it? If I did, how would you repay me, you Clodagh?"

She cocked her eyes, seeking to comprehend. God knows, at that moment I pitied the poor dumb waif, alone in all the whole round earth with me. The candle-flame, moved by the wind like a slow-painting brush, flickered upon her face, though every cranny was closed.

"Perhaps, then," I said, "I will teach you. You are a pitiable little derelict of your race, you know: and two hours every day I will let you come to the palace, and I will teach you. But be sure, be careful. If there be danger, I will kill you: assuredly—without fail. And let me begin with a lesson now: say after me: 'White.'"

I took her hand, and got her to understand that I wanted her to repeat after me.

"White," said I.

"Hwhite," says she.

"Power," said I.

"Pow-wer," said she.

"White Power," said I.

"Hwhite Pow-wer," said she.

"Shall not," said I.

"Sall not," said she.

"White Power shall not," said I.

"Hwhite Pow-wer sall not," said she.

"Prevail," said I.

"Fffail," said she, pronouncing the "v" with a long fluttering "f"-sound.

"Pre-vail," said I.

"Pe-vvvail," said she.

"White Power shall not prevail," said I.

"Hwhite Pow-wer sall not—fffail," said she.

A thunder which roared as she said it seemed to me to go laughing
through the universe, and a minute I looked upon her face with positive
shrinking fear; till, starting up, I thrust her with violence from my path, and
dashed forth to re-seek the palace and my bed.

Such was the ingratitude and fatality which my first attempt, four nights
since, to teach her met with. It remains to be seen whether my pity for her
dumbness, or some servile tendency toward fellowship in myself, will result in
any further lesson. Certainly, I think not: for though I have given my word, the
most solemnly-pledged word may be broken.

Surely, surely, her presence in the world with me—for I suppose it is
that—has wrought some profound changes in my mood: for gone now apparently are those turbulent hours when, stalking like a peacock, I flaunted my
monarchy in the face of the Eternal Powers, with hissed blasphemies; or else
dribbled, shaking up my body in a lewd dance; or was off to fire some vast city
and revel in redness and the chucklings of Hell; or rolled in the drunkenness of
drugs. It was mere frenzy!—I see it now—it was "not good," "not good." And it
rather looks as if it were past—or almost. I have clipped my beard and hair,
removed the ear-rings, and thought of modifying my attire. I will just watch to
see whether she comes loitering down there about the gate of the lake.

$$*\qquad*\qquad*\qquad*\qquad*$$

Her progress is like . . .

$$*\qquad*\qquad*\qquad*\qquad*$$

$$*\qquad*\qquad*\qquad*\qquad*$$

It is nine months since I have written, on these sheets, those words, "Her progress is like . . ." being the beginning of some narrative in which something interrupted me; and since then I have had no impulse to write.

But I was thinking just now of the curious tricks and eccentricies of my memory, and seeing the sheets, will record it here. I have lately been trying to recall the name of a sister of mine—some perfectly simple name, I know—and the name of my old home in England: and they have completely passed out of my cognizance, though she was my only sister, and we grew up closely together: some quite simple name, I forget it now. Yet I can't say that my memory is bad: there are things—quite unexpected, unimportant things—which come up in my mind with considerable clearness. For instance, I remember to have met in Paris (I think), long before the poison-cloud, a little Brazilian boy of the colour of weak coffee-and-milk, of whom she now constantly reminds me. He wore his hair short like a convict's, so that one could spy the fish-white flesh beneath, and delighted to play solitary about the stairs of the hotel, dressed up in the white balloon-dress of a Pierrot. I have the impression now that he must have had very large ears. Clever as a flea he was, knowing five or six languages, as it were by nature, without having any suspicion that that was at all extraordinary. She has that same light, unconscious, and nonchalant cleverness, and easy way of life. It is little more than a year since I began to teach her, and already she can speak English with a quite considerable vocabulary, and perfect correctness (except that she does not pronounce the letter "r"); she has also read, or rather devoured, a good many books; and can write, draw, and play the harp. And all she does without effort: rather with that flighty naturalness with which a bird takes to the wing.

What made me teach her to read was this: One afternoon, fourteen months or so ago, I from the roof-kiosk saw her down at the lake-rim, a book in hand; and as she had seen me looking steadily at books, so she was looking steadily at it, with pathetic sideward head: so that burst into laughter, for I saw her clearly through the glass, and whether she is the simplest little fool, or the craftiest serpent that ever breathed, I am not yet sure. If I thought that she has the least design upon my honour, it would be ill for her.

I went to Gallipoli for three days in the month of May, and brought back a very pretty little caique, a perfect slender crescent of the colour of the moon, though I had two days' labour in cutting through bush-thicket for the passage of the motor in bringing it up to the lake. It has pleased me to see her lie among the silk cushions of the middle, while I, paddling, taught her first words and sentences between the hours of eight and ten in the evening, though later they became 10 A.M. to noon, when the reading began, we sitting on the palace-steps before the portal, her mouth invariably covered with the yashmak, the lesson-book being a large-lettered old Bible found at her yali. Why she must needs wear the yashmak she has never once asked; and how much she divines, knows, or intends, I have no idea, continually questioning myself as to whether she is all simplicity, or all cunning.

That she is conscious of some profound difference in our organisation I cannot doubt: for that I have a long beard, and she none at all, is among the most patent of facts.

*　　*　　*　　*　　*

I have thought that a certain *Western-ness*—a growing modernity of tone—may be the result, as far as I am concerned, of her presence with me? I do not know. . . .

*　　*　　*　　*　　*

There is the gleam of a lake-end just visible in the north forest from the palace-top, and in it a good number of fish like carp, tench, roach, &c., so in May I searched for a tackle-shop in the Gallipoli Fatmeh-bazaar, and got four 12-foot rods, with reels, silk-line, quill-floats, a few yards of silk-worm gut, with a packet of No. 7 and 8 hooks, and split-shot for sinkers; and since red-worms, maggots and gentles are common on the island, I felt sure of a great many more fish than the number I wanted, which was none at all. However, for the mere amusement, I fished several times, lying at my length in a patch of long-grass over-waved by an enormous cedar, where the bank is steep, and the water deep. And one mid-afternoon she was suddenly there with me, questioned me with her eyes, and when I consented, stayed: and presently I said I would teach her bottom-angling, and sent her flying up to the palace for another rod and tackle.

That day she did nothing, for after teaching her to thread the worm, and put the gentles on the smaller hooks, I sent her to hunt for worms to chop up for ground-baiting the pitch for the next afternoon; and when this was done it was dinner-time, and I sent her home, for by then I was giving the lessons in the morning.

The next day I found her at the bank, taught her to take the sounding for adjusting the float, and she lay down not far from me, holding the rod. So I said to her:

"Well, this is better than living in a dark cellar twenty years, with nothing to do but walk up and down, sleep, and consume dates and Ismidt wine."

"Yes!" says she.

"Twenty years!" I said: "how did you bear it?"

"I was not closs," says she.

"Did you never suspect that there was a world outside that cellar?" said I.

"Never," says she, "or lather, yes: but I did not suppose that it was *this* world, but another where he lived."

"He who?"

"He who spoke with me."

"Who was that?"

"Oh! a bite!" she screamed gladly.

I saw her float bob under, and started up, rushed to her, and taught her how to strike and play it, though it turned out when landed to be nothing but a tiny barbel: but she was in ecstasies, holding it upon her palm, murmuring her fond coo.

She re-baited, and we lay again. I said:

"But what a life: no exit, no light, no prospect, no hope—"

"Plenty of *hope!*" says she.

"Good Heavens! hope of what?"

"I knew vely well that something was lipening over the cellar, or under, or alound it, and would come to pass at a certain fixed hour, and that I should see it, and feel it, and it would be vely nice."

"Ah, well, you had to wait for it, at any rate. Didn't those twenty years seem *long?*"

"No—at least sometimes—not often. I was always so occupied."

"Occupied in doing what?"

"In eating, dlinking, or lunning, or talking."

"Talking to your*self?*"

"Not myself."

"To whom, then?"

"To the one who told me when I was hungly, and put the dates to satisfy my hunger."

"I see. Don't wriggle about in that way, or you will never catch any fish. The maxim of angling is: 'Study to be quiet'—"

"O! another bite!" she called, and this time, all alone, very agilely landed a good-sized bream.

"But do you mean that you were never sad?" said I when she was re-settled.

"Sometimes I would sit and cly," says she—"I did not know why. But if that was 'sadness,' I was never miserlable, never, never. And if I clied, it did not last long, and I would soon fall to sleep, for he would lock me in his lap, and kiss me, and wipe all my tears away."

"He who?"

"Why, what a question! he who told me when I was hungly, and of the thing that was lipening outside the cellar, which would be so nice."

"I see, I see. But in all that dingy place, and thick gloom, were you never at all afraid?"

"Aflaid! *I?* of what?"

"Of the unknown."

"I do not understand you. How could I be *aflaid?* The known was the very opposite of tellible: it was merely hunger and dates, thirst and wine, desire to lun and space to lun in, desire to sleep and sleep: there was nothing tellible in that: and the unknown was even less tellible than the known: for it was the nice thing that was lipening outside the cellar. I do not understand—"

"Ah, yes," said I, "you are a clever little being: but your continual fluttering about is fatal to all angling. Isn't it in your nature to keep still a minute? And with regard now to your habits in the cellar—?"

"*Another!*" she cried with a happy laugh, and landed a young chub. And that afternoon she caught seven, and I none.

*   *   *   *   *

Another day I took her from the pitch to one of the kitchens in the village with some of the fish, till then always thrown away, and taught her cooking: for the only cooking-implement in the palace is the silver alcohol-lamp for coffee and chocolate. We both scrubbed the utensils, and boil and fry I taught her, and the making of a sauce from vinegar, bottled olives, and the tinned American butter from the *Speranza,* and the boiling of rice mixed with flour for ground-baiting our pitch. And she, at first astonished, was soon all deft housewifeliness, breathless officiousness, and behind my back, of her own intuitiveness, grated some dry almonds found there, and with them sprinkled the fried tench. And we ate them, sitting on the floor together: the first new food, I suppose, tasted by me for twenty-one years: nor did I find it disagreeable.

The next day she came up to the palace reading a book, which turned out to be a cookery-book in English, found at her yali; and a week later, she appeared, out of hours, presenting me a yellow-earthenware dish containing a mess of gorgeous colours—a boiled fish under red peppers, bits of saffron, a greenish sauce, and almonds: but I turned her away, and would have none of her, or her dish.

*   *   *   *   *

About a mile up to the west of the palace is a very old ruin in the deepest forest, I think of a mosque, though only three truncated internal pillars under ivy, and the weedy floor, with the courtyard and portal-steps remain, before it being a long avenue of cedars, gently descending from the steps, the path between the trees choked with long-grass and wild rye reaching to my middle. Here I saw one day a large disc of brass, bossed in the middle, which may have been either a shield or part of an antique cymbal, with concentric rings graven round it, from centre to circumference. The next day I brought some nails, a hammer, a saw, and a box of paints from the *Speranza;* and I painted the rings in different colours, cut down a slim lime-trunk, nailed the thin disc along its top, and planted it well, before the steps: for I said I would make a bull's-eye, and do rifle and revolver practice before it, from the avenue. And this the next evening I was doing at four hundred feet, startling the island, it seemed, with that unusual noise, when up she came peering with enquiring face: at which I was very angry, because my arm, long unused, was firing wide: but I was too proud to say anything, and let her look, and soon she understood, laughing every time I made a considerable miss, till at last I turned upon her saying: "If you think it so easy, you may try."

She had been wanting to try, for she came eagerly to the offer, and after I had opened and showed her the mechanism, the cartridges, and how to shoot, I put into her hands one of the *Speranza* Colts. She took her bottom-lip between her teeth, shut her left eye, vaulted out the revolver like an old shot to the level of her intense right eye, and sent a ball through the geometrical centre of the boss.

However, it was a fluke-shot, for I had the satisfaction of seeing her miss every one of the other five, except the last, which hit the black. That, however, was three weeks since, and now my hitting record is forty per cent., and hers ninety-six—most extraordinary: so that it is clear that this creature is the *protégée* of someone, and favouritism is in the world.

* * * * *

Her book of books is the Old Testament. Sometimes, at noon or afternoon, I may look abroad from the roof or galleries, and see a remote figure sitting on the sward under the shade of plane or black cypress: and I always know that the book she cons there is the Bible—like an old Rabbi. She has a passion for stories: and there finds a store.

Three nights since when it was pretty late, and the moon very splendid, I saw her passing homewards close to the lake, and shouted down to her, meaning to say "Good-night"; but she thought that I had called her, and came: and sitting out on the top step we talked for hours, she without the yashmak.

We fell to talking about the Bible. And says she: "What did Cain to Abel?"

"He knocked him over," I replied, liking sometimes to use such idioms, with the double object of teaching and perplexing her.

"Over what?" says she.

"Over his heels," said I.

"I do not complehend!"

"He killed him, then."

"That I know. But how did Abel feel when he was killed? What is it to be *killed?*"

"Well," I said, "you have seen bones all around you, and the bones of your mother, and you can feel the bones in your fingers. Your fingers will become mere bone after you are dead, as die you must. Those bones which you see around you, are, of course, the bones of the men of whom we often speak: and the same thing happened to them which happens to a fish or a butterfly when you catch them, and they lie all still."

"And the men and the butterfly feel the same after they are dead?"

"Precisely the same. They lie in a deep drowse, and dream a nonsense-dream."

"That is not dleadful. I thought that it was much more dleadful. I should not mind dying."

"Ah! . . . so much the better: for it is possible that you may have to die a great deal sooner than you think."

"I should not mind. Why were men so vely aflaid to die?"

"Because they were all such shocking cowards."

"Oh, not all! not all!"

(This girl, I know not with what motive, has now definitely set herself up against me as the defender of the dead race. With every chance she is at it.)

"Nearly all," said I: "tell me one who was not afraid—"

"There was Isaac," says she: "when Ablaham laid him on the wood to kill him, he did not jump up and lun to hide."

"Isaac was a great exception," said I: "in the Bible and such books, you understand, you read of only the best sorts of people; but there were millions and millions of others—especially about the time of the poison-cloud—on a very much lower level—putrid wretches—covetous, false, murderous, mean, selfish, debased, hideous, diseased, making the earth a very charnel of festering vices and crimes."

This, for several minutes, she did not answer, sitting with her back half toward me, cracking almonds, continually striking one step with the ball of her outstretched foot. In the clarid gold of the platform I saw her fez and corals reflected as an elongated blotch of florid red. She turned and drank some wine from the great gold Jarvan goblet which I had brought from the temple of Boro Budor, her head quite covered in by it. Then, the little hairs at her lip-corners still wet, says she:

"Vices and climes, climes and vices. Always the same. What were these climes and vices?"

"Robberies of a hundred sorts, murders of ten hundred—"

"What made them *do* them?"

"Their evil nature—their base souls."

"But *you* are of them, *I* am another: yet you and I live here together, and do no vices and climes."

Her astonishing shrewdness! Right into the inmost heart of a matter does her simple wit seem to pierce!

"No," I said, "we do no vices and crimes, because we lack *motive*. There is no danger that we should hate each other, for we have plenty to eat and drink, dates, wines, and thousands of things. (Our danger is rather the other way.) But *they* hated and schemed, because they were very numerous, and there arose a question among them of dates and wine."

"Was there not, then, enough land to grow dates and wine for all?"

"There was—yes: much more than enough, I fancy. But some got hold of a vast lot of it, and as the rest felt the pinch of scarcity, there arose, naturally, a pretty state of things—including the vices and crimes."

"Ah, but then," says she, "it was not to their bad souls that the vices and climes were due, but only to this question of land. It is certain that if there had been no such question, there could have been no vices and climes, because you and I, who are just like them, do no vices and climes here, where there is no such question."

The clear limelight of her intelligence! She wriggled on her seat in her effort at argument.

"I am not going to argue the matter," I said. "There *was* that question of dates and wine, you see. And there always must be on an earth where millions of men, with varying degrees of cunning, reside."

"Oh, not at all necessalily!" she cries with conviction: "not at all, at all: since there are much more dates and wine than are enough for all. If there should spling up more men now, having the whole wisdom, science, and expeience of the past at their hand, and they made an allangement among themselves that the first man who tlied to take more than he could work should be killed, and sent to dleam a nonsense-dleam, the question could never again alise!"

"It arose before—it would arise again."

"But no! I can guess clearly how it alose before: it alose thlough the sheer carelessness of the first men. The land was at first so vely, vely much more than enough for all, that the men did not take the tlouble to make an allangement among themselves; and afterwards the habit of carelessness was confirmed; till at last the vely oliginal carelessness must have got to have the look of an allangement; and so the stleam which began in a little long ended in a big long, the long glowing more and more fixed and fatal as the stleam lolled further flom the source. I see it clearly, can't you? But now, if some more men would spling, they would be taught—"

"Ah, but no more men will *spling*, you see—!"

"There is no telling. I sometimes feel as if they must, and shall. The tlees blossom, the thunder lolls, the air makes me lun and leap, the glound is full of lichness, and I hear the voice of the Lord God walking all among the tlees of the folests."

As she said this, I saw her under-lip push out and tremble, as when she is near to crying, and her eyes moisten: but a moment after she looked at me full, and smiled, so mobile is her face: and as she looked, it suddenly struck me what a noble temple of a brow the creature has, almost pointed at the uplifted summit, and widening down like a bell-curved Gothic arch, draped in strings of frizzy hair which anon she shakes backward with her head.

"Clodagh," I said after some minutes—"do you know why I called you Clodagh?"

"No? Tell me?"

"Because once, long ago before the poison-cloud, I had a lover called Clodagh: and she was a . . ."

"But tell me first," cries she: "how did one know one's lover, or one's wife, flom all the others?"

"Well, by their faces . . ."

"But there must have been many faces—all alike—"

"Not all alike. Each was different from the rest."

"Still, it must have been vely clever to tell. I can hardly conceive any face, except yours and mine."

"Ah, because you are a little goose, you see."

"What was a goose like?"

"It was a thing like a butterfly, only larger, and it kept its toes always spread out, with a skin stretched between."

"Leally? How caplicious! And I am like that?—but what were you saying that your lover, Clodagh, was?"

"She was a Poisoner."

"Then why call *me* Clodagh, since *I* am not a poisoner?"

"I call you so to remind me: lest you—lest you—should become my—lover, too."

"I am your lover already: for I love you."

"What, girl?"

"Do I not love you, who are mine?"

"Come, come, don't be a little maniac!" I went. "Clodagh was a *poisoner*. . . ."

"Why did she poison? Had she not enough dates and wine?"

"She had, yes: but she wanted more, more, more, the silly idiot."

"So that the vices and climes were not confined to those that lacked things, but were done by the others, too?"

"By the others chiefly."

"Then I see how it was!"

"How was it?"

"The others had got *spoiled*. The vices and climes must have begun with those who lacked things, and then the others, always seeing vices and climes alound them, began to do them, too—as when one lotten olive is in a bottle, the whole mass soon becomes collupted: but originally they were not lotten, but only became so. And all thlough a little carelessness at the first. I am sure that if more men could spling now—"

"But I *told* you, didn't I, that no more men will spring? You understand, Clodagh, that originally the earth produced men by a long process, beginning with a very low type of creature, and continually developing it, until at last a man stood up. But that can never happen again: for the earth is old, old, and has lost her producing vigour now. So talk no more of men *splinging*, and of things which you do not understand. Instead, go inside—stop, I will tell you a secret: to-day in the wood I picked some musk-roses and wound them into a wreath, meaning to give them you for your head when you came to-morrow: and it is inside on the pearl tripod in the second room to the left: go, therefore, and put it on, and bring the harp, and play to me, my dear."

She ran quick with a little cry, and coming again, sat crowned, incarnadine in the blushing depths of the gold. Nor did I send her home to her lonely yali, till the pale and languished moon, weary of all-night beatitudes, sank down soft-couched in quilts of curdling opals to the Hesperian realms of her rest.

So sometimes we speak together, she and I, she and I.

*   *   *   *   *

*   *   *   *   *

That ever I should write such a thing! I am driven out from Imbros!

I was walking up in a wood yesterday to the west—it was a calm clear evening about seven, the sun just having set. I had the book in which I have written so far in my hand, for I had thought of making a sketch of an old wind-mill to the north-west to show her. Twenty minutes before she had been with me, for I had chanced to meet her, and she had come, but kept darting on ahead after peeping fruit, gathering armfuls of amaranth, nenuphar, and red-berried asphodel, till, weary of my life, I had called to her: "Go away! out of my sight"—and she, with suddenly pushed under-lip, had walked off.

Well, I was continuing my stroll, when I seemed to feel some quaking of the ground, and before one could count twenty, it was as if the island was bent upon wracking itself to pieces. My first thought was of her, and in a great scare I went running, calling in the direction in which she had gone, staggering as on the deck of some labouring ship, falling, picking myself up, running again. The air was quite full of uproar, and the land waving like the sea: and as I went plunging, not knowing whither, I saw to my right some three or four acres of forest droop and sink into a gulf which opened to receive them. Up I flung my arms, crying out: "Good God! save the girl!" and a minute later rushed out, to my surprise, into open space on a hill-side. On the lower ground I could see the palace, and beyond it, a small space of white sea which had the awful appear-ance of being higher than the land. Down the hill-side I staggered, driven by the impulse to fly somewhither, but about half way down was startled afresh by a shrill pattering like musical hail, and the next moment saw the entire palace rush with the jangling clatter of a thousand bells into the heaving lake.

Some seconds after this, the earthquake, having lasted fully ten minutes, commenced to lull, and soon ceased. I found her an hour later standing among the ruins of her little yali.

*   *   *   *   *

Well, what a thing! Probably every building on the island has been de-stroyed; the palace-platform, all cracked, leans half-sunken askew into the lake, like a huge stranded ark, while of the palace itself no trace remains, ex-cept a mound of gold stones emerging above the lake to the south. Gone, gone—sixteen years of vanity and vexation. But from a practical point of view, what is a worst calamity of all is that the *Speranza* now lies high-and-dry in the village: for she was bodily picked up from the quay by the tidal wave, and driven bow-foremost into a street not half her width, and there now lies, look-ing huge enough in the little village, wedged for ever, smashed in at the nip like a frail match-box, a most astonishing spectacle: her bows forty feet up the street, ten feet above the ground at the stem, rudder resting on the inner edge of the quay, foremast tilted forward, the other two masts all right, and that bot-tom, which has passed through seas so far, buried in every sort of green and brown sea-weed, the old *Speranza*. Her steps were there, and by a slight leap I could catch them underneath and go up hand-over-hand, till I got foothold; this I did at ten the same night when the sea-water had mostly drained back from the land, leaving everything swampy, however; she there with me, and

soon following me upon the ship. I found most things cracked into tiny fragments, twisted, disfigured out of likeness, the house-walls themselves displaced
a little at the nip, the bow of the cedar skiff smashed in to her middle against
the aft starboard corner of the galley; and were it not for the fact that the air-
pinnace had not broken from her heavy ropings, and one of the compasses still
whole, I do not know what I should have done: for the four old water-logged
boats in the cove have utterly disappeared.

I made her sleep on the cabin-floor amid the *débris* of berth and everything, and I myself slept high up in a wood to the west. I am writing now lying
in the long-grass the morning after, the sun rising, though I cannot see him.
My plan for to-day is to cut three or four logs with the saw, lay them on the
ground by the ship, lower the pinnace upon them, so get her gradually down
into the water, and by evening bid a long farewell to Imbros, which drives me
out in this way. Still, I look forward with pleasure to our hour's run to the
Mainland, when I shall teach her to steer by the compass, and manipulate liq-
uid-air, as I have taught her to dress, to talk, to cook, to write, to think, to live.
For she is my creation, this creature: as it were, a "rib from my side."

But what is the design of this expulsion? And what was it that she called it
last night?—"this new going out flom Halan!" "Haran," I believe, being the
place from which Abraham went out, when "called" by God.

*   *   *   *   *

We apparently felt only the tail of the earthquake at Imbros: for it has rav-
aged Turkey! And we two poor helpless creatures put down here in the theatre
of all these infinite violences: it is too bad, too bad. For the rages of Nature at
present are perfectly astonishing, and what it may come to I do not know.
When we came to the Macedonian coast in good moonlight, we sailed along it,
and up the Dardanelles, looking out for village, yali, or any habitation where
we might put up: but everything has apparently been wrecked. We saw Kilid-
Bahr, Chanak-Kaleh, Gallipoli, Lapsaki in ruins; at the last place I landed,
leaving her in the boat, and walked a little way, but soon went back with the
news that there was not even a bazaar-arch left standing whole, in most parts
even the line of the streets being obliterated, for the place had fallen like a
house of dice, and had then been shaken up and jumbled. Finally we slept in a
forest on the other side of the strait, beyond Gallipoli, taking our few provisions, and having to wade at some points through morass a foot deep before we
reached dry woodland.

Here, the next morning, I sat alone—for we had slept separated by at least
half a mile—thinking out the question of whither I should go: my choice would
have been to remain either in the region where I was, or to go eastward: but
the region where I was offered no dwelling that I could see; and to go any distance eastward, I needed a ship. Of ships I had seen during the night only
wrecks, nor did I know where to find one in all these latitudes. I was thus, like
her "Ablaham," urged westward.

In order, then, to go westward, I first went a little further eastward, once more entered the Golden Horn, and once more mounted the scorched Seraglio steps. Here what the wickedness of man had spared, the wickedness of Nature had destroyed, and the few houses which I had left standing round the upper part of Pera I now saw low as the rest; also the house near the Suleimanieh, where we had lived our first days, to which I went as to a home, I found without a pillar standing; and that night she slept under the half-roof of a little funeral-kiosk in the scorched cypress-wood of Eyoub, and I a mile away, at the edge of the forest where first I saw her.

The next morning, having met, as agreed, at the site of the Prophet's mosque, we traversed together the valley and cemetery of Kassim by the quagmires up to Pera, all the landscape having to me a rather twisted unfamiliar aspect. We had determined to spend the morning in searching for supplies among the earthquake-ruins of Pera; and as I had decided to collect sufficient in one day to save us further pains for some time, we passed a good many hours in this task, I confining myself to the great white house in the park overlooking Kassim, where I had once slept, losing myself in the huge obliquities of its floors, roofs and wall-fragments, she going to the Mussulman quarter of Djianghir near, on the heights of Taxim, where were many shops, and thence round the brow of the hill to the French Embassy-house, overlooking Foundoucli and the sea, both of us having large Persian carpet-bags, and all in the air of that wilderness of ruin that morning a sweet, strong, permanent odour of maple-blossom.

We met toward evening, she quivering under such a load, that I would not let her carry it, but abandoned my day's labour, which was lighter, and took hers, which was quite enough: and we went back westward, seeking all the while some shelter from the saturating night-dews of this place: and nothing could we find, till we came again, quite late, to her broken funeral-kiosk at the entrance to the immense cemetery-avenue of Eyoub. There without a word I left her among the shattered catafalques, for I was weary; but having gone some distance, turned back, thinking that I might take some more raisins from the bag; and after getting them, said to her, shaking her little hand where she sat under the roof-shadow on a stone:

"Good-night, Clodagh."

She did not reply promptly: and her answer, to my surprise, was a protest against her name: for a rather sulky, yet gentle, voice came from the darkness, saying:

"I am *not* a Poisoner!"

"Well," I said, "all right: tell me whatever you like that I should call you, and henceforth I will call you that."

"Call me Eve," says she.

"Well, no," I said, "not Eve, anything but that: for *my* name is Adam, and if I called you Eve, that would be simply absurd, and we do not wish to be ridiculous in each other's eyes. But I will call you anything else that you like."

"Call me Leda," says she.

"And why Leda?" said I.

"Because Leda sounds something like Clodagh," says she, "and you are already in the habit of calling me Clodagh; and I saw the name Leda in a book, and liked it: but Clodagh is most hollible, most bitterly hollible!"

"Well, then," said I, "Leda it shall be, and I shan't forget, for I like it, too, and it suits you, and you ought to have a name beginning with an 'L.' Goodnight, my dear, sleep well, and dream, dream."

"And to you, too, may God give dleams of peace and pleasantness," says she; and I went.

And it was only when I had lain myself upon leaves for my bed, my head on my caftan, a rill for my lullaby, and two stars, which alone I could see out of the heavenful, for my watch-lights; and only when my eyes were already closed toward slumber, that a sudden strong thought pierced and woke me: for I remembered that Leda was the name of a Greek woman who had borne twins. In fact, I should not be surprised if this Greek word Leda is the same word etymologically as the Hebrew Eve, for I have heard of *v*'s, and *b*'s, and *d*'s interchanging about this way, and if *Di*, meaning God, or Light, and *Bi*, meaning Life, and *Iove* and *Ihovah* and *God*, meaning much the same, are all one, that would be nothing astonishing to me, as *widow*, and *veuve*, are one: and where it says, "truly the Light is Good (*tob, bon*)," this is as if it said, "truly the Di is Di." Such, at any rate, is the fatality that attends me, even in the smallest things: for this Western Eve, or Greek Leda, had twins.

*   *   *   *   *

Well, the next morning we crossed by the ruins of old Greek Phanar across the triple Stamboul-wall, which still showed its deep-ivied portal, and made our way, not without climbing, along the Golden Horn to the foot of the Old Seraglio, where I soon found signs of the railway. And that minute commenced our journey across Turkey, Bulgaria, Servia, Bosnia, Croatia, to Trieste, occupying no day or two as in old times, but four months, a prolonged nightmare, though a nightmare of rich happiness, if one may say so, leaving on the memory a vague vast impression of monstrous ravines, ever-succeeding profundities, heights and greatnesses, jungles strange as some moon-struck poet's fantasy, everlasting glooms, and a sound of mighty unseen rivers, cataracts, and slow cumbered rills whose bulrushes never see the sun, with largesse everywhere, secrecies, profusions, the unimaginable, the unspeakable, a savagery most lush and fierce and gaudy, and vales of Arcadie, and remote mountain-peaks, and tarns shy as old-buried treasure, and glaciers, and we two human folk pretty small and drowned and lost in all that amplitude, yet moving always through it.

We followed the lines that first day till we came to a steam train, and I found the engine fairly good, and everything necessary to move it at my hand: but the metals in such a condition of twisted, broken, vaulted, and buried confusion, due to the earthquake, that, having run some hundreds of yards to examine them, I saw that nothing could be done in that way. At first this threw me into a condition like despair, for what we were to do I did not know: but after persevering on foot for four days along the deep-rusted track, which is of that large-gauge type peculiar to Eastern Europe, I began to see that there were considerable sound stretches, and took heart.

I had with me land-charts and compass, but nothing for taking altitude-observations: for the *Speranza* instruments, except one compass, had all been broken-up by her shock. However, on getting to the town of Silivri, about thirty miles from our start, I saw in the ruins of a half-standing bazaar-shop a number of brass objects, and there found sextants, quadrants, and theodolites. Two mornings later, we came upon an engine in mid-country, with coals in it, and a stream near; I had a goat-skin of almond-oil in the bag, and found the machinery serviceable after an hour's careful inspection, having examined the boiler with a candle through the manhole, and removed the autoclaves of the heaters. All was red with rust, and the shaft of the connecting-rod in particular seemed so frail, that at one moment I was very dubious: I decided, however, and, except for a slight leakage at the tubulure which led the steam to the valve-chest, all went very well; at a pressure never exceeding three-and-a-half atmospheres, we travelled nearly a hundred and twenty miles before being stopped by a head-to-head block on the line, when we had to abandon our engine; we then continued another seven miles a-foot, I all the time mourning my motor, which I had had to leave at Imbros, and hoping at every townlet to find a whole one, but in vain.

*   *   *   *   *

It was wonderful to see the villages and towns going back to the earth, already invaded by vegetation, and hardly any longer breaking the continuity of pure Nature, the town now as much the country as the country, and that which is not-Man becoming all in all with a certain *furore* of vigour. A whole day in the southern gorges of the Balkan Mountains the slow train went tearing its way through many a mile of bind-weed tendrils, a continuous curtain, flaming with large flowers, but sombre as the falling shades of night, rather resembling jungles of Ceylon and the Filipinas; and she, that day, lying in the single car behind, where I had made her a little yatag-bed from Tatar Bazardjik, continually played the kittur, barely touching the strings, and crooning low, low, in her rich contralto, eternally the same air, over and over again, crooning, crooning, some melancholy tune of her own dreaming, just audible to me through the slow-travailing monotony of the engine; till I was drunken with so sweet a woe, my God, a woe that was sweet as life, and a dolour that lulled like nepenthe, and a grief that soothed like kisses, so sweet, so sweet, that all that world of wood and gloom lost locality and realness for me, and became nothing but a charmed and pensive Heaven for her to moan and lullaby in; and from between my fingers streamed plenteous tears that day, and all that I could keep on mourning was "O Leda, O Leda, O Leda," till my heart was near to break.

The feed-pump eccentric-shaft of this engine, which was very poor and flaky, suddenly gave out about five in the afternoon, and I had to stop in a hurry, and that sweet invisible mechanism which had crooned and crooned about my ears in the air, and followed me whithersoever I went, stopped, too. Down she jumped, calling out:

"Well, I had a plesentiment that something would happen, and I am so glad, for I was tired!"

Seeing that nothing could be done with the feed-water pump, I got down, took the bag, and parting before us the continuous screen, we went pioneering to the left between a rock-cleft, stepping over large stones that looked black with moss-growths, no sky, but hundreds of feet of impenetrable leafage overhead, and everywhere the dew-dabbled profusion of dim ferneries, dishevelled maidenhairs mixed with a large-leaved mimosa, wild vine, white briony, and a smell of cedar, and a soft rushing of perpetual waters that charmed the gloaming. The way led slightly upwards three hundred feet, and presently, after some windings, and the climbing of five huge steps almost regular, yet obviously natural, the gorge opened in a roundish space, fifty feet across, with far overhanging edges seven hundred feet high; and there, behind a curtain which fell from above, its tendrils defined and straight like a Japanese bead-hanging, we spread the store of foods, I opening the wines, fruits, vegetables and meats, she arranging them in order with the gold plate, and lighting both the spirit-lamp and the lantern: for here it was quite dark. Near us behind the curtain of tendrils was a small green cave in the rock, and at its mouth a pool two yards wide, a black and limpid water that leisurely wheeled, discharging a little rivulet from the cave: and in it I saw three owl-eyed fish, a finger long, loiter, and spur themselves, and gaze. Leda, who cannot be still in tongue or limb, chattered in her glib baby manner as we ate, and then, after smoking a cigarette, said that she would go and "lun," and went, and left me darkling, for she is the sun and the moon and the host of the stars, I occupying myself that night in making a calendar at the end of this book in which I have written, for my almanack and many things that I prized were lost with the palace—making a calendar, counting the days in my head—but counting them across my thoughts of her.

She came again to tell me good-night, and then went down to the train to sleep; and I put out the lantern, and stooped within the cave, and made my simple couch beside the little rivulet, and slept.

But a fitful sleep, and soon again I woke; and a long time I lay so, gradually becoming conscious of a slow dripping at one spot in the cave: for at a minute's interval it darkly splashed, regularly, very deliberately; and it seemed to grow always louder and sadder, and the splash at first was "Leesha," but it became "Leda" to my ears, and it sobbed her name, and I pitied myself, so sad was I. And when I could no longer bear the anguished melancholy of its spasm and its sobbing, I arose and went softly, softly, lest she should hear in that sounding silence of the hushed and darksome night, going more slow, more soft, as I went nearer, a sob in my throat, my feet leading me to her, till I touched the carriage. And against it a long time I leant my clammy brow, a sob aching in my poor throat, and she all mixed up in my head with the suspended hushed night, and with the elfin things in the air that made the silence so musically a-sound to the vacant ear-drum, and with the dripping splash in the cave. And softly I turned the door-handle, and heard her breathe in sleep, her head near me; and I touched her hair with my lips, and close to her ear I said—for I heard her breathe as if in sleep— "Little Leda, I have come to you, for I could not help it, Leda: and oh, my heart is full of the love of you, for you are mine, and I am yours: and to live with you, till we die, and after we are dead to be near you still, Leda, with my broken heart near your heart, little Leda—"

I must have sobbed, I think: for as I spoke close at her ears, with passionately dying eyes of love, I was startled by an irregularity in her breathing: and with cautious hurry I shut the door, and quite back to the cave I stole in haste.

And the next morning when we met I thought—but am not now sure— that she smiled singularly: I thought so. She may, she *may*, have heard— But I cannot tell.

*   *   *   *   *

Twice I was obliged to abandon engines on account of forest-tree obstructions right across the line, which, do what I might, I could not move, and these were the two bitterest incidents of the pilgrimage; and at least thirty times I changed from engine to engine, when other trains blocked. As for the extent of the earthquake, it is pretty certain that it was universal over the Peninsula, and at many points exhibited extreme violence, for up to the time that we entered upon Servian territory, we occasionally came upon stretches of the lines so dislocated, that it was impossible to proceed upon them, and during the whole course I never saw one intact house or castle; and four times, where the way was of a nature to permit of it, I left the imbedded metals and made the engine travel the ground till I came upon other metals, when I always succeeded in driving it upon them. It was all very leisurely, for not everywhere, nor every day, could I get a nautical observation, and having at all times to go at low pressures for fear of tube and boiler weakness, crawling through tunnels, and stopping when total darkness came on, we did not go fast, nor much cared to. Once, moreover, for three days, and once for four, we were overtaken by hurricanes of such vast inclemency, that no thought of travelling entered our heads, our only care being to hide our poor cowering bodies as deeply and darkly as possible. Once I passed through a city (Adrianople) doubly devastated, once by the hellish arson of my own arm, and once by the earthquake: and I made haste to leave that place behind me.

Finally, three months and twenty-seven days from the date of the earthquake, having traversed only 900 odd English miles, I let go in the Venice lagoon, in the early morning of the 10th September, the lateen sail and stone anchor of a Maltese *speronare*, which I had found, and partially cleaned, at Trieste; and thence I passed up the Canalazzo in a gondola. For I said to Leda: "In Venice will I pitch my Patriarch tent."

But to will and to do are not the same thing, and still further westward was I driven. For the stagnant upper canals of this place are now mere miasmas of pestilence: and within two days I was rolling with fever in the Old Procurazie Palace, she standing in pale wonderment at my bedside, sickness quite a novel thing to her: and, indeed, this was my first serious illness since my twentieth year or thereabouts, when I had over-worked my brain, and went a voyage to Constantinople. I could not move from bed for some weeks, but happily did not lose my senses, and she brought me the whole pharmacopœia from the shops, from which to choose my medicines. I guessed the cause of this illness, though not a sign of it came near *her,* and as soon as my knees could bear me, I again set out—always westward—enjoying now a certain luxury in travelling compared with that Turkish difficulty, for here were no twisted metals, more and better engines, in the cities as many good petrol motors as I chose, and Nature markedly less savage.

I do not know why I did not stop at Verona or Brescia, or some other neighbourbood of the Italian lakes, since I was fond of water: but I had, I think, the thought in my head to return to Vauclaire in France, where I had lived, and there live: for I thought that she might like those old monks. At all events, we did not remain long in any place till we came to Turin, where we spent nine days, she in the house opposite mine, and after that, at her own suggestion, we went on still, passing by train into the valley of the Isère, and then into that of the Western Rhone, till we came to the old town of Geneva among some very great mountains peaked with snow, the town seated at the head of a long lake which the earth has made in the shape of the crescent moon, and like the moon it is a thing of much beauty and many moods, suggesting a creature under the spell of charms and magics. However, with this idea of Vauclaire still in my head, we left Geneva in the motor which had brought us at four in the afternoon of the 17th May, I intending to reach the town called Bourg that night about eight, and there sleep, so to go on to Lyons the next morning by train, and so, by the Bordeaux *route,* make Vauclaire. But by some chance for which I cannot to this hour account (unless the rain was the cause), I missed the chart-road, which should have been fairly level, and found myself on mountain-tracks, unconscious of my whereabouts, while darkness fell, and a windless down-pour that had a certain sullen venom in its superabundance drenched us. I stopped several times, looking about for château, châlet, or village, but none did I see, though I twice came upon railway-lines; and not till midnight did we run down a rather steep pass upon the shore of a lake, which, from its apparent vastness in the moonless obscurity, I could only suppose to be the Lake of Geneva once again. About two hundred yards to the left we saw through the rain a large pile, apparently risen straight out of the lake, looking ghostly livid, for it was of white stone, not high, but an old thing of complicated white little turrets roofed with dark-red candle-extinguishers, and oddities of Gothic nooks, window-slits, and outline, very like a fanciful picture. Round to this we went, drowned as rats, Leda sighing and bedraggled, and found a narrow spit of land projecting into the lake, where we left the car, walked forward with the bag, crossed a small wooden drawbridge, and came upon a rocky island with a number of thick-foliaged trees about the castle. We quickly found a small open portal, and went throughout the place, quite gay at the shelter, everywhere lighting candles which we found in iron sconces in the rather queer apartments: so that, as the castle is far-seen from the shores of the lake, it would have appeared to one looking thence a place suddenly possessed and haunted. We found beds, and slept: and the next day it turned out to be the antique Castle of Chillon, where we remained five long and happy months, till again, again, Fate overtook us.

*   *   *   *   *

The morning after our coming, we had breakfast—our last meal together—on the first floor in a pentagonal room approached from a lower level by three little steps. In it is a ponderous oak-table pierced with a multitude of worm-eaten tunnels, also three mighty high-backed chairs, an old oak-desk covered still with papers, arras on the walls, and three dark religious oil-paintings, and a grandfather's-clock: it is at about the middle of the château, and contains two small, but deep, three-faced oriels, in each face four compartments with white-stone shafts between, these looking south upon shrubs and the rocky edge of the island, then upon another tiny island containing four trees in a jungle of flowers, then upon the shore of the lake interrupted by the mouths of a river which turned out to be the Rhone, then upon a white town on the slopes which turned out to be Villeneuve, then upon the great mountains back of Bouveret and St. Gingolph, all having the surprised air of a resurrection just completed, everything new-washed in dyes of azure, ultramarine, indigo, snow, emerald, that fresh morning: so that one had to call it the best and holiest place in the world. These five old room-walls, and oak floor, and two oriels, became specially mine, though it was really common-ground to us both, and there I would do many little things. The papers on the desk told that it had been the *bureau* of one R. E. Gaud, "*Grand Bailli,*" whose residence the place no doubt had been.

She asked me while eating that morning to stay here, and I said that I would see, though with misgiving: so together we went all about the house, and finding it unexpectedly spacious, I consented to stop. At both ends are suites, mostly small rooms, infinitely quaint and cosy, furnished with heavy Henri Quatre furniture and bed-draperies; and there are separate, and as it were secret, spiral stairs for exit to each: so we decided that she should have the suite overlooking the length of the lake, the mouths of the Rhone, Bouveret and Villeneuve; and I should have that overlooking the spit of land behind and the little drawbridge, shore-cliffs, and elm-wood which comes down to the shore, giving at one point a glimpse of the diminutive hamlet of Chillon; and, that decided, I took her hand in mine, and I said:

"Well, then, here we stay, under the same roof—for the first time. Leda, I will not explain why to you, but it is dangerous, so much so that it may mean the death of one or other of us: deadly, deadly dangerous, my poor girl. You do not understand, but that is the fact, believe me, for I know it very well, and I would not tell you false. Well, then, you will easily comprehend, that this being so, you must never on any account come near my part of the house, nor will I come near yours. Lately we have been much together, but then we have been active, full of purpose and occupation: here we shall be nothing of the kind, I

can see. You do not understand at all—but things are so. We must live perfectly separate lives, then. You are nothing to me, really, nor I to you, only we
live on the same earth, which is nothing at all—a mere chance. Your own
food, clothes, and everything that you want, you will procure for yourself: it is
perfectly easy: the shores are crowded with mansions, castles, towns and villages; and I will do the same for myself. The motor down there I set apart for
your private use: if I want another, I will get one; and to-day I will set about
looking you up a boat and fishing-tackle, and cut a cross on the bow of yours,
so that you may know yours, and never use mine. All this is very necessary: you
cannot dream how much: but I know how much. Do not run any risks in
climbing, now, or with the motor, or in the boat . . . little Leda . . ."

I saw her under-lip push, and I turned away in haste, for I did not care
whether she cried or not. In that long voyage, and in my illness at Venice, she
had become too near and dear to me, my tender love, my dear darling soul;
and I said in my heart: "I will be a decent being: I will turn out trumps."

*   *   *   *   *

Under this castle is a sort of dungeon, not narrow, nor very dark, in which
are seven stout dark-grey pillars, and an eighth, half-built into the wall; and
one of them which has an iron ring, as well as the ground around it, is all worn
away by some prisoner or prisoners once chained there; and in the pillar the
word "Byron" engraved. This made me remember that a poet of that name had
written something about this place, and two days afterwards I actually came
upon three volumes of the poet in a room containing a great number of books,
many of them English, near the Grand Bailli's *bureau:* and in one I read the
poem, which is called "The Prisoner of Chillon." I found it very affecting, and
the description good, only I saw no seven rings, and where he speaks of the
"pale and livid light," he should speak rather of the dun and brownish gloom,
for the word "light" disconcerts the fancy, and of either pallor or blue there is
there no sign. However, I was so struck by the horror of man's cruelty to man,
as depicted in this poem, that I determined that she should see it: went up
straight to her rooms with the book, and, she being away, ferreted among her
things to see what she was doing, finding all very neat, except in one room
where were a number of prints called *La Mode,* and *débris* of snipped cloth, and
medley. When, after two hours, she came in, and I suddenly presented myself,
"Oh!" she let slip, and then fell to cooing her laugh; and I took her down
through a big room stacked with every kind of rifle, with revolvers, cartridges,
powder, swords, bayonets—evidently some official or cantonal magazine—and
then showed her the worn stone in the dungeon, the ring, the narrow deep slits
in the wall, and I told all the tale of cruelty, while the splashing of the lake
upon the rock outside was heard with a strange and tragic sound, and her mobile face was all one sorrow.

"How cluel they must have been!" cries she with tremulous lip, her face at
the same time reddened with indignation.

"They were mere beastly monsters," said I: "it is not surprising if monsters were cruel."

And in the short time while I said that, she was looking up with a new-born smile.

"Some others came and set the plisoner flee!" cries she.

"Yes," said I, "they did, but—"

"That was good of them," says she.

"Yes," said I, "that was all right, so far as it went."

"And it was a time when men had al-leady become cluel," says she: "if those who set him flee were so good when the lest were cluel, what would they have been at a time when all the lest were kind? They would have been just like Angels . . .!"

* * * * *

At this place fishing, and long rambles, were the order of the day, both for her and for me, especially fishing, though a week rarely passed which did not see me at Bouveret, St. Gingolph, Yvoire, Messery, Nyon, Ouchy, Vevay, Montreux, Geneva, or one of the two dozen villages, townlets, or towns, that crowd the shores, all very pretty places, each with its charm, and mostly I went on foot, though the railway runs right round the forty odd miles of the lake's length. One noon-day I was walking through the main-street of Vevay going on to the Cully-road when I had a fearful shock, for in a shop just in front of me to the right I heard a sound—an unmistakable indication of life—as of clattering metals shaken together. My heart leapt into my mouth, I was conscious of becoming bloodlessly pale, and on tip-toe of exquisite caution I stole up to the open door—peeped in—and it was she standing on the counter of a jeweller's shop, her back turned to me, with bead bent low over a tray of jewels in her hands, which she was rummaging for something. I went "*Hoh!*" for I could not help it, and all that day, till sunset, we were very dear friends, for I could not part from her, we walking together by vor-alpen, wood, and shore all the way to Ouchy, she just like a creature crazy that day with the bliss of living, rolling in grasses and perilous flowery declines, stamping her foot defiantly at me, arrogant queen that she is, and then running like mad for me to catch her, with laughter, *abandon*, carolling railleries, and the levity of the wild ass's colt on the hills, entangling her loose-flung hair with Bacchic tendril and blossom, and drinking, in the passage through Cully, more wine, I thought, than was good: and the flaming darts of lightning that shot and shocked me that day, and the inner secret gleams and revelations of Beauty which I had, and the pangs of white-hot honey that tortured my soul and body, and were too much for me, and made me sick, oh, Heaven, what tongue could express all that deep world of things? And at Ouchy with a backward wave of my arm I silently motioned her from me, for I was dumb, and weak, and I left her there: and all that long night her power was upon me, for she is stronger than gravitation, which may be evaded, and than all the forces of life combined, and the sun and the moon and the earth are nothing compared with her; and when she was gone from me I was like a fish in the air, or like a bird in the deep, for she is my element of life, made for me to breathe in, and I drown without her: so that for many hours I lay on that grassy hill leading to the burial-ground outside Ouchy that night, like a man sore wounded, biting the grass.

What made things worse for me was her adoption of European clothes since coming to this place: I believe that, in her adroit way, she herself made some of her dresses, for one day I saw in her apartments a number of coloured fashion-plates, with a confusion like dress-making; or she may have been only modifying finished things from the shops, for her Western dressing is not quite like what I remember of the modern female style, but is really, I should say, quite her own, rather resembling the Greek, or the eighteenth century. At any rate, the airs and graces are as natural to her as feathers to parrots; and she has changes like the moon; never twice the same, and always transcending her last phase and revelation: for I could not have conceived of anyone in whom *taste* was a faculty so separate as in her, so positive and salient, like smelling or sight—more like *smelling*: for it is the faculty, half Reason, half Imagination, by which she fore-scents precisely what will suit exquisitely with what; so that every time I saw her, I received the impression of a perfectly novel, completely bewitching, work of Art: the special quality of works of Art being to produce the momentary conviction that anything else whatever could not possibly be so good.

Occasionally, from my window I would see her in the wood beyond the drawbridge, cool and white in green shade, with her Bible probably, training her skirt like a court-lady, and looking much taller than before. I believe that this new dressing produced a separation between us more complete than it might have been; and especially after that day between Vevay and Ouchy I was careful not to meet her. The more I saw that she bejewelled herself, powdered herself, embalmed herself like sachets of sweet scents, chapleted her Greek-dressed head with gold fillets, the more I shunned her. Myself, somehow, had now resumed European dress, and, ah me, I was greatly changed, greatly changed, God knows, from the portly inflated monarch-creature that strutted and groaned four years previously in the palace at Imbros: so that my manner of life and thought might once more now have been called modern and Western.

All the more was my sense of responsibility awful: and from day to day it seemed to intensify. An arguing Voice never ceased to remonstrate within me, nor left me peace, and the curse of unborn hosts appeared to menace me. To strengthen my fixity I would often overwhelm myself, and her, with muttered opprobriums, calling myself "convict," her "lady-bird"; asking what manner of man was I that I should dare so great a thing; and as for her, what was she to be the Mother of a world?—a versatile butterfly with a woman's brow! And continually now in my fiercer moods I was meditating either my death—or hers.

Ah, but the butterfly did not let me forget her brow! To the south-west of Villeneuve, between the forest and the river is a well-grown gentian field, and returning from round St. Gingolph to the Château one day in the third month after an absence of three days, I saw, as I turned a corner in the descent of the mountain, some object floating in the air above the field. Never was I more startled, and, above all, perplexed: for, beside the object soaring there like a great butterfly, I could see nothing to account for it. It was long, however, before I came to the conclusion that she has re-invented *the kite*—for she had almost certainly never seen one—and I presently sighted her holding the string in the mid-field. Her invention resembles the kind called "swallow-tail" of old.

*   *   *   *   *

But mostly it was on the lake that I saw her, for there we chiefly lived, and occasionally there were guilty approaches and *rencontres*, she in her boat, I in mine, both being slight clinker-built Montreux pleasure-boats, which I had spent some days in overhauling and varnishing, mine with jib, fore-and-aft main-sail, and spanker, hers rather smaller, one-masted, with an easy-running lug-sail. It was no uncommon thing for me to sail quite to Geneva, and come back from a seven-days' cruise with my soul filled and consoled with the lake and all its many moods of bright and darksome, serene and pensive, dolorous and despairing and tragic, at morning, at noon, at sunset, at midnight, a panorama that never for a moment ceased to unroll its transformations, I sometimes climbing the mountains as high as the goat-herd region of hoch-alpen, once sleeping there. And once I was made very ill by a two-weeks' horror which I had: for she disappeared in her skiff, I being at the Château, and she did not come back; and while she was away there was a tempest that turned the lake into an angry ocean, and, ah my good God, she did not come. At last, half-crazy at the vacant days of misery which went by and by, and she did not come, I set out upon a wild-goose quest of her—of all the hopeless things the most hopeless, for the world is great—and I sought and did not find her; and after three days I turned back, recognising that I was mad to search the infinite, and coming near the Château, I saw her wave her handkerchief from the island-edge, for she divined that I had gone to seek her, and she was watching for me: and when I took her hand, what did she say to me, the Biblical simpleton?— "Oh you of little Faith!" says she. And she had adventures to lisp, with the r's liquefied into l's, and I was with her all that day again.

Once a month perhaps she would knock at my outermost door, which I mostly kept locked when at home, bringing me a sumptuously-dressed, highly-spiced red trout or grayling, which I had not the heart to refuse, and exquisitely she does them, all hot and spiced, applying apparently to their preparation the taste which she applies to dress; and her extraordinary luck in angling did not fail to supply her with the finest specimens, though, for that matter, this lake, with its old fish-hatcheries and fish-ladders, is not miserly in that way, swarming now with the best lake trout, river trout, red trout, and with salmon, of which last I have brought in one with the landing-net of, I should say, thirty-five to forty pounds. As the bottom goes off very rapidly from the two islands to a depth of eight to nine hundred feet, we did not long confine ourselves to bottom-fishing, but gradually advanced to every variety of manœuvre, doing middle-water spinning with three-triangle flights and sliding lip-hook for jack and trout, trailing with the sail for salmon, live-baiting with the float for pike, daping with blue-bottles, casting with artificial flies, and I could not say in which she became the most carelessly adept, for all soon seemed as old and natural to her as an occupation learned from birth.

*   *   *   *   *

On the 21st of October I attained my forty-sixth birthday in excellent health: a day destined to end for me in bloodshed and tragedy, alas. I forget now what circumstance had caused me to mention the date long beforehand in, I think, Venice, not dreaming that she would keep any count of it, nor was I even sure that my calendar was not faulty by a day. But at ten in the morning of what I called the 21st, descending by my private spiral in flannels with some trout and par bait, and tackle—I met her coming up, my God, though she had no earthly right to be there. With her cooing murmur of a laugh, yet pale, pale, and with a most guilty look, she presented me a large bouquet of wild flowers.

I was at once thrown into a state of great agitation. She was dressed in rather a frippery of *mousseline de soie*, all cream-laced, with wide-hanging short sleeves, a large diamond at the low open neck, the ivory-brown skin there contrasting with the powdered bluish-white of her face, where, however, the freckles were not quite whited out; on her feet little pink satin slippers, without any stockings—a divinely pale pink; and well back on her hair a plain thin circlet of gold; and she smelled like heaven, God knows.

I could not speak. She broke an awkward silence, saying, very faint and pallid:

"It is the day!"

"I—perhaps—" I said, or some incoherency like that.

I saw the touch of enthusiasm which she had summoned up quenched by my manner.

"I have not done long again?" she asked, looking down, breaking another silence.

"No, no, oh no," said I hurriedly: "not done wrong again. Only, I could not suppose that you would count up the days. You are . . . considerate. Perhaps—but—"

"Tell Leda?"

"Perhaps . . . I was going to say . . . you might come fishing with me. . . ."

"O luck!" she went softly.

I was pierced by a sense of my base cowardice, my incredible weakness: but I could not at all help it.

I took the flowers, and we went down to the south side, where my boat lay; I threw out some of the fish from the well; arranged the tackle, and then the stern cushions for her; got up the sails; and out we went, she steering, I in the bows, with every possible inch of space between us, receiving delicious intermittent whiffs from her of ambergris, frangipane, or some blending of perfumes, the morning being bright and hot, with very little breeze on the water, which looked mottled, like colourless water imperfectly mixed with indigo-wash, we making little headway; so it was some time before I moved nearer her to get the par for fixing on the three-triangle flight, for I was going to trail for salmon or large lake-trout; and during all that time we spoke not a word together.

Afterwards I said:

"Who told you that flowers are proper to birthdays? or that birthdays are of any importance?"

"I suppose that nothing can happen so important as birth," says she, "and perfumes must be ploper to birth, because the wise men blought spices to the young Jesus."

This *naïveté* was the cause of my immediate recovery: for to laugh is to be saved: and I laughed right out, saying:

"But you read the Bible too much! all your notions are biblical. You should read the quite modern books."

"I have tlied," says she; "but I cannot lead them long, nor often. The whole world seems to have got so collupted. It makes me shudder."

"Ah, well, now, you see, you quite come round to my point of view," said I.

"Yes, and no," says she: "they had got so *spoiled*, that is all. Everybody seems to have become quite dull-witted—the plainest tluths they could not see. I can imagine that those faculties which aided them in their stlain to become lich themselves, and make the lest more poor, must have been gleatly sharpened, while all the other faculties withered: as I can imagine a person with one eye seeing double thlough it, and quite blind on the other side."

"Ah," said I, "I do not think they even *wanted* to see on the other side. There were some few tolerably good and clear-sighted ones among them, you know: and these all agreed in pointing out how, by changing one or two of their old man-in-the-moon Bedlam arrangements, they could greatly better themselves: but they heard with listless ears: I don't know that they ever made any considerable effort. For they had become more or less unconscious of their misery, so miserable were they: like the man in Byron's 'Prisoner of Chillon,' who, when his deliverers came, was quite indifferent, for he says:

> 'It was at length the same to me
> Fettered or fetterless to be:
> I had learned to love Despair.'"

"Oh my God," she went, covering her face a moment, "how dleadful! And it is tlue, it seems tlue:—they had learned to love Despair, to be even ploud of Despair. Yet all the time, I feel *sure* flom what I have lead, flom what I scent, that the individual man was stluggling to see, to live light, but without power, like one's leg when it is asleep: that is so pletty of them all! that they meant well—evely one. But they were too tloubled and sad, too awfully burdened: they had no chance at all. Such a queer, unnatulal feeling it gives me to lead of all that world: I can't desclibe it; all their motives seem so tainted, their life so lopsided. Tluely, the whole head was sick, the whole heart faint."

"Quite so," said I: "and observe that this was no new thing: in the very beginning of the Book we read how God saw that the wickedness of man was great on the earth, and every imagination of his heart is evil. . . ."

"Yes," she interrupted, "that is tlue: but there must have been some *cause!* We can be quite *sure* that it was not natulal, because you and I are men, and our hearts are not evil."

This was her great argument which she always trotted out, because she found that I had usually no answer to it. But this time I said:

"Our hearts not evil? Say yours: but as to mine you know nothing, Leda."

The semicircles under her eyes had that morning, as often, a certain moist, heavy, pensive and weary something, as of one fresh from a revel, very sweet and tender: and, looking softly at me with it, she answered:

"I know my own heart, and it is not evil: not at all: not even in the very least: and I know yours, too."

"You know *mine!*" cried I, with a half-laugh of surprise.

"Quite well," says she.

I was so troubled by this cool assurance, that I said not a word, but going to her, handed her the baited flight, swivel-trace, and line, which she paid out; then I got back again almost into the bows.

After a ten-minutes I spoke again:

"So this is news to me: you know all about my heart. Well, come, tell me what is in it!"

Now she was silent, pretending to be busy with the trail, till she said, speaking with low-bent face, and a voice that I could only just hear:

"I will tell you what is in it: in it is a lebellion which you think good, but is not good. If a stleam will just flow, neither tlying to climb upward, nor overflowing its banks, but lunning modestly in its fated channel just wherever it is led, then it will finally leach the sea—the mighty ocean—and lose itself in fulness."

"Ah," said I, "but that counsel is not new. It is what the philosophers used to call 'yielding to Destiny,' and 'following Nature.' And Destiny and Nature, I give you my word, often led mankind quite wrong—"

"Or *seemed* to," says she—"for a time: as when a stleam flows north a little, and the sea is to the south; but it is bound for the sea all the time, and will turn again. Destiny never could, and cannot yet, be judged, for it is not finished: and our lace should follow blindly whither it points, sure that thlough many curves it leads the world to our God."

"Our God indeed!" I cried, getting very excited: "girl! you talk speciously, but falsely! whence have you these thoughts in that head of yours? Girl! you talk of 'our race'! But there are only two of us left? Are you talking *at* me, Leda? Do not *I* follow Destiny?"

"You?" she sighed, with down-bent face: "ah, poor me!"

"What should I do if I followed it?" said I, with a crazy curiosity.

Her face hung lower, paler, in trouble: and she said:

"You would come now and sit near me here. You would not be there where you are. You would be always and for ever near me. . . ."

My good God! I felt my face redden.

"Oh, I could not *tell* you . . .!" I cried: "you talk the most disastrous . . .! you lack all responsibility . . .! Never, never . . .!"

Her face was now covered with her left hand, her right on the tiller: and bitingly she said, with something of venom:

"I could *make* you come—*now*, if I chose: but I will not: I will wait upon my God . . ."

"*Make* me!" I cried: "Leda! How make me?"

"I could cly before you, as I cly often and often . . . in seclet . . . for my childlen . . ."

"*You* cry in secret? This is news—"

"Yes, yes, I cly. Is not the burden of the world heavy upon me, too? and the work I have to do *vely, vely* gleat? And often and often I cly in seclet, thinking of it: and I could cly now if I chose, for you love your little girl so much, that you could not lesist me one minute. . . ."

Now I saw the push and tortion and trembling of her poor little under-lip, boding tears: and at once a flame was in me which was altogether beyond control; and crying out: "why, my poor dear," I found myself in the act of rushing through the staggering boat to take her to me.

Mid-way, however, I was saved: a whisper, intense as lightning, arrested me: "Forward is no escape, nor backward, but *sideward* there may be a way!" And at a sudden impulse, before I knew what I was doing, I was in the water swimming.

The smaller of the islands was two hundred yards away, and thither I swam, rested some minutes, and thence to the Castle. I did not once look behind me.

*　　*　　*　　*　　*

Well, from 11 A.M. till five in the afternoon, I thought it all out, lying in the damp flannels on my face on the sofa in the recess beside my bed, where it was quite dark behind the tattered piece of arras: and what things I suffered that day, and what deeps I sounded, and what prayers I prayed, God knows. What complicated the awful problem was this thought in my head: <u>that to kill her would be far more merciful to her than to leave her alone, having killed myself: and, Heaven knows</u>, it was for her alone that I thought, not at all caring for myself. To kill her was better: but to kill her with my own hands—that was too hard to expect of a poor devil like me, a poor common son of Adam, after all, and never any sublime self-immolator, as two or threee of them were. And hours I lay there with brows convulsed in an agony, groaning only those words: "To kill her! to kill her!" thinking sometimes that I should be merciful to myself too, and die, and let her live, and not care, since, after my death, I would not see her suffer, for the dead know not anything: and to expect me to kill her with my own hand was a little too much. Yet that one or other of us must die was perfectly certain, for I knew that I was just on the brink of failing in my oath, and matters here had reached an obvious crisis: unless we could make up our minds to part . . .? putting the width of the earth between us? That conception occurred to me: and in the turmoil of my thoughts it seemed a possibility. Finally, about 5 P.M., I resolved upon something: and first I leapt up, went down and across the house into the arsenal, chose a small revolver, fitted it with cartridge, took it up-stairs, lubricated it with lamp-oil, went down and out across the drawbridge, walked two miles beyond the village, shot the revolver at a tree, found its action accurate, and started back. When I came to the Castle, I walked along the island to the outer end, and looked up: there were her pretty cream Valenciennes, put up by herself, waving inward before the light lake-breeze at one open oriel; and I knew that she was in the Castle, for I felt it: and always, always, when she was within, I knew, for I felt her with me: and always when she was away, I knew, I felt, for the air had a dreadful drought, and a barrenness, in it. And I looked up for a time to see if she would come to the window, and then I called, and she appeared. And I said to her: "Come down here."

$$*\qquad*\qquad*\qquad*\qquad*$$

Just here there is a little rock-path to the south, going down to the water between rocks mixed with shrub-like trees, three yards long: a path, or a lane, one might call it, for at the lower end the rocks and trees reach well over a tall man's head. There she had tied my boat to a slender linden-trunk: and sadder now than Gethsemane that familiar boat seemed to my eyes, for I knew very well that I should never enter it more. I walked up and down the path, awaiting her: and from the jacket-pocket in which lay the revolver I drew a box of Swedish matches, from it took two matches, and broke off a bit from the plain end of one; and the two I held between my left thumb and forefinger joint, the phosphorus ends level and visible, the other ends invisible: and I awaited her, pacing fast, and my brow was stern as Azrael and Rhadamanthus.

She came, very pale, poor thing, and flurried, breathing fast. And "Leda," I said, meeting her in the middle of the lane, and going straight to the point, "we are to part, as you guess—for ever, as you guess—for I see very well by your face that you guess. I, too, am very sorry, my little child, and heavy is my heart. To leave you . . . alone . . . in the world . . . is—death for me. But it must, ah it must, be done."

Her face suddenly turned as sallow as the dead were, when the shroud was already on, and the coffin had become a stale added piece of room-furniture by the bed-side; but in recording that fact, I record also this other: that, accompanying this mortal sallowness, which painfully shewed up her poor freckles, was a steady smile, a little turned-down: a smile of steady, of slightly disdainful—Confidence.

She did not say anything: so I went on.

"I have thought long," said I, "and have made a plan—a plan which cannot be effective without *your* consent and co-operation: and the plan is this: we go from this place together—this same night—to some unknown spot, some town, say a hundred miles hence—by train. There I get two motors, and I in one, and you in the other, we separate, going different ways. We shall thus never be able, however much we may want to, to rediscover each other in all this wide world. That is my plan."

She looked me in the face, smiling her smile: and the answer was not long in coming.

"I will go in the tlain with you," says she with slow decisiveness: "but where you leave me, there I will stay, till I die; and I will patiently wait till my God convert you, and send you back to me."

"That means that you refuse to do what I say?"

"Yes," said she, bowing her head with great dignity.

"Well, you speak, not like a girl, Leda," said I, "but like a full woman now. But still, reflect a minute . . . O reflect! If you stayed where I left you, I *should* go back to you, and pretty soon too: I know that I should. Tell me, then— reflect well, and tell me—do you definitely refuse to part with me?"

The answer was pretty prompt, cool, and firm:

"Yes; I lefuse."

I left her then, took a turn down the path, and came back.

"Then," said I, "here are two matches in my grasp: be good enough to draw one."

Now she was hit to the heart: I saw her eyes widen to the width of horror, with a glassy stare: she had read of the drawing of lots in the Bible: she knew that it meant death for me, or for her.

But she obeyed without a word, after one backward start and then a brief hovering indecision of thumb and forefinger over my held-out hand. I had fixed it in my mind that if she drew the shorter of the matches, then she should die; if the longer, then I should die.

She drew the shorter . . .

* * * * *

This was only what I should have expected: for I knew that God loved her, and hated me.

But instantly upon the first shock of the enormity that I should be her executioner, I made my resolve: to drop shot, too, at the moment after she dropped shot, so disposing my body, that it would fall half upon her, and half by her, so that we might be close always: and that would not be so bad, after all.

With a sudden movement I snatched the revolver from my pocket: she did not move, except her white lips, which, I think, whispered:

"*Not yet* . . ."

I stood with hanging arm, forefinger on trigger, looking at her. I saw her glance once at the weapon, and then she fixed her eyes upwards upon my face: and now that same smile, which had disappeared, was on her lips again, meaning confidence, meaning disdain.

I waited for her to open her mouth to say something—to stop that smile— that I might shoot her quick and sudden: and she would not, knowing that I could not kill her while she was smiling; and suddenly, all my pity and love for her changed into a strange resentment and rage against her, for she was pur-

posely making hard for me what I was doing for her sake: and the bitter
thought was in my mind: "You are nothing to me: if you want to die, you do
your own killing; and I will do my own killing." And without one word to her, I
strode away, and left her there.

I see now that this whole drawing of lots was nothing more than a farce: I
never could have killed her, smiling, or no smiling: for to each thing and man is
given a certain strength: and a thing cannot be stronger than its strength, strive
as it may: it is so strong, and no stronger, and there is an end of the matter.

I walked up to the Grand Bailli's *bureau*, a room about twenty-five feet
from the ground. By this time it was getting dark, but I could see, by peering,
the face of a grandfather's-clock which I had long since set going, and kept
wound. It is on the north side of the room, over the writing-desk opposite the
oriels. It then pointed to half-past six, and in order to fix some definite moment for the bitter effort of the mortal act, I said: "At Seven." I then locked
the door which opens upon three little steps near the desk, and also the stair-
door; and then I began to pace the chamber. There was not a breath of air
here, and I was hot; I seemed to be stifling, tore open my shirt at the throat,
and opened the lower half of the central mullion-space of one oriel. Some
minutes later, at twenty-five to seven, I lit two candles on the desk, and sat to
write to her, the pistol at my right hand; but I had hardly begun, when I
thought that I heard a sound at the three-step door, which was only four feet
to my left: a sound which resembled a scraping of her slipper; I stole to the
door, and crouched, listening: but I could hear nothing further. I then returned
to the desk, and set to writing, giving her some last directions for her life, telling why I died, how I loved her, much better than my own soul, begging her to
love me always, and to live on to please me, but if she *would* die, then to be
sure to die near me. Tears were pouring down my face, when, turning, I saw
her standing in a terrified pose hardly two feet behind me. The absolute stealth
which had brought and put her there, unknown to me, was like a miracle: for
the ladder, whose top I saw intruding into the open oriel, I knew well, having
often seen it in a room below, and its length was quite thirty feet, nor could its
weight be trifling: yet I had heard not one hint of its impact upon the window.
But there, at all events, she was, wan as a ghost.

Immediately, as my consciousness realised her, my arm instinctively went
out to secure the weapon: but she darted upon it, and was an instant before
me. I flew after her to wrench it away, but she flew, too: and before I caught
her, had thrown it cleanly through two rungs of the ladder and the window. I
dashed to the window, and after a hurried peer thought that I saw it below at
the foot of a rock; away I flew to the stair-door, wrung open the lock, and
down the stairs, three at a time, I ran to recover it. I remember being rather
surprised that she did not follow, forgetting all about the ladder.

But with a horrid shock I was reminded of it the moment I reached the
bottom, before ever I had passed out of the house: for I heard the report of the
weapon—that crack, my God! and crying out: "Well, Lord, she has died for

me, then!" I tottered forward, and tumbled upon her, where she lay under the incline of the ladder in her blood.

*   *   *   *   *

That night! what a night it was! of fingers shivering with haste, of harum-scarum quests and searches, of groans, and piteous appeals to God. For there were no surgical instruments, lint, anæsthetics, nor antiseptics that I knew of in the Château; and though I knew of a house in Montreux where I could find them, the distance was quite infinite, and the time an eternity in which to leave her all alone, bleeding to death; and, to my horror, I remembered that there was barely enough petrol in the motor, and the store usually kept in the house exhausted. However, I did it, leaving her there unconscious on her bed: but *how* I did it, and lived sane afterwards, that is another matter.

If I had not been a medical man, she must, I think, have died: for the bullet had broken the left fifth rib, had been deflected, and I found it buried in the upper part of the abdominal wall. I did not go from her bed-side: I did not sleep, though I nodded and staggered: for all things were nothing to me, but her: and for a frightfully long time she remained comatose. While she was still in this state I took her to a châlet beyond Villeneuve, three miles away on the mountain-side, a homely, but very salubrious place which I knew, imbedded in verdures, for I was desperate at her long collapse, and had hope in the higher air. And there after three more days, she opened her eyes, and smiled with me.

It was then that I said to myself: "This is the noblest, sagest, and also the most loveable, of the creatures whom God has made in heaven or earth. She has won my life, I will live. . . . But at least, to save myself, I will put the broadest Ocean that there is between her and me: for I wish to be a decent being, for the honour of my race, being the last, and to turn out trumps . . . though I do love my dear, God knows. . . ."

And thus, after only fifty-five days at the châlet, were we forced still further westward.

*   *   *   *   *

I wished her to remain at Chillon, intending, myself, to start for the Americas, whence any sudden impulse to return to her could not be easily accomplished: but she refused, saying that she would come with me to the coast of France: and I could not say her no.

And at the coast, after thirteen days we arrived, three days before the New Year, traversing France by both steam, air, and petrol traction.

We came to Havre—infirm, infirm of will that I was: for in my deep heart was the secret, hidden away from my own upper self, that, she being at Havre, and I at Portsmouth, we could still speak together.

We came humming into the dark town of Havre in a four-seat motor-car about ten in the evening of the 29th December: a raw bleak night, she, it was clear, poor thing, bitterly cramped with cold. I had some recollection of the place, for I had been there, and drove to the quays, near which I stopped at the

Maire's large house, a palatial place overlooking the sea, in which she slept, I occupying another near.

The next morning I was early astir, searched in the *mairie* for a map of the town, where I also found a *Bottin:* I could thus locate the Telephone Exchange. In the *Maire's* house, which I had fixed upon to be her home, the telephone was set up in an alcove adjoining a very stately *salon* Louis Quinze; and though I knew that these little dry batteries would not be run down in twenty odd years, yet, fearing any weakness, I broke open the box, and substituted a new one from the Company's stores two streets away, at the same time noting the exchange-number of the instrument. This done, I went down among the ships by the wharves, and fixed upon the first old green air-boat that seemed fairly sound, broke open a near shop, procured some buckets of oil, and by three o'clock had tested and prepared my ship. It was a dull and mournful day, drizzling, chilly. I then returned to the *mairie,* where for the first time I saw her, and she was heavy of heart that day: but when I broke the news that she would be able to speak to me, every day, all day, first she was all incredulous astonishment, then, for a moment, her eyes turned white to Heaven, then she was skipping like a kid. We were together three precious hours, examining the place, and returning with stores of whatever she might require, till I saw darkness coming on, and we went down to the ship.

And when those long-dead screws awoke and moved, bearing me toward the Outer Basin, I saw her stand darkling, lonely, on the Quai through heart-rending murk and drizzly inclemency: and oh my God, the gloomy under-look of those red eyes, and the piteous out-push of that little lip, and the hurried burying of that face! My heart broke, for I had not given her even one little, last kiss, and she had been so good, quietly acquiescing, like a good wife, not attempting to force her presence upon me in the ship; and I left her there, all widowed, alone on the Continent of Europe, watching after me: and I went out to the bleak and dreary fields of the sea.

*   *   *   *   *

Arriving at Portsmouth the next morning, I made my residence in the first house in which I found an instrument, a spacious dwelling facing the Harbour Pier. I then hurried round to the Exchange, which is on the Hard near the Docks, a large red building with facings of Cornish moor-stone, a bank on the ground-floor, and the Exchange on the first. Here I plugged her number on to mine, ran back, rang—and, to my great thanksgiving, heard her speak. (This instrument, however, did not prove satisfactory: I broke the box, and put in another battery, and still the voice was muffled: finally, I furnished the middle room at the Exchange with a truckle-bed, stores, and a few things, and here have taken up residence.)

I believe that she lives and sleeps under the instrument, as I here live and sleep, sleep and live, under it. My instrument is quite near one of the harbour-windows, so that, hearing her, I can gaze out toward her over the expanse of the waters, yet see her not; and she, too, looking over the sea toward me, can hear a voice from the azure depths of nowhere, yet see me not.

*   *   *   *   *

I this morning early to her:

"Good morning! Are you there?"

"Good morning! No: I am there," says she.

"Well, that was what I asked—'are you there?'"

"But I am not here, I am there," says she.

"I know very well that you are not 'here,'" said I, "for I do not see you: but I asked if you were there, and you say 'No,' and then 'Yes.'"

"It is the paladox of the heart," says she.

"The what?"

"The paladox," says she.

"But still I do not understand: how can you be both there and not there?"

"If my ear is here, and I elsewhere?" says she.

"An operation?"

"Yes!" says she.

"What doctor?"

"A special one!" says she.

"An ear-specialist?"

"A heart!" says she.

"And you let a heart-specialist operate on your ear?"

"On myself he operlated, and left the ear behind!" says she.

"Well, and how are you after it?"

"Fairly well. And you?" says she.

"Quite well. Did you sleep well?"

"Except when you lang me up at midnight. I have had such a dleam . . ."

"What?"

"I dleamed that I saw two little boys of the same age—only I could not see their faces, I never can see anybody's face, only yours and mine, mine and yours always—of the same age—playing in a wood. . . ."

"Ah, I hope that one of them was not called Cain, my poor girl."

"Not at all! neither of them! Suppose I tell a stoly, and say that one was called Caius and the other Tibelius, or one John and the other Jesus?"

"Ah. Well, tell me the *dleam*. . . ."

"Now you do not deserve."

"Well, what will you do to-day?"

"I? It is a lovely day . . . have you nice weather in England?"

"Very."

"Well, between eleven and twelve I will go out and gather Spling-flowers in the park, and cover the *salon*, deep, deep. Wouldn't you like to be here?"

"Not I."

"You would!"

"Why should I? I prefer England."

"But Flance is nice, too: and Flance wants to be fliends with England, and is waiting, oh waiting, for England to come over, and be fliends. Couldn't some *lapplochement* be negotiated?"

"Good-bye. This talking spoils my morning smoke. . . ."

So we speak together across the sea, my God.

*   *   *   *   *

*   *   *   *   *

On the morning of the 8th April, when I had been separated thirteen weeks from her, I boarded several ships in the Inner Port, a lunacy in my heart, and selected what looked like a very swift boat, one of the smaller Atlantic air-steamers called the *Stettin*, which seemed to require the least labour in oiling, &c., in order to fit her for the sea: for the boat in which I had come to England was a mere tub, though sound, and I pined for the wings of a dove, that I might fly away to her, and be at rest.

I toiled with fluttering hands that day, and I believe that I was of the colour of ashes to my very lips. By half-past two o'clock I was finished, and by three was coasting down Southampton Water by Netley Hospital and the Hamble-mouth, having said not one word about anything at the telephone, or even to my own guilty heart not a word. But in the silent depths of my being I felt this fact: that this must be a 35-knot boat, and that, if driven hard, hard, in spite of the heavy garment of seaweed which she trailed, she would do 30; also that Havre was 120 miles away, and at 7 P.M. I should be on its quay.

And when I was away, and out on the bright and breezy sea, I called to her, crying out: "*I am coming!*" And I knew that she heard me, and that her heart leapt to meet me, for mine leapt, too, and felt her answering.

The sun went down: it set. I was tired of the day's work, and of standing at the high-set wheel; and I could not yet see the coast of France. And a thought smote me, and after another ten minutes I turned the boat's head back, my face screwed with pain, God knows, like a man whose thumbs are ground between the screws, and his body drawn out and out on the rack to tenuous length, and his flesh massacred with pincers: and I fell upon the floor of the bridge contorted with anguish: for I could not go to her. But after a time that paroxysm passed, and I rose up sullen and resentful, and resumed my place at the wheel, steering back for England: for a fixed resolve was in my breast, and I said: "Oh no, no more. If I could bear it, I would, I would . . . but if it is impossible, how can I? To-morrow night as the sun sets—without fail—so help me God—I will kill myself."

*   *   *   *   *

So it is finished, my good God.

On the early morning of the next day, the 9th, I having come back to Portsmouth about eleven the previous night, when I bid her "Good morning" through the telephone, she said "Good morning," and not another word. I said:

"I got my hookah-bowl broken last night, and shall be trying to mend it to-day."

No answer.

"Are you there?" said I.

"Yes," says she.

"Then why don't you answer?" said I.

"Where were you all yesterday?" says she.

"I went for a little cruise in the basin," said I.

Silence for three minutes: then she says:

"What is the matter?"

"Matter?" said I, "nothing!"

"*Tell me!*" she says—with such an intensity and rage, as to make me shudder.

"There is nothing to tell, Leda!"

"Oh, but how can you be so *cluel* to me?" she cries, and ah, there was anguish in that voice! "There *is* something to tell—there *is*! Don't I know it vely well by your voice?"

Ah, the thought took me then, how, on the morrow, she would ring, and have no answer; and she would ring again, and have no answer; and she would ring all day, and ring, and ring; and for ever she would ring, with white-flowing hair and the staring eye-balls of frenzy, battering reproaches at the doors of God, and the Universe would cry back to her howls and ravings only the one eternal answer of Silence, of Silence. And as I thought of that—for very pity, for very pity, my God—I could not help sobbing aloud:

"May God pity you, woman!"

I do not know if she heard it: she *must*, I think, have heard: but no reply came; and there I, shivering like the sheeted dead, stood waiting for her next word, waiting long, dreading, hoping for, her voice, thinking that if she spoke and sobbed but once, I should drop dead, dead, where I stood, or bite my tongue through, or shriek the high laugh of distraction. But when at last, after quite thirty or forty minutes she spoke, her voice was perfectly firm and calm. She said:

"Are you there?"

"Yes," said I, "yes, Leda."

"What was the colour," says she, "of the poison-cloud which destloyed the world?"

"Purple, Leda," said I.

"And it had a smell like almonds or peach-blossoms, did it not?" says she.

"Yes," I said, "yes."

"Then," says she, "there is *another* eluption. Evelly now and again I seem to scent stlange whiffs like that . . . and there is a purple vapour in the East which glows and glows . . . just see if you can see it. . . ."

I flew across the room to an east window, threw up the grimy sash, and looked: but the view was barred by the plain brick back of a tall warehouse: I rushed back, gasped to her to wait, rushed down the two stairs, and out upon the Hard. For a minute I ran dodging wildly about, seeking a purview to the East, and finally ran up the dock-yard, behind the storehouses to the Semaphore, and reached the top, panting for life. I looked abroad: the morning sky, but for a bank of cloud to the north-west, was cloudless, the sun blazing in a region of clear azure pallor. And back again I flew.

"I cannot see it . . .!" I cried.

"Then it has not tlavelled far enough to the north-west yet," she said with decision.

"My wife!" I cried: "you are my wife now!"

"Am I?" says she: "at last? Are you glad? . . . But shall I not soon die?"

"No! You can escape! My home! My heart! If only for an hour or two, then death—just think, together—on the same couch, for ever, heart to heart—how sweet!"

"Yes! how sweet! But how escape?"

"It travelled slowly before. Get quick—will you?—into one of the smaller boats by the quay—there is one just under the crane that is an air-boat—you have seen me turn on the air, haven't you?—that handle on the right as you descend the steps under the dial-thing—get first a bucket of oil from the shop next to the clock-tower in the quay-street, and throw it over everything that you see rusted. Only, spend no time—for me, my heaven! You can steer by the tiller and compass: well, the wheel is quite the same, only just the opposite. First unmoor, then to the handle, then to the wheel. The course is directly North-East by North. I will meet you on the sea—go now—"

I was wild with bliss. I thought that I should take her between my arms, and have the little freckles against my face, and taste her short firm-fleshed upper-lip, and moan upon her, and whimper upon her, and mutter upon her, and say "My wife." And even when I knew that she was gone from the telephone, I still stood there, hoarsely calling after her: "My wife! My wife!"

*　　*　　*　　*　　*

I flew down to where the steamer lay moored that had borne me the previous day. Her joint speed with the speed of Leda's boat would be forty knots: in three hours we must meet. I had not the least fear of her dying before I saw her: for, apart from the deliberate movement of the vapour that first time, I foretasted and trusted my love, that she would surely come, and not fail: as dying saints foretasted and trusted Eternal Life.

I was no sooner on board the *Stettin* than her engines were straining under what was equivalent to forced draught. On the previous day it would have little surprised me at any moment, while I drove her, to be carried to the clouds in an explosion from her deep-rusted steel tanks: but this day such a fear never crossed my mind: for I knew very well that I was immortal till I saw her.

The sea was not only perfectly smooth, but placid, as on the previous day: only it seemed far placider, and the sun brighter, and there was a levity in the breezes that frilled the sea in fugitive dark patches, like *frissons* of tickling; and I thought that the morning was a true marriage-morning, and remembered that it was a Sabbath; and sweet odours our wedding would not lack of peach and almond, though, looking eastward, I could see no faintest sign of any purple cloud, but only rags of chiffon under the sun; and it would be an eternal wedding, for one day in our sight would be as a thousand years, and our thousand years of bliss be but one day, and in the evening of that eternity death would come and sweetly lay its finger on our languid lids, and we should die of weary bliss; and all manner of dancings and singings—fandango and light galliard, corantoes and the solemn gavotte—were a-tune in my heart that happy day; and running by the chart-house to the wheel, I saw under the table a great roll of old flags, and presently they were flying in a long curve of gala from the main; and the sea rumpled in a long tract of tumbling milk behind me; and I hasted homeward, to meet my heart.

*   *   *   *   *

No purple cloud could I see as, on and on, for two hours, I tore southward: but at hot noon, on the weather beam I spied through the glass across the water something else which moved, and it was you who came to me, Oh Leda, my spirit's breath!

I bore down upon her, waving: and soon I saw her stand like an ancient mariner, but in white muslins that fluttered, at her wheel on the bridge—it was one of those little old Havre-Antwerp craft very high in the bows—and she waved a little white thing. And we came nearer, till I could spy her face, her smile, and I shouted her to stop, in a minute stopped myself, and by happy steering came with slowing head-way to a slight crash by her side, and ran down the trellised steps to her, and led her up; and on the deck, without saying a word, I fell to my knees before her, and I bowed my brow to the floor, with obeisance, and I worshipped her there as Heaven.

And we were wedded: for she, too, bowed the knee with me under the jovial blue sky; and under her eyes were the little moist semicircles of dreamy pensive fatigue, so dear and wifish: and God was there, and saw her kneel: for He loves the girl.

And I got the two ships apart, and they rested some yards divided all the day, and we were in the main-deck cabin, where I had locked a door, so that no one might come in to be with my love and me.

*   *   *   *   *

I said to her:

"We will fly west to one of the Somersetshire coal-mines, or to one of the Cornwall tin-mines, and we will barricade ourselves against the cloud, and provision ourselves for six months—for it is quite feasible, and we have plenty of time, and no crowds to break down our barricades—and there in the deep earth we will live sweetly together, till the danger is overpast."

And she smiled, and drew her hand across my face, and said:

"No, no; don't you tlust in my God? do you think He would leally let me die?"

For she has appropriated the Almighty God to herself, naming Him "my God"—the impudence: though she generally knows what she is saying, too. And she would not fly the cloud.

And I am now writing three weeks later at a little place called Château-les-Roses, and no poison-cloud, and no sign of any poison-cloud, has come. And this I do not understand.

It may be that she divined that I was about to destroy myself . . . she may be quite capable . . . But no, I do not understand, and shall never ask her.

But *this* I understand: that it is *the White* who is Master here: that though he wins but by a hair, yet he wins, he wins: and since he wins, dance, dance, my heart.

I look for a race that shall resemble its Mother: nimble-witted, light-minded, pious—like her; all-human, ambidextrous, ambicephalous, two-eyed—like her; and if, like her, they talk the English language with all the *r*'s turned into *l*'s, I shall not care.

They will be vegetable-eaters, I suppose, when the meat now extant is eaten up: but it is not certain that meat is good for men: and if it is really good, then they will *invent* a meat: for they will be *her* sons, and she, to the furthest cycle in which the female human mind is permitted to orbit, is, I swear, all-wise.

There was a preaching man—a Scotchman he was, named Macintosh, or something like that—who said that the last end of Man shall be well, and very well: and she says the same: and the agreement of these two makes a Truth. And to that I now say: Amen, Amen.

For I, Adam Jeffson, second Parent of the world, hereby lay down, ordain, and decree for all time, clearly perceiving it now: That the one Motto and Watch-word essentially proper to each human individual, and to the whole Race of Man, as distinct from other races in heaven or in earth, was always, and remains, even this: "Though He slay me, yet will I trust in Him."

Appendix

Vaila

E caddi come l'uome cui sonno piglia.—DANTE.

A good many years ago, a young man, student in Paris, I was informally associated with the great Corot, and eyewitnessed by his side several of those cases of mind-malady, in the analysis of which he was a past master. I remember one little girl of the Marais, who, till the age of nine, in no way seemed to differ from her playmates. But one night, lying a-bed, she whispered into her mother's ear: "Maman, can you not hear the *sound of the world?*" It appears that her recently-begun study of geography had taught her that the earth flies, with an enormous velocity, on an orbit about the sun; and that *sound of the world* to which she referred was a faint (quite subjective) musical humming, like a shell-murmur, heard in the silence of night, and attributed by her fancy to the song of this high motion. Within six months the excess of lunacy possessed her.

I mentioned the incident to my friend, Haco Harfager, then occupying with me the solitude of an old place in S. Germain, shut in by a shrubbery and high wall from the street. He listened with singular interest, and for a day seemed wrapped in gloom.

Another case which I detailed produced a profound impression upon my friend. A young man, a toy-maker of S. Antoine, suffering from chronic congenital phthisis, attained in the ordinary way his twenty-fifth year. He was frugal, industrious, self-involved. On a winter's evening, returning to his lonely garret, he happened to purchase one of those vehemently factious sheets which circulate by night, like things of darkness, over the Boulevards. This simple act was the herald of his doom. He lay a-bed, and perused the *feuille.* He had never been a reader; knew little of the greater world, and the deep hum of its travail. But the next night he bought another leaf. Gradually he acquired interest in politics, the large movements, the roar of life. And this interest grew absorbing. Till late into the night, and every night, he lay poring over the furious mendacity, the turbulent wind, the printed passion. He would awake tired, spitting blood, but intense in spirit—and straightway purchased a morning leaf. His being lent itself to a retrograde evolution. The more his teeth gnashed, the less they ate. He became sloven, irregular at work, turning on his bed through the day. Rags overtook him. As the greater interest, and the vaster tumult, possessed his frail soul, so every lesser interest, tumult, died to him. There came an early day when he no longer cared for his own life; and another day, when his maniac fingers rent the hairs from his head.

As to this man, the great Corot said to me:

"Really, one does not know whether to laugh or weep over such a business. Observe, for one thing, how diversely men are made! There are minds precisely so sensitive as a cupful of melted silver; *every* breath will roughen and darken them: and what of the simoon, tornado? And that is not a metaphor but a simile. For such, this earth—I had almost said this universe—is clearly no fit habitation, but a Machine of Death, a baleful Vast. *Too* horrible to many is the running shriek of Being—they *cannot* bear the world. Let each look well to his own little whisk of life, say I, and leave the big fiery Automaton alone. Here in this poor toy-maker you have a case of the ear: it is only the neurosis, Oxyecoia. Splendid was that Greek myth of the Harpies: by *them* was this man snatched—or, say, caught by a limb in the wheels of the universe, and so perished. It is quite a grand exit, you know—translation in a chariot of flame. Only remember that the member first involved was *the pinna*: he bent *ear* to the howl of Europe, and ended by himself howling. Can a straw ride composedly on the primeval whirlwinds? Between chaos and our shoes wobbles, I tell you, the thinnest film! I knew a man who had this peculiarity of aural hyperæsthesia: that every sound brought him minute information of the matter causing the sound; that is to say, he had an ear bearing to the normal ear the relation which the spectroscope bears to the telescope. A rod, for instance, of mixed copper and iron impinging, in his hearing, upon a rod of mixed tin and lead, conveyed to him not merely the proportion of each metal in each rod, but some strange knowledge of the essential meaning and spirit, as it were, of copper, of iron, of tin, and of lead. Of course, he went mad; but, beforehand, told me this singular thing: that precisely such a sense as his was, according to his *certain* intuition, employed by the Supreme Being in his permeation of space to apprehend the nature and movements of mind and matter. And he went on to add that *Sin*—what we call *sin*—is only the movement of matter or mind into such places, or in such a way, as to give offence or pain to this delicate diplacusis (so I must call it) of the Creator; so that the 'Law' of Revelation became, in his eyes, edicts promulgated by their Maker merely in self-protection from aural pain; and divine punishment for, say murder, nothing more than retaliation for unease caused to the divine aural consciousness by the matter in a particular dirk or bullet lodged, at a particular moment, in a non-intended place! Him, too, I say, did the Harpies whisk aloft."

My recital of these cases to my friend, Harfager, I have mentioned. I was surprised, not so much at his acute interest—for he was interested in all knowledge—as at the obvious pains which be took to conceal that interest. He hurriedly turned the leaves of a volume, but could not hide his panting nostrils.

From first days when we happened to attend the same seminary in Stockholm, a tacit intimacy had sprung between us. I loved him greatly; that he so loved me I knew. But it was an intimacy not accompanied by many of the usual interchanges of close friendships. Harfager was the shyest, most isolated, insulated, of beings. Though our joint *ménage* (brought about by a chance meeting at a midnight *séance* in Paris) had now lasted some months, I knew nothing of his plans, motives. Through the day we pursued our intense readings together, he rapt quite back into the past, I equally engrossed upon the present; late at night we reclined on couches within the vast cave of an old fireplace Louis Onze, and smoked to the dying flame in a silence of wormwood and terebinth. Occasionally a *soirée* or lecture might draw me from the house; except once, I never understood that Harfager left it. I was, on that occasion, returning home at a point of the Rue St. Honoré where a rush of continuous traffic rattled over the old coarse pavements retained there, when I came suddenly upon him. In this tumult he stood abstracted on the trottoir in a listening attitude, and for a moment seemed not to recognise me when I touched him.

Even as a boy I had discerned in my friend the genuine Noble, the inveterate patrician. One saw that in him. Not at all that his personality gave an impression of any species of loftiness, opulence; on the contrary. He did, however, give an impression of incalculable *ancientness.* He suggested the last moment of an æon. No nobleman have I seen who so bore in his wan aspect the assurance of the inevitable aristocrat, the essential prince, whose pale blossom is of yesterday, and will perish to-morrow, but whose root fills the ages. This much I knew of Harfager; also that on one or other of the bleak islands of his patrimony north of Zetland lived his mother and a paternal aunt; that he was somewhat deaf; but liable to transports of pain or delight at variously-combined musical sounds, the creak of a door, the note of a bird. More I cannot say that I then knew.

He was rather below the middle height, and gave some promise of stoutness. His nose rose highly aquiline from that species of forehead called by phrenologists "the musical," that is to say, flanked by temples which incline *outward* to the cheek-bones, making breadth for the base of the brain; while the direction of the heavy-lidded, faded-blue eyes, and of the eyebrows, was a downward *droop* from the nose to their outer extremities. He wore a thin chin-beard. But the astonishing feature of his face were the ears: they were nearly circular, very small, and flat, being devoid of that outer volution known as the *helix.* The two tiny discs of cartilage had always the effect of making me think of the little ancient round shields, without rims, called *clipeus* and *peltè.* I came to understand that this was a peculiarity which had subsisted among the members of his race for some centuries. Over the whole white face of my friend was stamped a look of woful inability, utter gravity of sorrow. One said "Sardanapalus," frail last of the great line of Nimrod.

After a year I found it necessary to mention to Harfager my intention of leaving Paris. We reclined by night in our accustomed nooks within the fireplace. To my announcement he answered with a merely polite "Indeed!" and continued to gloat upon the flame; but after an hour turned upon me, and said:

"Well, it seems to be a hard and selfish world."

Truisms uttered with just such an air of new discovery I had occasionally heard from him; but the earnest gaze of eyes, and plaint of voice and despondency of shaken head, with which he now spoke shocked me to surprise.

"À *propos* of what?" I asked.

"My friend, do not leave me!"

He spread his arms. His utterance choked.

I learned that he was the object of a devilish malice; that he was the prey of a hellish temptation. That a lure, a becking hand, a lurking lust, which it was the effort of his life to eschew (and to which he was especially liable in solitude), continually enticed him; and that thus it had been almost from the day when, at the age of five, he had been sent by his father from his desolate home in the sea.

And whose was this malice?

He told me his mother's and aunt's.

And what was this temptation?

He said it was the temptation to return—to fly with the very frenzy of longing—back to that dim home.

I asked with what motives, and in what particulars, the malice of his mother and aunt manifested itself. He replied that there was, he believed, no specific motive, but only a determined malevolence, involuntary and fated; and that the respect in which it manifested itself was to be found in the multiplied prayers and commands with which, for years, they had importuned him to seek again the far hold of his ancestors.

All this I could in no way comprehend, and plainly said as much. In what consisted this horrible magnetism, and equally horrible peril, of his home? To this question Harfager did not reply, but rose from his seat, disappeared behind the drawn curtains of the hearth, and left the room. He presently returned with a quarto tome bound in hide. It proved to be Hugh Gascoigne's *Chronicle of Norse Families*, executed in English black-letter. The passage to which he pointed I read as follows:

"Nowe, of thise two brethrene, tholder (the elder), Harold, beying of seemely personage and prowesse, did goe pilgrimage into Danemarke, wher from he repayred againward hoom to Hjaltlande (Zetland), and wyth hym fette (fetched) the amiabil Thronda for hyss wyf, which was a doughter of the sank (blood) royall of danemark. And his yonger brothir, Sweyne, that was sad and debonayre, but far surmounted the other in cunnying, receyued him with all good chere. Butte eftsones (soon after) fel sweyne sick for alle his lust that he hadde of Thronda his brothir's wyfe. And whiles the worthy Harold, with the grenehede (greenness) and folye of yowthe, ministred a bisy cure aboute the bedde wher Sweyne lay sick, lo, sweyne fastened on him a violent stroke with a swerde, and with no lenger taryinge enclosed his hands in bondes, and cast him in the botme of a depe holde. And by cause harold wold not benumb (deprive) hymself of the gouernance of Thronda his wif, Sweyne cutte off boeth his ere[s], and putte out one of his iyes, and after diverse sike tormentes was preste (ready) to slee (slay) hym. But on a daye, the valiant Harold, breking hys bondes, and embracinge his aduersary, did by the sleight of wrastlyng ouer-throwe him, and escaped. Nat-withstandyng, he foltred whan he came to the Somburgh Hed not ferre (far) fro the Castell, and al-be-it that he was swifte-foote, couth ne farder renne (run) by reson that he was faynte with the longe plag[u]es of hyss brothir. And whiles he ther lay in a sound (swoon) did Sweyne come sle (sly) and softe up on hym, and whan he had striken him with a darte, caste him fro Sarnburgh Hede in to the See.

"Nat longe herafterward did the lady Thronda (tho she knew nat the manere of her lordes deth, ne, veryly, yf he was dead or on live) receyve Sweyne in to gree (favour), and with grete gaudying and blowinge of bea-mous (trumpets) did gon to his bed. And right soo they two wente thennes (thence) to soiourn in ferre partes.

"Now, it befel that sweyne was mynded by a dreme to let bild him a grete maunsion in Hialtland for the hoom-cominge of the ladye Thronda; where for he called to hym a cunninge Maistre-worckman, and sente him hye (in haste) to englond to gather thrals for the bilding of this lusty Houss, but hym-self soiourned wyth his ladye at Rome. Thenne came this worckman to london, but passinge thennes to Hialtland, was drent (drowned), he, and his feers (mates), and his shippe, alle and some. And after two yeres, which was the tyme assygned, Sweyne harfager sente let-tres to Hialtlande to vnderstonde how his grete Houss did, for he knew not the drenchynge of the Architecte; and eftsones he receiued answer that the Houss *did wel*, and was bildinge on the Ile of Vaila; but that ne was the Ile wher-on Sweyne had appoynted the bilding to be; and he was aferd, and nere fel doun ded for drede, by cause that, in the lettres, he saw before him the mannere of wrytyng of his brothir Harold. And he sayed in this fourme: 'Surely Harolde is on lyue (alive), elles (else) ben thise lettres writ with gostlye hande.' And he was wo many dayes, seeing that this was a dedely stroke. Ther-after, he took him-selfe back to Hjalt-land to know how the matere was, and ther the old Castell on Somburgh Hede was brek doun to the erthe. Thenn Sweyne was wode-wrothe, and cryed, 'Jhesu mercy, where is al the grete Hous of my faders becomen? allas! thys wy-cked day of desteynye.' And one of the peple tolde him that a hoost of worckmen fro fer partes hadde brek it doun. And he sayd: 'who hath bidde them?' but that couth none answer. Thenne he sayd agayn: 'nis (is not) my brothir harold on-lyue? for I haue biholde his writinge'; and that, to, colde none answer. Soo he wente to Vaila, and saw there a grete Houss stonde, and whan he looked on hyt, he saye[d]: 'this, sooth, was y-bild by my brothir Harolde, be he ded, or bee he on-lyue.' And ther he dwelte, and his ladye, and his sones and hys sones sones vntyl nowe. For that the Houss is rewthelesse (ruthless) and withoute pite; where-for tis seyed that up on al who dwel there faleth a wycked madness and a lecherous agonie;

and that by waye of the eres doe they drinck the cuppe of the furie of the erelesse Harolde, til the tyme of the Houss bee ended."

I read the narrative half-aloud, and smiled.

"This, Harfager," I said, "is very tolerable romance on the part of the good Gascoigne; but has the look of indifferent history."

"It is, nevertheless, genuine *history*," he replied.

"You believe that?"

"The house still stands solidly on Vaila."

"The brothers Sweyn and Harold were literary for their age, I think?"

"No member of my race," he replied, with a suspicion of hauteur, "has been illiterate."

"But, at least, you do not believe that mediæval ghosts superintended the building of their family mansions?"

"Gascoigne nowhere says that; for to be stabbed is not necessarily to die; nor, if he did say it, would it be true to assert that I have any knowledge on the subject."

"And what, Harfager, is the nature of that 'wicked madness,' that 'lecherous agonie,' of which Gascoigne speaks?"

"Do you ask me?" He spread his arms. "What do I know? I know nothing! I was banished from the place at the age of five. Yet the cry of it still reverberates in my soul. And have I not *told* you of agonies—even within myself—of inherited longing and loathing. . . ."

But, at any rate, I answered, my journey to Heidelberg was just then indispensable. I would compromise by making absence short, and rejoin him quickly, if he would wait a few weeks for me. His moody silence I took to mean consent, and soon afterward left him.

But I was unavoidably detained; and when I returned to our old quarters, found them empty. Harfager had vanished.

It was only after twelve years that a letter was forwarded me—a rather wild letter, an excessively long one—in the well-remembered hand of my friend. It was dated at Vaila. From the character of the writing I conjectured that it had been penned *with furious haste*, so that I was all the more astonished at the very trivial nature of the voluminous contents. On the first half page he spoke of our old friendship, and asked if, in memory of that, I would see his mother who was dying; the rest of the epistle, sheet upon sheet, consisted of a tedious analysis of his mother's genealogical tree, the apparent aim being to prove that she was a genuine Harfager, and a cousin of his father. He then went on to comment on the extreme prolificness of his race, asserting that since the fourteenth century, over four millions of its members had lived and died in various parts of the world; three only of them, he believed, being now left. That determined, the letter ended.

Influenced by this communication, I travelled northward; reached Caithness; passed the stormy Orkneys; reached Lerwick; and from Unst, the most bleak and northerly of the Zetlands, contrived, by dint of bribes, to pit the weatherworthiness of a lug-sailed "sixern" (said to be identical with the "lang-schips" of the Vikings) against a flowing sea and a darkly-brooding heaven. The voyage, I was warned, was, at such a time, of some risk. It was the Cimme-rian December of those inter-boreal latitudes. The weather here, they said, though never cold, is hardly ever other than tempestuous. A dense and dank sea-born haze now lay, in spite of vapid breezes, high along the water, enclos-ing the boat in a vague domed cavern of doleful twilight and sullen swell. The region of the considerable islands was past, and there was a spectral something in the unreal aspect of silent sea and sunless dismalness of sky which produced upon my nerves the impression of a voyage *out* of nature, a cruise *beyond* the world. Occasionally, however, we careered past one of those solitary "skerries," or sea-stacks, whose craggy sea-walls, cannonaded and disintegrated by the in-ter-shock of the tidal wave and the torrent currents of the German Ocean, wore, even at some distance, an appearance of frightful ruin and havoc. Three only of these I saw, for before the dim day had well run half its course, sudden blackness of night was upon us, and with it one of those tempests, of which the winter of this semi-polar sea is, throughout, an ever-varying succession. During the haggard and dolorous crepuscule of the next brief day, the rain did not cease; but before darkness had quite supervened, my helmsman, who talked continuously to a mate of seal-maidens, and waterhorses, and *grülies*, paused to point to a mound of gloomier grey on the weather-bow, which was, he assured me, Vaila.

Vaila, he added, was the centre of quite a system of those *rösts* (dangerous eddies) and cross-currents, which the action of the tidal wave hurls hurrying with complicated and corroding swirl among the islands; in the neighbourhood of Vaila, said the mariner, they hurtled with more than usual precipitancy, ow-ing to the palisade of lofty sea-crags which barbicaned the place about; ap-proach was, therefore, at all times difficult, and by night fool-hardy. With a running sea, however, we came sufficiently near to discern the mane of surf which bristled high along the beetling coast-wall. Its shock, according to the man's account, had ofttimes more than all the efficiency of a bombing of real artillery, slinging tons of rock to heights of several hundred feet upon the main island.

When the sun next feebly climbed above the horizon to totter with marred visage through a wan low segment of funereal murk, we had closely ap-proached the coast; and it was then for the first time that the impression of some *spinning* motion in the island (born no doubt of the circular movement of the water) was produced upon me. We effected a landing at a small *voe*, or sea-arm, on the western side; the eastern, though the point of my aim, being, on account of the swell, out of the question for that purpose. Here I found in two feal-thatched *skeoes* (or sheds), which crouched beneath the shelter of a far over-hanging hill, five or six poor peasant-seamen, whose livelihood no doubt consisted in periodically trading for the necessaries of the great house on the east. Beside these there were no dwellers on Vaila; but with one of them for guide, I soon began the ascent and transit of the island. Through the night in the boat I had been strangely aware of an oppressive booming in the ears, for which even the roar of the sea round all the coast seemed quite insufficient to account. This now, as we advanced, became fearfully intensified, and with it, once more, the unaccountable conviction within me of *spinning* motions to which I have referred. Vaila I discovered to be a land of hill and precipice, made of fine granite and flaggy gneiss; at about the centre, however, we came upon a high tableland sloping gradually from west to east, and covered by a series of lochs, which sullenly and continuously flowed one into the other. To this chain of sombre, black-gleaming water I could see no terminating shore, and by dint of shouting to my companion, and bending close ear to his answering shout, I came to know that there *was* no such shore: I say *shout*, for nothing less could have prevailed over the steady bellowing as of ten thousand bisons, which now resounded on every hand. A certain tremblement, too, of the earth became distinct. In vain did the eye seek in its dreary purview a single trace of tree or shrub; for, as a matter of course, no kind of vegetation, save peat, could brave, even for a day, that perennial agony of the tempest which makes of this turbid and benighted zone its arena. Darkness, an hour after noon, commenced to overshadow us; and it was shortly afterward that my guide, pointing down a precipitous defile near the eastern coast, hurriedly set forth upon the way he had come. I frantically howled a question after him as he went; but at this point the human voice had ceased to be in the faintest degree audible.

Down this defile, with a sinking of the heart, and a most singular feeling of giddiness, I passed. Having reached the end, I emerged upon a wide ledge which shuddered to the immediate onsets of the sea. But all this portion of the island was, in addition, subject to a sharp continuous ague evidently not due to the heavy ordnance of the ocean. Hugging a point of cliff for steadiness from the wind, I looked forth upon a spectacle of weirdly morne, of dismal wildness. The opening lines of *Hecuba*, or some drear district of the *Inferno*, seemed realised before me. Three black "skerries," encompassed by a fantastic series of stacks, crooked as a witch's fore-finger, and giving herbergage to shrill routs of osprey and scart, to seal and walrus, lay at some fathoms' distance; and from its race and rage among them, the sea, in arrogance of white, tumultuous, but inaudible wrath, ramped terrible as an army with banners toward the land. Leaving my place, I staggered some distance to the left: and now, all at once, a vast amphitheatre opened before me, and there burst upon my gaze a panorama of such heart-appalling sublimity, as imagination could never have conceived, nor can now utterly recall.

"A vast amphitheatre" I have said; yet it was rather the shape of a round-Gothic (or Norman) doorway which I beheld. Let the reader picture such a door-frame, nearly a mile in breadth, laid flat upon the ground, the curved portion farthest from the sea; and round it let a perfectly smooth and even wall of rock tower in perpendicular regularity to an altitude not unworthy the vulture's eyrie; and now, down the depth of this Gothic shape, and *over all its extent*, let bawling oceans dash themselves triumphing in spendthrift cataclysm of emerald and hoary fury,—and the stupor of awe with which I looked, and then the shrinking *fear*, and then the instinct of instant flight, will find easy comprehension.

This was the thrilling disemboguement of the lochs of Vaila.

And within the arch of this Gothic cataract, volumed in the world of its smoky torment and far-excursive spray, stood a palace of brass . . . circular in shape . . . huge in dimension.

The last gleam of the ineffectual day had now almost passed, but I could yet discern, in spite of the perpetual rain-fall which bleakly nimbused it as in a halo of tears, that the building was low in proportion to the vastness of its circumference; that it was roofed with a shallow dome; and that about it ran two serried rows of shuttered Norman windows, the upper row being of smaller size than the lower. Certain indications led me to assume that the house had been built upon a vast natural bed of rock which lay, circular and detached, within the arch of the cataract; but this did not quite emerge above the flood, for the whole ground-area upon which I looked dashed a deep and incense-reeking river to the beachless sea; so that passage would have been impossible, were it not that, from a point near me, a massive bridge, thick with algæ, rose above the tide, and led to the mansion. Descending from my ledge, I passed along it, now drenched in spray. As I came nearer, I could see that the house, too, was to half its height more thickly bearded than an old hull with barnacles and every variety of brilliant seaweed; and—what was very surprising—that from many points near the top of the brazen wall huge iron chains, slimily barbarous with the trailing tresses of ages, reached out in symmetrical divergent rays to points on the ground hidden by the flood: the fabric had thus the look of a many-anchored ark; but without pausing for minute observation, I pushed forward, and dashing through the smooth circular waterfall which poured all round from the eaves, by one of its many small projecting porches, entered the dwelling.

Darkness now was around me—and sound. I seemed to stand in the very throat of some yelling planet. An infinite sadness descended upon me; I was near to the abandonment of tears. "Here," I said, "is Khoreb, and the limits of weeping; not elsewhere is the valley of sighing." The tumult resembled the continuous volleying of many thousands of cannon, mingled with strange crashing and bursting uproars. I passed forward through a succession of halls, and was wondering as to my further course, when a hideous figure, bearing a lamp, stalked rapidly towards me. I shrank aghast. It seemed the skeleton of a tall man, wrapped in a winding-sheet. The glitter of a tiny eye, however, and a sere film of skin over part of the face, quickly reassured me. Of ears, he showed no sign. He was, I afterwards learned, Aith; and the singularity of his appearance was partially explained by his pretence—whether true or false—that he had once suffered *burning*, almost to the cinder-stage, but had miraculously recovered. With an expression of malignity, and strange excited gestures, he led the way to a chamber on the upper stage, where having struck light to a vesta, he pointed to a spread table and left me.

For a long time I sat in solitude. The earthquake of the mansion was in
tense; but all sense seemed swallowed up and confounded in the one impres
sion of sound. Water, water, was the world—nightmare on my chest, a horror
in my ears, an intolerable tingling on my nerves. The feeling of being infinitely
drowned and ruined in the all obliterating deluge—the impulse to gasp for
breath—overwhelmed me. I rose and paced; but suddenly stopped, angry, I
scarce knew why, with myself. I had, in fact, found myself walking with a cer
tain *hurry*, not usual with me, not natural to me. The feeling of giddiness, too,
had abnormally increased. I forced myself to stand and take note of the hall. It
was of great size, and damp with mists, so that the tattered, but rich, mediæval
furniture seemed lost in its extent; its centre was occupied by a broad low mar
ble tomb bearing the name of a Harfagar of the fifteenth century; its walls were
old brown panels of oak. Having drearily observed these things, I waited on
with an intolerable consciousness of loneliness; but a little after midnight the
tapestry parted, and Harfager, with hurried stride, approached me.

In twelve years my friend had grown old. He showed, it is true, a tendency
to corpulence; yet, to a knowing eye, he was, in reality, tabid, ill nourished.
And his neck protruded from his body; and his lower back had quite the for
ward curve of age; and his hair floated about his face and shoulders in a disar
ray of awful whiteness. A chin beard hung grey to his chest. His attire was a
simple robe of bauge, which, as he went, waved aflaunt from his bare and hir
sute shins, and he was shod in those soft slippers called *rivlins*.

(RUDE IMPRESSION OF HARFAGER)

To my surprise, he spoke. When I passionately shouted that I could gather no fragment of sound from his moving lips, he clapped both palms to his ears, and thereupon renewed a vehement siege to mine: but again without result. And now, with a seemingly angry fling of the hand, he caught up the taper, and swiftly strode from the chamber.

There was something singularly unnatural in his manner—something which irresistibly reminded me of the skeleton, Aith: an excess of zeal, a fever, a rage, a *loudness*, an eagerness of walk, a wild extravagance of gesture. His hand constantly dashed the hair-whiffs from his face. Though his countenance was of the saffron of death, the eyes were turgid and red with blood—heavy-lidded eyes, fixed in a downward and sideward intentness of gaze. He presently returned with a folio of ivory and a stylus of graphite hanging from a cord about his garment.

He rapidly wrote a petition that I would, if not too tired, take part with him in the funeral obsequies of his mother. I shouted assent.

Once more he clapped palms to ears; then wrote: "Do not shout: no whisper in any part of the building is inaudible to me."

I remembered that, in early life, he had seemed slightly *deaf*.

We passed together through many apartments, he shading the taper with his hand. This was necessary; for, as I quickly discovered, in no part of the shivering fabric was the air in a state of rest, but seemed for ever commoved by a curious agitation, a faint windiness, like the echo of a storm, which communicated a gentle universal trouble to the tapestries. Everywhere I was confronted with the same past richness, present raggedness of decay. In many of the chambers were old marble tombs; one was a museum piled with bronzes, urns; but broken, imbedded in fungoids, dripping wide with moisture. It was as if the mansion, in ardour of travail, sweated. An odour of decomposition was heavy on the swaying air. With difficulty I followed Harfager through the labyrinth of his headlong passage. Once only he stopped short, and with face madly wild above the glare of the light, heaved up his hand, and uttered a single word. From the shaping of the lips, I conjectured the word, "Hark!"

Presently we entered a very long black hall wherein, on chairs beside a bed near the centre, rested a deep coffin, flanked by a row of tall candlesticks of ebony. It had, I noticed, this singularity, that the foot-piece was absent, so that the soles of the corpse were visible as we approached. I beheld, too, three upright rods secured to the coffin-side, each fitted at its summit with a small silver bell of the kind called *morrice* pendent from a flexible steel spring. At the head of the bed, Aith, with an appearance of irascibility, stamped to and fro within a small area. Harfager, having rapidly traversed the apartment to the coffin, deposited the taper upon a stone table near, and stood poring with crazy intentness upon the body. I too, looking, stood. Death so rigorous, Gorgon, I had not seen. The coffin seemed full of tangled grey hair. The lady was, it was clear, of great age, osseous, scimitar-nosed. Her head shook with solemn continuity to the vibration of the house. From each ear trickled a black streamlet; the mouth was ridged with froth. I observed that over the corpse had been set three thin laminæ of polished wood, resembling in position, and shape, the bridge of a violin. Their sides fitted into grooves in the coffin-sides, and their top was of a shape to exactly fit the inclination of the two coffin-lids when closed. One of these laminæ passed over the knees of the dead lady; another bridged the abdomen; the third the region of the neck. In each of them was a small circular hole. Across each of the three holes passed vertically a tense cord from the morrice-bell nearest to it; the three holes being thus divided by the three cords into six vertical semicircles. Before I could conjecture the significance of this arrangement, Harfager closed the folding coffin-lid, which in the centre had tiny intervals for the passage of the cords. He then turned the key in the lock, and uttered a word, which I took to be, "Come."

At his summons, Aith, approaching, took hold of the handle at the head; and from the dark recesses of the hall a lady, in black, moved forward. She was very tall, pallid, and of noble aspect. From the curvature of the nose, and her circular ears, I conjectured the lady Swertha, aunt of Harfager. Her eyes were red, but if with weeping I could not determine.

Harfager and I, taking each a handle near the coffin-foot, and the lady bearing before us one of the candlesticks, the procession began. As we came to the doorway, I noticed standing in a corner yet two coffins, inscribed with the names of Harfager and his aunt. We passed at length down a wide-curving stairway to the lower stage; and descending thence still lower by narrow brazen steps, came to a portal of metal, at which the lady, depositing the candlestick, left us.

The chamber of death into which we now bore the coffin had for its outer wall the brazen outer wall of the whole house at a point where this approached nearest the cataract, and must have been deep washed by the infuriate caldron without. The earthquake here was, indeed, intense. On every side the vast extent of surface was piled with coffins, rotted or rotting, ranged upon tiers of wooden shelves. The floor, I was surprised to see, was of brass. From the wide scampering that ensued on our entrance, the place was, it was clear, the abode of hordes of water-rats. As it was inconceivable that these could have corroded a way through sixteen brazen feet, I assumed that some fruitful pair must have found in the house, on its building, an ark from the waters; though even this hypothesis seemed wild. Harfager, however, afterwards confided to me his suspicion, that they had, for some purpose, been *placed* there by the original architect.

Upon a stone bench in the middle we deposited our burden, whereupon Aith made haste to depart. Harfager then rapidly and repeatedly walked from end to end of the long sepulchre, examining with many an eager stoop and peer, and upward strain, the shelves and their props. Could he, I was led to wonder, have any doubts as to their security? Damp, indeed, and decay pervaded all. A piece of woodwork which I handled softened into powder between my fingers.

He presently beckoned to me, and with yet one halt and uttered "Hark!" from him, we traversed the house to my chamber. Here, left alone, I paced long about, fretted with a strange vagueness of anger; then, weary, tumbled to a horror of sleep.

In the far interior of the mansion even the bleared day of this land of heaviness never rose upon our settled gloom. I was able, however, to regulate my *levées* by a clock which stood in my chamber. With Harfager, in a startlingly short time, I renewed more than all our former intimacy. That I should say *more*, is itself startling, considering that an interval of twelve years stretched between us. But so, in fact, it was; and this was proved by the circumstance that we grew to take, and to pardon, freedoms of expression and manner which, as two persons of more than usual reserve, we had once never dreamed of permitting to ourselves in reference to each other. Down corridors that vanished either way in darkness and length of perspective remoteness we linked ourselves in perambulations of purposeless urgency. Once he wrote that my step was excruciatingly deliberate. I replied that it was just such a step as fitted my then mood. He wrote: "You have developed an aptitude to *fret*." I was profoundly offended, and replied: "There are at least more fingers than one in the universe which *that* ring will wed."

Something of the secret of the unhuman sensitiveness of his hearing I quickly surmised. I, too, to my dismay, began, as time passed, to catch hints of loudly-uttered words. The reason might be found, I suggested, in an increased excitability of the auditory nerve, which, if the cataract were absent, the roar of the ocean, and bombast of the incessant tempest about us, would by themselves be sufficient to cause; in which case, his own aural interior must, I said, be inflamed to an exquisite pitch of hyperpyrexial fever. The affection I named to him as the Paracusis Willisii. He frowned dissent, but I, undeterred, callously proceeded to recite the case, occurring within my own experience, of a very deaf lady who could hear the fall of a pin in a rapidly-moving railway-train.* To this he only replied: "Of ignorant persons I am accustomed to consider the mere scientist as the most profoundly ignorant."

Yet that he should affect darkness as to the highly morbid condition of his hearing I regarded as simply far-fetched. Himself, indeed, confided to me his own, Aith's, and his aunt's proneness to violent paroxysms of *vertigo*. I was startled; for I had myself shortly before been twice roused from sleep by sensations of reeling and nausea, and a conviction that the chamber furiously spun with me in a direction from right to left. The impression passed away, and I attributed it, perhaps hastily (though on well-known pathological grounds), to some disturbance in the nerve-endings of the "labyrinth," or inner ear. In Harfager, however, the conviction of wheeling motions in the house, in the world, attained so horrible a degree of certainty, that its effects sometimes resembled those of lunacy or energumenal possession. Never, he said, was the sensation of

*Such cases are known, or at least easily comprehensible, to every medical man. The concussion on the deaf nerves is said to be the cause of the acquired sensitiveness. Nor is there any *limit* to such sensitiveness when the concussion is abnormally increased.

giddiness wholly absent; seldom the feeling that he stared with stretched-out arms over the verge of abysmal voids which wildly wooed his half-consenting foot. Once, as we went, he was hurled, as by unseen powers, to the ground; and there for an hour sprawled, cold in a flow of sweat, with distraught bedazzlement and amaze in eyes that watched the racing house. He was constantly racked, moreover, with the consciousness of sounds so very peculiar in their nature, that I could account for them upon no other hypothesis than that of *tinnitus* highly exaggerated. Through the heaped-up roar, there sometimes visited him, he said, the high lucid warbling of some Orphic bird, from the pitch of whose impassioned madrigals he had the inner consciousness that it came from a far country, was of the whiteness of snow, and crested with a comb of mauve. Else he was aware of accumulated human voices, remotely articulate, contending in volubility, and finally melting into chaotic musical tones. Or, anon, he was stunned by an infinite and imminent crashing, like the huge crackling of a universe of glass about his ears. He said, too, that he could often see, rather than hear, the parti-coloured whorls of a mazy sphere-music deep, deep, within the black dark of the cataract's roar. These impressions, which I ardently protested *must* be purely entotic, had sometimes upon him a pleasing effect, and long would he stand and listen with raised hand to their seduction; others again inflamed him to the verge of angry madness. I guessed that they were the origin of those irascibly uttered "Harks!" which at intervals of about an hour did not fail to break from him. In this I was wrong: and it was with a thrill of dismay that I shortly came to know the truth.

For, as once we passed together by an iron door on the lower stage, he stopped, and for several minutes stood, listening with an expression most keen and cunning. Presently the cry "Hark!" escaped him; and he then turned to me, and wrote upon the tablet: "You did not hear?" I had heard nothing but the monotonous roar. He shouted into my ear in accents now audible to me as an echo heard far off in dreams: "You shall see."

He lifted the candlestick; produced from the pocket of his garment a key; unlocked the door. We entered a chamber, circular, very loftily domed in proportion to its extent, and apparently empty, save that a pair of ladder-steps leaned against its wall. Its flooring was of marble, and in its centre gloomed a pool, resembling the impluvium of Roman atriums, but round in shape; a pool evidently deep, full of an unctuous miasmal water. I was greatly startled by its present aspect; for as the light burned upon its jet-black surface, I could see that this had been quite recently *disturbed*, in a manner for which the shivering of the house could not account, inasmuch as *ripples* of slimy ink sullenly rounded from the centre toward its marble brink I glanced at Harfager for explanation. He signed to me to wait, and for about an hour, with arms in their accustomed fold behind his back, perambulated. At the end of that time he stopped, and standing together by the margin, we gazed into the water. Suddenly his clutch tightened upon my arm, and I saw, not without a thrill of horror, a tiny ball, doubtless of lead, but smeared blood-red by some chymical pigment, fall from the direction of the roof and disappear into the centre of the black depths. It hissed, on contact with the water, a thin puff of vapour.

"In the name of all that is sinister!" I cried, "what thing is this you show me?"

Again he made me a busy and confident sign to wait; snatched then the ladder-steps toward the pool; handed me the taper. I, mounting, held high the flame, and saw hanging from the misty centre of the dome a form—a sphere of tarnished old copper, lengthened out into balloon-shape by a down-looking neck, at the end of which I thought I could discern a tiny orifice. Painted across the bulge was barely visible in faded red characters the hieroglyph:

"HARFAGER-HOUS: 1389–188."

Something—I know not what—of *eldritch* in the combined aspect of spotted globe, and gloomy pool, and contrivance of hourly hissing ball, gave expedition to my feet as I slipped down the ladder.

"But the meaning?"

"Did you see the writing?"

"Yes. The meaning?"

He wrote: "By comparing Gascoigne with Thrunster, I find that the mansion was *built* about 1389."

"But the final figures?"

"After the last 8," he replied, "there is another figure, nearly, but not quite, obliterated by a tarnish-spot."

"What figure?"

"It cannot be read, but may be surmised. The year 1888 is now all but passed. It can only be the figure 9."

"You are *horribly* depraved in mind!" I cried, flaring into anger. "You assume—you dare to *state*—in a manner which no mind trained to base its conclusions upon fact could hear with patience."

"And you, on the other hand, are simply absurd," he wrote. "You are not, I presume, ignorant of the common formula of Archimedes by which, the diameter of a sphere being known, its volume may be determined. Now, the diameter of the sphere in the dome there I have ascertained to be four and a half feet; and the diameter of the leaden balls about the third of an inch. Supposing then that 1389 was the year in which the sphere was full of balls, you may readily calculate that not many fellows of the four million and odd which have since dropped at the rate of one an hour are now left within it. It could not, in fact, have contained many more. The fall of balls *cannot* persist another year. The figure 9 is therefore forced upon us."

"But you assume, Harfager," I cried, "most wildly you assume! Believe me, my friend, this is the very wantonness of wickedness! By what algebra of despair do you know that the last date must be such, was intended to be such, as to correspond with the stoppage of the horologe? And, even if so, what is the significance of the whole. It has—it can have—*no significance!* Was the con-

triver of this dwelling, of all the gnomes, think you, a being pulsing with om-
niscience?"

"Do you seek to madden me?" he shouted. Then furiously writing: "I
know—I swear that I know—nothing of its significance! But is it not evident
to you that the work is a stupendous hour-glass, intended to record the hours
not of a day but of a cycle? and of a cycle of five hundred years?"

"But the whole thing," I passionately cried, "is a baleful phantasm of our
brains! an evil impossibility! How is the fall of the balls regulated? Ah, my
friend, you wander—your mind is debauched in this bacchanal of tumult."

"I have not ascertained," he replied, "by what internal mechanism, or vis-
cous medium, or spiral coil, dependent no doubt for its action upon the vibration of the house, the balls are retarded in their fall; that is a matter well within
the cunning of the mediæval artisan, the inventor of the watch; but this at
least is clear, that one element of their retardation is the minuteness of the aperture through which they have to pass; that this element, by known, though
recondite, statical laws, will cease to operate when no more than three balls
remain; and that, consequently, the last three will fall at nearly the same moment."

"In God's name!" I exclaimed, careless what folly I poured out, "but your
mother is *dead*, Harfager! You dare not deny that there remain but you and the
lady Swertha!"

A contemptuous glance was all the reply he then vouchsafed me.

But he confided to me a day or two later that the leaden balls were a constant bane to his ears; that from hour to hour his life was a keen waiting for
their fall; that even from his brief slumbers he infallibly startled into wakefulness at each descent; that, in whatever part of the mansion he happened to be,
they failed not to find him out with a clamorous and insistent *loudness*; and
that every drop wrung him with a twinge of physical anguish in the inner ear. I
was therefore appalled at his declaration that these droppings had now become
to him as the life of life; had acquired an intimacy so close with the hue of his
mind, that their cessation might even mean for him the shattering of reason.
Convulsed, he stood then, face wrapped in arms, leaning against a pillar. The
paroxysm past, I asked him if it was out of the question that he should once
and for all cast off the fascination of the horologe, and fly with me from the
place. He wrote in mysterious reply: "A *threefold* cord is not easily broken." I
started. How threefold? He wrote with bitterest smile: "To be enamoured of
pain—to pine after aching—to dote upon Marah—is not that a wicked madness?" I was overwhelmed. Unconsciously he had quoted Gascoigne: a wicked
madness! a lecherous agonie! "You have seen the face of my aunt," he proceeded; "your eyes were dim if you did not there behold an impious calm, the
glee of a blasphemous patience, a grin behind her daring smile." He then spoke
of a prospect, at the infinite terror of which his whole nature trembled, yet
which sometimes laughed in his heart in the aspect of a maniac *hope*. It was the
prospect of any considerable increase in the volume of sound about him. At
that, he said, the brain must totter. On the night of my arrival the noise of my

booted tread, and, since then, my occasionally raised voice, had caused him acute unease. To a sensibility such as this, I understood him further to say, the luxury of torture involved in a large sound-increase in his environment was an allurement from which no human strength could turn; and when I expressed my powerlessness even to conceive such an increase, much less the means by which it could be effected, he produced from the archives of the house some annals, kept by the successive heads of his race. From these it appeared that the tempests which continually harried the lonely latitude of Vaila did not fail to give place, at periodic intervals of some years, to one sovereign *ouragan*— one Sirius among the suns—one *ultimate* lyssa of elemental atrocity. At such periods the rains descended—and the floods came—even as in the first world-deluge; those *rösts*, or eddies, which at all times encompassed Vaila, spurning then the bands of lateral space, shrieked themselves aloft into a multitudinous death-dance of water-spouts, and like snaky Deinotheria, or say towering monolithic in a stonehenge of columned and cyclopean awe, thronged about the little land, upon which, with converging *débâcle*, they discharged their momentous waters; and the lochs to which the cataract was due thus redoubled their volume, and fell with redoubled tumult. It was, said Harfager, like a miracle that for twenty years no such great event had transacted itself at Vaila.

And what, I asked, was the third strand of that threefold cord of which he had spoken?

He took me to a circular hall, which, he told me, he had ascertained to be the geometrical centre of the circular mansion. It was a very great hall—so great as I think I never saw—so great that the amount of segment illumined at any one time by the taper seemed nearly flat. And nearly the whole of its space from floor to roof was occupied by a pillar of brass, the space between wall and cylinder being only such as to admit of a stretched-out arm.

"This cylinder, which seems to be solid," wrote Harfager, "ascends to the dome and passes beyond it; it descends hence to the floor of the lower stage, and passes through that; it descends thence to the brazen flooring of the vaults, and *passes through that* into the rock of the ground. Under each floor it spreads out laterally into a vast capital, helping to support the floor. What is the precise quality of the impression which I have made upon your mind by this description?"

"I do not know!" I answered, turning from him; "propound me none of your questions, Harfager. I feel a giddiness . . ."

"Nevertheless you shall answer me," he proceeded; "consider the *strangeness* of that brazen lowest floor, which I have discovered to be some ten feet thick, and whose under-surface, I have reason to believe, is somewhat above the level of the ground; remember that the fabric is at no point *fastened* to the cylinder; think of the *chains* that ray out from the outer walls, seeming to anchor the house to the ground. Tell me, what impression have I *now* made?"

"And is it for this you wait?" I cried,—"for *this*? Yet there may have been no malevolent intention! You jump at conclusions! Any human dwelling, if solidly based upon earth, would be at all times liable to overthrow on such a land, in such a situation, as this, by some superlative tempest! What if it were the intention of the architect that in such eventuality the chains should break, and the house, by yielding, be saved?"

"You have no lack of charity at least," he replied; and we returned to the book we then read together.

He had not wholly lost the old habit of study, but could no longer constrain himself to sit to read. With a volume, often tossed down and resumed, he walked to and fro within the radius of the lamp-light; or I, unconscious of my voice, read to him. By a strange whim of his mood, the few books which now lay within the limits of his patience had all for their motive something of the *picaresque*, or the foppishly speculative: Quevedo's *Tacaño*; or the mundane system of Tycho Brahe; above all, George Hakewill's *Power and Providence of God*. One day, however, as I read, he interrupted me with the sentence, seemingly *à propos* of nothing: "What I *cannot* understand is that you, a scientist, should believe that the physical life ceases with the cessation of the breath"— and from that moment the tone of our reading changed. He led me to the crypts of the library in the lowest part of the building, and hour after hour, with a certain *furore* of triumph, overwhelmed me with volumes evidencing the longevity of man after "death." A sentence of Haller had rooted itself in his mind; he repeated, insisted upon it: "sapientia denique consilia dat quibus longævitas obtineri queat, nitro, opio, purgationibus subinde repetitis . . ."; and as opium was the elixir of long-drawn life, so death itself, he said, was that opium, whose more potent nepenthe lullabied the body to a peace not all-insentient, far within the gates of the gardens of dream. From the *Dhammapada* of the Buddhist canon, to Zwinger's *Theatrum*, to Bacon's *Historia Vitæ et Mortis*, he ranged to find me heaped-up certainty of his faith. What, he asked, was my opinion of Baron Verulam's account of the dead man who was heard to utter words of prayer; or of the leaping bowels of the dead *condamné*? On my expressing incredulity, he seemed surprised, and reminded me of the writhings of dead serpents, of the visible beating of a frog's heart many hours after "death." "She is not dead," he quoted, "but *sleepeth*." The whim of Bacon and Paracelsus that the principle of life resides in a subtle spirit or fluid which pervades the organism he coerced into elaborate proof that such a spirit must, from its very nature, be incapable of any *sudden* annihilation, so long as the organs which it permeates remain connected and integral. I asked what limit he then set to the persistence of sensibility in the physical organism. He replied that when slow decay had so far advanced that the nerves could no longer be called nerves, or their cell-origins cell-origins, or the brain a brain—or when by artificial means the brain had for any length of time been disconnected at the cervical region from the body—*then* was the king of terrors king indeed, and the body was as though it had not been. With an indiscretion strange to me before my residence at Vaila, I blurted the question whether all this *Aberglaube* could have any reference, in his mind, to the body of his mother. For a while he stood thoughtful, then wrote: "Had I not reason to believe that my own and my aunt's life in some way hinged upon the final cessation of hers, I should still have taken precautions to ascertain the progress of the destroyer upon her mortal frame; as it is, I shall not lack even the minutest information." He then explained that the rodents which swarmed in the sepulchre would, in the course of time, do their full work upon her; but would be unable to penetrate to the region of the throat without first gnawing their way through the three cords stretched across the holes of the laminæ within the coffin, and thus, one by one, liberating the three morrisco bells to a tinkling agitation.

The winter solstice had passed; another year opened. I slept a deep sleep by night when Harfager entered my chamber, and shook me. His face was ghastly in the taper-light. A transformation within a few hours had occurred upon him. He was not the same. He resembled some poor wight into whose unexpecting eyes—at midnight—have glared the sudden eye-balls of Terrour.

He informed me that he was aware of singular intermittent straining and creaking sounds, which gave him the sensation of hanging in aerial spaces by a thread which must shortly snap to his weight. He asked if, for God's sake, I would accompany him to the sepulchre. We passed together through the house, he craven, shivering, his step for the first time laggard. In the chamber of the dead he stole to and fro examining the shelves, furtively intent. His eyes were sunken, his face drawn like death. From the footless coffin of the dowager trembling on its bench of stone, I saw an old water-rat creep. As Harfager passed beneath one of the shortest of the shelves which bore a single coffin, it suddenly fell from a height with its burthen into fragments at his feet. He screamed the cry of a frighted creature, and tottered to my support. I bore him back to the upper house.

He sat with hidden face in the corner of a small room doddering, overcome, as it were, with the extremity of age. He no longer marked with his usual "Hark!" the fall of the leaden drops. To my remonstrances he answered only with the words, So soon! so soon! Whenever I sought I found him there. His manhood had collapsed in an ague of trepidancy. I do not think that during this time he slept.

On the second night, as I approached him, he sprang suddenly straight with the furious outcry: "The first bell tinkles!"

And he had hardly larynxed the wild words when, from some great distance, a faint wail, which at its origin must have been a most piercing shriek, reached my now feverishly sensitive ears. Harfager at the sound clapped hands to ears, and dashed insensate from his place, I following in hot pursuit, through the black breadth of the mansion. We ran until we reached a round chamber, containing a candelabrum, and arrased in faded red. In an alcove at the furthest circumference was a bed. On the floor lay in swoon the lady Swertha. Her dark-grey hair in disarray wrapped her like an angry sea, and many tufts of it lay scattered wide, torn from the roots. About her throat were livid prints of strangling fingers. We bore her to the bed, and, having discovered some tincture in a cabinet, I administered it between her fixed teeth. In the rapt and dreaming face I saw that death was not, and, as I found something appalling in her aspect, shortly afterward left her to Harfager.

When I next saw him his manner had assumed a species of change which I can only describe as hideous. It resembled the officious self-importance seen in a person of weak intellect, incapable of affairs, who goads himself with the exhortation, "to business! the time is short—I must even bestir myself!" His walk sickened me with a suggestion of *ataxie locomotrice*. I asked him as to the lady, as to the meaning of the marks of violence on her body. Bending ear to his deep and unctuous tones, I heard, "A stealthy attempt has been made upon her life by the skeleton, Aith."

My unfeigned astonishment at this announcement he seemed not to share. To my questions, repeatedly pressed upon him, as to the reason for retaining such a domestic in the house, as to the origin of his service, he could give no lucid answer. Aith, he informed me, had been admitted into the mansion during the period of his own long absence in youth. He knew little of him beyond the fact that he was of extraordinary physical strength. Whence he had come, or how, no living being except the lady Swertha had knowledge; and she, it seems, feared, or at least persistently declined, to admit him into the mystery. He added that, as a matter of fact, the lady, from the day of his return to Vaila, had for some reason imposed upon herself a silence upon all subjects, which he had never once known her to break except by an occasional note.

With a curious, irrelevant *impressement*, with an intensely voluntary, ataxic strenuousness, always with the air of a drunken man constraining himself to ordered action, Harfager now set himself to the ostentatious adjustment of a host of insignificant matters. He collected chronicles and arranged them in order of date. He tied and ticketed bundles of documents. He insisted upon my help in turning the faces of portraits to the wall. He was, however, now constantly interrupted by paroxysms of vertigo; six times in a single day he was hurled to the ground. Blood occasionally gushed from his ears. He complained to me in a voice of piteous wail of the clear luting of a silver *piccolo*, which did not cease to invite him. As he bent sweating upon his momentous futilities, his hands fluttered like shaken reeds. I noted the movements of his muttering and whimpering lips, the rheum of his far-sunken eyes. The decrepitude of dotage had overtaken his youth.

On a day he cast it utterly off, and was young again. He entered my chamber, roused me from sleep; I saw the mad *gaudium* in his eyes, heard the wild hiss of his cry in my ear:

"Up! It is sublime. The *storm!*"

Ah! I had known it—in the spinning nightmare of my sleep. I felt it in the tormented air of the chamber. It had come, then. I saw it lurid by the lamplight on the hell of Harfager's distorted visage.

I glanced at the face of the clock. It was nine—in the morning. A sardonic glee burst at once into being within me. I sprang from the couch. Harfager, with the naked stalk of some maniac old prophet, had already rapt himself away. I set out in pursuit. A clear deepening was manifest in the quivering of the edifice; sometimes for a second it paused still, as if, breathlessly, to listen. Occasionally there visited me, as it were, the faint dirge of some far-off lamentation and voice in Ramah; but if this was subjective, or the screaming of the storm, I could not say. Else I heard the distinct note of an organ's peal. The air of the mansion was agitated by a vaguely puffy unease. About noon I sighted Harfager, lamp in hand, running along a corridor. His feet were bare. As we met he looked at me, but hardly with recognition, and passed by; stopped, however, returned, and howled into my ear the question: "Would you *see?*" He beckoned before me. I followed to a very small window in the outer wall closed with a slab of iron. As he lifted a latch the metal flew inward with instant impetuosity and swung him far, while a blast of the storm, braying and booming through the aperture with buccal and reboant bravura, caught and pinned me against an angle of the wall. Down the corridor a long crashing *bouleversement* of pictures and furniture ensued. I nevertheless contrived to push my way, crawling on the belly, to the opening. Hence the sea should have been visible. My senses, however, were met by nothing but a reeling vision of tumbled blackness, and a general impression of the letter O. The sun of Vaila had gone out. In a moment of opportunity our united efforts prevailed to close the slab.

"Come"—he had obtained fresh light, and beckoned before me—"let us see how the dead fare in the midst of the great desolation and *dies iræ!*" Running, we had hardly reached the middle of the stairway, when I was thrilled by the consciousness of a momentous shock, the bass of a dull and far-reverberating thud, which nothing conceivable save the huge simultaneous thumping to the ground of the whole piled mass of the coffins of the sepulchre could have occasioned. I turned to Harfager, and for an instant beheld him, panic flying in his scuttling feet, headlong on the way he had come, with stopped ears and wide mouth. Then, indeed, fear overtook me—a tremor in the midst of the exultant daring of my heart—a thought that *now* at least I must desert him in his extremity, now work out my own salvation. Yet it was with a most strange hesitancy that I turned to seek him for the last time—a hesitancy which I fully felt to be selfish and diseased. I wandered through the midnight house in search of light, and having happened upon a lamp, proceeded to hunt for Harfager. Several hours passed in this way. It became clear from the state of the atmosphere that the violence about me was being abnormally intensified. Sounds as of distant screams—unreal, like the screamings of spirits—broke now upon my ear. As the time of evening drew on, I began to detect in the vastly augmented baritone of the cataract something new—a shrillness—the whistle of an ecstasy—a malice—the menace of a rabies blind and deaf. It must have been at about the hour of six that I found Harfager. He sat in an obscure apartment with bowed head, hands on knees. His face was covered with hair, and blood from the ears. The right sleeve of his garment had been rent away in some renewed attempt, as I imagined, to manipulate a window; the slightly-bruised arm hung lank from the shoulder. For some time I stood and watched the mouthing of his mumblings. Now that I had found him I said nothing of departure. Presently he looked sharply up with the cry "Hark!"—then with imperious impatience, "Hark! Hark!"—then with rapturous shout, "The second bell!" And *again*, in instant sequence upon his cry, there sounded a wail, vague but unmistakably real, through the house. Harfager at the moment dropped reeling with vertigo; but I, snatching a lamp, hasted forth, trembling, but eager. For some time the high wailing continued, either actually, or by reflex action of my ear. As I ran toward the lady's apartment, I saw, separated from it by the breadth of a corridor, the open door of an armoury, into which I passed, and seized a battle-axe; and, thus armed, was about to enter to her aid, when Aith, with blazing eye, rushed from her chamber by a further door. I raised my weapon, and, shouting, flew forward to fell him; but by some chance the lamp dropped from me, and before I knew aught, the axe leapt from my grasp, myself hurled far backward. There was, however, sufficiency of light from the chamber to show that the skeleton had dashed into a door of the armoury: that near me, by which I had procured the axe, I instantly slammed and locked; and hasting to the other, similarly secured it. Aith was thus a prisoner. I then entered the lady's room. She lay half-way across the bed in the alcove, and to my bent ear loudly croaked the *râles* of death. A glance at the mangled throat convinced me that her last hours were surely come. I placed her supine upon the bed; curtained her utterly from sight within the loosened festoons of the hangings of black, and inhumanly turned from the fearfulness of her sight. On an *escritoire* near I saw a note, intended apparently for Harfager: "I mean to defy, and fly. Think not from fear—but for the glow of the Defiance itself. Can you come?" Taking a flame from the candelabrum, I hastily left her to solitude, and the ultimate throes of her agony.

I had passed some distance backward when I was startled by a singular sound—a clash—resembling in *timbre* the clash of a tambourine. I heard it rather loudly, and that I should *now* hear it at all, proceeding as it did from a distance, implied the employment of some prodigious energy. I waited, and in two minutes it again broke, and thenceforth at like regular intervals. It had somehow an effect of pain upon me. The conviction grew gradually that Aith had unhung two of the old brazen shields from their pegs; and that, holding them by their handles, and smiting them viciously together, he thus expressed the frenzy which had now overtaken him. I found my way back to Harfager, in whom the very nerve of anguish now seemed to stamp and stalk about the chamber. He bent his head; shook it like a hail-tormented horse; with his deprecating hand brushed and barred from his hearing each recurrent clash of the brazen shields. "Ah, when—when—when—" he hoarsely groaned into my ear, "will that rattle of hell choke in her throat? I will myself, I tell you—*with my own hand!*—oh God . . ." Since the morning his auditory inflammation (as, indeed, my own also) seemed to have heightened in steady proportion with the roaring and screaming chaos round; and the *râles* of the lady hideously filled for him the measured intervals of the grisly cymbaling of Aith. He presently hurled twinkling fingers into the air, and with wide arms rushed swiftly into the darkness.

And again I sought him, and long again in vain. As the hours passed, and the slow Tartarean day deepened toward its baleful midnight, the cry of the now redoubled cataract, mixed with the throng and majesty of the now climactic tempest, assumed too definite and intentional a *shriek* to be longer tolerable to any mortal reason. My own mind escaped my governance, and went its way. Here, in the hot-bed of fever, I was fevered; among the children of wrath, was strong with the strength, and weak with the feebleness of delirium. I wandered from chamber to chamber, precipitate, bemused, giddy on the upbuoyance of a joy. "As a man upon whom sleep seizes," so had I fallen. Even yet, as I approached the region of the armoury, the noisy ecstasies of Aith did not fail to clash faintly upon my ear. Harfager I did not see, for he too, doubtless, roamed a headlong Ahasuerus in the round world of the house. At about midnight, however, observing light shine from a door on the lower stage, I entered and found him there. It was the chamber of the dropping horologe. He half-sat, swaying self-hugged, on the ladder-steps, and stared at the blackness of the pool. The last flicker of the riot of the day seemed dying in his eyes. He cast no glance as I approached. His hands, his bare right arm, were red with new-shed blood; but of this, too, he appeared unconscious. His mouth gaped wide to his pantings. As I looked, he leapt suddenly high, smiting hands, with the yell, "The last bell tinkles!" and galloped forth, a-rave. He therefore did not see (though he may have understood by hearing) the spectacle which, with cowering awe, I immediately thereupon beheld: for from the horologe there slipped with hiss of vapour a ball into the torpid pool: and while the clock once ticked, another; and while the clock yet ticked, another! and the vapour of the first had not *utterly* passed, when the vapour of the third, intermingling, floated with it into grey tenuity aloft. Understanding that the sands of the house were run, I, too, flinging maniac arms, rushed from the spot. I was, however, suddenly stopped in my career by the instinct of some stupendous doom emptying its vials upon the mansion; and was quickly made aware, by the musketry of a shrill crackling from aloft, and the imminent downpour of a world of waters, that a water-spout had, wholly or partly, hurled the catastrophe of its broken floods upon us, and crashed ruining through the dome of the building. At that moment I beheld Harfager running toward me, hands buried in hair. As he flew past, I seized him. "Harfager! save yourself!" I cried—"the very fountains, man,—by the living God, Harfager"—I hissed it into his inmost ear—"*the very fountains of the Great Deep . . .!*" Stupid, he glared at me, and passed on his way. I, whisking myself into a room, slammed the door. Here for some time, with smiting knees, I waited; but the impatience of my frenzy urged me, and I again stepped forth. The corridors were everywhere thigh-deep with water. Rags of the storm, irrageous by way of the orifice in the shattered dome, now blustered with hoiden wantonness through the house. My light was at once extinguished; and immediately I was startled by the presence of *another* light—most ghostly, gloomy, bluish—most soft, yet wild, phosphorescent—which now perfused the whole building. For this I could in no way account. But as I stood in wonder, a gust of greater vehemence romped through the house, and I was instantly conscious of the harsh *snap* of something near me. There was a minute's breathless pause—and then—quick, quick—ever quicker—came the throb, and the snap, and the pop, in vastly wide circular succession, of the anchoring chains of the mansion before the urgent shoulder of the hurricane. And *again* a second of eternal calm—and then—deliberately—its hour came—the ponderous palace moved. My flesh writhed like the glutinous flesh of a serpent. Slowly moved, and stopped:—then was a sweep—and a swirl—and a pause! then a swirl—and a sweep—and a pause!—then steady industry of labour on the monstrous brazen axis, as the husbandman plods by the plough; then increase of zest, assuetude of a fledgeling to the wing—then intensity—then the last light ecstasy of flight. And now, once again, as staggering and plunging I spun, the thought of escape for a moment visited me: but this time I shook an impious fist. "No, but God, no, no," I cried, "I will no more wander hence, my God! I will even perish with Harfager! Here let me waltzing pass, in this Ball of the Vortices, Anarchie of the Thunders! Did not the great Corot call it translation in a chariot of flame? But this is gaudier than that! redder than that! This is jaunting on the scoriac tempests and reeling bullions of hell! It is baptism in a sun!" Recollection gropes in a dimmer gloaming as to all that followed. I struggled up the stairway now flowing a steep river, and for a long time ran staggering and plunging, full of wild words, about, amid the downfall of ceilings and the wide ruin of tumbling walls. The air was thick with splashes, the whole roof now, save three rafters, snatched by the wind away. In that blue sepulchral moonlight, the tapestries flapped and trailed wildly out after the flying house like the streaming hair of some ranting fakeer stung gyratory by the gadflies and tarantulas of distraction. The flooring gradually assumed a slant like the deck of a sailing ship, its covering waters flowing all to accumulation in one direction. At one point, where the largest of the porticoes projected, the mansion began at every revolution to bump with horrid shiverings against some obstruction. It bumped, and while the lips said one-two-three, it three times bumped again. It was the levity of hugeness! it was the mænadism of mass! Swift—ever swifter, swifter—in ague of urgency, it reeled and raced, every portico a sail to the storm, vexing and wracking its tremendous frame to fragments. I, chancing by the door of a room littered with the *débris* of a fallen wall, saw through that wan and livid light Harfager sitting on a tomb. A large drum was beside him, upon which, club grasped in bloody hand, he feebly and persistently beat. The velocity of the leaning house had now attained the *sleeping* stage, that ultimate energy of the spinning-top. Harfager sat, head sunk to chest; suddenly he dashed the hairy wrappings from his face; sprang; stretched horizontal arms; and began to spin—dizzily!—in the same direction as the mansion!—nor less sleep-embathed!—with floating hair, and quivering cheeks, and the starting eye-balls of horror, and tongue that lolled like a panting wolf's from his bawling degenerate mouth. From such a sight I turned with the retching of loathing, and taking to my heels, staggering and plunging, presently found myself on the lower stage opposite a porch. An outer door crashed to my feet, and the breath of the storm smote freshly upon me. An *élan*, part of madness, more of heavenly sanity, spurred in my brain. I rushed through the doorway, and was tossed far into the limbo without.

The river at once swept me deep-drowned toward the sea. Even here, a momentary shrill din like the splitting asunder of a world reached my ears. It had hardly passed, when my body collided in its course upon one of the basalt piers, thick-cushioned by sea-weed, of the not all-demolished bridge. Nor had I utterly lost consciousness. A clutch freed my head from the surge, and I finally drew and heaved myself to the level of a timber. Hence to the ledge of rock by which I had come, the bridge was intact. I rowed myself feebly on the belly beneath the poundings of the wind. The rain was a steep rushing, like a shimmering of silk, through the air. Observing the same wild glow about me which had blushed through the broken dome into the mansion, I glanced backward—and saw that the dwelling of the Harfagers was a memory of the past; then upward—and lo, the whole northern sky, to the zenith, burned one tumbled and fickly-undulating ocean of gaudy flames. It was the *aurora borealis* which, throeing at every aspen instant into rays and columns, cones and obelisks, of vivid vermil and violet and rose, was fairly whiffed and flustered by the storm into a vast silken oriflamme of tresses and swathes and breezes of glamour; whilst, low-bridging the horizon, the flushed beams of the polar light assembled into a changeless boreal corona of bedazzling candor. At the augustness of this great phenomenon I was affected to blessed tears. And with them, the dream broke!—the infatuation passed!—a hand skimmed back from my brain the blind films and media of delusion; and sobbing on my knees, I jerked to heaven the arms of grateful oblation for my surpassing Rephidim, and marvel of deliverance from all the temptation—and the tribulation—and the tragedy—of Vaila.

Printed in the United States
53920LVS00005B/118-123